Where Women are Kings

ALSO BY CHRISTIE WATSON FROM CLIPPER LARGE PRINT

Tiny Sunbirds Far Away

Where Women are Kings

Christie Watson

W F HOWES LTD

This large print edition published in 2014 by
W F Howes Ltd
Unit 4, Rearsby Business Park, Gaddesby Lane,
Rearsby, Leicester LE7 4YH

1 3 5 7 9 10 8 6 4 2

First published in the United Kingdom in 2013
by Quercus Editions Ltd

ISBN 978 1 47125 420 8

Typeset by Palimpsest Book Production Limited,
Falkirk, Stirlingshire
Printed and bound by
www.printondemand-worldwide.com of Peterborough, England

For Moyo who swallowed all the goodness of the world, and for Kike, who he loves like the world has never known love.

CHAPTER 1

Elijah, my lovely son,
    I want to tell you your life. Everyone has a story inside them, which begins before they are born, and yours is a bigger story than most will ever know. They say I shouldn't tell you some things, and that words can hurt little ears, but, son of mine, there are no secrets between a mother and son. A child has seen the insides of its mother's body, and who can know a secret bigger than that? And they say a lot of things, those English. What they call 'child abuse', us Nigerians call 'training'. So don't mind them.

Your story begins in Nigeria, which is a place like Heaven. There is continuous sunshine and everyone smiles and takes care of each other. Nigerian children work hard at school, have perfect manners, look after their parents and respect the elderly. Nigeria is brightness and stars, and earth like the skin on your cheeks: brown-red, soft and warm.

I am full up with proud memories from Nigeria. Most of all I remember my family. Mummy – your grandmother – was famous for shining cooking pots and shining stories. 'Long ago,' she would tell me and my sisters, 'a woman, so full of empty, sold her body as if it was nothing but meat for sale at the market. She travelled all over Nigeria, that woman, looking for something to fill up her insides, and learnt many languages, searching for words to explain the emptiness. And people liked this empty, clever woman: she was made of starlight; her heart glowed silver. They listened when she spoke her many-language words, telling the places she'd seen: of Jos, where the sky rained diamonds, and the North, where men disappeared inside walls of sand, and the Delta creeks, dancing with river spirits. And so the people made her king. And the land filled her up, and the emptiness was sky. Nigeria is a place where women are kings. Where anything is possible.'

All my childhood she cleaned her pots while I watched, listening to her stories, to her songs, contented as any woman who ever lived. Mummy's singing was loud, which was a good thing as my sister, your Aunt Bukky, from whom you inherited that beautiful skin tone, had the kind of voice that reached inside your face. I remember one day her begging Mummy to share secrets. The sun was only half risen, yet we'd been up for hours, listening to Mummy sing and Baba snore.

'Please,' Bukky whined. 'Please, Mummy. I won't tell a soul.'

'I'll never tell you my secret ingredient.' Mummy shook her head until her beaded plaits clicked together. She laughed. 'Never. You can pester me all day and my mouth will be closed tight as Baba's fist on pay day!'

'Please,' Bukky said, looking at the cloth with which she was wiping the pots. 'It could make us rich. Imagine, a formula that cleans pots that well for sale on Express Road!' Bukky was always looking for ways to make money, and she was foolish. Once, she'd nearly been arrested after a man told her he'd give her one hundred U.S. dollars to carry a bag through airport customs. If Baba hadn't driven past and seen her out of school and hanging around with a bag that wasn't hers, she would have been thrown in prison. And if it had been Mummy who'd driven past, then Bukky would be dead, for sure. And who knows if the gates of Heaven would open for such a crime, even if it was born of foolishness? But the things that sit in my heart are not Bukky's foolishness, or our parents' exasperation. Rather, the light in the compound, dancing on those cooking pots, making a thousand diamonds in the dust and on Bukky's pillow cheeks; Mummy's laughter; Baba's snoring. The tiny emptiness, where you would grow. A place where women are kings.

I remember the house, with broken stairs and a leaking roof, was centred around a middle courtyard where Mummy washed rice in one of those pots; I swear our rice was the cleanest in all of Nigeria. My sisters, Miriam, Eunice, Rebekah, Bukky, Esther, Oprah and Priscilla, spent their time looking in Mummy's other shining cooking pots, examining the thickness of their eyebrows, the distance between their eyes (Bukky always said you could have parked a car between Esther's eyes), the shape of their lips, the curl of their eyelashes. Baba chuckled with laughter whenever he saw them looking in the pots, and patted me on the head. 'Lovely Deborah,' he said. I never looked in a cooking pot. I knew, even from such a young age, that it was sinful to be vain. I was a clever child, Elijah. Gifted. I knew the Bible so well that I could recite Psalms from the age of one year. I'm not sure if it was my not looking in a cooking pot or my willingness to study the Bible that made me Baba's favourite. But I knew that I was. And every daughter who is her father's favourite grows up blessed, as I was.

Really, we were all blessed. We loved school and attended The Apostle of Christ Coming Senior Department, which was only a fifteen-minute walk away. But we loved coming home from school even more – to eat dinner together and talk through the day, and read the Bible, or the other books that Baba bought for us from the store near his work, or books given to us by Mummy, which were so well read that they stayed open, as if their stories were alive and wanted to be heard. We lived on the outskirts of Lagos, in the suburb of Yaba, near the bus stop on University Road towards the cemetery: me, Mummy, Baba, my seven sisters, aunts, grandparents, and my brothers, Othniel and

Immanuel – although Othniel was busy training to be a pharmacist, and always out at work or the university library, and Immanuel spent all his time with his girlfriend, who lived on Victoria Island. Immanuel's girlfriend was even more of a top secret than Mummy's cooking-pot paste; she had starred in a music video and her parents were separated and never attended church.

Church was always a big part of our lives. When you live in a place like Heaven, you cannot forget to thank God. And we had another reason to love God: our uncle, Baba's brother, was born with the voice of God in his heart. Uncle Pastor performed miracles. He could make a dying man live, and turn around a family's bad luck to make them the most fortunate family in all of Lagos. I've witnessed it with my own eyes. I've seen many things. One man prayed for the miracle of financial security and returned to church a week later with a winning Lotto ticket, a new Rolex watch and a girlfriend with breasts so large that Baba could not help commenting on them, and Mummy made him put all the naira from his pocket in the offerings bin. How we laughed, Elijah! Our church was a place of happiness and laughter, and your little face led me back to it, back to our parents' laughter. We'd all watch the way Mummy and Baba teased each other: his pretending to choke on her cooking; her calling him 'big-belly man'. Their laughter. The way they looked at each other, and at us. It was such a happy home. A family. There is nothing sweeter than that.

Mummy and Baba had strong foundations to their marriage, so, when the winds blew too hard, nothing fell over. They were friends first, for so many years, and when I became friends with Akpan, I remember Mummy and Baba looking at each other and the smile they shared. They wanted strong foundations for me, too. They were so happy when your baba led me under the palm tree, producing from his trouser pocket a ring that shone like a midnight star and must have cost six months' salary. They knew something of how marriage can work. They felt happiness, but also relief. Even in a place like Heaven, life is difficult for women. If it hadn't been for your baba, Akpan, asking for my hand in marriage, I do not know what would have become of me. And, son of mine, that is the situation for women the world over.

I was lucky. Akpan became my friend. He visited all of the time, and every time he visited I liked him a little more. He had a kind face and he believed in things, and often had a Marks and Spencer carrier bag full of gifts for us: a matching gold-plated jewellery set for my sisters and me, a travel alarm clock for Mummy, though she never travelled further than Ikeja and didn't have any AAA batteries, anyway.

Sometimes, when I was a child, I heard God in my ear – heard His voice as clear as the colours of morning. When I told him, Akpan said I had a spiritual gift. He said God had chosen me to whisper secrets to, because I was so beautiful. He called me his angel and my heart swelled so much I struggled to breathe. It was so many long years before we were married, and before Akpan got a visa for himself and a spouse visa for me so that we could leave our home and come to England, to the flat in London where we made you on the first try. The stars were bright that first night, Elijah, as though the Nigerian stars had travelled over to Deptford to light up our lovemaking. You were born from love and Nigerian stars and secrets believed.

You are loved, little Nigeria, like the world has never known love.

CHAPTER 2

Disgusting dirty horrible evil. Elijah heard the voice of the wizard all of the time. It told him to do bad things. Elijah knew he was bad. A disgusting boy. He wished the wizard would choose another boy, or just use superpowers for only good, like climbing really high or flying. The wizard could do anything. It could use super-human strength to lift heavy things, and read people's minds. It could turn into an animal, become invisible and fly through the night sky catching sticks of lightning in his hands. Elijah could use the wizard inside him to think right inside someone's brain. If Elijah could control the wizard, he could make it only do good things, like superpowers, and then Elijah would not be so afraid of it. Of what it might do next. Of what it might make him do.

Elijah was staying with Sue and Gary in a house that was filled with signs telling you what to do. He couldn't read, so he had to ask what each sign said, and Sue and Gary were bored with telling him. That is why it was lucky he could remember everything:

Keep Calm and Carry On
If It Isn't Broken, Don't Fix It
A House with Love Is a Home

They lived in something called a cul-de-sac, which was a place where every house was big and looked the same, and where no black-skinned people went. The neighbours were always washing their cars, or cutting their hedges, or weeding their front gardens whenever Elijah went past. But he knew they were really waiting to get a look at the wizard. Elijah wanted to warn them. He looked at them and opened his mouth to tell them to run from him but, whenever he did so, no words came out. They'd better go inside their houses at night, he thought, and pray to God. Please pray to God, he thought. And he prayed so hard himself that they too would pray. They would have to pray every night to protect themselves. Or the wizard might melt their houses with acid. Or eat them up.

Sue and Gary's house was very tidy and smelt of cabbage. They had no pets. They let Elijah play football on the grass outside but they didn't let him go out of the garden on his own. The living room was where they spent most of the time, watching a big television that was hooked on to the wall. He liked to watch *Spiderman* and *Superman* and, once, when Sue was at bingo, *Harry Potter*, which was about a boy wizard who had a matching scar on his head. But Elijah's scar was not the same shape: instead of being a zigzag it was a

9

straight line, and Harry Potter was a good wizard and Elijah was the evil type. He sat on the sofa, which had cushions with writing on them:

Grandmas Are Angels in Disguise!
An Old Rooster and a Young Chick Live Here
Welcome to the Nuthouse
Life Is Too Short to Drink Cheap Wine

Elijah had made Sue read them out to him.

Everywhere, there were pictures of children, all of them smiling, some with missing teeth. None of them looked like Sue or Gary. Sue and Gary had white skin with brown spots on their hands and hair you could see through. Sue was very short – Elijah came up to her shoulders – and her fingers were swollen and red all the time. Gary had glasses and wore slippers that had Mickey Mouse on them. They gave Elijah baths without oiling his skin afterwards and he felt dry and itchy and scratchy. The children in the pictures had different colours and different eyes and different hair. They must have been very itchy too. Elijah was so powerful he could read their minds, even in photos. They wanted their mamas.

'All those kids we've fostered.' Gary was behind him; Elijah could see him without turning around. 'So far, twenty-two emergency placements.' He laughed. 'And eighteen who stayed for quite a long time: one of them, until he was sixteen. They still come at Christmas, pop in and see Sue, bring their washing sometimes . . .'

Elijah wouldn't be staying for a long time. They wanted him to leave before the wizard killed them, and he couldn't blame them. He liked living with Sue and Gary but they didn't like living with a disgusting wizard. Gary kept talking to the air but Elijah blocked him out. All he could hear was the message sent directly from God. God sent messages sometimes. Twenty-two and eighteen. He had been told, and told to remember it well.

22:18 Exodus. Thou shalt not suffer a witch to live.

It was night when Sue made Elijah brush his teeth. Even with the minty toothpaste, all he could taste were the boiled vegetables they forced him to eat. He looked at Sue. Since Ricardo had left, she'd been watching him closely. She tried to hug him but Elijah managed to pull away from her arms. She was watching him now in the mirror but he knew that she couldn't see him because he didn't show up in mirrors. Sorcerers had no reflections or shadows. That's how you could tell if a sorcerer was living inside you. Sue was looking hard but she couldn't see Elijah at all. He couldn't believe she forced him to eat a vegetable called swede, which was orange and tasted of spit. Mama would never make him eat vegetables. Mama would never give him food that tasted like spit. Mama had no evil inside her at all. Mama was an angel. She was so kind that if a baddie were dying, she would save them, even if they were a real baddie. She would never give

11

boiled vegetables to anyone, not even the worst baddie in the world.

'That's right, Elijah. Brush for two whole minutes. You're doing a great job. You are such a clever boy, and you're so good at brushing your teeth.'

Elijah watched Sue looking at the empty mirror and pretending she saw a seven-year-old boy brushing his teeth. He used his laser eyes to steam the mirror up.

After brushing his teeth, Elijah followed Sue into his bedroom and climbed into bed. Sue pulled a blanket over him. 'Stop wriggling,' she said. 'You'll never drop off if you wriggle around like that. Maybe you're feeling a bit frightened today? You know you can always talk to me about anything at all.' Sue laughed and sighed at the same time. She looked at Elijah and patted his body. 'Are you feeling a bit unsafe? Because I want you to remember all the things that I told you: you're completely safe here; nobody will hurt you.' She lifted her head and pulled the blanket down to see more of Elijah. He wanted to pull it back up. He wondered if Mama had a blanket or if she felt cold.

Sue rested her head on her hand. 'I tell you, these social workers don't tell us half of it. Even Ricardo, as lovely as he is. Probably just as well, I suppose. Anyway, hun, you know you can always talk to me. It might help to talk it out. You know, share your problems.' Elijah looked at the brown spots on Sue's hand. The wizard was probably poisoning her.

12

Instead of looking at Sue's hands and thinking about things, he looked around the bedroom. There was a wardrobe with a picture of a bear on it that she said was called Winnie the Pooh. Sue read Elijah lots of stories. On the wall was a shelf with a lot of books, including the book about the bear. The book was Elijah's second favourite thing in the room.

His first favourite thing was next to his bed: a photo in a wooden frame. In the photograph, Mama had her hair in millions of tiny plaits and she was smiling, holding a King James Bible that her Uncle Pastor had given her. The colours of Nigeria were behind her: dark red, bright yellow, and green. And she was smiling.

'You have contact tomorrow, so we need to be up extra early.' Sue kissed the top of his head before he had time to move his head backwards. 'Sleep well.'

Elijah watched Sue walk out of the room and shut the door behind her. He touched the place where she'd kissed and pretended it was Mama who had kissed him instead.

Elijah stretched his hands, rubbing his fingers over a table scratched with a thousand pen marks, the light of day catching the dusting of glitter embedded into the wood, causing sparks as though the table held memories of children playing. Other children. It was morning and Ricardo had come to take him to the contact centre, but only after they'd had a chat. Elijah had sat down at the kitchen table while Ricardo spoke in a low voice to Sue outside the door. Then he came in and smiled and Elijah knew that he'd have to speak. Elijah didn't much like talking, and the sooner he started talking the sooner they would leave for the contact centre, which was like a sort of prison where they were keeping Mama. He closed his eyes and forced the words out one by one. 'Satan was here in the beginning, just like God.'

He opened his eyes widely and looked up at Ricardo, who had leant back in his chair and crossed his long legs in front of him. Wafts of Ricardo's aftershave travelled towards Elijah's nose, something fruity, and spicy. Ricardo had told Elijah once that he owned over fifty different after-shaves, and Elijah had imagined them all, bottle after bottle, lined up on a neat shelf. Ricardo shuffled Elijah's drawings, which were piled up in the middle of the table between them: dozens of penguins, a long branch of a tree with a line of marching ants carrying leaves across it, a butterfly wing in every colour possible – that had taken days – and a chalky white page that was meant to be a polar bear in the Arctic in the middle of a snowstorm. Elijah didn't like looking at that picture, even though he'd drawn it; it was so empty and secret. But he kept it, anyway, with the others and told Ricardo that it was important.

I am a wizard. Elijah wanted to tell Ricardo about the wizard inside him, but his promise to Mama, never, ever to tell about the wizard, echoed in his head. 'I'm a wicked boy,' he whispered instead. 'Full of evil and badness.' Elijah pushed the words out and thought of Mama waiting for him, of the way her mouth curled into a smile on one side and into a sad face on the other side.

Elijah reached his hand up to his face and touched the scar on his forehead with his fingertips. It felt lumpy and was the size of a matchstick. 'Look at my scar,' he whispered to Ricardo. 'Only baddies have scars on their face.'

Ricardo shrugged as if Elijah had said something uninteresting, or untrue. Elijah opened his eyes even wider until they began to fill with water and sting. He tried to ignore the stinging, looked down at the floor and took a big breath of Ricardo's aftershave. 'I don't want to be wicked. Can you help me?' Elijah's voice changed into a younger boy's voice. It moved in all directions as if the words didn't know the way into Ricardo's ears. He closed his eyes and listened to his insides: *Wizards bring sickness and bad luck and misery to anyone near. At night, they creep out of your skin and fly into the air before choosing a victim and eating their flesh, sometimes their very soul. I am full of evil spirits.*

'I am wicked, under the direct control of Satan himself. Bishop told me so.' Elijah began to sob, a large tear rolling slowly down to his jawline before falling to the table. He touched it with his thumb and rubbed it on the table until dry. 'I don't want to be wicked.'

'Who is Bishop? Is he from your church?'

Elijah opened his eyes but not his mouth.

Ricardo frowned. 'Well, whoever he is, you should know that you are not wicked in any way. You are a lovely boy who deserves to be happy and safe and playing.'

Elijah knew that Ricardo didn't believe he was evil. He tried to speak to him telepathically, which is when you think straight inside someone else's brain. It is true. Look at my eyes. It is true. 'I am Elijah,' he said, 'but I'm also full of evil. I bring sickness and bad luck and misery to anyone near me. I am full up with badness.'

Ricardo put his hand on top of Elijah's. 'It sounds very confusing. I'm so glad you managed to talk to me. Can you tell me about the Bishop?'

Elijah blinked quickly. 'He is a man of God.'

Ricardo squeezed Elijah's hand and then wrote something in his notebook. 'I'll try and get in touch with him: can you remember his name? Or the name of his church?'

Elijah shook his head.

'Don't worry. But, meanwhile, you must understand that, whatever anyone has ever said to you – even a man of God – you are a good, good boy. Anyway, everyone's a bit naughty sometimes. Even me, believe it or not!' Ricardo laughed deep from his stomach. 'And I'm sure that Bishop would never say that you are wicked. Sometimes, in Brazil, where I come from, the priests talk about heaven and hell and God and Satan. Is that what your Bishop was like?'

Elijah stopped blinking. His head nodded before he could stop it.

'Well, if your Bishop is anything like the priests I know, he will know that children are good and not wicked.'

Elijah felt his head begin to shake but he managed to stop it in time.

'And maybe if things weren't very good at home with Mummy then it was easy to get confused during church and think about bad things.' Ricardo lifted his head. 'It must be awful to think that you're bad inside.'

Elijah blinked slowly and pushed tears back inside his face by making his stomach twist tightly into a knot. Ricardo was wrong about everything. Things were always good at home with Mama. Always. He looked down at Ricardo's feet, stretching out in front of him under his side of the table.

'Thank you for telling me about Bishop; as I've said to you before, you can tell me anything at all. You're completely safe with me.' Ricardo put his hand across the table on top of Elijah's hand, but Elijah felt his hand shaking. He didn't want to risk touching Ricardo. Grown-ups said that he was completely safe with them but he was only completely safe with Mama.

Mama.

Even thinking of Mama changed everything.

When he thought of Mama, the table moved and shook and the ground fell away.

There was quiet in the kitchen for a short time, apart from the clock ticking above Sue's cupboards. Elijah looked at the window, and the plants lining the windowsill, which Sue had told him were called orchids. They only needed a tiny bit of water every few weeks and the flowers were the pinkest pink. One of the flowers was white with dots on it and crept up a thin green pole. He had felt a petal earlier that day with his thumb, and he couldn't work out if he was the petal or the thumb, both were so soft.

'How long have we known each other?' Ricardo smiled the smile he saved only for Elijah. Ricardo's face was usually square, his mouth flat, and when he smiled he showed his teeth. But the special smile he saved for Elijah was when his eyes twinkled. Elijah had never seen him use that smile on anyone else. It was like a secret between them. 'This is the first time you've told me properly that you feel like you're bad – and mentioned Bishop – with more than a sentence here or there. I know Mummy used to pray a lot and she's very religious. It's good that you're talking to me about things, Elijah. Talking is always good.'

But Elijah didn't feel good or safe. His heart was running across him and his stomach had moved. He looked past the orchids and out of the window into the daylight.

Ricardo smiled again but Elijah could see his

thoughts. Inside Ricardo's head he was running fast away, all the way back to Brazil where he could hide from such an evil wizard in the jungle that had neon-green frogs and spiders as big as a hand and you could keep lizards as pets in your living room.

'Do you want a biscuit?' Ricardo reached down into his bag and pulled something out. He waved a packet in the air: custard creams. Ricardo always brought custard creams.

'Wicked boys don't eat biscuits,' Elijah said. He sighed. 'You don't believe that I'm evil.'

'No, I actually know for sure that you're a good boy. I want to help you, and I can. We've got you to a safe place, and I've lined up some therapy. Now that you're settled with Sue and Gary, we can help you properly. Play therapy and art therapy, a nice school for you to start. I want you to see a special lady, Chioma, who helps children just like you. She's very nice. I think we can all help you, Elijah.'

'Nobody can help me. Even Mama couldn't help me.'

After the hospital, where he couldn't see Mama at all but could hear her howling like a wolf from somewhere far away, they had told him he had to stay with other families for a while. Elijah had stayed with many strange families in many strange houses. At first, when he had moved in with Sue and Gary, he had been allowed to see her three times a week, and she'd held him and whispered into his ear, 'I love you so much, and I promise everything will turn out well,' and pulled him close to her body, close enough for him to smell her skin, and everything was strange but bearable. But then the weeks went on and on, and he was waiting and waiting; they told him he had to stay with Sue and Gary for a while. Nobody told him when he could go home with Mama. Not even Ricardo. 'I want to go home.'

'I know you do, but it's our job – my job – to keep you safe. You deserve to be loved and to be safe.'

'I want to go home. I don't deserve anything.'

Ricardo opened the biscuits. 'You deserve so much, Elijah. But why don't you start with a biscuit, for now?'

I feast on human flesh. Elijah looked at the packet for a long time before reaching his small hand towards the biscuits, taking one, and putting it into his mouth whole.

Ricardo smiled, the special one. 'I think you're making real progress, Elijah. I'm so glad you're feeling settled enough here to talk about how you feel. And nothing has gone wrong for a long time. You're doing really well.'

Elijah shrugged back at Ricardo. He wanted to climb on his lap and go to sleep. Once, Ricardo had picked him up and carried him, and Elijah had liked it, the sense that Ricardo might be strong enough to carry a wizard, or even fight a wizard. Maybe Ricardo had special powers too. He felt close to safe. Almost. After Mama, Ricardo had known Elijah the longest in the world.

'Before we go for our visit today, I have to tell you about your Mama,' said Ricardo. 'There's some things we need to talk about. She's not doing so well, Elijah, I'm afraid. She's still being assessed for a while, but we need to talk about the future . . .'

Elijah ate his biscuit and closed his ears. Being a wizard could sometimes be useful. If he wanted to close his ears, he could, like they had tiny shutters that came down whenever he commanded. He didn't hear another word that Ricardo said.

The contact centre was a low building with windows that didn't open. There were children's pictures on the walls next to more notices telling you what to do. Elijah asked Ricardo to tell him what they all said. 'Nothing exciting,' he said, but then Elijah made him talk with mind control. Ricardo sighed, then read:

'In case of fire, assemble in car park.'

'Please ensure door is closed on way out.'

'C.C.T.V. in operation.'

Elijah followed Ricardo down the long corridor. Ricardo's flip-flops that day were green. Sometimes Elijah looked very closely at Ricardo's toes. His toes were smooth. Mama had hairy toes and so did Sue and Gary. Ricardo must have shaved them. 'Do you shave your toes?' Elijah asked.

Ricardo laughed. 'You're very funny, Elijah. You

make me laugh a lot. That's such a good skill, to make people laugh.'

Elijah felt his stomach turn when Ricardo said he was good at something. He knew it wasn't true. He wasn't really good at anything at all, except evil. They went into a room where there was a table in the middle and two sofas. On the other side of the room there was another door. They sat on a sofa. Elijah tried to see through the door but his eyes were wet. He wondered what Mama would look like today, what she'd be wearing, what she'd whisper into his ear. He felt the wizard push down low inside his body. Whenever Mama was near, the wizard got smaller, like it was scared of Mama.

It had been bearable when he saw Mama regularly, but when the visits became less and less, the wizard flipped around inside him and sometimes did something dangerous, like eat human flesh or cause sickness and misery. Elijah sat up straight and focused on the door without blinking, in case he missed the first look of her. He imagined exactly what she'd say to him: *Little Nigeria, you are the best thing that ever happened to me,* or, *My lovely son, I've missed you so much I can barely breathe.*

Ricardo tapped his foot on the carpet. The door they'd entered the room through opened, and the head of an old white man with a beard popped around the corner. 'Word, please?'

Ricardo looked at Elijah very quickly. 'Back in a minute, OK?'

Elijah smiled. He might get time on his own

with Mama. Maybe they'd let them cuddle, or even take a nap like they used to, tangled up in a ball until it was impossible to move and felt so safe and they both had dreamless sleep. Mama must be waiting the other side of the door. Elijah could smell her: slightly burning plantain and old library books.

He looked at the door and held his breath until small dancing lights filled his head. The other door opened. 'Elijah,' said Ricardo, sitting down on the sofa. 'Mama isn't here yet, I'm afraid.'

Elijah let out all of his breath in a rush. 'Where is she?'

'I'm afraid it's bad news, Elijah. It doesn't look like she'll be coming today.' Ricardo's voice sounded full of danger, like it was on a tightrope at the top of a circus tent, walking across very slowly.

'She will come,' said Elijah. He felt the wizard laugh inside him, a kind of rumbling in his belly. 'We just need to wait.' He started crying and let the tears spill down his face, no longer bothering to try and hold them in. 'She will come. She probably missed the bus.'

Ricardo pulled Elijah towards him and brushed his face dry with the palm of his hand. 'I'm sorry, Elijah. I did tell you this might happen.'

'We need to wait.' Elijah looked up at Ricardo and into his eyes. 'Please can we wait?'

Ricardo looked at his watch. 'We'll give it ten minutes, OK? But I really think that she won't make it this time.'

Elijah let Ricardo hold him while he watched the door. He prayed inside his body and inside his head. Open the door! his insides screamed. Open the door. He used all his powers until he felt empty.

The minutes ticked by and the door remained shut. Elijah became smaller and smaller and the wizard grew. The wizard laughed in Elijah's ear so loudly Elijah knew Ricardo must have heard it. But Ricardo just loosened his grip on Elijah. 'We have to go now, Elijah. I'm sorry Mama couldn't make it. I'm really sorry. She loves you very much.' Before Ricardo turned his head away and stood up, Elijah saw that Ricardo's eyes were wet. 'We better go before they kick us out,' said Ricardo.

But Elijah couldn't move. He just looked and looked at the closed door.

That night, it was so dark when Elijah woke up that he felt dead. He had to move his fingers and toes to know he was still alive. Elijah died once, the first night he had been away from Mama. He was so dead then that he couldn't move anything. Not even one toe. Being dead was like living inside a dream. Only some things were real, but you didn't know which ones.

It was quiet, but not too quiet. Elijah heard the snoring of Gary. Gary snored loudly and, before Gary, Marie never snored and, when Elijah stayed with Linda and Pete, Pete snored in bursts and then it went terrifyingly quiet, like Pete was dead, but then a sudden snore would come and Elijah knew he was all right, which was good because he liked Pete. He liked Pete so much he'd put a force field around the house to protect him from evil spirits. Before Pete and Linda's was Olu's house and, even though Olu's son, Fola, was only fourteen, he snored the loudest of all.

Listening to Gary snoring made Elijah think about all the other snores he'd heard in his life. He tried to focus really hard on the sound but he felt the badness inside him come alive like the snoring was waking it up. He felt the wizard grow bigger and bigger until he couldn't hold it down any more and the feeling made everything close in like the world was folding in half. He felt the wizard inside him wanting to get out. He knew the wizard would use its powers for evil but he had no fight left.

Creeping out of little boys' skins took a lot of effort, even for experienced wizards. First, it had to push Elijah's insides far down until it could sneak up his back. Then it moved itself up towards Elijah's head. When it was nearly there, it had to look for the nose or ear. Then was the tricky bit: getting itself really small – small enough to fit through a nostril. It pressed and pushed through and then it was free.

Elijah could feel the wizard crawling out of him and flying around the room, faster and faster. He shut his eyes tight and tried to keep them closed but something forced them open. He could hear the wizard slithering out of the door then swooping down the stairs. Elijah's heart was thumping like it was trying to get out. He thought of Sue and Gary asleep, and forced his legs to swing out of bed. Elijah walked down the stairs as quietly as possible with his thumping heart. The kitchen was quiet except for his heart and the clock, and everything was locked and closed. Even the fridge had a small lock on it. There was a sink with a washcloth hanging over the tap, the brightest yellow colour of the sun in Nigeria.

The wizard climbed back inside Elijah and filled him up until his stomach burnt and twisted. It picked up the dishcloth with Elijah's mind and made the cloth dance in the air. It danced all over the kitchen and above the cooker. The wizard liked making people sick and angry and mad. It liked the smell of things on fire. The cooker had tiny buttons on the side that Sue used to turn on the fire. Elijah had seen her do it. She cooked pasta for him sometimes, which was not so bad as swede, and she turned the buttons and fire appeared. 'Don't go near the oven,' she said, 'it's dangerous.' But it wasn't dangerous for the wizard. The wizard was laughing and Elijah was crying and crying. It felt like a belt on his tummy was pulling too tight. The wizard was squeezing. The fire made a sound like *puff!* and a tiny corner of the cloth started to turn black. Then there was orange on yellow. Elijah wanted to close his eyes and lie down and cry and cry, but the wizard didn't let him. It made him watch as the fire grew and grew. He watched the sun burning hot, and the fire rising and running, and the cupboards melting.

CHAPTER 3

'Right, now this is going to be a challenge for some of you, but it's very important we can talk about loss in an open way, in order that we are comfortable talking with our children about their losses surrounding the adoption process.'

Nikki found herself closing her eyes. She felt Obi's arm against hers stiffen. His leg twitched. They were sitting on plastic chairs, set out in a circle. A circle of childless couples, thought Nikki, and pushed her leg towards Obi's.

'I'm going to come around the room with this marker pen and clipboard, and I'd like you to list all the losses you've experienced – particularly in the last ten years, as time is ticking on –' the social worker flicked his head towards the clock – 'in chronological order.'

A couple to Nikki's right put their hands up at the same time, then laughed. 'We just have a few questions,' they said, also in unison.

'Yes? What is it, Sandra and Chris? It's good that you feel able to ask any questions, and that you're comfortable within the group to do that.'

'Do we list every loss? Sometimes Chris loses his keys, for example, or his temper. Or is it only major losses that we should write down? I mean, sometimes it does get him down, losing his keys.'

Everyone in the room tutted and shook their heads, except Obi, who Nikki could feel holding in laughter. She pressed his leg with hers. If he laughed out loud, she'd kill him. His laughter had always got them into trouble.

But he didn't laugh. Instead, the social worker, whose name was Ricardo, started laughing loudly. Then he coughed and pressed his mouth closed. 'Well, we like to leave it open to how it affected you,' he said. 'If you consider it a major loss, regardless of the cause, then write it down. Whatever led you to the adoption process.' He looked at the clock again, then clapped his hands. 'Right, let's get started; we have fifteen minutes before moving on to resolution.'

As Ricardo moved around the room, handing out marker pens, he hovered in front of Obi and Nikki until his aftershave filled the air between them and Obi coughed. Ricardo wore a pair of jeans and flip-flops, and a checked shirt with four undone buttons. There were two strings of beads around his neck. What was it about social workers that they had to dress like teenagers? And they were always late. Since starting the assessment process, Ricardo had been late every visit. Once he had not turned up, and e-mailed two days later to send his apologies and explain that he was on

29

a last-minute holiday. *Very good offer – too cheap to miss.* Obi wanted to ask for a different social worker, but Nikki managed to talk him out of it. 'They're probably all the same, anyway,' she'd said, but really, she liked Ricardo and felt relaxed around him. He was simply normal – like someone they'd have a drink with in the pub: friendly and unassuming, a normal, everyday man who made her feel relaxed enough to talk about the most private things, or the very worst of things. Perhaps that was a prerequisite for social workers – like hairdressers or taxi drivers – they had to be able to win trust, to get people talking to them, spilling their problems out in public. She had reminded Obi that the social workers were a means to an end. 'He's just doing a job. A very stressful job. There's a child at the end of this,' she'd said. 'Or a baby.'

Nikki held the marker tightly as she wrote her list:

Miscarriage aged 28
Miscarriage aged 30
Miscarriage aged 31
Miscarriage aged 32

She paused with the marker pen floating above the page. Then she forced her hand down and wrote the words

Stillbirth aged 33.

Nikki closed her eyes. In a second, Obi was behind her eyelids, pacing the room as she sat on the sofa and told him, for the fourth time, that she was bleeding. He had not worried at all after the first miscarriage, told her it was common, and even after the second; although he rushed her straight to hospital, he'd seemed relaxed, bought her a book about nutrition and a box of exotic fruits Nikki couldn't even name. After the third, he'd kept her doctors appointments in his diary and found her a specialist. But after number four Obi's expression had completely changed. He had that determined look on his face that meant he would fix things. He'd made sure that the G.P. had her referred to a team of experts, and another team of experts, and another he'd found himself. After their daughter was stillborn, he'd whispered that they would never ever go through it again. And after they eventually found what was wrong inside her – antiphospholipid syndrome, an autoimmune disease that meant her clotting was deranged – Obi took care of her. 'I will never ever put you through that pain again,' he whispered, and he'd thrown himself into researching adoption. 'We will be parents,' he'd whispered. 'But there will be no more loss.' And he was so certain that he made her feel certain.

Ricardo stood in front of them for a long time. He had very soft eyes, kind and caring, and his teeth were whiter than any teeth she'd ever seen.

There was a tiny hole in his left ear from a long-ago earring, and sometimes Nikki noticed him touch it. He'd been speaking to them for so many months already about their experiences, and watching them closely too. It unnerved Nikki, made her feel as if Ricardo knew everything about them, things that they weren't aware of. Nikki prayed that Obi would look directly at him. Maybe Ricardo was checking to see how well they could give eye contact. Was it a test? He stood in front of Obi for a long time before taking the pen. He was not sure about Obi. Nikki could tell. She wanted to tell him everything she knew: about how Obi was the best of all men; how he was proud and strong and soft and how the world simply was Obi. How he would be a father that a child would look up to. A constant: unchangeable in a world that changed too quickly. How Obi would love his child. How he held her after it happened, all night, and that, every night since, he'd put his hand on top of her chest and looked at her with such sadness in his eyes.

Her arms felt so empty. Too light.

'Now,' said Ricardo, after replacing the marker pens in a box and locking it with a tiny key. 'I'd like you to read out the losses you've experienced. And after each loss, describe how it made you feel.'

Obi shifted in his chair and crossed his long legs in front of him.

'You first,' said Ricardo, smiling and pointing directly at Obi.

Nikki closed her eyes. There was a long silence. When Nikki opened her eyes, Ricardo was still smiling, and looking directly at Obi.

'I don't mind going first,' said Nikki.

Obi was breathing deeply. He hated talking about his feelings. She could tell from the way he was breathing how much he wanted to run from the room, from the whole process. It was simply too important to him. 'We can help a child,' he'd said over and over. 'Really help someone.' And Obi's entire life had been about helping people. All his university friends had gone into private practice, and made a fortune in property or divorce law. But Obi worked for a much lower salary, often giving up time for free, as he felt so passionately about immigration, the rights of all people. She remembered when they'd first met, how different he was from anyone she'd ever known. Her previous boyfriends had not been conversationalists, or if they were they'd talked only of football, or the latest action film, but Obi had talked for hours about humanitarian issues and international affairs and opened up such a world to her. And now he would help a child in care. *They* would.

Nikki looked around the room at the mumsy women wearing court shoes and elastic-waisted trousers, and their husbands, quietly sitting beside them, at their lists written in marker pen – short, much shorter than theirs. She looked down at her jeans and wellies that she'd worn straight from her work at Battersea Dogs' Home; she'd been doing rehoming assessments all morning and had come straight from work and, because she'd stupidly forgotten her shoes, she was covered in mud and probably worse. She looked at Obi's three-piece suit and shining shoes from his court date, his cufflinks – how they mismatched. Him, a lawyer with an extensive publication record and a masters degree in ethics, and her, a helper in a dogs' home with an N.V.Q. level three. They would never get through it.

'OK, well, time is of the essence. Any loss in the family? Parents?' Ricardo looked at his watch. He seemed stressed. Nikki didn't envy him. Rehoming dogs was hard enough, but children? She couldn't imagine. 'I hate to rush everyone, but we are already cutting into resolution time.'

Nikki thought of her parents. She imagined her dad, his shuffling backwards and forwards between the kitchen and the living room, carrying cups of tea on a wooden tray, her mum with her legs stretched out in front of her on a pouffe, her feet spilling over her slippers, the look that always passed between them, even now, despite shuffling and puffy feet. 'Both of my parents are fit and well,' she said. 'They had me older, so it's something I will have to face in the future, but for now they're both fine.'

'Anything else?' said Ricardo 'Any losses that

may have led you here – particularly from the last ten years?'

Nikki took a deep breath. 'I had four miscarriages. I don't know if that counts. I mean, it was early on, really, so I'm not sure if it counts as loss. I've been quite lucky, I suppose.'

She could feel all eyes on her but she couldn't look up. Stupid tears. Now they would think she couldn't even cope. How could she adopt a baby? She couldn't even speak without crying.

'And then I had a stillbirth.'

People held their breath. Nikki heard them all inhale.

'I'm very sorry to hear that.' Ricardo looked at Nikki. 'What was the baby's name?'

She swallowed. Gulped. 'Sorry?'

'What did you call the baby you lost? I can see you're finding it hard, Nikki. But it's very important we can talk about loss in an open way. I can see, Nikki, that this is really difficult for you, talking about the stillborn.'

The stillborn. Still born. She was. The. Her. The wetness of it all. The smell of blood and dead things. Those things she could talk about. But saying her name, a simple name – that was impossible.

'Rosy,' said Obi. And then he whispered, 'Ify.'

'Tell us. Tell us. You need to be able to talk about these things. Imagine a child and the losses they would have suffered. If you can't talk about and resolve your own grief then how can a child talk to you? Especially if you want to consider the possibility of adopting an older child . . .'

A child. An older child. That was Obi's idea. But still: a child.

Any child.

Nikki pressed her leg into Obi. She took a breath.

'What was her name? The baby you lost? You need to say her name. We need to hear it from you as well as Obi.'

Nikki turned her head from Obi, let her leg move away from his. There's a child at the end of this, she told herself. A baby. Or a child we could really help. She remembered Obi's face when she'd agreed, how he'd held her, the sadness in his eyes completely lifted. 'This was meant to be,' he'd said. 'We are meant to help children, and that's right for us.' And she'd let her arms imagine holding something tightly. The weight of air.

'Ify,' she said. 'Our baby was Ify.' And Nikki suddenly remembered her wide-open eyes, gold-flecked and beautiful.

Obi started talking. 'I lost my mum when I was a teenager. Breast cancer.' He looked at Nikki. 'It was awful seeing her go through so much pain. Before that my dad and I didn't really spend much time together but we both looked after my mum as she was sick, and then cared for her at home while she was dying. It was horrendous but the one positive is that my dad and I are very close now. He lives around the corner, and we see him all the time.'

Nikki could hardly believe it. In their whole marriage, she'd managed to get this much out of him, in little puzzle pieces, and now he'd said it all at once. She wanted to hold his hand, hug him, but she didn't dare touch him.

'That must have been really traumatic, for both you and your dad.' Ricardo was really focusing on them today. He'd asked them so many questions, and Nikki wondered if it was some sort of test to see if they'd cope: a room full of strangers and personal information.

'Many thanks for sharing that with us, Obi. It's very important that we are able to talk openly about loss. Any child that you adopt will have experienced the loss of their birth mum. Even a tiny baby.'

Nikki looked up.

'For a child, there is no greater loss than that.' Ricardo paused and looked up at Obi. 'Or maybe there is no greater loss at all than that. Whatever the age. That wound will remain forever, and we need to help children live with it. We can't do that unless we talk openly.' He looked around the room. 'The children we're talking about have to feel safe enough to trust us, to talk to us. And some of them have a very disturbed background where they find it hard to trust, where their sense of reality is completely distorted.' Ricardo looked at Nikki. 'That's why it's so important, this open communication. Can you tell us a bit more, Obi? About your mum.'

Obi uncrossed his legs, sat up straighter. 'It's funny but, even though I was fourteen by then, I can't remember a lot of it. My memory is awful.'

Nikki flashed a look at Obi. His memory was perfect. He remembered in tiny details; everything, to the extent that she often joked he had a photographic memory.

He looked at her, then back at Ricardo. 'There is something else,' he said. 'After the miscarriages . . . After all those miscarriages.' Obi was breathing deeply. His voice had changed, become strained, as if he was forcing the words out. 'I felt them all too.' He stopped talking and everyone in the room held their breath. He had that effect on people. Then he turned towards Nikki, and picked up her hand. 'And after the stillborn, after losing our baby, I felt like I'd lost Nikki.'

Later, they ate tiny sandwiches in a room with no chairs. It was awkward, being in a room with people who knew intimate details of your life, yet were strangers. Everyone had a sad story. People ate their sandwiches carefully. Couples passed each other napkins and touched each other's arms. Everything was being watched. Even so, Nikki leant towards Obi in the corner of the room and kissed his cheek before whispering, 'Thank you for opening up – for talking. I love you,' quietly enough that nobody could hear. When she moved away from Obi, they laughed as they saw the mud she'd deposited from her boots on the bottom of

Obi's pinstripe suit. As they were laughing, Nikki noticed Ricardo across the room, looking at them and smiling before writing something down.

CHAPTER 4

Ricardo's car smelt like an exploded forest. Elijah leant forward and touched the air freshener dangling from the mirror and rubbed it with his finger and thumb, then brought his hand to his nose. He'd been to a forest once; Sue and Gary had taken him. The trees had dropped a soft carpet and Gary found a stick for him. Sue had made sandwiches and they ate them on the pine-needle blanket, watching squirrels jumping up the trees above. He tried to think about the smell of pine trees and not the water in Sue's grey eyes as the car pulled away, the way she lifted her hand up to wave but then let it drop down so quickly, or the way Gary didn't come out of the house. He tried not to remember the smell of burning but it stayed inside his nose and all he could smell was a forest on fire. But, even trying as hard as he could to forget the smell, it felt like his feet were burning. He couldn't believe what had happened, and what the wizard had made him do. The wizard controlled everything and was so powerful it could make Elijah burn down Sue and Gary's

40

kitchen, and make them hate him. The wizard could make Elijah lose everything, all over again. Elijah hated the wizard. He hated himself. He looked out of the window at the places he didn't recognise, and thought of Mama. Only Mama could save him. Only Mama could protect him from the wizard. Mama had done everything she could to help him, with the help of Bishop and the church, and God. But now she was gone.

How could anyone help Elijah if they didn't know about the wizard? Maybe Ricardo was safe to tell. Apart from Mama, no one else cared about Elijah more than Ricardo. But Elijah couldn't risk it. He looked up at Ricardo. 'How do you kill a wizard?' he asked.

Ricardo frowned, like a fly had buzzed in his face. 'I don't know, Elijah. Wizards aren't real.' He frowned harder then sighed and squeezed Elijah's hand, and Elijah sat back. Ricardo was wrong.

Ricardo kept glancing at Elijah and smiling a tight smile that was meant to say that everything would be all right. 'Nargis is a temporary carer but she can have you until we sort something more permanent out,' he finally said. 'She's really experienced and she has another boy staying with her around your age.' His voice sounded rehearsed and fed up, as though he was practising for a play he didn't want to be in, like when they made Elijah be the Angel Gabriel in the school Nativity and the other children laughed at the wings Sue had made him from coat hangers and feathers. It wasn't very good but she did her best. Sue had always done her best.

'What about school?' Elijah suddenly dropped his fingers from his nose. They had been driving for ages. How would he get to school?

'You'll have to go to a different school, I'm afraid. Just for a while.' Ricardo's eyes flicked from the mirror and back again. 'There just wasn't anyone available nearer to your old school.'

Elijah started crying. He couldn't help it. He could hear the wizard's voice laughing from deep within his belly and then it was quiet and not even the sound of the traffic outside the window could fill his empty ears. He thought about a new school and other children pulling and pinching him and laughing at how stupid he was, the teachers making huffy noises because he didn't know the work, and how they would have to do a project called 'family tree' and Elijah's tree always looked like the trees did then – the middle of winter – and when they'd take baby photos in to school and play 'guess the baby' and Elijah would have to take a photo from a catalogue and pretend it was him because he didn't have any baby photos, not a single one. Mama never had a camera. The tears popped out so quickly his entire face was wet in seconds. 'I want to go back to Sue and Gary's,' he said. He wanted Sue's stories so badly, as if stories were food and he was hungry. The air broke down in front of his face into a million different pieces.

'I know you do.' Ricardo continued to watch the

road, but he let his hand move over to Elijah's arm and gave it a gentle squeeze. 'I know you do. But Sue and Gary can't cope with your behaviours any more. They really wanted to but it's just not possible, I'm afraid.'

'Then I want to go with you. Can I stay with you? Just for a little while?'

Ricardo looked straight ahead of him. 'I'm sorry, Elijah, but that's against the rules.' He turned his face to Elijah then back to the road. 'As much as I would love to have you,' he whispered.

'I want Mama. I want my mama.'

There was quiet in the car and outside the car, but suddenly inside Elijah's head was the biggest noise of all. Ricardo looked out of the window, away from Elijah, but Elijah could see his eyes were wet too. 'We'll get you moved into somewhere more permanent as soon as we can. And we'll get you some help, Elijah.' He pulled the car into the side of the road and stopped it. The other cars whooshed past but their car was perfectly still. Ricardo turned off the engine and turned around. He held Elijah's arms tightly between his and looked straight at his face.

'You are a good boy, Elijah. You are a good boy and none of this is your fault.'

'I'm not a good boy,' Elijah cried. 'I'm a bad boy. I'm filled with badness.'

Ricardo held on to Elijah's arms even tighter. 'I'm so sorry you feel like that, Elijah. You're a good boy. There's no badness inside you at all.

Just hurt.' Then he kissed Elijah's head and turned the key to start the car. His hand was shaking. Elijah cried and cried louder than the radio. Even Ricardo cried a little bit and nobody bothered pretending that they weren't. Elijah tried to use his powers to time-travel backwards to before the fire but his powers were blocked. The wizard was only letting him use the evil ones.

Eventually they turned down a road that had lots of small houses, which looked the same, in a row. Ricardo pulled up outside one house and stopped the car. 'This is it,' he said. 'Nargis's house. And the other boy she's caring for is about your age. Maybe a little bit older. He's called Darren.' Ricardo sniffed. Just then the front door opened and there was shouting. Then a head poked out the front. 'Hello!'

An old lady came walking towards them, even older than Sue. She had brown skin the colour of a toffee, almost the same colour as Ricardo's. She wore a red draped dress and sandals over socks. 'Elijah, hello!' She waited until Elijah had come out of the car and stood on the pavement in front of her. 'Where's your bag?' Her face had a cold look that Elijah didn't like. He started crying again and thinking about Sue's warm face. He hated the wizard. He hated himself for letting the wizard be in charge. 'Now come on, Elijah. You'll be fine.' She took his arm and led him in. Elijah looked back to the car but Ricardo was busy lifting his case out of the back. It was getting dark but inside

44

the lights were still not on. Sue would have had her lights on. The house smelt funny. They walked through a hallway which had red carpet and no photos on the walls. There was a long, thin kitchen with a fruit bowl containing no fruit and there were lots of cups in the sink. 'Now, follow me outside and you can meet Darren.'

The woman led Elijah outside and she pointed to the back of a messy garden. There were no toys and the grass needed cutting. Elijah thought of Sue's garden with rose bushes that Gary watered every day. There was a sudden coughing noise. At the back of the garden were a few trees with something moving in them. Rustling. Elijah felt his legs wobble underneath him but he walked forwards to where Nargis pointed. As he turned around, he saw Nargis going back into the house, her red dress the exact colour of Sue's favourite roses. He watched the red disappear. At the back of the garden was a boy with white skin and grazed knees, sitting on a swing. He looked at Elijah and spat on the ground. It was only then that Elijah noticed what was in his hand. A cigarette! He was only a bit older than Elijah and smoking a cigarette. Elijah looked back at the house but Nargis wasn't there.

'Are you allowed to smoke?' Elijah asked.

'I do whatever I like,' said Darren. 'I'm in charge here. I've been here the longest, so I run things.' He spat again and that time it landed on Elijah's shoe. Then he stood up suddenly and grabbed

Elijah's arm, twisting really hard. Elijah closed his eyes. He'd felt hurt before and he knew that it was better to close your eyes. He heard voices in his ear: *Disgusting crybaby. The universe does not want you in it. Go back to burning hell. Then shall he say also unto them on the left hand, 'Depart from me, ye cursed, into everlasting fire.'*

Darren twisted harder, and Elijah opened his mouth to scream but then he closed it. He focused really hard on a stick on the ground, and imagined how it would feel between his fingers, the smooth coldness of it. He thought of a world with only trees, and no humans. How quiet it would be. Darren put his face very close to Elijah's face. His breath smelt of cigarettes and fire. 'If you scream,' he said, 'I'll burn you.'

'Don't forget, Elijah, what I told you. You're going to start work with Chioma, some therapeutic work, which is like special play. It will help you. She will help you. I promise. You are a good boy. And you're safe.'

Ricardo showed Elijah where the toilet was. There was a bucket next to the toilet and the bath was dirty. A rim of mould lined it, patches and circles with soft green edges. Balanced on the outside of the bath were almost-empty bottles: shampoo and bright blue shower gel, a half-used soap covered in tiny hairs, an empty plastic wrapper. Ricardo showed him the kitchen, which smelt funny, and the living room, which had a table in the middle of it where Nargis had left Elijah a plate of jam sandwiches for tea, but there was no pudding. There was a sofa against the wall, with a blanket thrown over it. Ricardo talked very loudly as he showed Elijah around.

Elijah looked and looked for Darren and his cigarette but he didn't see him again. Every time he thought of Darren he felt his stomach move quickly downwards, and his throat swelled closed. But Ricardo didn't notice. He was too busy talking loudly.

When it was time for bed, Ricardo stayed to tuck Elijah in. Elijah knew that he didn't need to stay; his job was over at five o'clock and by then it was almost eight o'clock. He knew that Ricardo was doing a job, looking after him. But it made Elijah feel like they were good friends when he stayed and stayed. Ricardo took Elijah to the bathroom and then to his bedroom. The bedroom was not really a bedroom at all because it was downstairs and it had a table and four chairs in the middle and Elijah's bed was a camp bed that squeaked every time he moved. 'I want you to be brave, OK, little man? You will be fine here. Safe. And after you've spent some time with Chioma, there will be somewhere more permanent soon, I promise.' Ricardo leant down and kissed Elijah's head and a tear fell on to Elijah's forehead.

Elijah felt so sorry for Ricardo, staying late and being sad, that he smiled the biggest smile he could and tried to ignore the wet on his head, on Ricardo's face. Elijah could smell the aftershave now. It was one he hadn't smelt before. Orangey. He wanted to press his nose against Ricardo's chest and breathe it in forever. 'I'll be OK,' he whispered.

But really, Elijah knew Ricardo was wrong about everything. Chioma couldn't help him – whoever she was. Ricardo was wrong to bring him away from Sue and Gary. He was wrong about Elijah being a good boy. And he was wrong about wizards. It wasn't his fault. He wasn't even Nigerian, so how would he know about wizards? Elijah knew. He could hear the wizard all the time, mixed up with Mama's voice, which whispered, *Little Nigeria, a thousand stars light up your face.* Elijah didn't know many things. He didn't know how to read, and he didn't know how to whistle, even though all the children he knew could whistle. But there were two things in life of which Elijah was certain:

His mama loved him.

And wizards were real.

CHAPTER 5

Chioma was the thinnest lady Elijah had ever seen. She was even thinner than Mama. It looked as if she wore a coat hanger across the top of her chest, made from her own bones. Her skin was exactly the same colour as Elijah's, exactly the same colour as Mama's. Around her neck there were three rows of coloured beads in bright yellow and turquoise and earth red. Chioma's legs stretched long and sharp, and her feet were thin, covered in brown leather sandals with tiny pink sequins sewn on. She even had silver beads in her hair, which was twisted in every direction and looked soft. Elijah suddenly wanted to touch it. And there was glitter on her eyelids. Everything about her glinted and twinkled, like she was made from starlight. But the thing that shone the brightest was her eyes; Elijah had never ever seen such bright, clear eyes in an older person. Her eyes were so fresh she must have only ever seen good things, he thought.

They were sitting opposite each other in a play room, which had a sand pit, a table, a small green sofa, boxes of toys – cars, dolls, a pirate ship, a wooden garage with motorbikes, and a castle surrounded by dragons and knights on tiny horses – a box with curtains and a basket of puppets. Everything looked normal in the room, and Elijah thought it could have been a school or club, with the blackboard and tray full of water, except there were bars on the window and a large red fire extinguisher hooked on to the wall. Elijah looked at Chioma's face, her wide smile and bright, square teeth, the colour of the glitter on her eyelids, and he listened to her humming quietly, the sound of her breathing softly. He felt sick and his head banged, but listening to Chioma breathing made the banging stop.

'It's good to finally meet you, Elijah. I've heard a lot about you. Ricardo has told me that you were feeling a bit nervous about coming to see me today but there's nothing to worry about at all. We're just going to have fun and play.'

Chioma's voice was low and soft. 'What toys do you like?'

Elijah didn't say anything, but looked over at the castle. It was tall and had two drawbridges, with secret hiding places. Grey flames were painted up the sides of it and, as he looked at them, they appeared to move. Elijah felt his heart speed up. The wizard crept around inside him. He looked at Chioma closely. Her sparkliness. Did she know about the wizard? Did she know about the fire? Was she really a special social worker or was she sent from God to fight the devil inside him? His heart lifted. Then he thought of other questions. Did she realise he could freeze her right then with laser eyes or point his finger at her heart and melt her to ash? Could she look inside him and see his body was filled with badness?

'We've got lots of work to do,' said Chioma. She laughed. 'Don't look so worried; it's special work – the playing kind. All we need to do is play. That is your work.' She pushed back the chair she was sitting on, stood and walked over to the castle. 'Do you like this?'

Elijah nodded.

'Do you want to play today?'

Elijah looked around at all the toys. He didn't play much. Sometimes he wasn't sure how to play. Other children made it look so easy, picking up toys and making them real, but other children didn't have a wizard trying to take them over. 'Do I have to?'

'No. You can just sit, if you want. Or play. Or even scream really loudly.' Chioma's eyes shone.

Scream really loudly? Who told a child to scream really loudly? Elijah looked at Chioma, who had walked away and was sitting next to the castle and picking up the knights on horseback. She began to make horse sounds and move them up and over the castle. It looked funny, seeing a grown-up play by themselves. Chioma played anyway, as if he wasn't there watching her. She looked as if she was having fun. She didn't look like someone sent to destroy an evil wizard.

51

She played for ages while Elijah just sat and watched. There were no toys to play with at Nargis's house. There was a box that she kept underneath the stairs, full of children's books and a ball, a noisy baby toy and a few cars, but Nargis only pulled that out when Ricardo visited. The rest of the time he watched Darren playing computer games where people exploded and their guts fell out. Elijah felt like playing with Chioma, but he stayed very still instead. He had to remind himself she wasn't his friend. She was a spy who wanted to find out about the wizard.

After ages, Chioma stopped playing. She sat back down on her chair and smiled. 'That was really good fun,' she said. 'We'll do some more playing next week, if you like.'

Elijah shrugged.

'Maybe next week you could play with me?'

He shrugged again. He could see Ricardo's outline against the glass of the window, tall and thin with spiked hair. He imagined Ricardo smiling behind the glass. Elijah suddenly looked right at Chioma. 'Can I see my mama?' he whispered.

'I bet that's what you want more than anything in the world,' she said, 'isn't it? All children want to be with their mummies. It's good to feel like that. But it's very sad when you can't be with Mama.'

Elijah nodded. He looked at Chioma very closely. Her eyes looked straight at his. Elijah focused on her bracelet, golden and filled with dark-red jewels. 'Are you Nigerian?' he asked.

'I am,' she said.

There was knocking on the door and Ricardo walked in. 'Hey, Elijah. I bet you've had great fun getting to know each other.' He looked at Chioma and raised his eyebrows up and down very quickly.

'Elijah has been watching me play with the castle, which is really great because that's my favourite toy. Apart from sand. I also love sand.'

Elijah had never heard of an adult who loved sand. She must be from God. 'Chioma is Nigerian,' he whispered.

Chioma smiled. 'I am very proud to be Nigerian. Nigeria is the best place on earth,' she said. 'In fact, better than earth.' Chioma's eyes sparkled. 'Like heaven.'

Elijah breathed her words in where they found other words inside him and stuck together like they were glued. *Nigeria is a place like Heaven.*

Every week, Elijah visited Chioma, and that was the only good thing about living with Nargis. If he could have lived in Chioma's play room, he would have done, but Chioma always told him after every session that it was time to go home. But Nargis's house was not home.

Some of the visits they would play, and sometimes they would draw or paint, and one visit all they did was drink lemonade and see who could do the loudest burp, and Elijah had laughed and laughed and laughed and felt just like a small boy laughing, which was a really good feeling. But then he had

53

to go back to Nargis's house. Elijah couldn't wait for that day when he would leave. He hated living with Nargis. Every room in her house screamed when he opened the door. Nobody else could hear it, but Elijah could. It was so hard to breathe at Nargis' that he wondered if even the air wanted to get away. He looked through the window every night at the patch of sky Mama would be looking at, and found her star. Then he wished and wished for her to come and find him. But she never did. Elijah knew in the bottom of his tummy that he was not going to live with Mama soon. He knew it because she felt so far away and her star wasn't shining as much as normal.

Elijah heard Mama's voice inside him: *Little Nigeria, you are in danger. If we ever get parted, you must find a Nigerian who believes in God and wait there. You will be safe.*

He also heard Bishop's voice inside him: *Ye make him twofold more the child of hell than yourselves. Ye serpents, ye generation of vipers, how can ye escape the damnation of hell?*

He knew Mama wasn't coming for him at Nargis' house. Elijah didn't feel safe at all. Not one little bit.

'Can I see Mama?' he asked Ricardo. They were outside Nargis' house in the garden in the cold air. Elijah brushed his hand back and forwards over the wooden bench and watched his breath explode in front of him. He couldn't feel the tip of his nose but it was still better than being inside with Nargis.

'She's not well enough to see you this week, Elijah. But she is feeling a little bit better and we are trying to set up regular contact so that you can spend some time with her every week. Also, when she's well enough, we'll have some letterbox contact, which means she'll be able to write you letters . . .'

Elijah looked up at Nargis' house. He saw a face at the window watching them. 'Can I come and live with you?' he asked Ricardo again.

Ricardo shook his head too quickly and too certainly. Ricardo's head definitely didn't want Elijah to live with him. 'It's not going to be possible, I'm afraid,' he said. 'But we are going to keep doing the therapeutic work with Chioma and we'll move towards finding something more permanent. OK?'

Ricardo looked up at Nargis' house too, but Elijah couldn't tell if he could see faces at windows or hear rooms scream or air trying to escape.

If he couldn't live with Ricardo, Elijah wanted to live with Chioma. She was a Nigerian and she believed in God – she must know all about hell and damnation. But Chioma said he wasn't allowed to live with her, either. Sometimes they played with the castle and sometimes they made shapes in the sand with tiny instruments: a small plastic knife, a bucket, a small scoop, a rake. Elijah liked the rake the best. No matter what they had been playing and what mess they had made, the rake smoothed the sand out completely until it was in neat flat rows. He liked touching the sand and holding it in his fist, then letting it fall slowly between his fingers until his hand was empty. Chioma let him play with water and make a big mess and she said it was good to make a mess sometimes. But Elijah didn't like making a mess; he liked cleaning it up afterwards. When he held sand in his hand, he pictured the sea above it – deep, dark blue – and the smell of salt. Sometimes, at night, he'd fly over the oceans and swim right down to the bottom, until it got darker than midnight and tiny fish flashed like miniature stars.

'Do you want to do some drawing today?' Chioma asked. She wore a long patterned dress and a scarf tied up high on her head. Elijah loved her clothes and the tiny slices of fried plantain she brought him to snack on, wrapped in kitchen roll.

'We're not supposed to eat in here,' she'd whisper, 'but who wants to play without a snack?'

Elijah looked out of the window. He felt closer to Mama when he was there. Chioma's play room was on the same road as the contact centre. He always wanted to stay in Chioma's play room in case Mama was searching for him, and he wouldn't mind sleeping on the floor. Mama only went to the contact centre when there was contact and there hadn't been contact for so long, since Mama was ill in the special hospital. Still, Mama had breathed the air in the contact room and her feet had walked on the path outside.

'I wanted to talk to you today,' said Chioma, 'about something important.'

Elijah flicked his eyes towards her.

'It's nothing bad,' she said. 'In fact, it's quite a good thing.' She smiled and shone and sparkled. It was impossible to not smile back. 'I think you are doing so well with our sessions that I wonder if you're ready to start thinking about a forever family. Have you heard of adoption?'

Elijah shook his head. He looked out of the window, past the bars, at the patches of sun changing the colour of the grass outside. Then suddenly he remembered. A boy from Sue and Gary's had been adopted and sent them letters every year and a photo of himself on a bike or on a skateboard or climbing a tree.

'I'd like you to have a think about it, and a talk with Ricardo. And we can talk lots and lots. But I think you might be ready to live with a family forever. A family who you would belong to, and who would belong to you.'

Elijah tried to shrug but his shoulders were frozen.

'Let's play now instead of all this chatting,' said Chioma, her eyes sparkling brightly. 'What would you like to play with?'

Elijah thought for a minute or two then knelt down near the giant dolls' house in the corner. He had never wanted to play with the dolls' house before. It was painted pink and white on the outside and had five different levels. Inside were different furnished rooms and miniature wooden people. A family. 'Shall we play mums and dads?' he asked.

'That's a good idea, Elijah.' Chioma put the pens and paper away, and walked towards the dolls' house and sat down next to him. 'I love this dolls' house,' she said.

Elijah looked at the rooms. There was a living room with tiny chairs and patterned wallpaper, and a bathroom with a real-looking bath and taps the size of ants. At the top of the house was the nursery, where a baby doll was lying in a cot. Elijah picked up the baby. 'The baby is crying,' he said.

'Poor baby,' said Chioma. 'Why is he crying?'

'He wants his mama.'

Chioma peered into the dolls' house and frowned. 'Where is his mummy?'

'I don't know.'

Elijah made crying sounds and lifted the baby into his fingers and gently out of the room to show Chioma. The crying sounds got louder and louder.

'Poor baby,' said Chioma. She stroked the doll's face with her thumb.

Elijah made the crying sounds really well until it sounded exactly like a baby was crying. He looked at the wooden baby and felt so sorry for it. He imagined how the baby must feel and how his cry would sound.

'Poor baby,' said Chioma. 'It must be so hard for him to miss his mummy so much.' She touched the doll's head, and her fingertips touched Elijah's hand. 'Look at the lovely baby,' she said. 'He deserves to have a mummy, and a daddy, and to be loved and to be safe forever.'

Elijah cried and cried like the baby. He let his hand fall into Chioma's and she held it tight before pulling him towards her. Chioma wrapped her arms around Elijah while he cried and cried. She held him so close that he didn't notice the doll fall to the floor. She wasn't supposed to hold him; Elijah knew that. On their very first week, Chioma had told him that she couldn't hold him or touch him, that it was the rules and her job was very different from Ricardo's. But she must have forgotten because she held him close enough that he could hear her heart beating slow and steady, and he felt his own heart beating over it, so quick, like it wanted to get away from his body.

'Poor baby,' Chioma whispered, over and over and over, straight into Elijah's ear.

CHAPTER 6

Obi and Nikki sat together on the sofa, but there was space between them where a pile of magazines waited, children's faces smiling from the covers: *Be My Parent!* one side, and *Children Who Wait* the other. Daddy sat in the chair opposite, grinning. It always surprised Nikki how much he looked like Obi, only slightly smaller with greying hair and smiling eyes.

'Can I get you anything, Daddy?' Obi asked.

'Stop fussing,' said Daddy, laughing. Then he looked up at Obi and half stood, reached across the table and patted Obi's leg before sitting back down. 'Such a good boy,' he said.

Obi rolled his eyes but Nikki could see the smile in them.

She looked around the living room and thought back to their first visits from Ricardo. Usually she hated cleaning, but now, as things became more real and the adoption was more than simply a possibility, she found herself nesting. Obi laughed whenever he saw her pottering around and, the day before, he'd grabbed her and lifted her up to him. 'I can't believe I'm saying this, but stop cleaning!' he'd said, and then they'd both laughed.

'I feel nervous,' said Nikki. She thought of Ricardo's questions about what she and Obi would feel able to accept when they got to matching:

Parental schizophrenia?

Child born of incest or rape?

Child with overtly sexualised behaviour?

What about a child who had had one parent killed by the other parent, or a child who had a life-limiting illness?

Obi had said yes to everything. But she'd said, 'A child with a life-limiting illness? I couldn't ever lose a child. Not another child.' Obi had held her, and nodded his head gently against hers. Then Nikki had looked at the list again. A child with overtly sexualised behaviour? How would she cope? How would she know what to do? The thought made her feel sick.

'These are real children, Nik. We can't be picky.'

'I'm not being picky, Obi. I'm being serious.'

He had shaken his head. 'This is what we've signed up for – any child we adopt will be damaged. How they behave is just a symptom of that.'

Nikki's heart hurt. She felt cruel. But what was the point in not being honest? 'It doesn't matter if it's just a symptom. It's their behaviour. It's them. And I don't think I could handle a child who . . . who . . .'

Obi had just stared, waiting, but the words wouldn't come. This was why Nikki wanted a baby:

a life too new to be too damaged; a child who'd be easy to care for. She closed her eyes and scolded herself. Why was she trying to limit their options? They wanted a child; she wanted to be a mother.

When Ricardo next visited, Obi told him that they weren't able to accept a child with a life-limiting disease. 'It's out of the question,' he said, looking at Nikki.

'That's fine,' said Ricardo. 'I think we're done with the home study. I think you're going to be wonderful parents,' he said, and Nikki's arms threw themselves around Ricardo before she could stop them.

Nikki shook Ricardo and the home study and difficult questions with difficult answers from her head. She took a big breath. They were finally going to be parents.

'This is exciting! We could be looking at our son or daughter.' Nikki touched the magazines, ran her finger over the faces. They had collected three months' worth and Ricardo had brought them a few that were much older.

'They're out of date,' he'd said, 'but they give you some idea of the ages and needs of children who are waiting to be adopted. I think all families should look at these to understand that most children who need adoption have special needs, or are sibling groups of three or more children, needing adopting together. It helps them if they have a fantasy of a single, healthy little baby.'

He looked at Nikki then, she was sure of it, but

Obi didn't notice. He had thanked Ricardo and put the magazines away. It was only now that they had felt able to look at them. Only now they were approved adopters. Only now it was real. A child.

'One of these children in here could be ours,' said Obi. 'Imagine that! What a thing we're doing. What an adventure.'

'A grandfather at last!' Daddy laughed out loud. 'I don't like these magazines,' he said. 'Feels like a sales conference. But I am very, very pleased that you are finding my grandson.'

'It might be a girl!' said Nikki, but when she looked at Daddy's face, she could see that look in his eye. He was teasing her.

Obi looked at Nikki for the longest time and touched her cheek with his thumb. 'You are going to be the best mum. This is what we've been waiting so long for. All those months and intrusive questions, and before, all that pain . . .'

Nikki closed her eyes and felt the softness of Obi's thumb, the certainty of his voice. He was right.

'All those miscarriages,' whispered Obi. 'All those children we lost. And here are children waiting to be found. It all makes so much sense.'

'I can't wait to see my grandchild. Honestly, having grandchildren is better than having children. You are older and wiser and can give them back at the end of the day when they're tired!'

Nikki smiled. Daddy had been such a support for them. He was the first person they called to tell they were pregnant and the first person to call to say they'd miscarried. Yet he'd never once told them to give up, or been any less excited each and every time, or less sad each and every time. When Obi had collected the magazines, Nikki had suggested they look at them with Daddy. 'He's been with us every step,' she'd said. 'Let's get his opinion.'

First there was giggling, loud enough to float into the house, then high heels clicking on the pavement outside. Then a guffaw. It sounded like two drunk teenagers were messing around in the street outside, but Nikki knew it wasn't.

'I'm not holding them,' said Jasmin's voice. 'I look like a baby.'

She heard her sister whoop in response and imagined her pulling a silly face at her daughter.

'Chanel,' said Obi. 'I told her not to come over until later.'

'You can't blame her. She's excited too.' Nikki looked at the outlines against the frosted glass: a tall, thin one and a shorter one with pigtails. The shorter one was passing a bunch of balloons to the tall, thin one. Her sister. Her niece. She smiled, ran to the front door and opened it before they could knock again.

'Approved adopters!' shouted Chanel. She handed over half a dozen pink balloons. 'A baby! We're going to have a baby!'

Nikki pulled them into the house and held the string on the balloons, not knowing what to say.

'Approved adopters,' said Chanel again. 'So exciting.' She walked into the living room with Jasmin trailing after her, and Nikki followed them in. 'Have you picked one yet?'

Chanel was hugging Obi, then Daddy, so they didn't notice the balloons at first, but then Obi started to laugh. 'We haven't actually got a child yet, you know. And what's with the pink? We are not specifying the gender.'

Jasmin suddenly looked interested. 'Ew. You're getting a boy? Maisie in my class has a baby brother and her mum spends all day cleaning snot off his nose.'

'Jasmin.' Nikki let the balloons go and dance in the air above them and put her arm around Jasmin's shoulder. 'It could be a boy, or a girl.'

'And it probably won't be a baby,' said Obi. 'Whoever we get matched with will be perfect for this family. Most children who need adopting are older. Look.' Obi picked up a magazine and laid it on his lap, flicking open the first page.

Nikki sat down next to Obi. Daddy got up from his chair and moved next to Obi, sitting on the arm of the sofa. Nikki made to move but he shook his head. 'I'm fine,' he said, looking down at the magazine on Obi's lap.

'I'm not sure we shouldn't save this for later,' said Nikki, gesturing with her eyes to Jasmin.

But Jasmin didn't move.

'She's fine,' said Chanel. 'It'll be her cousin, after all.'

Faces stared out at them: a few babies, but mostly older children in pairs or threes, most of them mixed race or black. Every single one of the children looked beautiful to Nikki. Children waiting to be adopted were all beautiful, unusually so, with thick, long eyelashes and eyes that opened wide and glistened. All the photos showed the children in their best clothes, ribbons in their hair, clean and neat. Underneath each photo was an advertisement for that particular child, as though the children were white goods – fridges or washing machines. Nikki tried not to focus on the babies' faces, but she felt her eyes drawn towards theirs, wide open, their smiling gums and chubby cheeks.

She touched the pages on Obi's lap. 'Ricardo said to read between the lines, whatever that means. I suppose like here, it says, "Sammy (not real name)", so that might mean the birth family are looking for them – want to take them back. There might be a possibility of abduction.'

'Abduction?' said Daddy. 'Really? Is that a possibility?'

Nikki nodded. It was true. There were so many possibilities. Abduction by birth families was just one of them. 'These children aren't given up, they're taken from their birth families due to the worst abuse you could imagine. Often families try and trace them; that's why they like to place children out of borough.' The words rang through Nikki as she looked at the photographs: *not real name*.

'Abducted by aliens,' whispered Jasmin.

'Or it might mean that they've got a ridiculous name,' said Obi. 'Look. There's one here called Lion; I mean, who calls a kid "Lion"? In seriousness?' He laughed.

'Lion!' Imagine a child in Nigeria called Lion,' said Daddy. 'Nobody would have him visit their house.'

Chanel laughed so loudly the balloons moved across the ceiling. Jasmin walked towards Daddy and he reached out and pretended to tickle her. He was the only person that Jasmin let treat her like a child, and her face lit up whenever Daddy was nearby.

They turned the next page, and the next. The adverts were all similar, but occasionally Obi would stop at one and read it out.

'*Lucy is a happy three-year-old girl who attends nursery part time where she is showing some difficulties but progressing well with support. She has some developmental delay, which may be due to her past experiences. Her foster carers describe her as a happy little rainbow who enjoys Peppa Pig and dressing up. Lucy would benefit from one parent being at home full time and no other children in the household.*' He paused. In the photo was a little girl with blond hair, blue eyes, pale skin. 'She looks lovely,' he said. 'Mind you, they all look lovely.'

'Aw, Nik, she looks perfect. I can picture her now in that new Rhianna collection they have for kids at River Island. O.M.G. Like clothes

67

for adults, but just miniature. She could totally pull off leopard print.'

Nikki hit Chanel's arm gently while Obi chuckled and shook his head.

Nikki looked down at the magazine again. She did look lovely to Nikki, but all Nikki could think of were alarm bells. Read between the lines, Ricardo had told them. Support, developmental delay, *cannot live with other children*. What would she do to the other children? thought Nikki. What had happened to her?

'Too white,' said Daddy.

Nikki leant forward and shot him a look.

'Well, she is,' he said, his eyes laughing.

'Or, look at these two. Gorgeous.' Obi pointed to two smiling children, a boy and girl, both mixed race – or 'dual heritage' as Ricardo kept correcting them – with beautiful happy faces. '*Talesha and Malika, age four and five, are a brother and sister who need to be adopted together. They have an older sibling who is to be adopted separately. Talesha has recently started reception and is settling well. She enjoys making cakes and flying kites. Talesha is a confident little girl who would benefit from clear boundaries. Malika is a boisterous boy who likes playing outside on his bike. He has shown some signs of attachment difficulties for which he is receiving extra support. Malika is very protective of his younger sister and finds it hard to let others care for her at times, though we anticipate that with time this will improve. Talesha and Malika's foster carers describe them as a cheerful handful.*'

'Cool names,' said Chanel.

'Nightmare,' said Nikki.

'What do you mean? They look lovely.'

'What kinds of names are those? They don't sound Nigerian!' said Daddy.

'Daddy, we've been over this,' said Obi. 'The child we adopt probably won't be Nigerian. At least not Igbo. And it really doesn't matter to us anyway.'

'Eh? I hope you're joking.' Daddy pretended to fall off the arm of the sofa.

Nikki ignored them and focused on the magazine. 'They do look lovely, but can you imagine how much work they'll be, how much help they will need? Maybe the older one cared for the younger one because they were so neglected. And I read somewhere that neglect is the worst form of abuse. It damages their brains. Anyway, look at this little fella!' Nikki pointed to a photo of a fat baby with a gummy smile.

Obi turned the page back to Talesha and Malika. 'What are you talking about?' He hadn't even looked at the baby. Nikki felt her eyes sting. He put his other hand on top of Nikki's. 'That's the whole point, isn't it? That we help someone who needs help the most?' He squeezed her hand.

She looked at Obi's kind face, the outline of Daddy's kind face behind him. 'You're right,' she said. 'It's just a bit scary, that's all, to think about a life, a life that we're in charge of.'

'I know, but what a thing to do! Look at these

kids. All of them. Of course they'll have issues but they need love. Love is the most important thing they've missed. And we have plenty of love.'

Nikki picked up a magazine from the pile and flicked through the pages. It was an older magazine, one that Ricardo had left them as it was out of date. 'Malika and Talesha,' she said. 'Look.'

It was definitely the children from the other magazine. 'It's the same two,' Obi said. 'A year ago. A whole year in care, being advertised and no parents coming forward. That should tell you everything you need to know if you're feeling unsure about what we're doing here.'

'Poor little things,' said Chanel. She leant towards Jasmin, but Jasmin stepped away from her.

Nikki breathed deeply. Obi was right. It made perfect sense. They should help someone who needed help the most. Poor kids.

'They are not the right ones for you,' said Daddy.

'We're not shopping for a new car, Daddy. We're looking at children. And lives. Imagine all these children and what they've been through.' Obi moved the magazine over to Nikki's lap.

Daddy moved back over to his chair and sat down, leant forwards. 'I know. I am making light of dark work,' he said. 'And I want you both to know that I will be on this journey with you every step of the way. We all are. I love you both and I'm so proud of you.'

Obi laughed and pulled Nikki's hand towards

his mouth and kissed her fingers. 'With us all together, we'll be fine,' he said.

'We'll help, Aunty Nikki,' said Jasmin.

'Of course we will,' Chanel agreed.

'I mean it,' said Obi. 'We are going to give a child a chance, a real chance.'

Nikki looked back down to the magazine.

So many children with read-between-the-lines stories. So many older children still waiting. Nikki tried to focus on them. But her eyes kept moving away and landing on the babies.

'You don't need the magazine,' said Daddy. 'Our boy isn't in there.'

'Here we go,' said Nikki, loud enough for Daddy to hear.

'I'm serious. My grandchild is a boy,' he said. 'A Nigerian boy.' He looked to the ceiling and put his hands together as if praying. 'A *Nigerian* boy.'

Later that afternoon, Obi was called into work. Something important. He had kissed her hair, grabbed his keys and run out. Nikki went for a walk to clear her head. She usually walked through the park towards the river – almost daily, if the weather allowed it. She loved to be near the water. Growing up, she'd lived close to the sea, her childhood filled with brawny, yellow-booted fishermen, whose laughter rattled like her mum and dad's house. But that day Nikki found herself walking towards the swing park, in the opposite direction to the water that usually drew

71

her. Their plans whirled round and round inside her. She understood why Obi wanted to help an older child, a child who needed help and who might be overlooked. And, seeing those children in the magazines getting older and older, she had felt his excitement that they might be able to rescue one. But still, her head was filled with the sound of a baby crying and her arms were too light and empty.

She walked past the thick trees, and the playground full of children. The sun was shining brightly, making the grass look AstroTurf green. The park was filled with the smell of summer. An ice-cream van perched on the side of the path; a small queue of children formed in front of it, looking up longingly at the pictures on the side of the van of different-coloured ice creams. As Nikki walked past, she smiled at a young girl pointing to a 99 Flake. Her mother shook her head.

'No,' she said. 'You can have a small natural-fruit lolly only. Don't want to spoil your dinner.' She looked over the girl's head and winked at Nikki.

But Nikki didn't wink back. She'd have loved the chance to give her child an ice cream. Nikki walked on towards the playground, which was filled with mothers. Some were talking while their children went up and down slides; some pushed younger children and babies on the swings while texting or talking on mobile phones. One mum, though, was completely focused on her child. Her boy, who was around six or seven years old, was climbing a tree and she was standing below it, her arms outstretched as if to catch him.

'I won't fall, Mum,' he shouted.

He was almost hanging upside down. But his mum laughed. 'I'll catch you.'

'Am I allowed to go higher?'

'Yes, but be careful.'

Nikki stood next to the gate and found that she was gripping the railings and holding her breath. He was so high up in the tree that she only saw a trainer poking out from the branches.

His mum stood, looking up, still smiling.

Eventually he climbed down and jumped the last part, and then ran towards his mum's outstretched arms. 'I did it, Mum! I did it!'

Nikki found her eyes glued to the mother and son. She'd give anything to be that mother standing under the tree. She thought about the girl without an ice cream. Nikki looked around the playground in front of her.

I can do it, she thought. I don't need a baby. A child is a child. I will have a son or daughter at last. I'll let them climb really high, and be ready to catch them if they fall.

CHAPTER 7

My Elijah,

As I write this, I can see the colours of spring bursting through the ground. I can see everything here from the shade of this tree, sitting on my 'writing bench', as I've named it. I like looking out. Especially at this time of year. The best thing about England is surely the spring, here reminding us that after every winter come flowers and sunshine, with tiny buds of colour and hope. With the air like it is today – blowing so soft on my face, smelling of all things pure – and the lawn laid out green in front of me, anything feels possible. Even in England. But I know the truth of it. That, of course, after every colour comes another, and after spring, summer and autumn comes winter, dark and cold like a terrible dream. There is never winter in Nigeria. Even now, as I look at the first hint of the best English spring, my stomach rolls into a ball when I think of home, spiny like a hedgehog curled up inside me. I remember everything as if it all happened in a dream last night. Leaving Nigeria was the most difficult thing of all. I'll never forget the look on my mother's face at the airport, the pain in her eyes wider than the earth. But I was young, and excited, and going to England. I imagined a place as sweet-tasting as my childhood breakfast cereals. The reality I was confronted with was not sweet at all, but bitter and sour.

We had a small flat, Akpan and I, which was difficult to clean, and smelt of the dead mouse that, despite our best efforts, we could never find. We lived on the eighth floor of a tall building with lifts that were stained with urine. Nigeria is a much cleaner place. We had two neighbours: the first, a Ghanaian, was an unregistered childminder and had somehow found a way to hide twenty or so young children whenever the authorities came knocking, and would take down the note from her door that said, *One hour, one pound, per child.* I waved at her a few times but she was hardly ever on the balcony and kept the children inside with the curtains closed and television on loud. The flat on the other side was quieter and always smelt of burning plantain, sweet and fiery at the same time. Men went in and out, and hung around the doorway. Bad-looking men. Those kinds of men would have been arrested in Lagos, simply for looking the way they did – shifty-eyed and furtive, like they'd committed a crime. Akpan told me to stay away from that doorway as bad people lived there, but, son of mine, I had a brain in my head and could see for myself. I made the sign of the cross whenever I walked quickly past. But they didn't bother us, and so we didn't bother them. Our flat was desperate for decoration; the carpet had lived many generations and the pattern was difficult to see, but cleanliness is next to Godliness, as you know, and so I did my best, keeping the surfaces clean, filling the air with the smell of jollof rice. I had Akpan buy plenty of bleach and small wipes in a yellow packet that removed the smell of the mouse, for a few minutes at least. We were not rich, and it was not a palace, but those first few months of living in Deptford were magical, filled with brightness. We lived in our own little cloud. Akpan would return from his work and we'd sit on the balcony and look out across London, while I fried some plantain and listened to his stories. He liked to tell me about his childhood and the games he played, the school he loved where he was president of the chess society. We heard of a church, Deliverance Church, which was at the end of Deptford High Street, next to the stalls selling coats and bathroom products, bin bags and trainers, and was run by Bishop Fortune, a Nigerian man from Jos.

The church was beautiful, the pulpit filled with gospel singers, the floors clean enough to eat off, the Nigerian congregation pressed into their neatest clothes. When we first met him, Akpan shook Bishop's hand so enthusiastically I thought he was hurting the poor Bishop, but he simply laughed. 'Welcome! Welcome!' he said. 'I'm Bishop Fortune Oladipo Jerusalem Pilgrim at your service, sir! If our Muslim brothers and sisters can have their Mecca, then why can we not?'

Akpan had laughed and lit up like a star. He'd taken home a card, given to him by the Bishop, and Blu-tacked it to the wall above our bed:

Bishop Fortune Oladipo J.P. (The Doctor of Souls). Owner and Manager of Deliverance Church, 41 Hill Street, Deptford –
where the Devil is
NOT WELCOME.

Fighting Evil with God-Given Powers
by Bishop Fortune Oladipo
is for sale at £4.99 from Evangelical Book Shop,
London SE5 7RY

We attended that church all the time, Elijah. We were so impressed by the four-wheel-drive cars parked outside, the flash of the Rolex watches coming from the men in the congregation. The Bishop impressed us the most: he wore a different silk suit every time we saw him, and had a reputation for exorcising evil spirits.

'He has a private jet,' one of the congregation, a smart man, whispered during the Sunday sermon. He always wore a waistcoat, and Akpan always nodded to him. 'He uses it to fly back to Nigeria whenever he feels like it.'

It didn't surprise me at all, Elijah. My own Uncle Pastor was a miracle maker, and so he was, by then, a famous man, and also very rich. He owned four television sets as big as wheelbarrows, a fleet of Mercedes, and had his suits imported directly from Italy. It was Uncle Pastor who'd paid for our large house and school uniforms, as Baba's mechanic's salary was barely enough to cover Mummy's cooking pots, and my grandparents were too old to work. Uncle Pastor performed miracles at Guaranteed Success Ministries. His sermons were a concert of the greatest music ever played. The Holy Ghost Night Programme at Guaranteed Success Ministries attracted people in their masses, falling over and around each other; even though the church was as big as an aircraft hangar, there simply was not enough floor space. The women who did not have room to jump down on to the floor would complain loudly. They were so dramatic, the women of my childhood church. And Bishop reminded me of them, those women, of my Uncle Pastor, of my family.

It must be strange to you, Elijah, that we were so impressed by such a wealthy man of God, but we were. In Nigeria, there were pastors who had their own television channels, a fleet of Mercedes, private jets, bodyguards, and were millionaires – some actually billionaires. They were more popular than movie stars, or pop stars, more popular than kings and presidents. They wore the finest clothes – imported, fine Italian silk suits, or designers such as Dolce and Gabbana, Gucci, Moschino – and their shoes were one hundred per cent crocodile skin. They were smart and shining, those men, groomed so far that the Rolexes on their wrists didn't even appear to shine in comparison. And I don't mean my Uncle Pastor, although he was famous and had a congregation of millions, but some of the others had their own recording studios. They were so famous that people, women usually, fainted and screamed and queued through the night to get glimpses of them speeding past in their new-series BMWs. These men are the reason that BMW brings out the new series in Lagos before any other place. They know wealth like I could never understand.

Elijah, it is common knowledge how pastors make their wealth, how they take ten per cent of their congregation's earnings, how the congregation has to give this ten per cent, these alms, to maintain the upkeep of the church. It is tricky to explain this to you when you've only known England, and the churches filled with six people at best on a Sunday, and terrible singing. Elijah, the Nigerian church is the pastor, and who would want to belong to a church that did not have enough faith in God to keep their pastor well? Every Nigerian knows that this money will come back tenfold. I have seen it with my own eyes, time and time again. And the reality, Elijah, is that when you are so poor you have to step over the dead bodies on your way to market as you cannot take on the funeral costs of a stranger, when you are that poor, Elijah, the dream of two Ferraris is just as reachable as the dream of good roads to drive them on, or food for all your neighbours, adequate healthcare. You get what you put into this world, and prayer is no different.

I explain all this to you, Elijah, so that you understand a little bit. Being English now, it will be hard for you, but I pray that one day you will find yourself in Nigeria and at church and see the pastors preaching, and the millions listening and literally throwing money at the pastor's feet – money they don't have, they cannot afford. But if you follow those people home you will understand something more; for how can they afford not to?

We began to settle, enjoying living in our own private world, talking to each other until late in the night, whispering across a pillow. Akpan removed any of my worries. When I first saw a red car and noticed the men inside it looking up at our balcony, Akpan convinced me I was imagining it. He pulled me towards him and kissed my worries gone, a kiss for each worry.

'There's nobody there.' He looked out of the window and down into the street below, where I'd seen the red car and noticed something black pointing upwards. A camera? Why would anyone photograph our flat?

'Honestly, there's nobody there.' Akpan stroked the back of my neck with his fingertips. 'My love, you worry so much. Even if there was a car following us, I have all the correct documents. They are after that childminder. In the UK they have to be registered so the government can take most of the money. Please try not to worry.'

'I'll try. I don't want you to worry about my worrying!'

We laughed, and how I loved him. I loved him so. I read my notebooks to Akpan while he slept, sending the words of Nigeria and God into his dreams. I recited psalms and Egyptian love poetry. Elijah, you were inside me by then, but Akpan did not know. It was a secret between you and me and God. I could feel a soft warmth running through me, God whispering to my body. I spoke to you all the time, sang songs from my own childhood. I felt like an old woman and a young girl all at once; everything looked so clear, even the grey colour of England seemed beautiful. Akpan and I made love all the time. Elijah, your very first foundations were strong, and I hope those early months of strength will help. When the wind blows hard, as it surely will, I pray you will only shake a little.

CHAPTER 8

It was a gloomy day. Not cold, but with a wind that whipped up around Nikki's face, blowing her hair in all directions. The kind of day she loved most: a Wales-weather day, as she always told Obi. Good for growing. She looked upwards. It might rain but she didn't mind being outside, even then. This was the best bit. Assessing the dogs for rehoming; watching and analysing and sometimes treating their behaviours; the way she gained their trust; how they went from being scared, ears down, flinching, to jumping and running towards her excitedly. It was remarkable how quickly they improved with the right sort of care and attention.

Nikki had fallen into charity work, starting in the office in the fundraising department, full of glamorous colleagues with perfect hair. Everyone was friendly but she'd found herself taking lunch breaks with the animals instead of her colleagues. A few courses and a lot of experience later, and Nikki was a valued member of the rehoming team. She still attended all the fundraising events, which was how she had met Obi, but her heart was outside with the dogs. She smiled as she remembered the night she and Obi had met. It was at the Dorchester Hotel, every bit as opulent and luxurious as she'd imagined, and Nikki had for once taken the entire afternoon to get ready. She'd worn a long, backless, jade-green silk dress and the highest heels imaginable, and tamed her hair into submission before arriving a fashionable ten minutes late. Nikki had always been able to talk to anyone and was more than happy circulating, a glass of champagne in her hand, cool and composed when she thought of the dogs and how much money she'd be able to raise. And then she'd seen him. A tall, strong, handsome man with the smoothest skin and widest smile, dressed in a petrol-blue suit. He'd smiled at her and suddenly she'd felt nervous. Nikki threw back her head and took a mouthful of champagne, and somehow it had ended up going down the wrong way, and she was spluttering and coughing and making noises that sounded barely human and there he was, the handsomest man in the room, patting her on the back of her backless dress, his skin on hers.

The Staffy at her feet barked and yapped and spun around in circles, chasing his tail. She focused and was back in the training yard, the grey day wrapped around her. Instead of a silk dress, she looked down at her muddy boots, the thick dog weaving between them. Nikki laughed. 'All right, little one,' she said. 'What an excited boy you are!' And he ran at her and jumped up knocking her off balance until he could get a good lick of her face.

'Nikki! Phone call!'

She pushed him away and wiped the slobber from her cheeks. Still laughing, she went into the office to answer the phone. Sometimes Chanel phoned her with some drama or other, but the voice wasn't Chanel's.

'Nikki? It's Ricardo. I'm so sorry to bother you at work, but I knew you'd want me to. I wonder if you're home this evening?'

Nikki's heart began thumping so hard it hurt. Why would he phone? Was there a problem with their application? 'We can be. Is everything OK?'

'Well, it's nothing to get excited about yet, but there is a child I wanted to discuss with you. A lovely boy who needs an extra-special family. But, as I said, this is very early days, so don't get too excited.'

Nikki listened to all the words that Ricardo said, and looked out of the window at the Staffy jumping up and down and spinning round and round like her heart. Ricardo spoke for another five minutes but all Nikki could hear were the words 'there is a child' over and over again: Thereisachildthereisa childthereisachildthereisachildthereisachildthereisa child.

Later that evening, they looked out of the window and watched Ricardo's car pull up outside, the car window open and techno music blaring out for a

84

few seconds before he switched the engine off. They watched Ricardo walking up the path towards the house wearing the widest-brimmed hat Nikki had ever seen and it took effort, even with all the stress and importance of the visit, not to laugh. It stretched out either side of his head like an umbrella and, as Ricardo neared the door where they stood, Obi squeezed her hand hard, and coughed. Obi was holding his stomach in, trying not to laugh. If he burst out laughing, she would be so angry. Everything rested on this visit.

'Hello, my loves,' Ricardo said, reaching an arm out from the shade of his hat. 'Thanks for seeing me today.'

'Hello. Come in.' Nikki stepped backwards to allow Obi and Ricardo to move through the doorway. She had already laid out cookies and cake, juice and a pot of tea in the living room. Ricardo followed her, sat down and whipped off the hat in one movement.

Underneath the hat, Ricardo's hair was blue.

Nikki and Obi stood looking at him for what seemed like ages, and quiet filled every corner of the room. Nikki tried to speak but no words came out. Obi started to laugh, holding his stomach with his hand: a real belly laugh, without any attempt to hide it. Nikki wanted to cry. How she loved Obi, and how she felt like killing him some-times. But part of her wanted to burst out laughing too.

'Oh, this,' said Ricardo, beginning to laugh too,

while rubbing his hair. 'I do apologise. It's much brighter than I'd intended.' He laughed again and all Nikki could hear was two men giggling like children, and she imagined her happiness hovering in the air between them, like a hummingbird, too fast, too small for them to notice.

'But, seriously – I must look very unprofessional. I'm a very professional person, honestly! It was supposed to wash out. Still, you should never believe the packet . . . Doesn't always do what it says on the tin!' Ricardo threw back his head, his laughter punctuated by snorts every few seconds.

'Right,' said Obi, sitting down eventually, after he had stopped laughing, 'would you like some tea?'

'Lovely,' Ricardo said.

Nikki sat on the chair opposite, trying not to look at the electric-blue hair or the giant hat on the back of the sofa, like a satellite dish. She tried to focus on the image of a child, of them as parents.

Ricardo drank some tea and ate three pieces of cake, dropping crumbs all over himself. Nikki could almost hear Obi's thoughts: *We can't trust a man who looks like this, with blue hair; how is this man a practising social worker?*

'Like I said, there's a child, and I must tell you that I think you'd be a very good match for my lovely Elijah. I've brought the paperwork with me to go through it, but I'm afraid it's not been done in great detail. But, of course, I can fill you in on the details. He really is a lovely little seven-year-old boy. Of course, there are plenty of things for us to discuss, factors that may affect his future behaviours.' He paused. 'He's had very challenging behaviours in the past. He might have been involved in a fire – even trying to hurt one of the other foster children in his last placement.'

Obi's face was neutral. But, even then, Nikki swore she noticed the corners of his mouth turning upwards.

'He's had some terrible experiences, but he appears to be resilient. He has suffered, though, a great deal of trauma, multiple moves and abuse – both neglect and physical – and his birth mum has a history of mental-health difficulties, some of which may be genetic. I know this is a lot to take on board, and we weren't considering adoption for Elijah at all; we were looking at long-term fostering. However, he's done so amazingly well in therapy that we think he would do well in a family environment. With the right family, of course. In terms of contact, it's currently letterbox only but ideally we'd like twice-yearly face to face. The birth mother has been encouraged to start writing letters but we're not sure how that'll go. If they're too age-inappropriate or disturbing in any way, we'll keep hold of them and make sure he gets them when he's older. Meanwhile, I've asked if she can send cards or write more age-appropriate, general letters. Anyway, let me tell you about the boy, Elijah, my lovely Elijah.'

He smiled and Nikki found her anxiety lifting.

'He's charming and such a character. He adores animals, so, Nikki, you'd have plenty in common. He likes anything to do with nature. He loves learning about different habitats. His temporary foster carer says that's his favourite thing – documentaries about natural history. He has quite a collection of animal textbooks that he likes looking through. He can't read and is way behind with his schooling, but that's more about his lack of opportunity than ability.' Ricardo smiled again. 'Now, you need to be aware that caring for him will probably be the hardest job you've ever done. And we'd expect you to drop everything to care for him. I know we discussed this before, but you'd have to be based at home.'

'My manager has said I can work flexibly.' Nikki looked at Ricardo. Being outside with the dogs was part of who she was. 'I could work a few hours a day when Elijah is at school.'

Obi looked straight at her. 'Of course, you'd stay at home if you had to,' he said.

Nikki nodded. 'Of course.'

Ricardo took another sip of tea. 'It might work. But there's so much to think about and discuss. If we want to proceed, then it will go to a matching panel – experts who will either agree that you're a good match for each other or not. Very rarely do we have any disagreements at that stage, I have to say. And Elijah is a very special case so you'd probably be one of two, if not the only family we're looking at for him.' He frowned. 'Elijah has difficulties separating fantasy from reality. He's even talked about thinking he is evil. There's an investigation going on as to whether he was subjected to some kind of ritual abuse.'

Ritual abuse. Nikki felt her stomach sinking inside her. What did that mean? 'Sounds serious,' she said.

'Well, it is, but we don't know anything yet. As for Elijah saying he's bad, my own feeling is that he's been made to feel bad and evil, and so that's exactly what he believes, but it's not naturally a part of him. You'll see. There's a pattern. Elijah's behaviours only become serious when something goes wrong – with his birth mum or in a placement – which all seems understandable but obviously needs to be addressed. So you see there'll be lots of work to do, and that will mean leaving work at a moment's notice if he's having a bad day, or something happens at school.'

'Of course. We're fully prepared for that.' Obi leant forwards and put his hand on top of Nikki's knee. 'And we're committed together. I would be able to take some time off work too, in special circumstances.'

Obi's job was important, dealing with asylum seekers who had just arrived in the country, terrified and alone, often suffering physical and psychological scars. Nikki knew that she'd be the primary carer. She remembered the mum she saw in the park, letting her son climb high up a tree, her arms outstretched ready to catch him. She could do this. They could do it. They were so close to having a child. 'What if we're not a suitable family for him?' Nikki asked. 'You said we might be the only ones?'

'Well, that's complicated. But, essentially, Elijah may be at the age now when a residential unit might be more appropriate than a family setting.'

'You mean a children's home?'

'They're not as bad as you'd think,' said Ricardo. 'And for some children family life may just be impossible. Elijah may be heading that way, and people don't come forward for older children—'

'He's seven years old,' said Obi.

'I know. It seems crazy, doesn't it? But Elijah has had a number of moves, which will all have affected his attachment. And he was with his birth mother until he was five. I don't want to paint a completely negative picture, but Elijah will have major difficulties and you need to be prepared.'

'Seven years old,' said Obi, shaking his head again.

'It's important to remember that all children needing adoption will have special needs of some description or other. All of them. And the key factor seems to be how resilient they are; certainly Elijah appears extremely resilient.' He paused. 'The other important factor is that Elijah will need to be an only child. I know medically you're not exactly in a position to have another child, but I still wanted to say – because of that tiny possibility. I can't stress it enough. We wouldn't go through the process if there were any way that you planned to have birth children soon. I think maybe when he's much older, depending on how he's doing, you could consider it, but you'd need to leave a significant gap or it could really affect Elijah's placement. He's suffered too many moves and too much abuse to share his parents and he needs to be cared for as a much younger child since he missed out on those experiences and so is emotionally very demanding.'

'We aren't trying to have children of our own,' said Obi. 'Not any more. I don't think we could go through that again.'

'We were told by so many doctors,' said Nikki. 'The doctors said it would be very hard, almost impossible, for me to get pregnant in the first place, now, after the stillbirth. And, even if it wasn't, I take contraceptives to regulate my periods. So there's really no chance.'

'Well, that's clarified.' Ricardo leant forwards. 'I think it's a great thing you're thinking of doing,' he said. 'I'd love to adopt one day myself, in Brazil. I think I'd choose to consider an older child too.' Then he started talking about Elijah again. 'The most beautiful boy,' he said. 'The kindest, the sweetest,' and his face changed too, and he spoke about Elijah as if they were old friends, or even family. Nikki saw that he loved this boy, this Elijah. And the hat or the blue hair didn't matter at all. He loved him. 'Would you like to see a photo before we go through his paperwork?'

Nikki could feel her breath coming out quickly, her heart beating faster. He was there, suddenly, in front of their eyes: a boy, smiling, dimples, tiny teeth.

'What's that on his forehead?' Nikki pointed to the photo. There was a mark, a line.

'He has a small scar from an incident where he was admitted to hospital. He had to have a small operation and the injury was never fully explained, but he's fine now. No health problems at all.'

'OK,' said Nikki. It was just a small scar.

'He's very handsome!' said Obi.

Nikki studied Elijah's eyes and for a split second tried to imagine what those eyes would have seen, and all she wanted to do was hold him. She clutched Obi's hand tightly and looked straight at Ricardo. 'Thank you,' she said.

CHAPTER 9

Elijah had been to Nikki and Obi's house before, four times, during introductions, but nothing had felt real. Elijah would stay for two nights, then go back to Nargis' and talk with Ricardo before coming back. Now it was 14 July and Elijah had moved in. For good. Even when Ricardo had told Elijah that he'd found a forever family, parents he could live with until he was grown up, it hadn't felt real at all. Obi looked a bit like Mama and, even though Nikki didn't look like Mama at all, she had a kind face. Calm and soft. Like water, if you kept really, really still in the bath.

When he thought of Mama, Elijah wanted to curl into a ball and never uncurl. But Ricardo had smiled and told him everything would work out fine. 'You deserve to love and be in a family and be safe. You're a good boy, Elijah, who deserves a loving family.' He'd looked at the photograph again and searched and searched. Ricardo had told him all through visits and introductions and overnight visits, 'It will all feel OK, I promise. It's a good match.' But nothing had felt real. The only thing that was real was the wizard and Mama's love, her voice in his head: *We belong together, you and me, for eternity and even after that.*

Now he was here, sleeping in his new bed, in his new room, in his new house, with his new family and all he could think of was Mama. Did Mama know that he was in another woman's house? Ricardo had said she was too unwell to have a visit at the moment, even though they would have liked a goodbye visit. 'We just call it that,' said Ricardo. 'We know that you will have contact with Mama twice a year.'

Goodbye visit.

Twice a year.

Mama would want to die.

'It might help, I think,' Ricardo had said, 'calling Nikki and Obi "Mum" and "Dad". It's not always appropriate for every child but I know you very well Elijah and, if you can, I think it will help.' He'd looked at the photograph again and again and again for the last month. Mum and Dad. He couldn't ever call them that. But Nikki and Obi had said that was OK. They said that, even if he did call them Nikki and Obi forever, they wouldn't mind because being a mum and dad was about a lot more than a name. And Chioma said he should call them whatever he wanted. As long as it wasn't a bad word, she'd said. And they'd both smiled. There was a boy, three schools ago, who'd said the f-word all the time and, once, Elijah had asked what it meant and got sent to sit outside the headmaster's office. The headmaster wasn't smiling, but Chioma's smile was never cross. He could probably shout the f-word and she would still smile and give him a hug.

But even Chioma's smile couldn't stop Elijah thinking about forever. Forever was scary. What if the wizard made him do something bad? The dark was darker and morning further away. Nikki had put some pyjamas on the bed that had pictures of dinosaurs on them. Elijah hated dinosaurs; he liked living, breathing daylight creatures that survived, not ones that walked the earth with wizards and died a million years ago, but he knew it would upset Nikki if he said that to her, and he didn't like making people upset even more than he didn't like dinosaurs. He put them on anyway and climbed into bed, pulling the cover over; he watched the shapes in the darkness become dinosaurs and start moving, growling and flying around his room. After a few minutes, there was a gentle knock on the door. 'Elijah, are you dressed? Can I come in?'

Nikki walked over and knelt down on the floor next to the bed. She smelled nice and fresh like the air outside. She wore tiny earrings that sparkled and reminded Elijah of the game he'd play with Mama, of catching the best stars. 'Do you want a story?'

Elijah stretched and opened his eyes. He looked up at the shelf of stories that were waiting. Nikki stood and reached for one. 'This one is lovely. It's called *The Little Prince*.'

Elijah smiled in the half darkness. Mama called him little prince sometimes.

Nikki read one whole chapter about a boy who liked drawings of animals and he found a drawing of a boa constrictor, which was Elijah's favourite type of snake. When Nikki showed him the picture of a boa constrictor swallowing an animal, Elijah's mouth dropped open. He wanted to look and look at the picture and listen and listen to the story. Nikki had a lovely soft voice and it made his body feel less heavy. But Nikki closed the book. 'Shall I stay with you while you fall asleep? It must be a bit scary staying here tonight, now you've officially moved in.' Elijah saw her teeth pressed so closed together there was no gap at all between them.

He shook his head. She must be tired and, even though he would have liked her to stay, Elijah knew that really she didn't want to. He could tell by the way Nikki glanced at the door, and how her voice shook a bit, her closed-together teeth. Nikki had very straight shoulders, and her back was long, even sitting down. She looked very different from Sue, and Linda and Marie, Nargis and Olu. She looked a little bit beautiful, but not as beautiful as Mama. Mama was so beautiful because she was an angel. Nikki was probably a junior angel, an angel in training. He would make sure he didn't like her. It was not safe for him to like her. His powers were very weak but he still might burn her with his laser eyes or turn her skin into molten lead. He looked at her face for something ugly to focus on but there was nothing. Her freckles were beautiful and already Elijah had noticed how they changed colour. When Nikki was really excited or happy they became darker, and when she was quiet or looked a bit sad her freckles became lighter. Mama told him that God sent down angels to kiss special people and their kisses were so powerful each kiss left behind a mark that people called a freckle. She said you could trust people with lots of freckles.

'Do you want to talk about anything? Or ask me anything? I think we've had enough of the story tonight, but I could sing you a song if you want – though, I must warn you, I'm not a great singer.'

Her eyes rested on Elijah. He couldn't remember the sound of anyone singing. Mama used to sing all the time and he couldn't remember how it sounded in his heart. Inside him was emptiness so wide and deep: the hole that used to be filled with Mama.

Nikki sat very still for a while and then she patted Elijah through the cover and went out of the room. 'I'll leave this little lamp on,' she said, 'and if you want us in the night, just come into our room. We don't mind. If you have a bad dream or feel a bit lonely, just wake us up. Anything at all. OK?' Her voice wobbled around. 'Obi will come and say goodnight too in a minute.'

As she walked away, Elijah could hear her humming. She turned her head back. He made sure to smile, even though he wanted to cry. He didn't want her to worry or not get any sleep, because it wasn't nice when you couldn't sleep. Elijah couldn't sleep a lot of the time and he knew how horrible that was, how slowly time could turn. On those nights, he pressed his eyes shut so tightly that he saw shapes behind them, and colours moving inside him. He felt like he was inside a boa constrictor waiting to be digested. He would have to wait a very long time until his body would be nothing, only dust.

Obi came next. He had arms that were as wide as legs and big teeth like a shark. But he didn't look evil at all. Elijah's heart was chattering. But Obi bent down from his high-up place and put his face close to Elijah's until Elijah was breathing Obi's breath. The air between them became warm. Then Obi kissed his giant hand and touched the side of Elijah's face where he had kissed his hand, so softly. 'Goodnight, Elijah,' he said, and then he was gone, too. Elijah lay very still but inside him his heart chattered on. Elijah prayed. Dear God, please tell Mama where I am. Please help me fight the wizard. Amen. Everything was strange. Even with the lamp on, the darkness was too full and the morning too far. Elijah felt wetness fall out of his body and he knew Nikki and Obi would smell it and probably send him away. Red crept from his cheeks to his neck until everything was hotter than fire. He closed his eyes tightly and dreamed of Mama. But in the dream it was night, and

Mama was howling at the moon, like a wolf, and scratching her face until she was not beautiful at all, and nothing existed, not even angels, or dinosaurs.

The next morning, Elijah woke late. The sun was poking through the gap underneath the curtains and changing the colour of the room. There was a clock next to his bed that said 9:05. He listened for sounds and heard clanging and laughing coming from downstairs. For a few seconds he closed his eyes and looked for Mama but he couldn't see her there, but smelt her instead: a mixture of burning plantain and Scotch-bonnet chillies. And he felt her combing his hair, gently tugging the knots and rubbing olive oil on his scalp, then kissing his cheek, and then he heard her: *Little son, my heart beats in perfect time with your heart.*

Elijah got up slowly, breathing through his mouth. He pulled on a dressing gown over his pyjamas and tied it tightly. The wet was dry but he could smell it, even through the dressing gown. At least Ricardo would come if Elijah was sent away. He walked down the stairs slowly, holding on to the rail. There were photographs on the wall of Nikki and Obi and children and old people. And dogs. But Elijah only stopped to look again at the dogs. He reached his arm out and touched the photo, running his fingertips over each dog's face. Some were square-shaped with big shoulders and short necks, some were scruffy with mud on their hair, and one dog had one ear sticking up and one ear sticking down so that he looked surprised. All the eyes in the photos watched him walk past them.

'Here he is.' Nikki was standing in the kitchen, holding a pan. 'I've made porridge and I bought some syrup and we've blueberries as well. I thought we'd have porridge today then pancakes tomorrow when Daddy comes to say hello, because he absolutely loves pancakes. Obi likes his with butter, which I think is horrible, but you get to choose. Do you want porridge?'

Elijah didn't say anything. He knew they would be able to smell the wet. Nikki's face was so upset and hurt. The room was really quiet for a few seconds, filled with only the bad smell. Obi pulled a chair out and Elijah sat on it. Obi's arms looked even longer in his T-shirt. He had a newspaper in front of him and a cup of coffee. There was a plant in the middle of the table with tiny round yellow flowers on long thin branches like fingers; they all pointed at Elijah.

Nikki knelt beside Elijah. 'Did you have an accident, Elijah? It's not a problem. Come with me and we'll give you a quick wash, OK? And then later on, after breakfast, you can have a soak in the bath.'

Elijah filled up with redness. Obi didn't look up from his paper once, but his eyes weren't moving between the words. They were fixed on one word the whole time. Then suddenly Obi's eyes lifted upwards and it made Elijah's heart speed up; his eyes were so perfectly brown, like a conker that Mama had once found for him in the park. Elijah smiled at Obi, and Obi smiled back.

Elijah followed Nikki back upstairs, past the eyes looking at him, and let her undo his dressing gown. In the bathroom, Nikki waited while Elijah pulled his pyjama bottoms down, and she filled the sink with warm, bubbly water, dipped a sponge in it and handed it to Elijah. He washed his bottom half and she handed him a towel.

'That's better,' she said. She felt the bottom of his pyjama top with her fingers. 'It's a tiny bit wet,' she said. 'Let's have a quick wash of your top, too, OK?' Then she pulled his pyjama top over his head. Suddenly she gasped. She put her hand to her mouth but then let it drop back down quickly. Elijah had seen that look before, every time someone saw the pattern on his body. His back and chest were covered with criss-crosses, faint lines in different shades of darkness, raised bumps and circular patches: dots of discoloration.

Elijah kept his eyes straight ahead. He didn't want to look at his patterns. He didn't want to look at Nikki's face, full of questions. Elijah pulled the robe back around him but the tie had fallen to the floor.

'Oh, Elijah,' she said. She held her hand towards him. 'Who did this to you?'

20:27 Leviticus: A man or a woman who is a

101

medium or a necromancer shall surely be put to death. They shall be stoned with stones; their blood shall be upon them.

Elijah could remember the exact words he'd heard over and over because they had made him learn them off by heart and say them out loud until his throat was sore. He could feel the wizard crawling round his stomach, creeping towards his throat, starting up the lasers in his eyes. If Nikki didn't turn away, the wizard would burn Nikki and eat her up. It would zap her blind so she couldn't stare any more.

'Stop looking at me,' he said.

But Nikki kept looking. Her hand hovered over his chest, over his robe, and then dropped to the bottom of his legs where you couldn't notice much but, if you looked hard, you could see the skin was patchy and different, and her eyes filled with tears because she couldn't love a boy like Elijah. She couldn't love a boy with a pattern. No one could. Elijah tried to press the wizard down but the wizard gripped Elijah's arm and used it to shove Nikki's hand away. Nikki squeaked and jumped back, holding her wrist, rubbing it, but she was still staring and the wizard was ready to pounce. Elijah wanted to warn her. He opened his mouth and words came out.

'The devil prowls around like a roaring lion, seeking someone to devour.'

Nikki's eyes widened and her face twisted as the wizard used its powers to reach inside Nikki's body and squeeze her intestines while Elijah just stood there, watching. She knelt down, all her breath leaving her with the pain of the wizard in her guts, and then at last she closed her eyes. She reached out and touched his arm.

'I'm sorry, Elijah.' Her voice came out all wobbly with lots of gasps. The wizard wasn't letting her breathe. 'I didn't mean to stare. It was just . . . Oh, poor Elijah.' She shook her head and pressed a hand to her eyes.

Elijah wrestled with the wizard. Nikki wasn't bad. She was good and kind and only wanted to help him and it wasn't her fault the wizard had made Elijah so no one could love him. He breathed deeply and slowly like Chioma had taught him and the wizard left Nikki. She looked straight into his eyes. 'There's nothing wrong with you, Elijah. I was shocked, but scars can't stop you from being perfect.' She tried to smile. 'You're a good boy and you don't deserve anything that's happened to you. And that's why you're here, why Obi and I are here. We're here to take care of you and love you.'

And Elijah closed his eyes and concentrated everything on pushing the wizard back down, squashing it so small it couldn't harm anyone. The wizard was still. He opened his eyes and Nikki made a face like she was trying to smile. 'Let's just have breakfast, OK?'

Nikki helped him put on his dressing gown and did the belt up so softly that it fell open as they walked downstairs.

Obi looked up from the newspaper he was reading, which was spread out on the kitchen table, but then he looked down again. Nikki helped Elijah get dressed with the clothes she'd put over the top of his chair, and then served Elijah some porridge and, when he'd finished, Obi put the paper down. 'Are you ready?' he asked. 'Shall we have a game of football in the garden?'

Elijah nodded. He liked being in the garden and being around Obi. He couldn't stop looking at Obi's arms and wondering if he was the strongest man in the world. He followed Obi out through the glass doors at the back of the kitchen. Nikki walked in front of them. She was breathing really quickly.

The garden was long and thin with a stretch of grass and two lines of flowers at the outsides, bursting with roses in all colours and tiny white flowers, which climbed up the fences and twisted through the gaps at the top. Near the kitchen there was a stone area where Nikki sat on a chair next to a table with a giant umbrella over it. On the table, she had laid a tray with a jug of lemonade and three small glasses. Nargis would never have made lemonade and Sue hadn't let him drink from a glass, but Olu let him have lemonade once from a bottle and he remembered the taste and Fola filling his glass up three times and putting his finger to his lips when Olu told them to not drink too much.

The other end of the garden had a trampoline

and swing set and a small white net with a football in it. Obi ran towards it and kicked the ball towards Elijah.

'Mind my flowers!' shouted Nikki. 'Let Elijah kick it and you be in goal.' Her words were normal but her voice wobbled a bit. Elijah checked but he couldn't feel the wizard.

Obi rolled his eyes so that Elijah could see but Nikki was probably too far away to notice. Elijah kicked the ball towards the net. The ball hit the post and bounced backwards as if it was alive. 'Nearly!' shouted Obi. 'Good kick.'

He held his hands in front of him as though he was a real goalie and moved from side to side. His body was so big that Elijah couldn't even see the net; the net was smaller than Obi's back but, even so, the next time he kicked it, Obi dived the wrong way and the ball flew in. 'Wow!' Obi stood up and ran towards Elijah, lifting him on to one of his shoulders. He ran around the garden shouting, 'Goal! Goal!'

Elijah smiled. When he'd finished running and shouting, he didn't put Elijah down. Instead, he walked towards the tree behind the swing and pointed upwards. 'Get me one, please,' he said. 'They're not ripe until autumn, but I love the sour taste.'

Elijah looked in front of him at the tree, full of tiny apples. He touched them one by one, hard and small and green. He had never picked apples from a tree before. Obi lowered him to the ground.

'Thanks,' he said, biting into his apple. 'Don't forget to check it for maggots.'

Elijah turned his apple around and around in his hands. He smelt it – sharp – and bit into the skin. 'Yuck,' he said, and Obi laughed. They walked back towards the house and Nikki poured them some lemonade. 'That was good football,' she said. 'Hey! You shouldn't eat the apples yet – they're not ripe.' She looked at Obi. 'Though it's hard to wait – I love apples.'

Elijah took a big breath and looked at Nikki right in the eyes. 'There are some riper ones,' he said, and he ran all the way down the garden. When he got to the tree, he jumped up as high as he could and swung his arm but he couldn't catch one. It was too high. He turned to Nikki who was waving. 'Don't worry,' she shouted. 'You can pick me one in September, when they're ready.' Her arm wasn't shaking at all. It looked strong, like the trunk of the tree.

Elijah looked up at the big tree and saw one apple, lower than the others, that was slightly red and not as small. He crouched down and pushed on to the grass, propelling himself as high as possible, grabbing the apple.

'I got one that's ready!' he shouted and ran back towards Nikki and Obi.

Nikki laughed. 'You did, Elijah. Thank you. And in September or October I'll get you a basket and you can pick the apples for me. We could make apple pie together.'

He sat down next to her. Instead of moving away, Nikki moved a little bit closer. He watched the light twinkling between the leaves of the apple tree. September or October, he thought.

'You look like you're concentrating,' said Obi, looking at Elijah's face. Obi's hand was on top of Nikki's.

'I really like that tree,' said Elijah.

Nikki turned her head to look at Elijah. 'That's exactly what I was thinking too,' she said.

Before bed, Elijah walked over to the window and looked across the street. He tried to figure out which patch of sky Mama would be looking at, but he couldn't think properly. He suddenly felt a little bad about having fun with Obi, but he didn't know why. The houses opposite were all different shapes and sizes, but all tall with chimneys. Nikki stood behind him. He could see her hand above his shoulder. It waited and waited before she put it down by her side again.

As Elijah was about to turn, something caught his gaze. In the flats opposite, there was a window and standing in front of it was a girl. He couldn't see her clearly but he could tell she had two plaits, one each side of her head, and white skin, and behind her on the wall of her room was a poster of a giant map. She was flashing a torch at the window, straight at them. 'Who's that?'

'Oh, yes; that's a new friend for you. She's my niece, Jasmin. She lives across the street, and she's your age – you'll be in the same year at school. I'm sure you'll be great friends. When you're a bit more settled, I'll introduce you. She's quite a funny character.'

Elijah looked at the girl and tried to count the flashing. Maybe she was doing a code. Maybe she needed help.

'I don't have any friends,' whispered Elijah. 'Except Ricardo. He's my best friend.'

Nikki swallowed really hard, like she had something she didn't want to eat in her mouth, like a boiled vegetable.

CHAPTER 10

'He has so many scars,' Nikki said. 'Obviously there's the one on his forehead, but we knew about that one. I mean, they're all over him. Even his legs and feet. Only tiny, but still noticeable. All over his body.' It was really late – she'd waited until she'd heard Elijah's slow breathing from outside his bedroom door before creeping in next to Obi and pulling him towards her – and she was half asleep. 'Thin scars in lines across his chest and back.' Her voice was breaking even as she spoke, and their bedroom felt too hot. She moved even closer to Obi, pressing herself against him until it bordered on painful. She needed to feel him right next to her, to know that she wasn't alone. The first night having Elijah with them, everything had been better than she could have imagined; he was polite and kind and helpful, not the troubled child they'd been expecting but a sweet and lovely boy. It was only when she'd seen the scars that Nikki felt anxious, questioning.

Obi kissed her cheek and pulled his arm around her back. 'I've seen clients with the worst scars imaginable, and they've absorbed them. Of course they're always a reminder of trauma, but people learn to live with things.'

Nikki shuddered.

'And Elijah's scars are not extensive. He'll probably grow out of them. They will fade out, at least, as he gets older.'

'I know they told us about the physical abuse, the way he was neglected, and I was prepared for him to be really frightened and obviously have some issues. But I just didn't expect . . .' She took a breath. 'And he had this look in his eyes.'

'He was upset.'

'I know, but . . . what he said; it was really strange. I think it was biblical, about the devil. I wish I could remember the words. It was something like, "the devil is prowling round".'

'Maybe it's something we should mention to Elijah's team. But Ricardo said his mother was very religious. Lots of religious people quote the Bible when they're scared – it's just something he's picked up.'

'I know, I know; I'm not saying anything – it was just so strange and awful and I didn't handle it well at all. I'll talk to Ricardo.'

Obi pulled away and looked at her face. 'It's all new to us, that's all. You're doing so well. *We're* doing so well. Of course there will be things that we didn't know. But he's resilient. Maybe he got upset this morning, but look how much fun we had in the garden! A few scars on his body will be something he can deal with, and we'll help him.'

Nikki smiled despite herself. Obi was becoming an expert in post-adoption issues from the textbooks he'd devoured. She looked at Obi's books on the nightstand: *Parenting a Traumatised Child*; *Healing with Love*; *Resilience and Outcomes*; *Case Studies of Neglect*.

Obi traced her jawline with his thumb. She closed her eyes. He was right. Everything was better than they'd hoped and of course she couldn't expect that there would be no shadows from his past. 'And he wet the bed. I know it was the first night, but I worry about that as well. Which is irrational because a lot of seven-year-olds wet the bed.'

'Of course he wet the bed,' said Obi. 'And, incidentally, I have to remind you that Chanel told me you wet the bed until you were ten.' He laughed. 'And you were scared of the dark. She said you had to have the landing light on otherwise you'd cry all night.'

Nikki smiled in the darkness. 'You're right,' she said. 'I was a nightmare.'

'Exactly. Look at all our friends' kids. Tia bites; she nearly bit another child's nose off at nursery – he had to have *stitches*. Frankie has A.D.H.D. and hasn't slept since he was born and, as for Jasmin, don't get me started!'

'Hey! That's our niece. There's nothing wrong with her!'

'Well, with Chanel as a mother, she's come off pretty lightly but still . . .'

Nikki punched Obi's arm. He winced and pretended to cry, rubbing his eyes and shaking his shoulders. 'That will be the day when you cry!'

He dropped his hands and grinned. Nikki looked at his face, his strong jaw, perfect eyebrows. 'We need to introduce them to Elijah. They're desperate to meet him. I was hoping to stall them for a week or so but Chanel keeps phoning.'

'I know. Daddy's done really well not to pop in but I'm not sure we'll manage to keep him away much longer.'

'Elijah's so lovely, isn't he?' said Nikki. She thought of his eyes and the way he smiled using only his mouth, the softness of his skin and how she was desperate to hold him but scared it would be too much and too soon.

'He's brilliant. He's continuing his therapy with Chioma. It's good that they'll carry that on, to get him settled.'

Nikki closed her eyes. Family therapy. Wet beds. Scars. It wasn't how she'd imagined things, but she had to believe Obi was right. Elijah was theirs and resilient and wonderful. She was a mum at last and Obi was a dad. That's how they had to look at it, even though it was such early days. She held Obi close until the alarm shook her fully awake.

Chanel phoned as usual first thing in the morning. It was their third morning with Elijah. This wasn't a visit. Elijah was home. Nikki took the phone to

112

the living room. 'Can we come over? Please, we can't wait any longer!'

Nikki laughed. 'Not yet. Give him a chance. I promise it won't be long, Chanel.'

'Can't you put him in front of the window then? Or at least text me some photos. I need his exact size, as well, and shoe size. We're going to the shops today.'

'Please, please don't buy him anything. Chanel, I know you mean well but let him settle in, please . . .'

'How are you coping? Are you feeling weird? It must be so strange . . .'

'It's a bit strange at times. He's wet the bed. And he got upset – I got upset – when I saw all the scars on his body. He has so many. But it's like it was always meant to be.'

'What colour is he?'

'What do you mean, what colour is he?'

'Well, is he as dark as Obi? Darker? Lighter? He looked really, really dark in the photo you showed us, and I need to know if he'll take neon. I'm going to Westfield later and I've seen a few bits—'

'I'm going now, Chanel,' said Nikki. She hung up the receiver and looked through her curtain. Chanel was standing in the flat opposite their house, wearing her leopard-print dressing gown and what looked like a shower cap, the phone next to her ear. Nikki breathed slowly and found herself smiling, imagining Chanel holding up a thousand different boys' outfits and Jasmin rolling her eyes at every single one.

113

When Nikki came back into the kitchen, Elijah was high in the air. 'Put him down, Daddy, please.' Nikki laughed and put the phone down before holding her hands up towards the space where her father-in-law held Elijah above his head. 'He's not a baby.'

'Please,' she said, towards Obi, who finally looked up from his newspaper.

'She's right, Dad.' Obi's voice was calm and clear, as usual, and his dad put Elijah straight down. Elijah wobbled a little when his feet touched the ground and he reached out for the chair. He was smiling broadly and looking up at Daddy. Daddy wore Nigerian clothes as usual, beautifully bright, and reminding Nikki of a flower in the kitchen.

'Little grandson,' Daddy said, softly. 'You are such a strong boy.' He turned to Nikki, screwed his nose up. 'I'm sorry,' he said. 'Anyway, he's not crying.' He reached towards Elijah, put his hand on his face and stroked his cheek. 'I was so excited and happy that I couldn't hold it in.' He laughed. 'I've been waiting a long time for a grandchild to spoil.'

'He's not crying because he's a tough cookie,' said Obi, putting his hand on Daddy's arm. He looked at Nikki, eyes sparkling. 'But we need to let him settle in a bit, don't we, Elijah? It's early days. Your third proper morning and all this fuss!' Obi stood in front of Elijah and dropped to his knees, making their eyes level. He smiled with such certainty that Elijah's shoulders relaxed. Nikki watched them, father and son, and felt her heart beat faster. It was the best feeling – almost better than holding Elijah herself. Obi would be such a good parent. She felt her eyes sting with tears, and smiled at herself. She was so emotional. Being a new adoptive mum was like being any new mum, her feelings seemed enhanced as if she was full of unstable hormones.

Elijah looked up with his wide eyes at Obi and Daddy. He was such a handsome boy, just like his photograph.

'Come, sit next to Granddad. We'll eat breakfast together.' Daddy patted the chair next to him and Elijah sat down. Nikki raised her eyebrows at Daddy. She wondered if Elijah would call him Granddad. So far, Elijah had only called them Nikki and Obi, but she wasn't upset about it. It felt strange calling herself Mum. When Nikki thought of Mum she imagined a baby crying. An image of Ify shot through her head suddenly – gold-specked eyes wide open, toffee skin and spiral curls – and she pushed it away.

'You don't have to call me Granddad,' Daddy continued, winking at Nikki. 'But you can if you want to. My name is Ozoemena – Ozo – which is an Igbo name, and my parents called me that because my brother died before I was born and my name means, "May it never happen again." Every name in Igbo culture has an important meaning.'

Elijah looked straight in front of him. 'Your brother died?' he whispered.

Daddy shrugged. 'Don't worry yourself too much,

Elijah. I was born hundreds of years ago; in fact, I don't even know my true age as I have no birth certificate. And back in the old days, when I was born, many children did not survive childhood; the hessian mat that women gave birth on was only washed if it produced a death, as women were giving birth all the time. These days things are very different. Better, and worse. Anyway, tell me about your name. Elijah is a beautiful name.'

Elijah blinked slowly. 'My name is in the Bible,' he said. 'Elijah brought fire down from the sky. He was a prophet.'

'Igbo names are the best,' said Daddy. 'But Bible names are the second best. I'm really glad that you know the Bible so well.'

There was quiet around the table for too many seconds but, despite trying to think of something, anything, to say, all Nikki thought of was Elijah's history – what Ricardo had told them. *There was a fire in his previous foster placement and some uncertainty about what caused it. But now we believe that Elijah was involved.*

Nikki watched Elijah's unblinking eyes. She'd only known him a few days and yet she was certain that he'd never harm anyone. Social workers got so many things wrong, and Obi was always right. Of course it had shocked her when Elijah had looked at her so coldly, pushed her away. But he was terrified. Elijah only needed love and he would thrive. 'Do you want some pancakes?' she asked.

Elijah looked up at her. 'Yes, please,' he whispered.

116

There was no way that this innocent boy could have been involved with starting fires. Nikki saw his character clearly: kind, loving, but frightened. And she could help him. Already he seemed to be settling in. He hadn't wet the bed last night and, when she went in to wake him up, he'd reached out to her on his way to the bathroom. It was only a second of touch, but he'd come to her, rested his hand on her arm.

She poured syrup on top of two pancakes. He ate quickly, not looking up until his plate was clean, and that made her happy. He was too skinny, with knees the widest part of his legs, and ribs you could see. Nikki thought of holding him, of how fragile he'd feel in her arms, how much she wanted to hold him. The hand on her arm was only the start.

'I have been so looking forward to meeting you,' said Daddy, reaching for the coffee and dropping in sugar cube after sugar cube. 'I'm going to teach you all about Nigeria, about your own culture. We have one of the richest cultures in the world, with some of the best literature, food, music. Of course, you'll need time to settle in, but I know it's going to be so wonderful. I've always wanted a grandson, my whole life.' Daddy's eyes were shining so it was impossible not to smile. He looked ten years younger.

Elijah smiled and looked up at Daddy the whole time. 'I never had a Granddad before,' he said.

Obi was downstairs next morning when she padded down in her slippers and dressing gown, and Elijah was already sitting at the table, watching Obi. They were laughing. 'Good morning,' said Obi, kissing her as she walked past.

'Good morning.' She smiled, looking over his shoulder at the pan of porridge, which was bubbling on the stove.

She sat next to Elijah and he suddenly stood up and moved his chair closer to hers so that their arms were touching. 'Could you be any closer?' Obi asked. 'Not that I blame you. Nikki does look very snuggly in that dressing gown.'

'Shall we go outside for a walk after breakfast? Show Elijah around the sights and sounds of the park and shops?'

Elijah moved away. 'Yes, please,' he said. 'I love going for walks.'

'So do I,' said Nikki. She looked at Obi. The air seemed to brighten between them. Obi turned to fill his bowl.

Nikki winked at Elijah and spoke to Obi's back. 'Are you coming with us, lazy bones?'

Obi turned around with a porridge spoon in his hand. 'Are you calling me lazy?' he said. 'Was she calling me lazy?' he asked Elijah. He wagged the spoon, and a large glob of porridge fell on to the front of his shirt. Elijah giggled.

Elijah swung between their hands as they walked, taking in the park, the pond, the ducks, the bus stop, the school where he'd be going. He stopped every few hundred yards and looked up at the sky, or picked up a stone and rubbed it between his finger and thumb, ran the palm of his hand over a bush, smelt the swollen-headed roses that spilled from the front gardens. She'd been told about his love of nature and animals but to see how he really enjoyed life was a surprise. It made everything seem fresh and clear to Nikki, as though she were looking at the world through his eyes.

She noticed people smiling at them. The woman in the bakery gave Elijah an extra doughnut. They were a good-looking family, Nikki realised. 'Cute as a button,' the woman said to Elijah.

Nikki held Elijah's hand as they went into the newsagent's. His skin was hot and slightly wet. She felt fiercely protective of him, with his slight frame and huge eyes. She realised she loved him already, within days, how she'd kill anyone who hurt him.

'Who are you, handsome boy?' A woman Nikki recognised was in front of them in the queue – a neighbour from the next street, stocky with wispy hair that had been cut badly. 'Who are you?' she repeated, looking at Elijah.

At first Nikki ignored her neighbour and tried to distract Elijah by pointing out the *Spiderman* comic. 'Do you want one?' she asked while she smiled, tight-lipped to the woman. It was none of this woman's business who Elijah was. Part of Nikki knew that the woman was just curious – friendly, even – but another part was ready, suddenly, to attack.

'What a handsome boy,' the woman said, looking at Obi. 'Is he family come to stay with you?' Nikki had known people would talk. After all, a white woman didn't suddenly give birth to a black child of seven. Still, she wished people would mind their own business.

Obi smiled and handed over some coins for the newspapers. He looked down at Elijah. 'He's my son,' he said.

'Ours,' Nikki said, finding courage in Elijah's hand.

'Of course,' she said, looking again at Obi, turning her head from Nikki. 'He looks exactly like you.'

CHAPTER 11

'Baby!' Jasmin said, and then she poked her tongue out and ran away, her ponytail jumping up and down on her head. Elijah couldn't take his eyes off her. He'd never seen anyone so small and fierce-looking, with such big eyes.

They were in the garden and Elijah had been playing catch with Nikki when the doorbell rang and she'd come back outside shouting, 'Elijah! Chanel and Jasmin are here to say hello.' Elijah had looked up at the sky and felt his heart tapping, and suddenly heard a whispering. *You contain such evil, the world is not safe.* He pushed the wizard down by breathing like Chioma had taught him to whenever he felt frightened. He clenched his fists, unclenched them and wiggled his toes and tapped his cheek with his fingertip. His breathing slowed. He was in control. The wizard was still. He looked through the kitchen window at Obi's Nigerian face and Nikki's, covered in freckles. I might be safe here, he thought.

'Come back here, Jasmin! That's not nice, is it?' Her mother was tall and had a pair of giant

121

sunglasses on top of her head. 'Look at you! I'm your Aunty Chanel,' she said, shaking Elijah's hand so hard his whole body shook. She knelt down to get a closer look at him and he got a closer look at her. He'd seen a photograph of Aunty Chanel standing next to Nikki, but in the photograph she'd been wearing a rain jacket and had white skin and no make-up. In real life she was strange looking. She had bright orange skin, the colour of a tangerine, which smelt of swimming pools. On top of her eyes were two butterflies. She looked like a woman in a fashion magazine where they'd printed the colours wrong, or it had been raining and the colours got all mixed up. She wore a lot of make-up and her face and neck did not match.

'What a handsome boy! So gorgeous! Like a mini supermodel.' She flicked her head at Nikki and they shared a smile, then turned her head back to Elijah. 'You're a cool dude. Jay-Z! Oh my God, you look exactly like a young Jay-Z!'

'Chanel!' Nikki tutted and moved over to them, pulling Elijah backwards towards her. 'Really!'

'What? I'm just pointing out to my little gangsta rapper here how coolio he is.'

Nikki took a breath so suddenly that Elijah heard the air travel into her mouth. She put her face next to Aunty Chanel's ear and hissed, 'Chanel, stop it!'

Aunty Chanel rolled her eyes.

Nikki looked at Aunty Chanel for a long time, then she turned to Elijah and smiled. 'Why don't you go and play with Jasmin?' she said, and pointed over to the other end of the garden where Jasmin had run and was already on the swing, swinging really fast. Elijah had lots of questions, like why Chanel was wearing butterflies, and why her skin was orange, and why she was calling him J.C. (which is what Mama sometimes called Jesus Christ). But Nikki pushed him gently towards Jasmin and so he walked away.

As he turned around, Chanel was blowing a big bubble from bubblegum and it popped on her face and she laughed. Elijah had never seen an adult pop bubblegum. Aunty Chanel was wearing a pair of jeans that had been cut into shorts, but whoever cut them hadn't done a very good job as the edges were all squiggly and the pockets hung down. Elijah wasn't very good at cutting but he could have done a better job than that. Maybe Jasmin cut the jeans for her mum.

Aunty Chanel threw her arm around Nikki. 'He's a miracle,' she said. 'So gorgeous and no sleepless nights! I might adopt, myself, next time.'

Nikki smiled at Elijah.

Elijah walked slowly towards the swing at the other end of the garden, taking deep breaths on the way. The wizard was walking around inside him again. He looked at Jasmin swinging against the sky, scattering birds above her against a cloud, her ponytail whooshing. Jasmin swung her legs really high and kicked out with each swing. She was so high but she didn't look scared at all. Elijah

kept his eyes on her swishing brown ponytail but
he could see her face underneath it, her round
cheeks, big, dark-brown eyes and the small jumping
skin at the side of her eye.

'Jasmin, sweetie, play with Jay-Z!' Aunty Chanel
burst into laughter. 'Come on, Jasmin; remember
what we talked about.'

Elijah felt his face get hot. Everyone talked about
him. She probably knew Elijah wasn't allowed to
live with Mama any more. Suddenly Jasmin
stopped swinging her legs and jumped from really
high up, straight on to the grass. She looked at
Elijah, then grabbed his hand and pulled him to
the plastic swingball set, where she put a plastic
racket in his fist and raised the ball high, before
letting it drop down. Elijah tried to hit it back but
the wizard was laughing at him inside his tummy.
It was loud enough that he felt sure Jasmin could
hear it, but she didn't say anything. The ball flew
between them, bouncing off their rackets without
them having to move much. Elijah could hear
Aunty Chanel making barking sounds then laughing
loudly. She mooed like a cow then shouted out,
'Did anyone see any animals in the garden? I can
hear farmyard animals.'

Jasmin tutted and hit the ball really hard. 'I hate
her,' she said, looking at Aunty Chanel.

Elijah gasped. Jasmin's face was crunched up,
angry.

'She won't let me live in America with my dad.
And she always tries to put me in scratchy dresses

and she says the same thing about a hundred times. It's so embarrassing.' Jasmin opened her mouth, poked her tongue at the house then put her tongue back in and grinned. One of her teeth was missing. She noticed Elijah staring at it and shut her mouth quickly. 'There's a girl in my class who has fourteen plastic ponies. She's totally crazy and her toenails are painted purple. She's not my best friend. She told my mum that there was a bubblegum at the bottom of my ice cream and my mum took it away and said I was too young and ate it herself! She used to be my best friend, but not any more.'

Jasmin moved her body close to Elijah. She put her hand on top of his hair and rubbed her thumb over the top of his head. 'I'm going to America soon to be with my dad. America is the best place in the world. You don't have to go to school and everyone is normal in America. There are no weird people like Mum. And Lady Gaga lives there and she's my favourite.'

Jasmin dropped her hand from Elijah's head and then touched his arm. There was a small round mark at the top of his arm where Darren had burnt him with a cigarette. It was the size of a pea. Jasmin put her fingertip on it until it disappeared. Elijah held his breath. 'We're cousins,' she said. 'I've never had a cousin before.' She looked at Elijah's face with unblinking eyes. 'But I won't be friends with you just because my mum said I have to. You are totally crazy.'

★   ★   ★

That night, Nikki tucked Elijah in and read him a few pages of *The Little Prince*, and kissed his head twice.

'Can I ask you something?' he said.

'Of course. You know that.'

Elijah breathed deeply. Asking for things was quite hard. 'Do you have a torch I can use?'

Nikki laughed. She opened the curtains slightly and then closed them again. 'I can imagine why you need a torch,' she said. 'How was it, meeting Jasmin?'

'She can swing really high,' he said.

'She certainly can,' said Nikki. She tucked the quilt up around Elijah's ears. 'She's completely fearless.'

Elijah felt his ears open to take in these words. 'She's not scared of anything?'

Nikki shook her head. 'Nothing at all. And – yes – I'll get you a torch; we've got one in the drawer downstairs. But you must promise me five minutes only please, OK? No staying up all night playing torches with Jasmin.'

'I promise,' said Elijah and he looked right into her eyes so she knew he meant it.

As Nikki went to look for the torch, Elijah tried to imagine not being frightened of anything at all. He had never not been frightened of anything. Not ever. And he had never met anyone who wasn't frightened of anything. Jasmin must have superpowers. He wished he had that superpower, of not being frightened of anything at all.

'Here it is.' Nikki walked back into his room carrying a torch. She showed him how to switch it on and then kissed his head again before leaving him in darkness. 'You can kiss me goodnight too, if you want,' said Nikki.

Elijah looked at the skin on her cheek. It was very pale. He worried that, if he kissed her, the wizard would leap out of his mouth. But her smile was still in her eyes and her freckles were darker than ever, so he leant towards her and risked just a very quick kiss, right on the part of her cheek where her freckles were all crowded together, and he didn't feel the wizard move at all.

'Goodnight, Elijah,' whispered Nikki. She smiled so widely that Elijah could see a silver tooth right at the back of her mouth.

'Why do you have treasure in your mouth?' he asked. He pointed to the tooth.

Nikki didn't say anything, but she kissed his head and laughed as she left the room and closed the door.

Elijah crept out of bed and opened his curtains. Jasmin was already standing there, in front of her map. He saw her in the light and then she disappeared. Suddenly she flashed her torch three times.

He held his torch in front of him and flashed the torch on and off five times. Jasmin would be so surprised to see him with a torch.

He looked down at the torch in his hand, making out the shape of it in the darkness. When he looked back up, Jasmin had turned her light on and was banging her head with her hand. She poked out her tongue and then shut her curtains.

Elijah could feel Mama smiling whenever he saw Granddad's face. Granddad's face was even more Nigerian than Obi's and he went to church all the time. Elijah felt wrapped up whenever he was nearby, like he was inside a blanket. He loved seeing Granddad's soft hair at the doorway, and seeing how Obi lit up like a torch when his dad was around. Elijah's skin matched Obi's and Granddad's almost exactly, but Granddad's was dry and loose around the elbows as he had lived in his skin for so many years. When Granddad had started bringing him dead things and Nigerian things last week, Nikki had rolled her eyes but allowed it. At first it was a rabbit skin, so velvety and the exact shape of a squashed rabbit. Elijah held it all day and slept with it underneath his pillow. He had spent hours staring at the wooden masks with their wide grins and slits where the eyes should be, and laughed when Nikki said they made her shiver. The morning after the torches, Granddad brought a drum made from a stretched skin, so soft. Elijah suddenly remembered Mama holding his hand in a bowl and filling the bowl with holy water. His hand was badly cut, stinging, and balloons of blood had filled the bowl and brushed against his fingertips. Mama had sung a song and smiled at him with her eyes and it was the softest thing he'd ever felt.

But that day, when Granddad appeared at the back door, his hair was outlined by something else. Antlers! Nikki looked at Obi and muttered, 'No way.'

But Obi grinned and whispered, 'Wow! Where is he getting all this stuff?'

'Hello, Elijah; I'm glad I caught you. I have something for your collection.'

'Collection?' Nikki folded her arms into triangles and put her hands on her hips. 'He's not collecting dead things, that's for sure. I don't mind the Nigerian things – even those gruesome masks – but any more dead things are out of the question. The rabbit skin is bad enough.'

Obi laughed and Granddad waved the antlers slightly. They were beautiful: white and smooth and the shape of jagged mountains. 'Not dead things,' said Granddad. 'These nature items are alive.'

Then he put the antlers on top of his head and danced around the kitchen making a sound that wasn't human. Elijah looked at Nikki, who was smiling by then.

After lunch, Granddad helped put the antlers on Elijah's wall. 'You can use them for hanging up your dressing gown,' he said. 'Your room is becoming much better. More suited to your interests.'

Elijah looked at his room. Already, the football

posters were down, along with any hint of dinosaur. It felt more like home. And with his rabbit skin, the stones that Granddad had started collecting in a large, clear jar and the antlers making shadows on his wall, it felt like the best room he'd ever stayed in.

'Mum and Dad want to speak to Ricardo, so I thought we'd take a walk,' said Granddad. He knelt down. 'I know you believe in God. Ricardo said you wanted to know if we believed in God before you would agree to meet us all, so I thought maybe I could take my grandson to church.' He smiled at Elijah. 'Or we could just go find some squirrels in the park. It's up to you.'

Something wriggled in Elijah's stomach and he swallowed. Mama always said he must pray to God to help him with the wizard. Mama thought the church was the safest place of all. Maybe, if he went, he would find someone to help him, or the wizard would be so scared in such a sacred place that it would just run away.

Elijah nodded. 'I'd like to go to church, please.' He smiled and took Granddad's hand.

Granddad laughed. 'What a good boy,' he said.

But Elijah could feel the wizard, churning up his stomach, and he had to hold tight to Granddad or the wizard might take hold of Elijah's body and fly him far away.

'Come on,' said Granddad.

They left the house and walked for about ten minutes. Granddad talked about a fox he wanted

130

to buy Elijah – dead, but stuffed so it looked alive. 'I've been watching it for five days, but too many are bidding,' he said. Elijah nodded but he couldn't speak. He focused on pushing the churning away.

'Just down here,' said Granddad, and they turned down a little alley and the wizard slid up into Elijah's eyes and pulled the walls in close about them and the pavement up high. Elijah tried to breathe slowly.

They came back on to the street, which was filled with too-bright light and the sound of angels singing. 'We're late!' Granddad tugged Elijah across the road towards a low brick building with a spire stuck in its flat roof, and the sound of angels got louder. They were so, so happy and the wizard was so, so angry, swirling round inside Elijah.

The wizard would not let Elijah go in. It had glued Elijah's feet to the ground and Granddad was looking back at him. He would know now. Granddad would see that Elijah was so full of wizard he couldn't enter a church and he would tell Nikki and Obi and they would send him away.

'Is something wrong, Elijah?' Granddad said, pressing a hand to his forehead.

Elijah tried to shake his head but he could not.

'Maybe today isn't a good day for the church,' said Granddad. 'They have a visiting pastor, and he's not as good.'

Elijah blinked. The wizard stopped pounding in his ears and left his limbs and went back to pacing in his belly. Elijah nodded.

'Yes, I think today it's better to worship God in the park.'

Elijah felt his forehead wrinkle. Why was God in the park?

'Elijah, God is everywhere. You don't have to go into church to speak to him. He is even in here.' Granddad held a hand to Elijah's chest and it was as if Granddad was putting a little bit of God in him and the wizard froze and shrivelled up.

They walked away from the church. 'Let's talk about something cheerful,' said Granddad.

'OK,' said Elijah. He spotted a thrush darting under a hedge and paused to watch it. Granddad tugged his ear and Elijah looked up at him. 'Thank you for my antlers.'

'Of course!' said Granddad. He smiled and they moved on. 'I'll look out for other things for your collection,' he said. 'It's amazing what you can get on eBay these days.'

Elijah didn't know what eBay was but he nodded anyway. They turned into a large park with a big hill, and he imagined running down it, arms out.

'So you met Jasmin, then.' Granddad walked quickly. 'She's a real character.'

'She poked her tongue out,' said Elijah.

Granddad laughed. 'Yes, that's Jasmin.' He was a very old man but his legs went as quick as a young man's. The air was cool and Elijah's own legs felt strong. He liked how the cold air felt on his nose, and how the trees looked.

'The Greenwich planetarium is not far and we're

free for an hour,' said Granddad. 'Let's go in.' He walked ahead. Elijah watched Granddad's back, and kept his legs moving fast so he wouldn't get lost. It was a long climb upwards in Greenwich Park and Elijah's breath was quick. He tried to count the steps but there were too many. Lots of people on the way were smiling and taking photographs of each other. Lots of families. His heart bit him inside.

Finally, they came to a shining dome, glittering in the sunshine. Elijah looked down at the whole of Greenwich and saw the shining tower blocks in the distance.

'Canary Wharf,' Granddad said. 'You can see nearly the whole of London from up here.' He took Elijah's hand and they walked through the gate.

Inside, there were photos of space rockets and everywhere was suddenly dark. It felt like he was inside a dream. A good one. He looked for the wizard but couldn't feel it. Granddad bought some tickets for a short show and his eyes twinkled in the low light. They sat down together in the darkness. 'This is one of my favourite places,' he said. 'I like to come here and see the Nigerian stars. London is so full of dirt and pollution that you can't actually see the night sky. I miss the sky most of all.' He whispered towards Elijah's ear but the words spilled out everywhere, and someone behind them coughed. 'I miss everything, living in exile like this.'

Elijah could only see Granddad's outline, the softness of his white hair. Elijah suddenly thought of his schoolbag, sitting by the door, waiting for Monday. Of Nikki holding his hand too tightly. Of Ricardo talking to Nikki and Obi. Of Mama.

There was music and a blanket of stars fell on top of them.

'This is like Nigeria,' whispered Granddad. He looked up with Elijah and they listened to a man tell them about all of the stars and planets and Elijah felt very, very small, like an ant. He thought about sitting in Nigeria with Granddad, and how hot they would feel and how many stars they'd see. The stars seemed to fall inside Elijah's body and fill in the empty spaces. The wizard was nowhere inside him. He was full of Nigerian stars. Granddad put his arm around Elijah's shoulder and they watched and watched, and for a few minutes, Elijah felt as though his Mama was very, very near. He closed his eyes tightly and let himself remember her voice, her smell, her love – bigger than the sky.

'Obi usually takes only a few minutes for lunch,' said Nikki as she pressed the door buzzer to his office. 'But I've talked him into taking the whole hour with us.'

They stood on a busy street with lots of cars and people rushing by. Obi's office had a cluster of women outside who were wearing long black sheets and only the eyeholes cut out. Elijah tried to look at their eyes but the women were too busy moving their heads and talking loudly in a language that sounded like coughing. He wondered if the women had come to get help from Obi. Obi's job was all about helping people. He took care of human rights, which was the rights of humans, like Nikki took care of dog rights. Humans had lots of rights and Obi had told him some of them.

Nikki buzzed again and smiled down at Elijah. Obi's head appeared. He threw the door open, swooping Elijah into his arms and carrying him into the building, with Nikki grinning at Elijah from behind Obi's wide shoulders. The room was not at all what he expected. Fola's favourite show was *Crime Scene Investigation* and he couldn't remember much about it, because it was so long since he lived with Fola, but he did remember the lawyers' offices, all sparkling and full of white-skinned blonde women wearing high heels. Obi's office had lots of old Blu-tack on the walls and there was only one white-skinned blonde woman sitting behind a small desk, but she didn't look like the ones in *C.S.I.*: she wore a T-shirt that had an orange stain on the front.

'Pauline, this is Elijah,' said Obi, and he spun Elijah around in the air before setting him down in front of the woman.

'You're all he talks about,' said Pauline. She held out her hand. 'It's so nice to finally meet you.'

Elijah shook her hand. Her fingers were sticky.

Obi turned to Nikki. 'I just have one phone call

to make, then I'm all yours.' He kissed her cheek then went into another room and shut the door behind him.

Nikki squeezed Elijah's shoulder. Pauline reached into her desk drawer and pulled out a tub filled with sweets. 'Flying Saucers are my favourites,' she said, and opened the tub towards Elijah.

Elijah looked at Nikki. She nodded. 'One won't hurt.'

Elijah could hear Obi talking on the phone in a loud voice. He sounded cross.

'In fact, I might steal one myself.' Nikki put her hand in and took a round purple sweet.

Elijah took a sweet for himself and popped it in his mouth. Obi's voice was saying, 'She will be deported. It's as simple as that. We will be sending her to . . .'

Elijah wondered what 'deported' meant.

'I think we'll wait outside,' said Nikki.

Elijah took her hand. 'Thanks for the sweet,' he said.

Pauline reached over the desk and pinched his cheek with her sticky fingers. 'Any time,' she said.

It was sunny outside and there was a traffic jam, lots of cars honking and people with their arms dangling out of rolled-down windows. He would have liked to stay inside to get a proper look around but, when they got outside, the women wearing sheets were still there, so it was just as interesting. He tried to look at all of their eyes, so he could guess what kind of people they were underneath the sheets. They carried on talking with their coughing language, one of them making big round gestures with her hands.

Nikki leant against the wall and pulled Elijah closer, running her fingers over his hair. 'Who knew hair could grow so fast?' she said. He closed his eyes so he could concentrate on the feeling of her fingers on his scalp, so gentle.

The office door opened and Obi came out. He looked at Nikki and shrugged. 'I'm so sorry guys, but I'm not going to be able to come and have fun with you.' He bent down and waggled his head at Elijah. 'I'm sorry to miss out, but it's really, really important.' He kissed Nikki on the cheek and patted Elijah's head. 'I want you to save some cake for me, OK? And I'll have it at home tonight.'

Nikki sighed. 'But we were really looking forward to it.'

'I'm sorry – I can't afford the time.' He reached out to run his thumb across her cheek. 'Do you remember the case I told you about? Amira and Youssef?'

She nodded.

He shook his head, slowly.

Nikki winced and bit her lip. 'Of course,' she said, reaching up to squeeze Obi's arm, but she pulled a sad face.

'I really can't.'

'OK, no, I understand,' she said. 'We might just have to eat your cake, though.'

Obi laughed. 'Elijah, can I trust you to keep an eye on Nikki? Make sure she doesn't eat my cake?'

Elijah looked up at Nikki, who shook her head and rubbed her belly. 'Probably not,' said Elijah. Nikki and Obi laughed as Nikki pulled Elijah away. As they walked up the street, Elijah looked back to see Obi talking to the women outside. They followed him into his offices. He wondered if Pauline would give them a Flying Saucer and, if she did, how would they eat it? There was no hole for their mouths. How did they even speak?

CHAPTER 12

My little son, my love, my heart,
You were born at Lewisham Hospital in a room that had too many men and not enough women, and cold metal instruments pulling you out of me. Elijah, childbirth is a lie that women tell each other and themselves. I will not lie to the only one who was there with me, because, as bad as it was for me, so it was for you.

It is the worst of all things. But mine was even worse than any other childbirth, and I'm not just saying that in the way of all first-time mothers. It was worse. You must remember. They ripped you out from inside me, and your first few hours were spent shaking softly like an autumn leaf about to fall.

The cracking came first. There was no stretching and no waves getting stormier and stormier, only sudden cracking and breaking and splitting. I had seen babies being born to aunties and cousins, of course, back home where women gathered around and held each other, and sang and cried and laughed. Those women helped the labouring woman stretch out, pull and swell and become

139

wider, wide enough to be a doorway for a baby into this world. My body did not stretch at Lewisham Hospital. Instead, I smashed. Every crack of metal brought you closer and every crack took me further. Both of us could not survive, I thought. For a few seconds after you left my body, we remained one person.

And that, Elijah, is the centre of everything.

And then we were separate. We did not scream, but the world screamed around us.

Akpan sang and whispered and prayed next to me – us – and did his best, but even the best of men is not a woman in that situation. I would have given anything for my mummy, or a sister or two. 'You are beautiful,' said Akpan as I sweated and vomited and shit and pissed, everything but you coming from inside me. But he meant it, Elijah. His eyes were filled with happy tears the entire time. He rubbed my back and my feet and my stomach and he held my hand and I squeezed his hand until I heard crunching, yet he never once complained.

Finally there was an emptying. Hot stickiness. I shook – shakes on top of shakes. I had no centre; my centre was you, and you were gone.

'Congratulations!' A voice flew into my popped brain. 'You have a son.'

A son, I thought. Akpan kissed me on the mouth and kissed you on your mouth and his face was bloody but he didn't care at all. I'd never seen such a happy man.

You looked straight at me and frowned. Your nose was pressed flat against you, and your head coned upwards, lips soft and pink. I picked my shaking hand up and touched your cheek with my thumb. I was the thumb and I was the cheek. You cried suddenly and I cried with you.

Gradually your face took shape, your little eyes closed, your body uncurled, and when I pressed my thumb to your cheek, all I felt was my thumb. You were real and alive, and I had made you, created you. All other things in my life were nothing. Those few moments when I held you were the happiest minutes of my life, and the pain was worth it.

I was in the place where women are kings.

It's true, Elijah. There are three places where women are kings. One is in that moment after birth, when generations of women stir up inside a woman's body and the whole world shakes and nature reminds us who is king. The second place is Nigeria, where – you remember – a woman, a prostitute even, was so respected she was made king. And in Heaven women must be kings, for in Heaven all the wrongs of earth are righted. Nigeria, and Childbirth, and Heaven: these are the places where anything is possible for women.

Akpan leant towards me – us. 'Look what we have done,' he said. 'God is truly blessing us.'

In the moments after you were born, the other mothers held their new babies to their breast and lay back and closed their eyes, but not me. I lifted you up right in front of my eyes to see Nigeria looking back at me. You were born in Lewisham, England, but your face belonged in Nigeria. I prayed so hard that night, Elijah, to thank God for such a gift as you. I remember Akpan and I walking you over to the window and showing you the night filled with Nigerian stars and the fullest moon I'd ever seen, swelling in the sky like a heart in love. 'My little son, Elijah,' whispered Akpan. 'Look, now. Even the moon loves you.'

CHAPTER 13

'How many dogs are there?' Elijah asked. 'Hundreds!' Nikki couldn't wait to see his face; sometimes she found him in the living room, looking at photos of her with the dogs. 'But remember what I told you. We can't take any home, OK? Maybe in a few years' time.'

It was Sunday morning and raining, but that wasn't going to spoil her mood. She was finally going in to Battersea for a 'keeping in touch' day, and to show Elijah around. Also, she was planning to speak to her line manager about her return-to-work date. Elijah was doing so well, there was really no reason to delay once he started school. The summer holidays were whizzing by and she knew September would come quickly. They walked hand in hand towards the entrance, past the long, high wall. A couple passed them excitedly – obviously talking about a dog they'd seen. The woman linked her arm with the man. They looked at each other. 'He's adorable,' the woman said.

Elijah looked at Nikki. 'Have they got a dog?'

She nodded. 'I think so.' They came to the heavy gate and Pete, a thickset security guard, who sometimes fostered the dogs if they were going kennel-crazy, opened the door. He looked at Elijah with one eyebrow raised.

'Hi Pete,' said Nikki, smiling. 'We've come to visit. This is the famous Elijah.'

Pete smiled back, winked at Nikki. 'Hello there,' he said.

'Can we see the dogs?' asked Elijah, excitement making his voice squeak.

Pete laughed and opened the door. 'Go on. Have fun,' he said.

Elijah almost ran. There were two large dog-statues outside the reception doors, and a few people were walking dogs in front of them. Nikki picked up Elijah's hand and led him towards reception where she was greeted with hugs and kisses from all her colleagues who came out to see Elijah, patting his head, making a fuss of him. He didn't seem to mind. How far they had come, Nikki thought, in a matter of weeks.

'Shall we go see the dogs, then?' Nikki asked.

'Yes, please!' Elijah shouted and her colleagues laughed. They knew how long she'd waited for Elijah. And what she'd been through.

She took Elijah's hand and led him through the door and up the ramp towards the dogs. 'You have to be quiet,' she said, 'and try not to stare too much. Dogs hate people staring at them.'

The first dog, a husky, came to the front of its kennel and raised a paw. 'Wow! It looks like a wolf.'

'I know. We're getting more and more of these dogs at Battersea. We're not sure why,' said Nikki.

'Why is the cage so small?'

'Well, it's not a cage,' said Nikki, 'more of a temporary kennel. And the dogs can go in and out of the back – look. Also, they get one hour out of their kennel every day. And they love their walks. Look at this,' Nikki pointed to the small material pouch hanging on the outside of the kennel. 'It's lavender and other herbs to calm the dogs down.'

'But why do they need calming down?'

Elijah had his face pressed towards the cage bars. He was looking straight at the dog's eyes and his breathing was getting quicker. Nikki started to feel anxious. What if the dogs triggered some sort of memory in Elijah? Of course, there were parallels. Where were their owners? Where was Elijah's mum? She scanned the viewing area, the notes above each cage, the one in front of them:

Edith is a lovely, kind lady approaching her later years. She needs a special family who are used to the breed and are at home for most of the time. Edith will make a lovely pet to a family with older children, and no other pets.

Nikki pulled Elijah towards her. 'I think we should go to the office. Every single day there is a dog that gets to be the office dog. I bet if we ask really nicely we could take the office dog for a quick walk.'

'Yes, please!'

They walked quickly out of the viewing area and didn't look back. Nikki put her arm around Elijah's shoulder.

That afternoon, all Elijah could talk about was the dogs: how the dog they'd taken for a walk was shaped like a sausage and barked at the birds in the park. When Elijah was out of the room, Nikki told Obi how the visit had nearly triggered something in Elijah, the way he'd started getting anxious about the dogs waiting to be rehomed.

'He's going to have loads of triggers,' Obi said. 'But look how well you dealt with it.' He leant towards her and kissed her mouth.

But that night a scream filled the house and brought them both running to Elijah's bedroom. He was covered in sweat, every muscle stiff and tense, his face twisted into a much older face. He was crying and screaming and had red scratches all over his arms.

'Elijah, what is it? Elijah?' Nikki ran towards him and put her hand on to his boiling-hot head. She stared at the scratches on his skin. 'Shall we phone an ambulance?' She looked at Obi but he was motionless, standing in the doorway, his mouth half open.

Nikki jumped on to the bed and held Elijah

close, his body rigid against hers, his eyes far away. 'Shhhh.' She rocked him back and forth. But Elijah reached out suddenly and scratched a raw line just below her eye.

She pulled backwards. 'Elijah! Elijah!' She touched her face. It stopped hurting almost immediately.

Elijah curled in a ball on the bed. He was sobbing.

'We should phone for advice, and not crowd him. Remove anything that could be harmful,' said Obi as he reached for the bedside lamp and moved it away.

Nikki dropped back on to the bed next to Elijah.

'No,' said Obi. 'We mustn't crowd him.'

But she curled her body around Elijah.

Obi knelt beside the bed. 'Check his arms,' he whispered. 'Does he need some antiseptic or plasters?'

Nikki lifted her head from Elijah's. 'He's not bleeding,' she said. 'They're just shallow scratches.' She rested against him again. 'You're OK, Elijah.'

Elijah's sobbing quietened down until the only noise was his breathing.

Obi knelt beside the bed. 'Elijah, do you want to come and sleep in our room?'

'I don't think he can hear you,' she said. 'You go back to bed and I'll stay here. You've got court first thing.'

Obi coughed. 'We should ask for advice.'

'Who're we going to call at this time? It's OK,'

said Nikki. 'Honestly. He was just having a nightmare.'

'OK, if you're sure.' Obi looked at Elijah for a long time. His eyes were closed tight and his breathing was regular. Obi kissed Nikki before switching the light off and leaving the room.

Nikki felt her own heart thumping against Elijah's back. Ricardo had warned them about rages and that Elijah might lash out, but, since she'd first seen his scars, Elijah had been nothing but calm and loving. She felt the skin underneath her eye. What had happened to her son? She held him close.

Eventually Elijah turned around and faced her. She could see his wide-open eyes in the almost darkness. He looked terrified. 'I'm sorry,' he whispered.

'If we lie close enough,' she said, 'you'll be able to share my dreams and I never have nightmares, only good dreams.'

Nikki couldn't see Elijah's smile, but she felt it.

'Thank you for seeing us at short notice,' Nikki said to Chioma. She liked her already. She had one of those faces that was expressive and open, and, Nikki imagined, truthful. After she'd spoken to Ricardo and told him about the incident, he reassured her it was only to be expected, and that Elijah was acting out his inner anxieties. Nightmares and tantrums were fairly normal in the early days of placement. But he had told her to get in touch with Chioma as soon as possible and Nikki was glad that he had. She'd only ever seen Chioma through the window before, when dropping Elijah off. Elijah had insisted he didn't need her to come in with him. He didn't want her to come in with him.

'Thanks to you all for coming.'

Elijah looked up at Chioma. Nikki could tell from his body language that he was relaxed around Chioma. His shoulders were relaxed and he was slouching slightly. On the way there in the car, Elijah had been tense. He'd asked Nikki to sit in the back with him and held her hand for the entire journey. Obi, on the other hand, had his shoulders raised up to his ears. He was flicking a pen on, off, on, off.

He had woken up early with a headache and gone rummaging around in the bathroom for a painkiller. 'But is play therapy enough?' he'd asked. 'We still don't know what he's dealing with and, with outbursts like this, maybe he needs a more clinical approach.' He went thudding down the stairs and she heard him banging the cupboards open and shut. She yawned and sat up as he came back into the bedroom again. 'Maybe it's time for another psychiatric assessment. He could even benefit from drug therapy.' He disappeared back into the bathroom and there was a crash as the toothbrush holder fell into the bath and Obi swore. 'Do we not have any aspirin in this house? Really?' The bathroom cabinet slammed shut and Obi stood in the doorway. 'Aspirin?'

Nikki shrugged.

'I can live with this headache, but what about you?'

'Come on, Obi,' she said.

'I'm serious! Really? There's no aspirin?'

Aside from making her lose babies, Nikki's condition made her susceptible to deep-vein thrombosis, among other nasty conditions, which needed to be kept in check with aspirin. 'There've been other things on my mind,' she'd said, frowning at him.

He frowned back and they stared at each other for a moment. But then he'd apologised and told Nikki about a new case he'd been dealing with: a woman from the Democratic Republic of Congo who, along with her sisters, had been brutally attacked and raped by men and their guns. One sister had bled to death following the attack. 'The other had to have reconstructive surgery,' Obi told her.

Nikki blinked. So that's what he'd been worrying about. She sighed. 'What a world we live in. What a world *you* live in.' The horror of it made her shudder. 'How do you do it? How do you come home from that?'

He shrugged. 'I always do my best and, if there's nothing more I can do, I move on to the next case. I have to. There's always another case.'

Nikki had curled up against him.

'Right, let's get started,' said Chioma. 'Don't look so nervous, Dad; Elijah will tell you, there's nothing to be nervous of here.' She smiled.

Elijah nodded and Obi laughed. 'I'm not nervous,' he said. 'And we'll do anything at all,' he added, 'to help our son.' *Son*. He put the pen down and smiled.

Chioma nodded back at him. 'OK, then. Well, today I thought we'd start with some music. Grab yourselves a drum and a stethoscope.' She pointed to a selection of drums, and a large pile of black doctors' stethoscopes.

Nikki and Obi looked at each other. 'Er, OK,' said Nikki, picking up both.

Elijah jumped up. 'I love this game!' he said. 'These are Nigerian drums.'

Nikki laughed. They all sat in a semicircle, with Chioma opposite. 'OK, now, Elijah, whenever we've done this before, you've listened to your own heartbeat, but this time I'd like you to drum to Mum or Dad's heartbeat.'

Elijah looked at Nikki, then Obi. 'Who should I choose?' he asked.

'Whoever you like. You can have a turn with the other afterwards.'

Elijah picked up his stethoscope and popped the earpieces into his ears. He stretched out and lifted Nikki's T-shirt, then moved the stethoscope underneath. His fingers were warm. With one hand he held it in place and with the other he began tapping on the drum. The sound was loud and steady and strong. Elijah began rocking his body in time to the beat. Then Nikki rocked with him.

They both started laughing. Obi took his

151

stethoscope and put it on to Elijah's back, then began drumming too. The sound was quicker and lighter and matched the other drum perfectly. The two drums together sounded exactly like a heart beating. Nikki closed her eyes. She listened to her husband and son, their drumming, her heartbeat. When Chioma told them to stop, Elijah pulled the stethoscope out from underneath Nikki's T-shirt, but he didn't move away. Nikki breathed in the smell of Elijah's skin.

'That was lovely, Elijah. What about Dad now?' said Chioma.

Elijah reached his stethoscope up underneath Obi's shirt. He began tapping a beat. Obi joined in again, drumming on both his and Elijah's drum, then Chioma grabbed a drum and began too. The room was filled with sound.

When they finished, Obi was breathless.

'Drumming to heartbeats,' Nikki said to Obi.

'I read a piece of research in the *Lancet* about the therapeutic effects of music. It was in last month's.' He looked at Chioma.

'Excellent,' said Chioma. 'It's extremely therapeutic. And, more than that, it's great fun. What shall we play now? I think you should choose, Elijah.'

'Mums and dads.' He beamed and looked at Nikki. 'Let's play mums and dads.'

'Good idea. Another of my favourite games. Who will everyone be?'

'You be the dog,' said Elijah, pointing at Chioma, who immediately said, 'Woof!'

'And you be the dad –' pointing to Obi, who smiled and winked – 'and you be the mum,' he said, looking up at Nikki.

'What will you be, Elijah?'

'Shall I be the baby?'

Nikki glanced at Chioma. 'Very good idea,' she said.

They began to play the game. Elijah pretended to cry and Nikki stroked his head, and Obi went out of the room and came back in. 'I've had a terrible day at work,' he said. 'Where's my dinner?' He laughed.

'Woof! Woof!' said Chioma. She was crawling on all fours and pretending to wag an imaginary tail. Nikki imagined it must hurt her knees, crawling around on the floor, but if it did she didn't seem to mind.

'Mama,' said Elijah holding his arms out to Nikki. Nikki pulled him into her arms and stroked his head. Obi walked towards them and placed his hand over Nikki's, and Chioma smiled.

Dinner was salmon baked in tinfoil with sesame oil and soy sauce, spring onions, chilli, garlic and ginger. Nikki had set aside two small portions of salmon and added only honey to those before baking all the fish in the oven, but when Elijah saw Obi's fish, he licked his lips. 'Can I have one like that?' He looked at his honey salmon and then back at Obi's plate. He was completely normal, as if the other night had never happened.

If Nikki hadn't been so tired, she'd have thought it was all a dream. The kitchen was alive with spicy, sweet smells and the sound of the family talking over one another. Nikki looked at them all for a few minutes, gathered around the wooden table: Elijah, Obi, Chanel, Jasmin and Obi's Daddy. It was as if they had always been there together. Elijah was laughing at jokes and whispering with Jasmin, Daddy was holding court and even Chanel seemed to be on her best behaviour. It was light outside and the sun was still shining, but Nikki had lit candles anyway and the scene looked cosy and warm. Obi caught her eye from across the other side of the table and smiled. She'd been a bit angry with him the other night, for standing back and talking rather than simply holding Elijah, and then being more upset about work than his own son, but with Chioma he'd been perfect. She heard again the beating of the drums. She smiled back.

'I'll have two plain honey ones,' said Jasmin. 'Salmon is good for brain development and, if I am going to be a marine biologist, I need a good brain.' She reached across the table and pulled Elijah's fish on to her plate. 'And I like your honey salmon. It's much better than Mum's fish fingers.'

'Hey!' said Chanel. 'That's Captain Birdseye you're offending.'

'Good job you made extra, then,' said Obi, winking at Nikki.

'What's a marine biologist?' Elijah was already

154

digging into his dinner, piling couscous on to his plate next to the fish.

'Marine biologist!' Chanel laughed. 'You won't even do your homework now, so how will you study something like that?' She was sitting next to Jasmin, but moved away as Jasmin tried to elbow her. 'Hey! You know that's true. You're always trying to get out of your homework.'

'I am not,' said Jasmin. She was wearing a T-shirt that said *Pop Star* in pink glitter. 'Mrs Pullen says I've got the best brain in class and, if I applied myself, I could do anything.'

'Exactly,' said Chanel. 'So apply yourself. That means do your homework without complaining. I bet Jay-Z will work super hard at his new school, won't you, little man?'

Nikki tutted at Chanel. 'Stop calling him that.'

'I don't mind,' said Elijah.

He's kind to everyone, even Chanel, thought Nikki.

'Anyway, I do apply myself.' Jasmin turned to Elijah. 'A marine biologist is someone who swims with dolphins,' she said. 'Like a human mermaid.'

Daddy rolled his eyes and snorted. 'In Nigeria, when I was growing up, there were only three professions: medicine, law and engineering. The kids were given a book and slapped around the head for playing too much football. Now they're slapped around the head for reading books and given a football instead.' He began to laugh. 'How times have changed!'

'What do you want to be when you're older?' asked Obi, looking at Elijah. 'Do you have a grand plan, like Jasmin?'

Elijah looked around the table at everyone's faces.

'You don't have to decide now,' Nikki said. 'You have years and years and years at school.'

Elijah laughed. 'I already know what I want to be,' he said.

'A marine biologist with me?' Jasmin asked. 'Then we could both live in California, because that's the best place to do it. There are millions of dolphins there and Hollywood movie stars who live in mansions.'

Elijah shook his head again but he was smiling. Nikki could tell that he liked Jasmin. His face lit up when she was around. He looked at Nikki. 'I want to work with you,' he said. 'I want to be an animal helper at Battersea Dogs' Home.'

CHAPTER 14

Elijah hadn't liked any of the schools he'd been to, but some were worse than others. Horton School was bigger than Appletree School, and it had more grass than St John's School, more buildings than Grove Field and St Anne's, and more cars parked outside than Lowry Park School, but fewer flowers outside than St Peter's and definitely bigger children than Kennedy Court Primary School. The worst turned out to be St Peter's, where Elijah learnt that flowers outside the gate did not mean kind hearts inside the teachers.

'Come on, slow coach,' Jasmin pulled him by the mittens that Nikki had sewn on to his coat sleeves. Just in case they get lost, she'd said, or your hands get cold. Jasmin had rolled her eyes back into her head. 'It's only September. It's not even winter yet.' She snorted but Elijah didn't mind. He liked having warm hands.

He looked behind him at Nikki and Aunty Chanel, who were talking and laughing. Nikki was wearing a thin coat like his and had a patterned scarf wrapped around her neck. Aunty Chanel was wearing leopard-print trousers and a bright pink vest underneath a leather jacket, and had high heels that tapped on the pavement. He wished he wasn't walking to school. He wished he was going to the park and the river, which was where Nikki took him sometimes, to sit on a bench and look at the water.

'That's OK,' said Nikki when she noticed him looking. 'You can go ahead a bit with Jasmin. Mrs Pullen will be waiting at the gate, anyway. But come here first.'

Elijah pulled his mittens away from Jasmin's grasp. He stood in front of Nikki.

'Now, remember everything I told you? This is a first day, that's all. If it is too hard then tell the teacher and she'll phone me and I'll get you straight away. Just tell Mrs Pullen.' Nikki kissed him on the cheek. She smelt of mint. Nikki took a small piece of paper out from her back pocket and showed Elijah. It was a picture she'd drawn of a prince wearing a crown and there was a heart and two kisses. 'Keep this in your pocket and you can think of me,' she said. Obi had already given him another note with the words *carpe diem* written on it. He said it meant 'seize the day' but, even in English, it didn't really make sense because Obi told him that 'seize' meant hold really suddenly and tightly, and you couldn't hold a day. If you could hold a day, Elijah would have held the day when he last saw Mama's face. But he didn't tell Obi that.

'I'll be OK,' he murmured. He knew Nikki was worried about him; he'd heard her talking to Ricardo on the telephone the night before: *too soon, not ready, it might trigger a relapse in behaviour.* But, although he heard Nikki's words in his ear: 'Don't worry about school too much – it's not important', Elijah heard Mama's words in his heart: *My little son, when you are well, you will be lucky going to school. School is like a ticket to any place you want to go and, if you work really hard, you will be able to travel in first class.*

But, although Elijah carried Mama's words, no matter how much he tried, he didn't like school. The work was too hard for his eyes and the wizard made everything blur so he wouldn't see and laughed in his ear so that he wouldn't hear the teachers. The teachers would put on cross faces and, if Elijah wasn't very careful, the wizard would take over completely. And then the teachers would get really angry, shouting at him for saying bad words or kicking or breaking the window, when Elijah had no idea what they were talking about. That would make them angriest of all. He hadn't felt the wizard at all for a few days, but he felt sure that it would be back on his first day at his new school. As the days went on and school became closer, the dreams had come every few days. The other night, Elijah had thought the wizard was back, torturing him with bad dreams, and he had screamed and scratched himself to get rid of it, but in the end it was just a bad dream. As Nikki slept next to him, he had searched and searched in himself for any sign of the wizard and it was not there. But the wizard always came back. Elijah looked up at the sun. He felt cold.

He leant towards Nikki and hugged her quickly, taking the note and putting it into his pocket. 'Don't come to the gate,' he said. Even though he thought Nikki was a special and kind person, he didn't want Nikki standing beside him in case the other children saw her and then they would know he didn't live with his real mum. If only Obi had been able to join them. But then he saw Nikki's puzzled face and he felt bad. She had held him so close the other night. Closer than Ricardo. As close as Mama. He ran back and gave her another quick hug.

'I'll be fine,' he said, and she smiled and looked up at Aunty Chanel, who held her hand over her heart and said, 'Ahhh.'

They walked towards the gate and Jasmin began speaking quickly. 'I wanted to talk to you the other night but I couldn't because Mum and everyone was there. I have to tell you about the spy code for the torches. The other day you did something totally embarrassing.'

Elijah looked back at Nikki and Aunty Chanel, who were talking and walking slowly behind them. 'Is it a code? The way you flash the torches?'

'Of course it's a code. And, if you want to message me, it's very important. Three flashes and then one quick flash means I'll knock for you in the morning to walk to school, three quick flashes means I'll come over to play, and four flashes means you come over to mine to play. But you did five slow flashes!'

'What does it mean?' Elijah touched the note Nikki had put into his pocket. The paper felt very smooth on his fingertips, like the skin on Mama's cheek.

'Five slow flashes must never be used! The only time I would use five slow flashes is if Justin Bieber moved in, and you don't look anything like Justin Bieber and, anyway, we're cousins, which is like brother and sister, anyway, so five slow flashes is gross.'

He had no idea what Jasmin was talking about but he liked her saying they were like brother and sister. He'd never had a cousin or friend or brother or sister before.

Jasmin looked towards the school. 'It's fine for you to use the code. In fact, we have to use the code because Mum won't let me have a walkie-talkie, which would be better. But don't ever, ever use five flashes.' She leant towards Elijah's ear. 'Five slow flashes means, "I love you."'

A lady came out of the gate and walked towards them. 'Good morning, Jasmin,' she said. 'How are you?' They both stopped walking and stood still until Nikki and Aunty Chanel caught up.

Jasmin smiled. 'Hello, Mrs Pullen. I had a good summer holiday. I went to America and saw the

Statue of Liberty, and I went to the top of the Empire State Building.'

Elijah giggled and quickly put his hand over his mouth.

'Jasmin,' said her mum, shaking her head. 'Stop making up stories.' She turned to Mrs Pullen. 'We went to my friend's caravan in Great Yarmouth for two nights and it pissed down with rain.'

'Chanel!'

'Sorry,' said Aunty Chanel. 'I meant to say, "poured". Poured with rain.'

Jasmin turned towards her teacher. 'See what I'm dealing with?' Then she took Elijah's hand and flicked her ponytail. 'You will have to put a pound in the swear jar, Mum. Come on, Elijah. Let's go.'

'Are you OK, Elijah?' Nikki looked lost, as if she was on a strange street even though they were only two roads away from their house.

Elijah nodded. Mrs Pullen picked up his other hand. 'Come with me; I'm your new teacher,' she said.

'He'll be fine, Aunty Nikki. Won't ya?' Jasmin smiled at Elijah. He nodded again.

They walked towards the school and through the big metal gates and Elijah didn't look backwards once because he knew Nikki would be crying and that might make him cry. Jasmin flicked her ponytail again. 'In America, you don't have to go to school,' she said.

'Jasmin, that's not entirely true, is it?' said Mrs

Pullen, winking at Elijah. She had bushy red hair and black circles around her eyes.

'Some kids are homeschooled. That means they just watch TV all day. I wish I lived in America so I didn't have to go to school to sit on my hands when I'm fiddling in class.'

'Then don't fiddle!' Mrs Pullen laughed then and Jasmin smiled at her and Elijah realised they must be friends. 'She can't keep still, can you, Jasmin?'

Jasmin rolled her eyes. Elijah had never known a girl like Jasmin. She wasn't like a boy, but she wasn't like any other child he'd ever met. Part of him wanted to be her friend, but he was worried about the wizard. The wizard hurt everyone he ever liked. It would be safer for Jasmin if they weren't friends, but when Jasmin was near he felt a bit better – like she was full of sunshine that filled all Elijah's darkness. It was impossible not to like her. Even if she said she wouldn't be friends with him. And Chioma had taught him how to breathe so slowly it stopped time and helped him think and that made the wizard really small. It did mean he didn't have any special powers – no wizard meant no special powers – but he didn't mind. He'd give up anything in the world to make the wizard go. If the wizard went, he would be safe and Mama might get better and see how he was a normal boy.

Inside the playground, Elijah suddenly stopped

walking. He stood still for a few minutes because his legs wouldn't work. Then he walked towards the big door where lots of children were screaming inside. He let go of Mrs Pullen and Jasmin and covered his ears. Children were whizzing past him and he didn't know any of them. The whole world was filled with children who were not friends. Some of them pushed him and he moved to the side and looked at the wall where there was a big peeling-paint mark.

Mrs Pullen knelt down in front of him and gently moved his hands from his ears. 'Come on, let's get out of this chaos. Let me take you to your classroom. You'll see – it's a very friendly class and we do so many fun things.'

Everything went blurred as if there was a problem with his eyes. Maybe the wizard was making them blurred. He followed Mrs Pullen and Jasmin through the school corridors to a room with a glass door. The children had gone into the class already and everything was quiet inside the classroom. As they walked in, Elijah felt everyone looking at him. He wondered which child would be the first to hit him, or call him a name, or laugh at him. He looked up. Jasmin was there right next to him. She smiled a wide smile.

'OK, Elijah, welcome to class 3F. You can sit next to Jasmin. She insisted! I know better than to argue with Jasmin when she insists!' Mrs Pullen winked at Jasmin again.

Elijah sat on a chair at the front; Jasmin sat next to him. As Mrs Pullen read the names out, Jasmin took a pencil from her pencil case and drew a skull with bones around it, like a pirate skull-and-crossbones, on the piece of paper on Elijah's desk. She began to fiddle with her pencil case, getting everything out then putting everything in again. She was humming loudly.

Elijah looked at the classroom. It was the same as all the others he'd been in: a big blackboard and a big whiteboard, hundreds of drawings, drawers and drawers of equipment with stickers on the front that he couldn't read, a large globe on the front desk and lots of children looking at him. In all the places he'd been to, he'd hated school. He'd never had any real friends, not a single one. But suddenly, sitting beside Jasmin, he felt like something important might change. He could breathe easily and the wizard was completely silent. He sat up straighter and nobody laughed at him. Not even the wizard. For the first time, Elijah had a friend. Even better than a friend. A cousin. He knew it was dangerous to make friends with people, that the wizard could hurt anyone. But, sitting next to Jasmin, he realised that the wizard never woke up when she was near. If it did start to wake up, Elijah could control it how Chioma taught him. It was like being near Jasmin made him stronger. Jasmin wasn't scared of anything. Not even a wizard. Elijah decided to risk it. He looked straight up at Jasmin's face and smiled.

But Jasmin was too busy sharpening all her pencils one by one to notice.

Mrs Pullen sighed. 'Jasmin,' she said. 'Sit on your hands, please.'

CHAPTER 15

Nikki asked if October was a bit late in the year for a barbecue, but Obi told her she was being ridiculous. 'It must be twenty degrees. We'll put gloves on, if necessary. I've got the best marinade recipe for chicken and I can't wait until spring to try it.'

Nikki laughed. 'Obi is always barbecuing,' said Nikki. 'It's the only time he cooks. Like a king, only he's allowed near the barbecue. He says I'm messy, but wait until you see him barbecuing. That's when we can really understand mess!'

Elijah had never had a barbecue but he didn't tell Nikki that. Once, Mama had fried plantain on the balcony, but she liked it blackened, which was when it was the sweetest, she'd said. She'd forgotten to take it off the fire that she'd made from wrapping-paper and an old chair. And the armchair on the balcony had caught fire somehow and she'd had to throw the burning chair over the edge of the balcony. She'd burnt her hands and cried with pain.

Later that day, Nikki took Elijah with her to Aunty Chanel's flat so that Obi could get the barbecue ready. The flat was covered in large posters that were Blu-tacked to the wall, of pop stars wearing not very much clothing. Jasmin rolled her eyes when she saw Elijah looking at them. 'It's Mum,' she said. 'So embarrassing.' She looked around the room and leant closer to Elijah. 'She's actually going to audition for *X-Factor* but you won't know what that is because you don't have a TV. It's a singing competition but like the coolest show on earth.'

Elijah tried to imagine Aunty Chanel on the stage, singing. He giggled.

'It's not funny,' whispered Jasmin. 'Don't tell anyone at school.'

'I won't,' he said. He could hear Aunty Chanel in the shower, singing loudly. 'Maybe she'll win.'

Jasmin huffed. 'Don't be ridiculous. She's too strange.' She took Elijah's hand and they went into her bedroom. It was funny being inside the room that he'd often looked at from across the road. He liked the way her curtains were always open and the horses on her duvet cover. She had a globe on her desk and a giant map on her wall, covered in tiny sticking-out pins. 'These are all the places that I will visit when I'm older,' she said. 'I want to see the whole world.' She ran her fingers over the map and read out the names: 'Peru, Brazil, Australia, Russia, Mongolia, Sudan, Alaska—'

'Ricardo is from Brazil,' said Elijah. 'He said there's a great big forest.'

Jasmin looked up at the map. 'Of course, I will

have to go to Nigeria as well,' she smiled. 'Because, the way Granddad Ozo goes on about it, you would think it's the best place in the world.'

Nigeria is a place like Heaven. Elijah heard the voice inside him. He looked at Nigeria on Jasmin's map. Russia was bigger. He always thought that Nigeria would be as big as the sky, but it was small, really, and squashed between other countries.

He put his thumb on Nigeria and moved across the other countries. Nigeria felt no different on his skin. He'd expected it to be hot.

'I'm going to see the whole world,' said Jasmin.

Elijah reached into his pocket. He took out the postcard he'd seen in the shop and begged Nikki to let him buy. It was a photo of the Empire State Building in black and white, and it had the words *I Heart NYC* written underneath. 'I got this for you,' he said. He handed the card to Jasmin.

Her smile was big enough to fill up the room. 'Thanks,' she said. She looked closely at the photo. 'It looks better in real life,' she said. Then she shrugged. 'You can come with me, if you want.'

'Can I really?'

'Of course. But you have to carry the bags. We need to take loads of sweets. You can't get really good sweets in Russia, only potatoes.'

Elijah nodded fast. 'OK,' he said. And, as he touched the giant map, he felt his thumb get hot after all.

Jasmin propped up the card on the table next

to her bed, then moved to stand beside Elijah. She reached out and put her thumb on top of his. 'Wherever we touch thumbs on the map is where we'll go, OK?'

Elijah nodded. They moved their stuck-together thumbs all over the map until there was hardly any place in the world where they wouldn't go. As they did it, Elijah's thumb became hotter and hotter but it wasn't hot like when the wizard started fires using Elijah's body. In fact, the wizard was not walking around inside him at all. It was true that whenever Jasmin was nearby, the wizard shrank to nothing. Maybe the wizard was scared of Jasmin's super-power, scared that she wasn't frightened of anything in the world. Maybe the wizard needed Elijah to feel scared so that it would grow. It was like he was finally in charge of the wizard, or the wizard was starting to disappear. Whatever the reason, Elijah looked up at Jasmin, pressed his thumb hard against hers and whispered, 'Thank you.'

She laughed. 'That's all right, silly. Of course you can come on my round-the-world trip.' She raised her eyebrows. 'Anyway. You need to be my lookout. In L.A., the police kidnap children to steal their skin and put it on the faces of old, wrinkly people.'

When they got back, Elijah could smell burning. Granddad arrived wearing a blanket wrapped around him. 'I know your dad,' he said to Elijah. 'He wants to eat outside in the freezing cold.'

But when Aunty Chanel arrived, she was wearing a vest and no jumper. 'Hey Jay-Z,' she said. 'You get more handsome every day, doesn't he, Jas?'

Jasmin was standing behind her, wearing a big coat with the hood up but Elijah could see her face turning red inside the hood.

He could feel his own face turning red. He focused on the garden, on Nikki's flowers and the small mud patch at the bottom where she said Elijah could grow vegetables. She said she thought he'd have green fingers, like hers.

'Stop embarrassing the poor boy,' said Nikki, walking past them carrying a big bowl of coleslaw that Elijah had helped make. 'Come on now, you two, you can give me a hand.'

They carried bowls of food to the table outside: rice, salad, potatoes, sauces, cutlery, serviettes, a jug of juice, glasses, a bottle of red wine for Aunty Chanel and a can of beer for Granddad. Obi put on some music and then stood by the fire, turning pieces of chicken over. The garden filled with music and the sound of talking and the smell of chicken with Obi's special marinade, and Elijah closed his eyes for a few seconds to keep it all inside his body. Obi's mobile phone rang and he pulled it from his pocket and spoke in a low voice, rushing back towards the house. 'You be in charge of the chicken,' he mouthed to Elijah, and winked before going back indoors. 'Let's do it together,' said Nikki, rushing over and picking up the tongs.

'I'll probably live in California,' said Jasmin.

'That's where all the cool people live. I'll surf on the beach and see loads of famous people. I'll probably have to get two or even three autograph books for all the names.'

Jasmin talked about America the same way Granddad talked about Nigeria, but differently as well. When Granddad talked about Nigeria, Elijah could see it in his head, but when Jasmin talked about America, all he could see was her looking for it.

They ate and ate, licking their fingers and the garden filled up with slurping happy noises. By the time Obi came back into the garden Elijah had eaten three pieces. Obi waved but was still on his mobile. 'First thing, though, OK?'

Aunty Chanel sipped her wine and raised an eyebrow at Nikki.

'I'm counting on you,' Obi said. He tucked the phone back into his pocket. He came to sit the other side of Elijah, and Nikki reached out to grab his arm as he lowered himself to the ground.

'I wish you'd put that thing away.'

'It's away!' He held his hands up, showing they were empty.

She shook her head but Elijah could see her smile.

'Did you like the chicken?' Obi asked.

Everyone made satisfied noises and nodded.

'You are some chef,' Aunty Chanel told Elijah.

'It is in his blood,' said Granddad.

Aunty Chanel laughed and Jasmin went to sit in

Granddad's lap, even though he always said she was too big.

'I think I'm going into a food coma,' said Aunty Chanel.

Elijah looked up at the sky and, even though it was lit up orange with city lights, he could count many stars.

CHAPTER 16

Ricardo was wearing purple flip-flops even though it was a really cold day and you could see your breath like a puff of smoke. He had new beads around his neck that he kept touching. If he went to the same school as Elijah, Mrs Pullen would have made him sit on his hands to stop him from fiddling. They were sitting in McDonald's, which was a big treat for Elijah because Obi would never let him go. Nikki had taken him once and they'd both had a Happy Meal. 'Let's not mention it to Obi,' Nikki had said, and they had laughed. Obi said that fast food was poison and he would never give such bad food to a loved one. That made Elijah smile.

'So, how is everything going? You seem to be really settled! I can't believe you've been with Nikki and Obi for three months already. It really has flown by!' Ricardo bit into his veggie burger. He was vegetarian and ate no meat at all. He had told Elijah that was why he didn't live in Brazil. 'No vegetarians live in Brazil,' he'd explained. 'It's against the law. When I cannot stay away from Brazil any longer, then I'll have a good-quality

174

steak. But, until that day, I'll stick to this terrible vegetarian burger.' He took another bite and pulled a face. 'Nikki says you're settling in really well.'

'Obi is teaching me to play football. School is really good. And Nikki took me to her work and let me play with the dogs.' Elijah laughed. 'They're funny. They licked my face.'

'Did you say school is really good? Fantastic. And Nikki said you're a natural with the dogs,' said Ricardo. 'And that you're a great helper.' He paused. 'But she also said it was a bit hard for you seeing the dogs. And that night you were angry.'

Elijah shrugged. 'They looked very sad,' he said, 'which is why I want to help them, like Nikki.'

'Well, I'm sure they'll have a forever family, just like you do, before long. Nikki and Obi said the anger was only for a short time and then you were back to your old lovely self again. So you've now spent some time with all the family? Have you got to know everyone?'

'Aunty Chanel is really funny. She's an adult but she acts like a child. And Jasmin sits next to me at school. I like Jasmin. In the Easter holidays, we're going to Wales so I can meet my other new nan and granddad. I've spoken to them on Skype and they made me laugh. And also,' Elijah smiled widely, 'Obi said he'd take me to Nigeria next year.'

Ricardo laughed. 'Sounds busy! And how are you feeling about the adoption day?'

Elijah stopped eating. 'Do I have to talk?'

'No. An adoption day is just a special day in court when Nikki and Obi sign the papers to become your mum and dad forever. It's a celebration when we can have cake and go for a special meal afterwards. You don't have to talk, but you do need to look smart.' Ricardo laughed. 'For example, I will be wearing proper shoes. No sandals, no Havaianas. And my very best aftershave, that I save only for fabulous occasions.'

Elijah couldn't imagine Ricardo wearing shoes.

'So you like being with your forever family?'

Elijah thought about it. Living with Nikki and Obi was like nowhere else he'd ever lived. He didn't want to go anywhere else. He still missed Mama very much, but Nikki said that was OK. She said that was normal.

Forever family.

'When can I see Mama?'

'She's not well at all, Elijah, and as we discussed it might be better for you to stick to twice-yearly contact. Any more than that and it might make you not do so well.'

'Is she still sick?'

'Yes, she's sick,' said Ricardo, 'and she has some other problems, which won't get better. She can't keep you safe, even when she's not sick any more, and you deserve to be safe. You can keep contact with her. You might be ready to write a letter to Mama. Nikki and Obi will help you with that.'

Elijah slumped down. 'Mama kept me safe.'

176

'And now Nikki and Obi are keeping you safe too.'

Elijah sat upright. 'I think so.' He ate a chip, chewing it slowly. 'I think the badness has gone.'

Ricardo put the rest of his burger down. 'You haven't mentioned being bad in a long time, Elijah.' He paused. 'Do you think that maybe, now you are settled with Nikki and Obi, you have stopped feeling like there is a badness inside you? Maybe you've started to believe me that you're a good boy. Maybe you're even ready to talk about what happened to you?'

Elijah popped a chicken nugget into his mouth. The wizard had not been in control for quite a while. The last time he felt it was on his first day at school, but, even then, being near to Jasmin meant the wizard's powers were not strong at all. In fact, he couldn't feel it creeping around at all any more. Elijah was in charge. He smiled. 'The wizard might have gone,' he said. He jumped off his seat and hugged Ricardo. He thought of Mama and how happy she'd be.

Elijah caught the look on Ricardo's face: his eyes stuck open and his mouth was full of burger but not chewing. He had told Ricardo about the wizard; he would never see Mama again.

'The wizard?' said Ricardo, swallowing and wiping his mouth.

Elijah sat very still, but nothing happened. If the wizard was really gone, then maybe it didn't matter?

'Elijah?'

He opened his mouth to speak. He really couldn't feel the wizard. 'I am free of evil.'

Ricardo leant forwards. 'But you said, "wizard".'

Yes. He had said 'wizard', but the ground was still there and the sun was still up in the sky and no one was dragging him away or saying he couldn't see Mama again. Elijah shrugged. 'The evil inside me has gone.' It was true. Mama was right – to be safe, all he had to do was find a Nigerian who believed in God, and he had found Granddad and Obi. And Nikki, who was not Nigerian but was covered in angel kisses called freckles, and Jasmin, who wasn't scared of anything. Not even a wizard.

Ricardo nodded. 'OK.' He drew Elijah in for a hug.

Maybe Elijah could stay with Nikki and Obi until he was a bit older. And then perhaps he could live with Mama again? Maybe she'd get better now and be able to come and live with Nikki and Obi too.

After McDonald's, Aunty Chanel took Elijah out so that Ricardo could have a chat with Nikki and Obi.

Aunty Chanel put her hand on top of Elijah's head and laughed. 'We get to hang out, Jay-Z! It's going to be so cool.' Aunty Chanel was wearing another set of butterflies on her eyelids but they looked broken, like half their wings were missing, and it made her eyes look in different places, one near and one far. She had a pair of panda earmuffs covering her ears. He'd never seen an adult wear animal earmuffs. 'We need to sort this hair out, little man,' she said, and put her hand on Elijah's head again. She was wearing four rings and, when she touched him, tiny sparks came between her hand and his shoulder, which made him jump. 'You're electric,' she said.

Elijah followed her to the bus stop, where she took a packet of chewing gum out of her bag and gave him one. He'd never had chewing gum before.

'Don't tell Mum I gave you gum,' she said. Elijah shook his head and chewed really fast. The gum tasted like toothpaste. Aunty Chanel always called Nikki 'Mum'. It sounded strange inside Elijah's head. She was sort of his mama, but she wasn't Mama.

Jasmin ran out of the gate. 'Yippee! School's finished! How was your meeting?'

'Good,' said Elijah.

'We're going to get Elijah's hair cut,' said Aunty Chanel. 'A cool haircut.'

'Great!' said Jasmin. And she slipped her hand into Elijah's.

'I don't think I'm allowed to have my hair cut,' Elijah said, imagining Nikki's face, her telling Aunty Chanel off. Nikki loved his soft, tight curls; she'd said so. They had grown so suddenly in the time that Elijah had been living with Nikki and Obi, like they'd been hiding inside his head. He'd never had much hair before; it was always shaved close. He touched his hair.

'Listen, little man – when you're with me, you're allowed to do anything I say, OK?' Aunty Chanel's face was close to Elijah's and he could smell the chemicals that Nikki had said came from Aunty Chanel's fake tan, which was why she looked orange. At first he thought the smell was horrible, but now he was used to the smell of Aunty Chanel's skin and he liked it. He knew Jasmin didn't, though; she turned her nose into a smaller nose every time her mum got too close, by pinching it really hard.

'Come on, this is our bus.' Aunty Chanel pulled Elijah towards her and the three of them ran across the road. They got on to the bus and sat at the front. Aunty Chanel sat on the seat that had a sign which had a picture of two people holding sticks, but Aunty Chanel didn't get up when an old man got on the bus; she just looked out of the window at the streets flashing past. Jasmin's seat didn't have a sign and she looked straight out of the window with her face pressed to the glass. The old man had crooked legs that looked like they might hurt a bit. Elijah stood up and pointed to his seat with his head. But the old man didn't sit down in Elijah's seat. He pretended he couldn't see him. Elijah wondered if he was invisible, but the wizard wasn't moving inside him any more. The wizard seemed to be gone completely. And when a lady got off the bus, the old man sat down in her seat instead. Maybe he liked the look of her seat more. Elijah didn't care. The wizard was gone! He couldn't wait until Mama was better so he could tell her.

Elijah stayed standing up, anyway, until Aunty Chanel and Jasmin got up and they climbed off the bus on to a busy street filled with people. Some had the same colour skin as Elijah and others had white skin like Nikki, but nobody had orange skin like Aunty Chanel, so Elijah put his hand in hers. He didn't want her to feel lonely.

She looked down at him really quickly. 'I feel like Beyonce,' she said. Jasmin rolled her eyes so far her head rolled too.

'Here we are, at last! After this, we need to sort out your clothes. I mean, trainers: essential – and not those hideous ones my sister has you in! She doesn't get you at all, little man. Good job for your Aunty Chanel!'

Jasmin stood behind a lamppost.

'But this will be a start, anyway. Your first proper haircut!' Aunty Chanel pointed to the shop in front of them where lots of boys and men were sitting in chairs. They all looked bald. Elijah touched his hair, curly, exactly how Nikki liked it. As they walked closer to the window, Elijah's mouth dropped open and his hand squeezed Aunty Chanel's. 'A barber shop. This is where you need to come; you need a black-boy's hairdresser to sort that mop out!'

A boy glanced out of the window at Elijah. He

looked about his age and very smart. The boy had skin the same colour as Elijah, and dark brown eyes. He was wearing a shirt and jeans and big boots with the laces undone. He looked like a pop star.

Aunty Chanel went into the shop and, as they followed her, Jasmin whispered, 'You're going to look so cool; I wish I was having my hair cut.' So far, Aunty Chanel had taken him to a funfair and given him candyfloss, and she'd even taken him to a pub where she'd given him and Jasmin two Cokes and two bags of crisps each. He liked everywhere Aunty Chanel had taken him to.

In the shop, a big man came towards them. 'Hello, cheeky,' he said. 'What you looking for?'

He wanted to be as smart as the boy in the window, but he was too scared to talk – the man was bigger than Obi.

Aunty Chanel was too busy talking. 'He needs it buzzed then I'd like a design on one side – I was thinking of the Nike symbol. Something cool. You know, something that will suit him.'

Jasmin made a noise in the background like a small mouse.

Aunty Chanel talked and talked and didn't notice the man raise his eyebrows to the ceiling. Elijah wasn't sure why he was raising his eyebrows. He didn't know what she meant by 'the Nike symbol' but he kept quiet. He thought of Nikki. Would she be cross when his hair was gone? Nikki was cross with Obi sometimes. Especially if

Obi told her off when he got home from work because the house was a tip. Then Nikki's face would change and she would say, 'Stop! Please.'

'Come on, here.' The man put Elijah into a chair next to the boy, and reached over for a buzzing machine that started moving over Elijah's head.

'He's going to look great!' said Aunty Chanel, then she leant towards Elijah's ear. 'She's just jealous!' Aunty Chanel and Jasmin stood in front of the mirror next to each other but they didn't touch arms. Aunty Chanel looked at herself for a long time. 'I need mine doing. It's getting too much rootage.' She pulled her earmuffs off, then parted her hair to show a line of black through the middle.

Jasmin looked up at the ceiling. She'd stuck a small star-shaped sticker with sellotape on the front of her school tie. A teacher had given her the sticker a long time ago and, even though it had lost its stick, Jasmin still wanted to wear it.

'What shall we have for dinner?' Aunty Chanel laughed. 'I should cook you up some jerk chicken. I'm in the mood for that. Or maybe some soul food: crab callaloo.'

Elijah didn't know what soul food was, but it sounded nice.

Jasmin flicked her ponytail. 'You never cook anything except fish fingers,' she said.

That night, Obi woke him up by gently shaking Elijah's arm. He sat up suddenly. Obi put his finger to his lips. Maybe he was going to tell Elijah off about his haircut?

'Your Aunty Chanel,' he laughed. 'Don't look so worried,' he said. 'It's OK. We're going on an adventure.' He flashed a torch in front of Elijah's face.

'Where are we going?' Elijah rubbed his eyes and swung his legs out of bed. Obi had laid out some clothes – jeans, jumper, coat, scarf, socks and boots – and he helped Elijah to get dressed. Elijah didn't know what time it was but the chink of light underneath his curtain wasn't there at all. It must have been the middle of the night.

'I know you have school tomorrow, so it will be a quick adventure, but I wanted to show you something. Hurry, now; we might miss it.'

They sneaked out of the house so quietly that Elijah could hear his own heart beating. He panicked. Maybe Obi was going to send him away? Even though the wizard was gone, maybe they wanted another child to adopt. A baby. Everyone wanted a baby. It was probably Elijah's hair, with the large tick at the side of his head, that had made them change their minds.

After they'd come home, Nikki had answered the door and gasped. Then she'd held Elijah for a long time before sending him out to the garden. Then she'd gone over to Aunty Chanel's flat to speak to her, which meant they had a secret. Could it be that she wanted him to live in another place? When Nikki came back, she gave Elijah another hug but he was still worried. Her favourite thing was his old curly hair. She said it reminded her of a newborn baby's hair. Nikki must have told Obi that she couldn't love him any more without his hair, and told Obi to take him away.

Obi pulled Elijah's arm and they were running towards the park. The air smelt wet, though it hadn't been raining. In the moonlight, everything looked the darkest blue, and the bushes at the side of the park rustled and moved. Elijah began to cry. He didn't want to leave.

Obi stopped suddenly. 'What is it? What's wrong?'

'Where are we going?' he whispered, sniffing. He hated being a leaking boy. 'I'm sorry about my hair.'

Obi laughed. 'Well, I know Nikki doesn't like it. And I know Aunty Chanel has very unusual ideas. But I'll tell you a secret.' He put his hand on Elijah's shoulder. 'I think it looks pretty cool.'

'Really?' Elijah reached up and touched the tick at the side of his head.

'Of course! Now, don't be frightened,' he said. 'We're looking for creatures. I had a really long day at work today and, as I was walking home through the park, I saw something you'd love. That's all. No need to worry.' He lifted Elijah high up and put him on top of his shoulders and held his legs with his giant hands. Elijah put his hands on top of Obi's and held on really tightly.

They walked through the cold night and Elijah watched the shadows and the emptiness of the park, the quiet of the world. The moon was a slice.

Obi's shoulders were warm underneath him and he liked being high up. He could see everything, even in the darkness. Obi handed Elijah a torch and told him to flash it around. Suddenly, a small black shape flashed past them. Elijah heard a screeching sound, like a high echo in a big room. 'There!'

'What is it?' The creature swooped again and then another and another. Much faster than a bird.

'A bat!' he said. 'Bats! Have you ever seen one before?'

Elijah couldn't answer. He was too busy shining the torch to catch a bat in the light, its wings almost see-through and so beautiful he couldn't even speak.

The next morning, Elijah ate a giant breakfast: two bowls of cereal and then two slices of toast. Nikki smiled and looked at Obi, but he was reading the paper. He held it high in front of his face, like a wall between him and Nikki. Granddad watched Elijah eat and listened about the bats. 'I like your hair!' he said. 'Except that side bit. The rest of it looks very smart. In Nigeria, we go to the barber's much more than people do here. You wouldn't see a scruffy boy in Nigeria. Aunty Chanel has unusual ideas about fashion sometimes, but this wasn't one of them. I like it.'

Elijah couldn't stop talking or eating. 'There must have been a hundred bats,' he said. 'Or maybe five. And they fly so fast. And they use the echo sounds to help them find their way. I could hear them screeching.'

Nikki kept touching his hair. 'That sister of mine!' she said. But she laughed. 'Sometimes,' she said, her eyes sparkling. 'Sometimes, children can hear bats but adults can't.' She walked to the sink.

Obi put down his paper and looked at her. 'Maybe we can all go bat watching again at the weekend,' he said.

And Elijah walked over towards Nikki, and threw his arms around her neck.

CHAPTER 17

'So, this is your second review meeting and you're now fifteen weeks into placement.' Paula, who they'd not met before but who had introduced herself as another social worker on the team, tapped her pen on the table and looked at Nikki.

Nikki nodded. She looked round the cramped kitchen table at Elijah, sandwiched between Obi and Ricardo as though they were his bodyguards, and Chioma, with another social worker, Meena – a petite woman with an uneven fringe, who kept smiling at Nikki reassuringly. Nikki looked at Ricardo. His face was always warm, yet he had a line between his eyebrows, as if he'd frowned too much. He smiled at her.

'We are all pleased with how things are going,' Ricardo said. 'Of course, it's early days and a few hiccups are only to be expected, but a pretty solid start of placement.'

Everything was different from what Nikki had expected. They'd been told so many times that Elijah would have significant needs, how damaged he was, and they'd been anxious, expecting trouble.

Yet he was the most loving child. He'd settled at home, and even settled in at school. His teachers reported that he was catching up academically, and had impeccable behaviour. There had been the issue with taking him to Battersea, and she hadn't been able to go back to work yet, but – Obi was right – Elijah was empathetic, thoughtful and kind. At first, he'd seemed more comfortable with men, sitting on Obi's or Daddy's lap whenever he got the chance. But now he was really relaxed around Nikki too.

Meena smiled, and Paula wrote something down quickly in a large notebook, then looked at Elijah. 'How are you, Elijah?'

'I'm good, thanks.' His voice was quiet. He was probably terrified. Nikki tried not to imagine how many meetings he'd had to go through in his short life. She'd put a colouring book on the table and a box full of crayons, but so far he seemed to want to sit and listen. He kept looking at her and she found herself nodding.

Paula turned to Nikki. 'Now, is Elijah registered with a G.P.? Any health concerns?'

She asked question after question and ticked some sort of list in her giant notebook. Nikki tried to focus on Paula's questions: what time does Elijah go to bed? Get up? Eat dinner?

Nikki answered most of the questions. Obi had gone back to work shortly after Elijah's arrival and Nikki spent all of her time with him. She felt a little sad that Obi missed the small moments:

Elijah helping her to cook, his delight in watering the garden, the warmth of his hand when it slipped into hers. She was looking forward to getting back to work but she knew how much she'd miss Elijah.

'How is Elijah getting on with family members? Obi's dad, your sister, Chanel? Your niece? Jasmin, isn't it?'

Suddenly Elijah spoke and everyone stopped talking. 'Jasmin is my friend,' he said. 'We're cousins, but we're best friends too.'

Nikki looked at Obi and smiled. Paula wrote in her notebook.

'Well, look at you,' said Chioma. 'What a proud boy you are! That's a very good feeling to have, Elijah.' She beamed at Nikki. 'From my point of view, the family therapy is working really well. Both Obi and Nikki are maximising any opportunity to promote attachment.'

Paula scribbled in her book as Chioma spoke. This wasn't entirely true. While Obi had made time to get to the meetings with Chioma, he wasn't often able to play at home. But he was certainly trying. Elijah had said that seeing those bats the other night was one of the best things he'd ever done.

Chioma turned to Elijah. 'What games do you enjoy the most?'

'I like mums and dads. They're really good at it. Obi's always moaning about work like a real dad and Nikki always rolls her eyes like a real mum and it's really funny – but she doesn't know about babies. When a baby cries, you have to give it a bottle.'

Nikki's eyes opened wide. Elijah was smiling, but Obi frowned. 'But you're a big boy, Elijah; you don't need a bottle!' He laughed.

'It's only a game,' said Elijah.

Paula stopped writing. 'That's right. And, anyway, is that such a bad idea?'

Nikki looked at Obi and Ricardo. Ricardo shrugged. 'He didn't have any time with you as a baby,' he said. 'Maybe he needs to make up lost ground.'

'Children take what they need,' said Chioma. 'If Elijah wants to play mums and dads and have a bottle, then I'd let him,' she said.

Nikki felt her face get hot. She imagined holding Elijah like he was a baby. There was a sudden pain in her stomach and an emptiness afterwards. She felt Chioma's eyes on her.

'Sometimes we even recommend this kind of thing for much older children.' She smiled at Elijah. 'Now. Let's you and me go for a walk and let Mum and Dad talk for a while, OK? I really want an ice cream.'

Elijah looked at Nikki.

'In this cold?' Nikki said, laughing. 'It's nearly November! But I think an ice cream would be a good idea. Elijah knows the way to the best ice-cream shop.'

Chioma held Elijah's hand on the way out, and Nikki heard his chatter fade as they left the house.

'Right, the first thing to say is thank you for letting us know about what happened when you first saw Elijah's scars. And, also, it's good to talk about these things openly with Elijah. I'd say you dealt with it really well, before it escalated into something further,' said Paula.

'Also thanks for telling us about the Bible quotes.' Ricardo sat up in his chair. 'Deborah's psychiatrist has been trying to get her to talk about her religion, but she's so far been too ill to respond coherently. Mostly she talks about her family in Nigeria, but we've been unable to contact them.'

Paula stopped writing and looked up. 'Has Elijah had any more nightmares?'

Nikki shook her head. 'Not recently. There were a few before school began, but not since then.'

'He's been great,' said Obi.

'There are bound to be little problems, but Elijah is more settled with you than anywhere I've ever seen him.' Ricardo beamed. 'Perfect for each other.'

'He adores Obi's dad,' said Nikki. 'If he's around, we don't get a look in.'

Obi laughed. 'He may as well live here, he's been popping in so often. He's had a key cut for Elijah, so that when he's old enough he can let himself into Granddad's house any time!'

'That's wonderful,' said Paula. 'I think that's it for today. The only other point is this wizard business that you mentioned, Ricardo.' She tapped her pen on the list written in the notebook in front of her. 'Has he mentioned anything about it?'

Nikki frowned. She looked up at Ricardo.

'It's probably nothing,' he said. 'I thought I was Batman until I was eleven.'

'He hasn't mentioned anything to us. What do you mean, "wizard"?'

'Well, a while ago, Elijah asked me if I knew how to kill wizards. I didn't think anything of it at the time, but then at our meeting he said something again, that "the wizard has gone". That sounds positive, whatever he means, but with his extremely religious upbringing, and those Bible quotations, it's something to be aware of – maybe ask him about.'

Paula let her pen drop to the notebook. 'I don't think we need to be adding worries. At this stage, jumping to conclusions, especially culturally sensitive ones, is likely to be damaging.'

Nikki nodded. 'Do you mean a belief in witch-craft? I saw a documentary on Channel Four about children being branded as witches.' She was appalled.

Paula raised her shoulders. 'Well, possibly, but we really don't know enough and what we do know doesn't point to—'

Ricardo cut in, 'We're certain that the physical abuse Elijah suffered came from the birth mother, and that would be very unusual. And, as we said, the birth mother is much more focused on her home and family than she is on the church.'

'As you told us when we talked about this the first time,' said Paula, 'it's not unusual for kids to pick up phrases they've heard, and I think it's important not to overreact. Keep an eye out, but don't push it. As long as Elijah's making progress, we can get to the bottom of things naturally, rather than unsettling him.'

'All young kids believe in magic and super-heroes,' said Obi.

'Exactly.' Paula snapped her notebook shut. 'You're doing a wonderful job.' She smiled at Nikki and Obi. 'Wonderful. Do contact us if there are any issues. Our manager is on sick leave and I'll be away on annual leave until the sixth, but there's always someone on duty if it's an emergency.'

Nikki gave a tiny smile to Obi. He opened his eyes slightly wider.

The following morning, Ricardo was back. Nikki spotted him through the bedroom window, carrying a briefcase and wearing a business suit and proper shoes that clicked on the pavement. She ran down the stairs, only to find a letter on the doormat. She opened the door but he was already walking back down the path.

'Ricardo! Ricardo!'

He turned quickly and walked back. 'Sorry. I'm so pushed today, I just wanted to drop off the L.A.C. report from yesterday. I can't stop – I have to be in court in fifteen minutes and I'm on duty as well – three of my colleagues are off sick today, would you believe.'

If Ricardo hadn't been carrying the briefcase and

a stack of papers, Nikki imagined he would have been waving his arms with every word. 'OK,' she smiled. 'Poor you! But I did want to talk to you about the meeting yesterday. So if you can make some time . . .'

'I know, I know. It's ridiculous, the pressure we're under. Awful when you feel like you can't do your job properly because you're stretched so thin.' He shrugged. 'But at least you, my lovely family, are doing so well that I don't need to worry about you.' He turned and walked away. 'I'll be in touch,' he called, before opening his car door and climbing in, a flurry of papers landing all around him.

Nikki watched him drive away. She knew she shouldn't worry, that if Elijah's team was happy to let things unfold naturally, then she should be happy too. But occasionally she caught Elijah looking sad, and every time she saw his scars her heart broke. There was so much she didn't know about her own son.

L.A.C. Review Decisions and Planning 2:

1. The review supports Obi and Nikki's wish to submit an application to adopt Elijah. They have completed the paperwork and will send this week.
2. Social worker visits will become monthly. Ricardo will visit at an agreed date.
3. Chioma will continue therapeutic-play work. This has been identified as enormously beneficial for Elijah.

4. Life-Story work will not start until Elijah is completely settled, as it has triggered so many behaviours in the past. This work will be done in conjunction with therapy.

5. Contact agreements will remain, though face-to-face contact is looking less likely as Deborah has remained unable to fulfil these agreements for a significant period of time. The letters are being kept by Ricardo. Deborah's art / writing, intended for Elijah, is inappropriate for him at this age and she is refusing to modify them to make them suitable. There is an agreement that the pieces are being kept by the team.

'Can we play mums and dads?' Elijah asked at bedtime. Nikki looked at the clock. It was already eight. 'OK,' she said.

In the lamplight she looked around at the shadows in his bedroom. Once, long ago, it was going to be a nursery. They had a cot, which Obi had spent hours fitting together, only to find he had one screw left over and no idea where it should go. He'd sworn so loudly she'd come rushing up the stairs. They'd had curtains, pink and white gingham, and a changing table with a matching pink and white gingham changing mat.

But the memory was already fading, and here in front of her Elijah's face was shining and real. Now she was a mum with a son who liked animals and playing games and was perfect. For the first time in so long, the present mattered much more than the past. Elijah looked up at her with perfectly clear eyes.

He was making crying noises and closing his eyes, curling into a ball, making his voice babyish. 'Pretend I've just been born,' he whispered. 'Pretend you're my mama.'

Nikki stroked his face. 'We don't need to pretend,' she whispered. 'I am your mum.'

CHAPTER 18

My little son,
This will be a difficult letter. I have to tell you some awfulness now because, as I've told you many times, there should be no secrets between a mother and her son. But this will be hard for you to read, so I pray this finds you with a family who love you well.

Elijah, sometimes things shift in the universe and everything moves backwards or turns inside out. God likes to remind us, now and then, of his wrath. In the Book of Kings, your own namesake, Elijah, controlled fire from the sky and flew up to Heaven in a whirlwind. If you, my little son, can control fire and fly, well, imagine then what God himself can do. And if God can do such things for the greater good then the devil can surely match him.

Akpan was gone for a long time. He was studying Estate Management at the University of East London and working evenings in a security job to fund our family, but he always came home on time, always. I watched the clock at dinner time, the pan of stew bubbling away in a large pot, you on my back as I moved around in the flat, tidying things and folding clothes. I could sense that you were awake, even though I couldn't see your face, but you were happy, breathing softly and quiet, curled high up against me like a small question mark. Night fell and the clock ticked. You began to cry, not because you were upset or hungry, but you sensed the change in me – the worry. We were still tied by that cord between us, visible or not.

'Where can he be?' I said. 'Where is your baba?'

I turned off the stew and turned off the light and we stood in darkness for a few seconds. Something awful was biting my insides. Panic filled me up and I began to cry, and then we heard it. The siren. I wrapped the blanket around us and we ran out of the flat, pressing the lift button again and again and listening to more sirens. Different sirens. The sound of screaming and shouting. By the time the lift took us down to the ground and we had run out of the building, there was a crowd gathered, two ambulances, a police car. I remember it so clearly: a woman in a blue anorak, the shape of her eyes, a man next to her talking loudly on his mobile telephone and others too, forming a circle around something. You cried and shook; I felt your little heart drumming quick-quick. The moon was covered by half a cloud and there were no stars at all, not a single one. I walked slowly towards the crowd. The ambulance drivers were rushing around with giant forest-green backpacks and luminous yellow jackets, brighter than the half-moon. I couldn't see anything yet as the thick crowd were gathering close together, shouting, and the air sped through my ears, your cry. Then the moon went out. By the light of those jackets I could see a black shoe. Your baba's shoe.

Elijah, your baba was rushing home to us when that car hit him. He died in the street outside our flat. He died instantly with his head facing up towards our window, imagining you and me, me and you, us three together. Akpan loved me like no man has ever loved a woman. He loved you like no father has ever loved a son.

After it happened, everything changed. I fell into such a hole of depression that I thought I'd never get up. But I had to. There was a funeral to organise. My pain was too big for me to speak it to Akpan's people, to my family, and so I had a funeral with no singing, and only a handful of people, and I didn't shed a single tear. The Bishop put his arms around my shoulders and told me Akpan was a good man, and all good men go to Heaven. He told me Heaven was a better place. But I didn't want Akpan in Heaven. I wanted him there with me and with you, our future lying before us. I stood in front of your baba, my insides made of ice. That was how I knew something had broken inside me. And I didn't tell anyone in Nigeria that he was dead. I knew I was protecting them. I wanted them to continue believing that he was happy and successful living in London with a family. I wanted to believe that myself. I had a plan, though. I would allow a month for my sadness to eat me and then, as soon as I had money and strength for the journey, we would take a plane home for good. But that plan never happened.

The month came and went and I stopped eating, stopped washing or combing out my hair. I could hear you cry a lot, but I couldn't do anything to help you. You didn't feed properly and I had to start you on bottles, but the effort of making a bottle was sometimes so hard. Such a simple thing, making a bottle. You cried and cried and I did nothing but feel dizzy and disconnected from my body. Some days I simply wanted to die and see Akpan's face once more, hear his voice tell me he loved me. But every day the sun managed to rise. Somehow. The only thing that stopped me was you in my arms. I did what I could, Elijah, and it was probably not good enough, but I did what I could. You looked at me with such sad eyes. I prayed and prayed. But every day I became more lost, deep in a dark place and I didn't know my way back.

I was so alone, Elijah, that I almost jumped when I recognised someone. It was on the walk home from getting some nappies that he walked past. 'Hello,' I said, without even realising I'd spoken.

He turned, raised one eyebrow.

'You weren't in church.'

As he turned, I noticed the man was wearing jeans halfway down his legs. I looked at his face. Was it the man from church? I did know a man from church who was friendly and had known Akpan well. Where was his waistcoat? My head was confused, back and forth, round and round. Everything had been so clear while I was praying but now, in the street, on the side of the busy road with traffic rushing and rain and grey, I felt unsure who I was, Elijah, suddenly unsure of anything, which is a terrifying thing when you are as certain a woman as me. Where was I? Who was he?

'Hi,' he said. 'Church?'

It must be him. He had the same jacket. The same smile. 'Where were you?' I said. 'Was it you? I mean— I'm sorry. I don't know . . . Akpan, I mean . . .'

I felt lost. Missing. My legs felt heavy. I moved forwards and tripped over one of my own feet, as though it belonged to another person. Was it him? Akpan's friend? Did he know that he'd died? I'd been so sure. But there was no lined waistcoat wrapped around him. He wore a T-shirt that had writing on the front, but I couldn't read it as everything had become blurred. He had folded his T-shirt sleeves up and I could see a drawing on his skin.

He smiled. 'I was late,' he said, 'for church. I'm always late for church!' He laughed. He looked behind me. 'That church,' he said. 'Always late, me.' Then he drew his breath inwards so sharply it made a sound like a rattlesnake. 'Listen, sister, you look cold. You want me to take you home?'

I was cold. My body shivered and shook. I looked past the man, at the group behind him who were clustered like tadpoles. I heard laughing and spitting noises. A whistle. One of them was shouting. Where was I? Was I home at the estate already? I looked at the buildings beside me, but they looked different. How would I get home? Was I lost? The grey sky and the concrete of the buildings were exactly the same colour, as though things were dripping into each other or the world was closing over on itself. A few birds flew past and landed by our feet, pecking around the dry and empty ground. I did not know who I was any more. Then I saw it: the red car that followed me everywhere, even into my dreams. It was moving slowly along the road next to us, and the windows were so dark I couldn't see inside. But, even so, my heart hammered through me. You were upstairs in the flat alone in your cot. I'd only popped out for a minute, but that car was watching me. Had I been gone too long? I grabbed the man's arm.

The man took my arm in his other hand. 'You're safe,' he said. 'You're safe. Let me take you home.' And his voice was soft and he was from church.

And I let him walk me towards the steps and past the tadpoles and they laughed and we got to the flat and he came in, and I looked at him again and it did not look like him, the man from the third row who was friends with Akpan. I noticed his stranger's eyes there, right in the flat, and he was talking softly, dropping me down on the bed and his teeth were sharp and I was saying nothing – not even 'No' – and he was talking and talking and then he was pushing into me and saying, 'It's me, from church; you're safe; you're safe,' but then his voice was changing and his breath was changing and I knew he wasn't from church. And you were there, Elijah, in the cot next to the bed, looking at me with eyes sadder than the moon, and you didn't cry but you didn't look away, not once.

Elijah, I can't write any more. Not even in English.

CHAPTER 19

Another few months sped by and school was going really well. Elijah began looking forward to school and playing with Jasmin and going for long walks with Granddad. It felt to Elijah that he'd been living with Nikki and Obi forever. He still saw Chioma, and Ricardo came once every month. Christmas came and went, filled with presents and food and Nikki and Obi singing Christmas carols off key. Jasmin and Chanel and Granddad had come over for Christmas dinner, and they had beef and turkey, and crackers with terrible jokes. Everyone had planned his present and it was Elijah's best gift ever: a special children's camera that took photographs and films. Elijah took photographs of the garden, the trees, the sky, a bird. Then Jasmin borrowed the camera and filmed Granddad, who'd fallen asleep after lunch, and they recorded his snoring too, and played it back to him when he woke up. 'That is not me,' he said, laughing. 'You've added sound effects.'

On 18 January, it was finally time for Nikki and Obi to have the special adoption day for Elijah. It was a day, Ricardo had said, which would mean they all belonged to each other forever. Elijah had let himself love Nikki and Obi a tiny bit and nothing bad had happened to them and so every day he let himself love them a tiny bit more. He loved the way Nikki brushed her hair one hundred times before bed because she said that was what her own grandmother used to do. And he loved the way that Obi had a globe with all the countries of the world on it, and he would let Elijah spin it around with his eyes shut and point his finger until it landed on a mystery country. No matter what country it landed on, Obi had met someone from there. But Elijah still thought of Mama when he woke up in the morning.

The court was a big, cold building made from brick, which had notices everywhere on the walls. Elijah read the notices. Elijah's reading was getting quite good because he was learning at school and Nikki let him read stories every night. They were on *Treasure Island* and, even though it was really hard, Nikki helped him read a few pages every night. The words in the court were much easier than the words in *Treasure Island* but much less interesting because there was nothing about pirates:

No Mobile Phones
No Eating
Silence Please

Elijah was wearing a suit and tie and shoes that had slid around in the ice and snow outside. It was the most grown-up outfit he'd ever worn and his shoes tapped on the floor. Nikki told Elijah that all the family could be there for his special day. Jasmin wore a purple dress and her hair was held away from her face with a small red clip. She had lost another tooth, so the only teeth she had were two big ones at the front and she kept putting her lip underneath them to make herself look like a rabbit. Elijah laughed, and Aunty Chanel – in leather trousers and a bright red shirt with a golden belt around her middle – tutted.

Nikki and Obi held hands all day, and they looked so happy and smart – Nikki in a light-blue dress that matched her eyes and Obi in a smart suit like Elijah's. Granddad wore a patterned tunic and trousers in matching colours, green and blue, and a tiny hat. His tunic had golden thread woven across the chest in swirly shapes.

'What a special day!' said Ricardo, when he came in with a man who wore a big white wig.

'Hello,' the man said. 'You must be Elijah. Do you want to come into my special courtroom? Today is a special day!'

They followed the judge into his room, which was very big and had rows and rows of wooden chairs and benches and a higher-up bench with a chair facing them. Jasmin and Elijah took turns sitting on different chairs while the judge spoke to Nikki and Obi.

'Elijah, can we have a chat as well?' he asked. 'I have a very special form to fill in and this form means you will be adopted by Nikki and Obi as your mum and dad. I've read all about you and I think that the very best thing would be for them to adopt you and be your parents forever. How do you feel about that?'

Elijah sat down in a chair with a high back. 'I'm happy,' he said. 'But I want to see my mama too.'

'Well, I'm happy about that too. And your mum and dad tell me that you write to your birth mummy, Deborah, and that they will support you if you want to have contact with her in the future.'

Elijah looked at Nikki and Obi. They would let him see Mama. He knew that. But Mama was never well enough to go and see. He was sure she'd get better, though, because the wizard was gone.

The judge stamped a piece of paper and then signed it with an expensive-looking silver pen. He held it up for Elijah to see. 'Your adoption certificate,' he said. 'It's official. You are officially adopted.'

Everyone clapped loudly and Nikki hugged Elijah. She breathed out very deeply. Granddad whooped and lifted Elijah high into the air. 'My grandson!' he shouted. Then everyone followed Nikki and hugged Elijah.

Afterwards, they went to Pizza Express. They had a long table and Nikki and Aunty Chanel drank a lot of red wine. Everyone laughed and was happy. The wizard was nowhere and Elijah knew that Mama would be pleased. She would get better and then they would see each other again.

CHAPTER 20

Before Elijah came, Nikki had dreamt often of the same place: a closed room where she could somehow hear the sound of the sea and a far-away baby crying. But, now, Elijah was there in her dreams, laughing, and the baby was there too – Rosy-Ify, in her arms – the three of them laughing. The room was warm and lit by firelight. Obi was not there in person but she could hear the drumming of his heart.

Nikki wanted to stay in the room and, as the dream lifted away, she pushed her feet into the carpet. Rosy-Ify was around her and inside her still, her breasts ached and bubbles popped in her belly. The heaviness of her breasts became sharper and Nikki was forced awake, the dream leaving a memory of something sweet, already the details fading, until all she remembered was Obi's giant heart and the sharpness of her breasts. *Sharpness of my breasts.*

Nikki pushed her hand underneath her pyjama top and pressed them and sleep flew fast away. She sat up suddenly. Her breasts. It couldn't be, can't be. Impossible; completely impossible. But when was her period? She counted backwards: eight weeks. Eight weeks! She thought of everything she knew, tried to stay calm. They couldn't have children. They had tried and tried and every time lost them and, after the last horrific time, the doctors had said there was very little chance of Nikki ever getting pregnant again. They'd had to do surgery; there was so much blood, so much scraping away at her insides. So many doctors told her. Almost. Impossible. The room spun around and she lay down again. It was impossible for her to get pregnant. She said aloud, 'Impossible. *Almost* impossible.' Almost! She remembered conversations, second opinions, painful words: too much damage, scar tissue, trauma.

She remembered taking the pill religiously, until they ran out and she didn't have time to go and get her repeat prescription. With Elijah, her head had been all over the place; she'd been forgetting to take her vitamins, her pill, aspirin for her condition.

Almost impossible. Suddenly she felt so guilty. She had told Ricardo she was still taking her contraceptive. She had barely given it a second thought – just forgot to take it one morning, rushed back for the packet then realised she hadn't picked up her prescription. It hadn't seemed to matter because *Nikki could not get pregnant.* Oh God; she hadn't even told Obi. It couldn't be. But her breasts and the soreness of them her body remembered from long ago. Before Elijah. Elijah!

Ricardo had said again and again how important it was for Elijah to be their only child. That, if they did want to try again, to wait for as long as possible – till Elijah was much older.

But Elijah had been home for just over six months and Nikki was pregnant. He would feel like he was being replaced. Ricardo had told them that Elijah's trauma meant that he needed stability and no major changes. That his attachment depended on it. She could hear Ricardo's voice: *Elijah might not be able to cope, or you might not be able to cope with his behaviours, and the last thing any of us want is to see him going back into care.* They could lose their son.

When Nikki got out of bed later that morning she couldn't shake the taste out of her mouth. Every time she moved, her breasts felt heavy and sore. She went downstairs as normal, and kissed Elijah and Obi, and chatted with them about how lovely the adoption day had been. For the first time in years, she wanted her mum. She pictured her sitting with her dad in front of the television, feet up on a footstool. She'd promised to take Elijah to Wales to visit them during the Easter holidays. She imagined her mum's voice, her using the same tea bag between her and Dad, and telling Nikki that that was what marriage was in the end: the sharing of a tea bag between two old cups.

'We'll get the photos framed,' said Obi, his voice full of pride. 'There were so many lovely photos;

we'll have to choose a selection. And I'm sure Daddy will want one.'

Nikki closed her eyes briefly. Daddy. What would he think? How would he react? No, it was silly. There was no way she could be pregnant.

'We're going swimming this morning,' said Obi. 'We already decided before you came down. There's a wave machine at the local pool on Saturdays and Jasmin said she'd come too. Do you fancy it?'

Nikki frowned. 'In the snow? Anyway, I thought you said you had to go to work.'

Obi's face tensed. 'No need. I've filed the appeal. All I can do now is wait.' He relaxed. 'So I'm going to have fun while I wait – snow or not! You coming?'

'No, I think I'll stay here and relax. Get some peace and quiet for once.'

'Suit yourself. Go and get your swimming shorts, little man,' he told Elijah.

Elijah looked at Nikki with big eyes. 'Are you OK?' he asked. He put a hand on her arm and Nikki gathered him up and pressed him to her, trying to squeeze away the pain in her breasts.

'I'm OK,' she breathed into his hair, the Nike tick long grown out. 'I'm just tired after yesterday.' She pushed Elijah gently away. 'I think Aunty Chanel poured me a little too much wine.'

Obi laughed and Elijah grinned. She couldn't be pregnant. She couldn't go through losing a baby again. And she couldn't risk upsetting Elijah. Things were too good.

After they left, she let the quiet of the house fold around her for a few minutes before putting on her boots and coat and leaving, almost running all the way to the chemist. She nearly slipped on the frozen ground a number of times. She grabbed a pregnancy test, then another. She knew them all, the tests, but still new brands had appeared since she'd last had to use one. Her heart was thumping as she paid, and she felt like a teenager. Get a grip, she told herself. I'm a grown woman, a mother. And anyway, this won't be positive. It can't be.

She let herself into the house and ran upstairs, opening the wrapping of the test and pulling down her clothes before peeing on the stick as she'd done hundreds of times before.

She pulled up her knickers, trousers, washed her hands, paced the bathroom and counted out loud. 'One hundred and seven, one hundred and eight.' She counted to five hundred, not because she needed to, but because she couldn't bear to look.

But eventually she stopped, took a big breath, and glanced over at the test on the side of the sink:

Pregnant 8–9

Eight to nine weeks! How was it possible? She looked in the mirror. Her face looked worried, *terrified*. But inside her head, despite everything, was an image of her holding a baby.

Over the next month, Obi came home later and later, his face drawn and his jaw tight. He relaxed around Elijah, but when they were on their own he sighed and told her about the three sisters whose case he was managing, who would surely be deported. They had lived in the U.K. for six years. Nikki had decided not to tell Obi yet. She'd lost all her babies except Ify at eleven weeks and the chances were she'd lose this one too. She hated keeping secrets from him, but it was for the right reasons. It was her fault she was in this situation, and she didn't want Obi suffering too. He was under so much stress.

Nikki found herself googling her syndrome, treatment plans for pregnancy, outcomes. She went to the doctor, saw the specialist and began taking aspirin every day instead of her contraception. It was probably too late, she told herself, but she had to try. The doctors told her that she should've been taking the aspirin regularly, but it looked very hopeful. She wouldn't let herself believe them. Doctors were often wrong. They had scheduled her in for another check-up, when they said they would know for certain.

She tried to carry on as normal and not think about it, pushing thoughts of being pregnant away every time they entered her head. But keeping a secret from Obi made her wake up at night in a cold sweat, her heart thumping. It was only while she watched his steady breathing, his strong chest rising up and down, that she'd finally relax. Then, as she began to fall asleep again, she would feel something inside her, the tiniest hope that this time would be different. During the days, she focused on loving Elijah. That was easy.

The first time he said it, they were in the park on a bright February day, the first clear day after four days' rain, and Elijah was running fast, then stopped suddenly and ran back. 'Look at me!'

She and Obi were walking along a muddy path in their wellies, and Elijah, in his trainers, was covered in mud. It looked lovely to her, him covered in mud.

'Let him be muddy,' said Nikki, laughing at Obi's concerned face. 'Boys are meant to be muddy.'

'There's muddy and there's muddy,' he said. Elijah ran back towards them. 'And you are like a mud king. A mud monster from the swamp of mud, from a deep land where the earth is made of nothing but thick, thick mud . . .' Obi ran towards Elijah, his own boots squelching in the mud.

Elijah squealed and ran, but Obi was quicker. He caught Elijah and swung him around by his arms, both of them laughing and laughing.

As Nikki watched them – her husband, her son – she felt something stirring inside her that she'd never felt before. A sense that anything was possible.

She'd tell him, she promised herself; she'd tell Obi next weekend, after her appointment. She'd explain that it might work this time, that it had to work this time. They would need to be strong

216

enough to help Elijah cope. She knew they could do it.

Elijah turned again. 'Look at me! Look at me, Mum!'

Mum!

Nikki's insides flooded with happiness. She looked at Obi and smiled and his outline seemed to glow, and everything became clear and bright until it was as if the sun was shining right through his body. Everything would work out. A family. Mum. Mother of two children. Nikki let the feeling sink deep inside her.

CHAPTER 21

Nikki applied her lipstick, looking at her reflection in the mirror. Time's up, Nik, she said silently to her own eyes. Time's up and you need to tell him. She finished her make-up, sprayed some perfume behind her ears and turned towards Chanel.

'Right; you've got both our numbers, and I've stuck the number of the restaurant and the number of the G.P. and Daddy's number on the fridge.'

'Chill out, will you?' Chanel had walked across the street in her pyjamas and dressing gown. 'I couldn't be bothered to get dressed at all today,' she said.

Jasmin rolled her eyes. 'So embarrassing.'

Elijah giggled.

'You look really nice,' Chanel told Nikki. She'd put on a black dress and high heels, and twisted her hair up in a knot. Chanel looked at Nikki's waist. Nikki dropped her arms in front of herself. She was starting to thicken around the middle – only a tiny bit, but her sister noticed everything about weight. Chanel frowned. 'You are –' she paused, looking up at Nikki's eyes – 'glowing.'

Nikki glanced away quickly, and tried not to blush. She looked in the mirror and fiddled with her hair, but she sensed Chanel behind her, staring.

'Wow!' Obi walked into the bedroom. 'Hi, Chanel. Thanks for babysitting.'

'That's OK. I won't see them all evening. Apparently they're developing their secret code in Elijah's room.'

Obi laughed. 'Are you ready?'

'Oh, she's ready,' said Chanel. 'You have a lovely evening.' She smiled at Nikki. 'I'm sure it'll be interesting.'

'Er, OK then,' said Obi. 'I'll just go and say goodbye to Elijah.'

He disappeared out of the room and left them facing each other. 'What the fuck?' Chanel hissed. 'When were you going to tell me?'

'What are you talking about?' said Nikki. She tried to keep her voice neutral but it waved up and down.

'Come on. I've been your sister forever; I know what you're hiding. Why put yourself through that again? I thought that was the whole point of adopting!'

Nikki pushed past Chanel. 'Don't you dare say anything,' she whispered. Then she held her sister's gaze. 'Please.'

Chanel sighed. 'Look, I'm just worried, that's all. I don't want you losing another baby; look what you went through. And how would Elijah feel about it? He's only just settled.'

'Are you ready?' Obi shouted from across the hallway.

'Yes; I'll be down in a sec,' Nikki hugged Chanel quickly. 'Please. Please don't say anything. Not to anyone. I'm going to tell Obi tonight but I don't want Elijah to know. Not yet.'

Chanel hugged Nikki back. Then she put her hand on Nikki's stomach. 'I won't say anything,' she said.

The restaurant was chosen by Obi, so was French and stylish, with small tables and candles everywhere, a menu written only in French and bored-looking waiting staff. Nikki had wanted to go to the new, fun-looking Mexican restaurant that served cocktails in fishbowls, but, since she wasn't drinking anyway, she'd let Obi choose. How different they were! Still, at least she looked the part. Not a wellington boot in sight. Obi chose a bottle of red and ordered. Nikki let him pour the wine, but she sipped a tiny amount only and hoped he wouldn't notice until she'd told him. Not that a glass would make any difference, but the metal taste still filled her mouth and she didn't feel like drinking anything except water. He hadn't noticed that she wasn't drinking tea or coffee, but Obi was working long hours. Nikki was still not back at work. Now, with the possibility of a baby, the chance of working seemed further and further away. But she didn't seem to mind. She had the strangest sense that everything would turn out well. She remembered how she'd worried about Elijah so much, and how well things had turned out. This would be the same.

The starters came and went. Obi talked and occasionally lifted Nikki's hand from the table and kissed it.

'This is lovely, to get some time on our own. Now Elijah's really settled, we should do this more often.'

Obi looked handsome in the candlelight, his features strong, his skin so soft. 'Thank you,' he said. 'Thank you for being such a great mum. I knew he was meant to be ours.'

'You were right,' said Nikki. 'You were so sure.' She smiled, but her hand was shaking. 'I have something to tell you; something else.'

Obi looked up. 'What do you mean?'

She paused, let the moment breathe. 'I'm pregnant,' she whispered.

Obi was silent and Nikki thought for a second or two that he was taking the moment in, like she was. But then his face changed. 'What do you mean? How?'

'I know,' she said. 'I know – I had the same reaction – I couldn't believe it either. All the things we were told . . .' Something about Obi's face made her stop talking. 'I know it's a shock, Obi, but I never meant this to happen – I didn't even think it was possible.'

'Pregnant? What do you mean? How pregnant?' His voice became tighter. 'And you want to . . .

We need to think about this.' His eyes were flicking up to her face then down to her lap. 'Have you thought about how risky this is? How Elijah will be affected?'

Nikki closed her eyes. How would Elijah react to a brother or sister? Or – worse – how would Elijah react to losing a brother or sister? She'd kept telling herself that they would be strong enough to help him cope with it, but suddenly all Nikki could see was Elijah's face. She snapped her eyes open. She remembered Ricardo's words about how Elijah would find any further losses extremely difficult, and how, at best, a birth sibling would affect his attachment and, at worst, he could be dangerous, abusive even, towards a younger child.

'I can't believe it's true.' Obi's voice was breaking.

'It's true,' whispered Nikki. 'I'm three months already.'

The waiter came towards them with a small pad. 'Shall I tell you about the desserts?' he asked.

Obi looked up. 'No,' he said, and then looked straight back at Nikki. The waiter walked backwards, then turned away.

'That was rude.'

Obi sighed. 'OK,' he said. 'We need to talk about this; think carefully how we handle things.'

'I've only known for sure for a month. It'll be all right,' she said. 'I just know it. This time I won't lose it.' She felt tears sting her eyes. 'I'm taking the right medication and the specialist said I could carry to term. You remember what they said: an eighty per cent chance, when on medication.'

'I thought you were on the pill!'

'My head's been all over the place, Obi. I guess I just missed a few. I didn't think it was that important – I only took them, really, to regulate my periods. I didn't think this was possible. When Elijah was settling in, I forgot to take them a couple of times. But they told me, Obi, they told me it was almost impossible . . .'

'Oh, Nikki,' said Obi, his breathing slowing down. 'What about Elijah? What about our talking, living, breathing son who needs us, who we have a duty to protect? Remember what Ricardo told us. It's best for him to be an only child – that, if we want to think about having a baby of our own, to wait, to leave a significant gap. Years, Nikki; years and years, not months. There's a reason they tell us these things, Nik. And we could still lose this baby. There's still a twenty per cent chance of that. How do you think Elijah will cope with that? Why didn't you tell me you missed the pill? Why didn't you tell me as soon as you found out?'

Obi closed his eyes. Nikki wanted him to pick up her hand again and kiss it. But his arms were folded across his chest.

'I'm sorry. I'm so sorry. I wanted this baby,' said Nikki, her voice breaking. 'I didn't tell you because I assumed I'd lose it. And anyway, exactly what could I do? Have an abortion? After spending my entire adult life losing so many babies?' She watched Obi's eyes. 'I want this baby,' she said.

Obi looked away, then snapped his head back towards her. 'I can't believe you've done this. Lied to me. I can't believe you would do this to our son. The doctors didn't say it was impossible. They said it would be very hard, almost impossible, which is very different, Nik. How could you miss your pill? Why would you think it wasn't important?'

Nikki shut her eyes. She didn't want to see Obi's face changing.

'Elijah's stability is in our hands and you didn't tell me when you missed a pill – didn't think to take extra precautions? What's Ricardo going to say? He thinks this is impossible.'

'You were there when I talked to Ricardo. We both talked to him—'

'Yes, I was there. "Nearly impossible" and the contraceptive pill equals impossible. But you've lied to me.'

Nikki opened her eyes. She wanted to crawl underneath the table and cover her ears. Instead, she reached across and tried to put her hand on top of Obi's, but he snatched his hand away, shaking the table so the glasses rattled.

When they got home, Elijah and Jasmin were asleep and Chanel was reading a magazine. 'How was your dinner?' she asked. Her eyes narrowed.

'Fine,' said Nikki.

Obi walked through to the kitchen.

Chanel blinked quickly. 'OK, well, I'm just going

to get Jasmin.' She laughed. 'I could hear her still talking, long after Elijah was quiet. I'm sure she chats even in her sleep.'

Chanel walked upstairs and Nikki followed. Nikki peered through the open bedroom doorway to see Jasmin curled around Elijah, her arm protectively draped over his shoulders. 'How was it?' hissed Chanel.

'Awful.'

Chanel put her hand on Nikki's cheek and pressed softly. 'We'll talk tomorrow.'

She woke Jasmin and half-carried her down the stairs, with Nikki following.

Chanel kissed Nikki on the cheek and smiled at Obi. 'See you tomorrow.'

'Thanks,' said Obi. Nikki let Chanel out and shut the door behind her.

When she went back into the kitchen, Obi was standing up.

'I'm going to bed,' he said.

The following day, he seemed even more distant. When Elijah was having a bath, he came and sat next to her in the kitchen. 'We need to speak to Ricardo,' he said. 'But my feeling is that we don't tell Elijah right away. Not for another few weeks, at least. We need to get our own heads around this. If we tell him, then lose the baby, that's another loss for him to deal with.' Obi put his head into his hands. 'Oh, God, and we'll have to tell Dad.' He looked up. 'Does Chanel know?'

Nikki nodded. 'She guessed last night.'

'You need to make sure, absolutely sure, that she doesn't tell Jasmin. OK?'

Nikki nodded. 'I'm sorry I didn't tell you. I've felt so awful keeping something from you – seeing the doctors and panicking then hoping, or beginning to hope, but I had good, *good* reason. I didn't want you to suffer any more, the same way you didn't want me to. But the doctors all said the same thing – especially now I'm over the twelve-week mark. They said it is perfectly possible that I'll carry to term. And I'm sorry about the timing and all the worry about how Elijah will handle it, and most of all for keeping it from you. But it wouldn't have changed anything.'

'I would never have kept such a secret from you. Not ever,' said Obi, and he stood up and left the room without even kissing her cheek.

Ricardo was silent for a while on the other end of the telephone when she told him. 'And have you discussed this? Made any concrete decisions yet?'

Nikki held her breath and closed her eyes. 'Ricardo, I can't have an abortion. I've wanted a baby all my life. We're keeping the baby. The doctors say there's no reason I shouldn't carry to term.'

Ricardo sighed. 'But there's no guarantee.'

'There's never a guarantee,' said Nikki.

'Well then, congratulations.' He sighed again. 'I'll have a chat with colleagues but this will need handling sensitively. My advice is to not tell Elijah yet – not until you're showing. But then you should involve him in every way: take him to the scans and everything. If he feels part of this, there's a better chance that he'll cope with the arrival of a sibling. I don't want to scare you unnecessarily but, in our experience, children with Elijah's traumatic background can be seriously affected by something like this. It will need open and honest communication. Let him know you have a condition, that there's a small chance the baby might not make it.' He paused. 'You should prepare him for the possibility of a loss, even if it's a small chance. He has to be prepared, Nikki, either way, and of course I hope the doctors are right, that you have this baby, but, either way, it's going to be hard on Elijah.'

Elijah had gone to Jasmin's house and Daddy was sitting at their table as Obi told him the news. Nikki closed her eyes. She couldn't take any more negative reactions.

There was quiet for a long time, then Daddy slowly got up from the table, came round the other side and hugged Nikki's back.

'A baby!' he shouted. 'Congratulations!'

Obi coughed. 'Daddy, do you not understand?'

Daddy let go of Nikki, went back to his seat, sat down and raised his eyebrows. 'Understand?'

'We lost so many,' whispered Obi. 'What happened before could happen again. And Elijah – they said it will affect him very badly.' Obi shook his head. 'It's a disaster.'

Daddy laughed. Both Nikki and Obi looked at each other.

'A disaster?' Daddy shook his hands in front of him. 'A baby is never, ever a disaster, no matter how difficult the circumstances.' His eyes shone. 'A baby,' he continued, 'is a gift from God.'

CHAPTER 22

Elijah couldn't get to sleep. Mum and Dad didn't kiss like they used to and they didn't hold hands. And now they said they were going to postpone the trip to see his grandparents in Wales until summer. He knew something was happening. He'd been watching them closely, but they seemed very far apart, like they weren't best friends any more. He lay awake for what seemed like hours, his eyes open in the darkness, looking at shadows. He could see the antlers, and the curtains, and the door. He thought about Mum and Dad, and how Dad seemed a bit far away, even when he was in the same room, and how Mum had fewer freckles on her face. Fewer angels' kisses. For some reason, the angels' protection was rubbing off a bit. He closed his eyes tight, but Mum and Dad kept popping behind his eyelids, turned away from each other. Then Elijah felt something inside his tummy. Something crawling. His mouth filled with sick. He quickly swallowed and forced all the crawling away. The wizard was gone. He would not let it come back. He would not.

But as the night hours went on, Elijah's head filled with worries and his tummy filled with crawling.

Obi and Nikki were sitting across the table, holding hands. Elijah hadn't slept all night; his eyes were sore and red. What had happened? They were holding hands again, so that was back to normal, but Ricardo hadn't visited for a long time and, even though Obi told Elijah it was good news and nothing to worry about, his mouth had turned completely dry. Had something happened to Mama?

Ricardo's hair was shaved at the sides. The middle bit was sticking up. He looked worried, even though he had funny hair. And that made Elijah feel worried. Feeling worried was like being a sun with a cloud in front of you, and you couldn't see the people or even shine. Elijah looked at Ricardo's face to see what it said. Ricardo noticed him looking at his funny hair and put on a hat that had the words, *Lose weight real quick, ask for Rick.*

'I'm trying to change careers,' he said when he saw Elijah watching his hat instead of his hair. 'You know I love looking after girls and boys, but my job is changing and I haven't got time to do it properly.' He looked at Dad. 'It's impossible now – so unsafe – nobody has time to do their job as they'd want to and, of course, it's always the social worker who gets scapegoated at the first sign of trouble.' He squeezed Elijah's arm. 'I'm so happy that you're all sorted and safe with your lovely family, Elijah. That's been the best part of my job and, if every child and family I looked after was like you, it would be an easy job.' He laughed, then he tapped his hat. 'I have these herbal diet pills from Brazil – completely organic and safe – and I've started a small business to sell them to private clients.' He looked Obi and Nikki up and down. 'But you, my lovely family, don't need any. So fit and healthy.'

Mum's eyes flashed at Dad.

'Do they help any illness?'

Ricardo laughed. 'I'm afraid not, Elijah. If they did, I'd be a very rich man.'

The doorbell rang, followed by knocking. 'Now,' said Ricardo, 'I have to talk to Mum and Dad, so Jasmin has come over to play.'

'Really?' Elijah looked at Mum. Her face was blotchy.

'Really,' she said. She stood up and walked to the door. Jasmin came in with a rush.

'Hi! Bye!' said Jasmin running up the stairs and waving her hand behind her head.

Elijah followed her up. He didn't look back to see what Ricardo was talking to Mum and Dad about, but he thought it might be something bad. The air was thicker than usual and there were shadows in corners.

'You are the best in the class, Jasmin,' said Jasmin to Elijah. 'The very best pupil I've ever taught and you will probably go on to be an astronaut or the President of the United States. In fact, the most well behaved pupil I've ever taught, Jasmin.'

Jasmin was the teacher and Elijah was a girl called Jasmin. She had a blackboard in front of her and was drawing on it in white chalk. 'Jasmin,' she said, 'come here. You can be class monitor and you can be in charge of ringing the lunch bell.'

Elijah walked to Jasmin and made a sound like a bell.

'Good. You can be the monitor today . . .' Jasmin stopped talking when raised voices travelled up the stairs. Elijah heard Nikki's voice and then Obi's. He didn't hear Ricardo's voice.

'Wow, they're talking loud for a meeting.'

Elijah moved closer to Jasmin. His arm was shaking.

'My mum and dad talked a lot louder than that. Actually, my mum and dad shouted all the time, had blasters every day before my dad moved to America.' Jasmin looked at Elijah's face filling up with tears. 'But your mum and dad are not like my mum and dad. All adults have louder voices sometimes.' She put her arm around Elijah's shoulder. 'Come on. Let's carry on playing schools. You can be teacher now, if you want.'

After Jasmin had gone, Ricardo was still there at the table and an empty coffee cup sat beside his hand.

Elijah leant towards Mum.

'Well, I've come along today, Elijah, to help Mum

and Dad give you some big news. Mum and Dad and I thought it might be even better if we all tell you together. We want to tell you lots of things, so please ask questions as it's confusing news – even for us!'

Then Mum smiled a smile that didn't look cheerful at all, and Ricardo stopped tapping his hat. Elijah had heard Mum and Dad talking about Ricardo. Mum and Dad laughed about Ricardo sometimes, and how he once had blue hair. Elijah thought they must like Ricardo a lot, even though they thought he was a little bit odd. Elijah liked Ricardo too. He used to be his best friend of all, but now Jasmin was his best friend of all.

'Well,' Ricardo said, before getting a notepad out and putting it on the table in front of him. 'I'm so happy about how things are going.' He smiled at Elijah and his smile looked angry, like Mum's. 'How are things, Elijah? It's been a month since I've seen you.'

'I'm good, thank you.' Elijah's voice sounded outside even though it was coming from inside him, like it wanted to fly into another room. 'We went to the aquarium, where I touched a stingray on the back. And I watched a show at Granddad's called *Frozen Planet* that had a caterpillar that dies every year when it gets really cold and then comes back to life. Granddad helps me collect nature things too.'

Ricardo moved his papers on the table in front of him. 'Wow,' he said. 'Overall, it sounds like you've been having a great time.' Ricardo's laugh made his hat jump up and down on top of his head. 'Mum and Dad tell me you're doing really well, and you've settled in completely. Which is great.'

Ricardo laughed again but Elijah didn't. He suddenly thought of how many other boys there were who were like him, and how many mamas were like Mama, all alone. Ricardo made Elijah feel very happy then a bit sad, quickly. He bit the inside of his mouth.

Mum's eyes were not looking for his. Usually Mum's eyes looked for his all the time.

'First –' Ricardo smiled and stopped moving his head around – 'you should know that this could be a very good thing, but it's completely fine for you to have feelings. You might feel confused, or even angry, and we're all here to help you to understand what's happening. Feelings are good. In fact, we are going to arrange for you to do some more playing with Chioma. She's very good at helping people with their feelings.'

Elijah looked around at them all. Maybe they couldn't love him because he was so wicked. 'I don't need to play with Chioma,' Elijah said. Mama was hurt. He just knew it. Tears filled his face and dropped on to the table one by one. Mum let Dad's hand drop like Elijah's tear and moved her chair even closer, next to him.

'Elijah, don't cry,' she said, pulling him towards her. 'Everything will be all right.' But Elijah knew there was something wrong because Mum smelt different.

'There's nothing to panic about,' she said. 'In fact, I think it's very good news and I think you will be happy.' Mum took a bite of the air with her teeth. 'You are going to be a brother. A big brother.'

And Elijah thought of Mama and a baby, who was not him, growing inside her tummy: a normal baby with no wizard inside it. And she would be able to look after it and she would get better and be able to see him again. The tears stopped straight away.

But then he saw it: the look on Mum's face. He smelt her as she pulled him back towards her. 'I'm so glad you're happy. It's going to be really great,' she said, and he suddenly realised. He felt the warm from deep inside her. A real baby inside Mum. Her baby and Dad's baby.

There was no baby in Mama's tummy. Mama was all alone.

Mum wanted a newborn baby as much as Elijah wanted Mama. But he couldn't have Mama. He couldn't ever have Mama.

Ricardo leant forwards. 'You might be a big brother,' he said. He looked at Mum for a long time. 'But the sad part of this news is that Mum has an illness inside her body which doesn't make her sick, but it does make it difficult for babies to grow in her tummy. It makes them come out too early for them to live in the world. We don't think that will happen with this baby because Mum is taking special medicine to help it grow, but it might.'

Dad reached over and put his hand on Elijah's shoulder.

'What happens to the baby if it comes out too early?' Elijah looked at Mum.

Mum was shaking her head.

'We hope it won't, but it's important that we discuss everything,' said Ricardo. He looked at Elijah. 'A baby that comes out too soon would be too small to live outside of her tummy. The baby would die, and it would be very sad, but the baby wouldn't suffer.'

The ground suddenly moved and everything swirled around Elijah's head. Why was Mum ill? She had always been healthy before. Illness. Death. It followed Elijah everywhere. This was the work of the wizard. If the baby died, then it would be his fault. The wizard's. And, if the wizard failed, then the baby would grow inside Mum where Elijah had never ever been. A baby who they would love and look after. A baby would have his bedroom and he would have to go back to Nargis' house and Darren would burn him with his cigarettes and everything would be FIRE and he would melt the whole world and suddenly he was screaming and screaming and screaming and, even though he was screaming, he could see Dad move back in his chair and raise his hands up and he could see Nikki's hands cover her mouth. He could see the look between them that he caused, full of fire and hate and burning hell, and he shouted and shouted with no words. This was the wizard. It must be the wizard. Everything was spinning. He tasted blood and in his ears was ringing and he felt pressed up high against the ceiling, looking down on his own head, then falling, falling quick so his stomach flipped and flew up inside him. His chair threw itself against the wall with a bang and everyone reached towards him, but they were too slow for a wizard, and Elijah watched as a tower of plates by the sink crashed to the floor, a million pieces, sharp and dying, screeching out at him, and he looked down at his hands, full of pieces cutting into his skin then flying across the room.

He could feel Ricardo's arms around him as he thrashed and bit and screamed and punched and finally he cried and cried and Ricardo carried him up the stairs, holding his body so tight.

'Shhh. It's all right,' he whispered. 'It will be all right, Elijah.'

But in the background Elijah heard Dad's voice change to evil, and say, 'This is your fault,' to Mum, and he knew that nothing would ever be right again.

After Ricardo left, Elijah felt the wizard walking around inside him once more, like it had shrunk itself and was trying to escape. Coldness spread around. He tried to block the wizard in by pinching his nostrils and holding his hands over his ears but, that night, the nightmares were back. He dreamt of Babylon the Great, the Mother of Prostitutes and Abominations of the Earth, and woke up screaming and scratching and Mum and Dad came in and shushed him and stroked his hair until he fell back asleep and the whispering in his ears was gone and replaced with shouting:

BEAST, FULL OF NAMES OF BLASPHEMY, HAVING SEVEN HEADS AND TEN HORNS.

CHAPTER 23

Obi paced the room as Nikki sat with her legs curled under her. She couldn't think straight. His voice was so loud it filled her entire body.

'I've read it, over and over again, when the parents have a birth child after adoption there is a higher percentage of failure. Of disruption. Do you know what that means? I think we've been over this before. I think I explained it to you a little after you took me for a nice dinner and threw a twelve-week pregnancy at me. Do you remember what a failed adoption means? Do you remember our adoption training all that time ago, when they told us that twenty per cent of adopted children go back into care?'

Obi paced round and round.

'A life in care. Completely preventable. A childhood ruined by the parents' selfishness.'

'My selfishness,' she said, quietly.

'Yes!' said Obi, swivelling to face her. He locked his eyes on hers. 'Elijah was settling in, Nikki. We had a family. We had a son.'

Nikki uncurled her legs. 'We have a son,' she said.

239

But Obi didn't draw breath. 'And there might not even be a baby! Even with anticoagulants, how is he supposed to cope with an eighty-per-cent chance? The worry, the rushing to the hospital in the middle of the night, all those tests and all that waiting and all your tears? How can he feel safe if you're in bits? What will happen when the baby dies? Elijah is covered head to toe in scars. He has lost his mother. You want him to lose a baby too? To lose you?'

'Please!' Nikki thumped the sofa. 'We have been over this. What does it change? We have said all this.' Her voice sounded muffled, like she was talking through glass.

'So, once it's been said, that's it? We can move on? These are the facts. Elijah has a twenty-per-cent chance of losing a sibling. He had a twenty-per-cent chance of ending up back in care. But that has gone up, now you've been so stupid.'

Nikki felt her mouth open, the air rush in. 'What can I do? What can I do?'

'Elijah should not be put through this.'

'But this is the situation and I don't know what you expect me to do. It's your baby too. You want me to have an abortion? Is that what you want? You want me to kill our baby?'

Obi turned on her and pushed his face towards hers. 'Did I say that? Would I say that?' He pulled back. 'You know full well that, by leaving it till twelve weeks, you took that discussion off the table.'

Nikki was burning up from the inside out. She cradled her arms over her stomach and watched Obi closely. 'It's still possible,' she said, slowly, not blinking.

His lips made a tight line and he shook his head. 'You knew. You knew. Twelve weeks! When you found out at eight! Of course it's possible.'

'And?'

'You know my views on this! You knew! So now we're stuck again with something that may or may not survive and will ruin everything either way.'

'Just say it. You want me to have an abortion, anyway.' She clenched her fists. 'I won't do it, Obi; I won't do that to our baby. But we might as well be clear about what you're saying.'

'That is not what I'm saying.'

'Then what are you saying? What are you saying?' She was screaming now.

'Everything was working. Did you hear Ricardo? Did you see how worried he was as soon as we told him? He knows Elijah. He knows he won't cope.'

'Stop saying this!'

'That tantrum? All those scratches on Elijah's arms?'

'What? *What?*'

Obi wasn't looking at her any more. He shouted on and on, going over and over the same ground: how good it had been, what they had promised the team, the research, how Nikki had let Elijah down. He was stuck. Obi could not get past the facts of the situation.

Nikki wiped her eyes and sat forwards. She made her voice soft again. 'Obi, I am pregnant with your baby and we have Elijah. That is the situation and I have taken all the blame and now we need to start dealing with it.'

'Oh, it's so simple, is it? I don't think you understand the magnitude of this, Nikki, I really don't.'

'Please; I understand, and we need to work together now.'

'Work together?' Obi laughed.

'What Ricardo said – we need to include him in everything. Ricardo said it was natural for Elijah to feel like he was being replaced, like we didn't love him any more.'

Obi just stared and shook his head. 'This didn't need to happen,' he said.

Nikki closed her eyes. 'Please, Obi, we need to try. More than ever, we can't be fighting now. It will unsettle Elijah.'

'I think that's already taken care of, don't you, Nikki?'

Nikki's eyebrows creased together. What did he want her to say?

'This shouldn't be happening to Elijah.'

Nikki nodded. 'I know,' she said.

'This shouldn't be happening.'

She closed her eyes again and sighed. 'We agree on that, Obi. I promise, I agree.' Huge tears pressed out from under her lids and her whole body shook.

Eventually, Obi sat at the table and pulled his

papers towards him. He opened a file and got out his pen.

When Elijah came downstairs later, she tried to hold his hand, but he twisted away. They ate dinner in near-silence, and Nikki couldn't stomach more than a few bites. Neither Obi nor Elijah would look her in the eye.

As she washed the dishes, Elijah disappeared out into the garden with his torch to look for bats, and Obi went back to his work. After a while, Obi stood up. 'I'm going for a walk.'

Nikki leant against the counter and tried not to cry. She folded the drying-up towel and wiped the hob. It was dark outside, now. She peered into the shadows then pushed through the door. 'Elijah?' she called. She squinted.

He was crouching by the pond. It was cold and she pulled her cardigan around her as she hurried across the lawn.

'Elijah?' She squatted down next to him, but he wouldn't look at her. She wrapped both arms around him and pulled him close. 'I'm sorry Dad and I were fighting, Elijah. Dad was upset with me. But it's OK now.'

She felt his hot tears on her neck.

'Poor Elijah,' she whispered. 'We love you, Elijah. Nothing will change that.'

He leant into her. He was so small. She scooped him up and carried him back to the house. When she tucked him in he clung to her hand, so she sat down on the mattress next to him. He pulled at her so she lay down and he curled against her, squeezed as close as he could, and she buried kisses in his hair. Slowly, he fell asleep and his body relaxed, and Nikki lay stroking his hair as she waited for the sound of Obi.

CHAPTER 24

When Elijah woke up, he felt empty, as though there was nothing inside him at all. Over the next few days, Mum watched Elijah like he was a television and Dad started coming home from work on time to play with him, but Elijah couldn't stop pinching his nostrils to stop the wizard getting out. He could feel it pressing against him from the inside, pushing everything out of its way. The wizard was going to make Elijah do something really bad. At school, he could try not to think about it and concentrate on his lessons. His teachers told him he was learning well, and the wizard was quiet. But at home all he could think of was the wizard. Sometimes, Elijah watched Mum and the wizard whispered in his ear, *She doesn't belong to you.* And, even when he told it to be quiet, it still carried on. *She's not your mum. You stole her.*

At night, he could feel there was something very wrong. Dad was sitting in the living room opposite

Mum when he went to find them. They both looked up from the books they were reading, and smiled. Mum was reading a book about gardening, with a picture of a beautiful flower on the cover, wide open and yellow. Dad was reading a book that had no picture on the front and only long words. Dad's book couldn't have been a very good one at all because he suddenly threw it down on the sofa.

In the weeks since they had told him about the baby, even though sometimes things were almost normal, it was too quiet and Dad kept his eyes on Elijah the whole time, as if he knew Elijah had some badness inside him.

'Are you OK, son?' Dad's eyes narrowed.

'I'm fine,' said Elijah, but everything felt different. The wizard was crawling all the time, creeping around inside him. And, even as he said the words, they didn't sound real.

'Go up to bed, Elijah,' said Mum. 'I'll be up in a minute, OK?'

He looked at Dad but Dad's eyes were not looking at him any more. They were looking at Mum's growing tummy.

Elijah climbed the stairs and into his empty bed. It seemed bigger somehow. It matched the size of the emptiness he felt inside his chest. Mum came into his room and looked out of the dark window. She pulled the curtains.

'There's no story tonight, Elijah,' said Mum, leaning close to his face. 'I'm just too tired. Being pregnant makes you very tired . . .' She looked down at her middle and smiled. Her face kept changing since Ricardo had come. Sometimes it looked frightened, and sometimes happier than he'd ever seen it.

'OK,' he said. But it was the first night she'd not read him a story. He looked at Mum's face. Then he looked closer. Elijah could only count five freckles. He clenched his fists and knew that the angels were losing. God was losing. The air became dangerous. He looked at her tummy, at the space where something was growing inside her.

'Goodnight, Elijah,' Mum whispered. The room was darker than ever and there was a big feeling in his tummy, like he was hungry and was never going to get food again. He heard the Bishop inside him: *But the cowardly, the unbelieving, the vile, the murderers, the sexually immoral, THOSE WHO PRACTISE MAGIC ARTS, the idolaters and ALL LIARS – their place will be in the fiery lake of burning sulphur. This is the second death.*

Elijah watched the shadows for a while, then he felt what was happening. The Bishop's voice couldn't stop it. The wizard was pushing out of him. He could feel it. It was making itself small and pushing and pushing and squeezing through him until everything went quiet and dark and he couldn't move any more. All he could do was listen to the wizard's voice tell him over and over again: *Her freckles are nearly gone. I will eat her baby and then eat Nikki. She's not your mama. Nobody will ever love you. The evil inside you killed your own father and hurt your own mother.*

CHAPTER 25

They went to the hospital in Nikki's car, and were all quiet on the way there, looking out of the window at the trees against the sky, the roads almost clear of traffic. She stopped at the lights and looked around at Obi and Elijah, but they were both looking out of their windows. She found herself biting her lip. It had to be OK. It had to be.

They walked through the hospital, a maze of corridors that Nikki knew too well. They were ushered in quickly, past the women in the waiting room who had babies already, or big swollen bellies. Nikki looked down at her stomach, hugged herself. She climbed on to the couch. 'If you can lower your trousers, please, and pull up your top.' A woman she hadn't seen before moved around the room, grabbing bits of equipment and tubes of things, a handful of paper towels.

The room was silent and dark, but it was more than no noise; the only light was coming from a monitor; there was a feeling, a heaviness, contained in the air. She imagined the people who'd been in that room: the babies, the mothers who'd looked on the screen in front of them, waiting for the heartbeat, as they did now, waiting for that one moment when everything changes, when life forks.

And so they watched the screen together, and Elijah couldn't possibly understand the significance of it all, he couldn't possibly, and yet Nikki knew that Elijah picked up on clues in the air better than she did. Nikki wanted to reach across and pull him closer to her, but he was out of reach. She looked at Obi. His face was completely unreadable.

She stopped trying to guess what he was thinking and focused on the screen, the picture of the scan: flickering, unidentifiable. Then suddenly something came into focus. And there it was. There *she* was; Nikki knew in a rush.

'The points where the lady is marking with the computer is to measure the head circumference,' said Obi. Elijah's eyes opened wide. 'And the long bone there is very important, in terms of scans, too. That's the femur. If those bones are within normal ranges, it tells us a lot of information about the exact bone age of the baby.'

Nikki tried to tune out Obi's hard voice and looked straight at the screen.

A flickering. A heart, beating. A life.

And all the worry and pain she felt suddenly melted. She. Her. A heartbeat. She smiled and her own heart flickered and beat inside her chest. She grabbed Obi's hand and he let her hold it. She reached for Elijah's hand – he had to shuffle his chair forwards – and then she held that too, and the three of them watched the screen.

'There's the heartbeat.' The woman performing the scan started moving the scanner over and around Nikki's stomach. 'Yes, just one healthy heartbeat. All looks normal. All the measurements are good. A healthy baby. And I estimate you're sixteen weeks plus four already. I'll get Doctor Seaton to review the scan right now, as requested, and get you back for a routine anomaly scan in a few more weeks. If you can wait, you can see him this morning.'

'Sixteen weeks,' Nikki said. 'Yes, please; we'll see Doctor Seaton.' Apart from Ify, all her babies had fallen away earlier, at ten or eleven weeks. 'Sixteen weeks,' she said again, to Obi. 'Healthy.'

'Are you sure?' asked Obi. 'Sixteen weeks?'

Obi was studying the angles of the picture, reading the numbers that appeared on the screen, asking the technician questions about the measurements of the head circumference, the femur, the amniotic fluid levels. As he read out the measurements, his frown disappeared and a slow smile appeared on his face. He looked from the screen to Nikki's stomach then back to the screen. 'This is real,' he whispered.

Nikki closed her eyes. They wouldn't lose anyone. Not this time. 'Are you OK, Elijah?' she kept asking him. And, although he was so quiet, he nodded. He looked overwhelmed. They took photos and gave one to Elijah. He folded it up very small, almost the size of a stamp, and kept it inside his clenched fist, before putting it in his pocket. He touched his pocket every so often on the way back, as though checking it was still there. Nikki took this as a sign that he was happy about things.

Doctor Seaton was a tall, painfully thin man who smelt of turpentine and had one section of hair that he'd combed over the top of his head. 'At this stage, everything is fine. We'll keep monitoring your platelets and levels, so continue to take the medications I prescribed, but baby is doing very well and, actually, now we're treating you, I don't envisage any problems at all.'

Nikki wanted to lift the piece of hair out of the way and kiss the top of his bald head.

'Thank you, doctor,' said Obi. He kept peering at the door. Elijah was outside, within shouting distance, playing a Nintendo. He'd wanted to come in with them, but then a boy in the waiting room took his computer game out and they started playing together. It was good seeing him make friends.

'I also want to start heparin injections for the remainder of the pregnancy. It's a tiny injection that you can do at home, once a day, just underneath the skin. Most people do it in the skin on their tummy. It doesn't hurt and it's a sort of extra treatment to make sure your blood doesn't get sticky any more.' He began to write out a prescription. 'Take this to the nurses and they'll get you sorted with the injections.'

Nikki took the prescription. All that was needed was a simple injection to thin her blood. She thought of all the tests she'd had, all the times she'd been told that miscarriages were common and it was just one of those things. And then, after Ify, they'd finally been referred to Doctor Seaton. Referred too late to save their daughter – Nikki put her hands over her stomach – but not too late for this baby.

Obi picked up Nikki's hand and kissed it. She looked up at him. He didn't say he was sorry but he didn't need to. She blocked out all his earlier words. Now he had seen their daughter, and heard himself what the doctor said, he couldn't be angry any more. They just had to concentrate on making Elijah feel safe and loved.

On the way home, Obi turned around in the car to face Elijah. 'What a great big brother you'll be,' he said.

Nikki watched Obi and Elijah all day, the warmth of the air between them. She felt bubbles inside her, the baby beginning to move. Nikki smiled, let her heart grow. This baby was going to make it. They would be parents of two children. A family.

The three of them curled together on the sofa, listening to music chosen by Obi: a Cuban band that Nikki had not heard before. Elijah was tapping his knee with the drums. He seemed so much more relaxed. After his initial reaction to the pregnancy, it crossed Nikki's mind that he wouldn't cope at all. But seeing how he calmed down after hearing the news, how he folded the photo, he was nearly back to his usual loving self already and it had only been a couple of weeks since he'd been told. 'He did react extremely,' Ricardo had said. 'But that doesn't mean he won't adapt. The news triggered something in him: a rage. It will calm down the more involved he is.'

And Ricardo had been right. After taking Elijah with them to the hospital, he was calmer, and he hadn't twisted to get away from her touch all afternoon.

'What's it like being a big brother?' he asked.

Obi grinned. He had completely forgotten his anger at Nikki. 'It's like having a friend to play with all day long.'

'Like Jasmin?'

'Well, yes,' said Obi. 'But the baby will be a lot younger, so you will be able to teach him or her things.'

'But only if your blood doesn't get sticky,' said Elijah.

Nikki nodded. 'That's right. But, like we told you earlier, I have special medicine for that now. The medicine will stop the sticky blood.'

Obi hooked his arm through Elijah's. He looked as if he was deciding something. 'Everything will be fine,' he said.

Nikki pressed herself towards Obi and kissed him hard on the mouth above Elijah's head.

'Jasmin would say that's gross,' said Elijah.

'What about you, Elijah? What do you say? Do you think it's gross?' Nikki tickled him, and he smiled and tried to wriggle away.

Obi pulled her towards him that night. He rested his hand on her stomach. She exhaled for so long, it was as if she'd been holding her breath for days on end. 'I'm sorry I kept the pregnancy from you,' she said. 'I hated not telling you. I really thought I was doing the right thing.'

Nikki rested her face on his neck. 'I'm sorry,' she whispered again.

They fell asleep next to each other and, when she woke, his hand was still on top of her stomach. She looked over his shoulder at the books on the nightstand, which were a mixture of adoption books – *Parenting a Challenging Child*; *When Trauma Affects Behaviour*; *Underlying Health Issues Caused by Negative Attachments* – next to his new pregnancy books: *A Normal, Healthy Pregnancy*; *Attachment Begins Before We Are Born*.

CHAPTER 26

Elijah took the folded-up photo from his trouser pocket and smoothed it out. He looked at the curves and angles, the shapes and shades of the baby. It didn't look like a baby at all, more like an alien. Mum and Dad and Ricardo kept telling him things that he didn't want to hear. They told him that the baby Mum had in her tummy might not grow big enough to be born, that it might die. And Elijah didn't know what to say. There were no words he could think of.

Elijah studied the photograph. He could see the baby's nose. 'You have to grow really big,' he said. And he knew that photos couldn't hear and even the baby might not have ears yet, but he said it again anyway. 'You have to grow really big and don't die.'

And then he curled into a ball on his bed and tried to pretend he was growing in Mama's tummy. He heard the whooshing, and felt the warm. Then he heard something else and sat up.

The medicine won't work. When you're asleep, I sneak into Mum's body to make Mum sick and hurt her baby. Medicine can't stop a wizard.

Elijah pressed the photo to his chest and tried to slow his breathing.

Dad was hidden behind the biggest bunch of flowers that Elijah had ever seen. Nikki ran to the door, to Dad and the flowers. Elijah was in the kitchen doing a drawing and trying not to think that his wizard could be eating Mum's baby.

'They're gorgeous!'

Dad poked his head above the flowers. 'Hi, Elijah. Me and Mum are going to have a quick chat, OK? Then I'll come and we'll play football before dinner. I've booked Chimichanga's at seven, and Jasmin and Chanel and Granddad are coming.'

Elijah didn't answer, but Dad didn't notice. He heard them talking from the other room, even though they closed the door:

'He's fine. He's been fine all day.'

'I know. I was so scared about how he'd react. I was scared about how he did react. But since then, nothing. No outbursts; no rages.'

'And Doctor Seaton was so positive.'

'I have such a good feeling about it all now, Nik. I'm so sorry about before . . .'

'I'll have a margarita please.' Granddad had studied the menu for ages before choosing.

'Are you sure, Dad? That has tequila in it . . .'

'I'll have one, too.' Aunty Chanel didn't look at the menu once. 'I always have chicken fajitas,' she said.

257

'I'll have a margarita, too, please.' Jasmin had her hair in two pigtails and she'd put five clips on the middle section of her hair.

'You can't have a margarita, Miss.' The waiter looked bored. 'It has alcohol.'

Jasmin turned to Aunty Chanel. 'So unfair. All the children in Mexico drink tequila. They have it in their bottles to help them sleep because everyone knows that Mexico is so noisy because of people playing those annoying pan pipes all day.' She looked at the waiter and narrowed her eyes. 'Are you even from Mexico?'

'Jasmin –' Aunty Chanel stood up – 'a word, please.'

Jasmin followed Aunty Chanel, tutting.

Granddad shook his head and then chuckled. 'She'll have a lemonade, please,' he said.

As usual when Jasmin was nearby, Elijah didn't worry too much about the wizard. He looked at Granddad. Granddad was still looking at the menu and reading out all the words, asking the waiter to recommend a dish.

'I'll come back with the drinks, sir,' he said, 'and give you more time to choose.'

Obi laughed. He had his hand on top of Nikki's. 'He always takes ages deciding. He likes to think carefully about everything.'

'All wise people think carefully about things,' said Granddad.

Elijah flicked his head to Granddad's eyes. Granddad was wise. And clever. He knew everything about Nigeria and lots about stars. And then he realised something important:

Granddad must know about wizards.

'Can we go to the park today?' Elijah asked. He looked out of the window. It was a beautiful spring day; his favourite kind. Mama's favourite kind.

Dad looked up at Elijah. Since the baby scan, Dad had been holding Mum's hand again, and he kissed her all the time, even when Elijah was looking. He put his hands on her belly and they smiled and smiled at each other, as if Elijah wasn't in the room. As if Elijah wasn't anywhere. He hadn't seen Granddad since the dinner and he hadn't had any time alone with him. But, even if he was alone with Granddad, he wasn't sure he could tell him about the wizard. Of course, Granddad might know what to do and be able to help. Granddad would believe Mama and believe Elijah. But bad things would happen if he told.

'I'm afraid I have to go to work later, and sort out a few things. But when I get home maybe we could play a game?'

Elijah shrugged. 'OK.'

'I have to work really, really hard from now on so I can take all my leave when your baby brother or sister arrives.' He smiled and looked at Mum. The air between them had a force field around it so that Elijah couldn't understand what the look said. 'I'm so proud of you, Elijah, how well you're coping. It's quite a change to be a big brother.'

Mum looked at Elijah and smiled. 'We're very proud of you,' she said.

Mum's belly was rounder and rounder, as if it was growing at superhuman speed. Mum bent down and hugged Elijah. He tried to hug her back; he tried so hard. But her belly was getting in the way.

Elijah had been waiting for Dad to come up to tuck him in for hours. He heard Dad when he first came in and held his breath, but Dad didn't rush up the stairs like usual and eventually Elijah had to let out all his breath. He heard Mum and Dad, and the baby inside Mum, laughing from downstairs.

'I'm sorry,' Dad said, tucking Elijah's quilt up around his ears. Dad looked at the bedroom door as if he couldn't wait to get back to them. 'We could have a story now, if you want? A very quick one?'

Elijah shook his head. 'It's OK.'

'I'm sorry. Maybe tomorrow. I just have so much to get through over the next few months, before . . .' Dad sniffed. 'Do you smell that?' Suddenly there was a loud screeching noise. Dad jumped up from Elijah's bed and ran towards the door. Elijah ran after him. When they got to the kitchen, it was filled with smoke and Mum was standing on a chair with a magazine, fanning the smoke alarm.

'Sorry!' she shouted. 'I burnt your dinner.'

Elijah coughed. Dad ran towards the back door and opened it. 'Outside!' he shouted. 'Come on. Out until the smoke clears.'

But Elijah didn't want to be sent outside. He felt his head bang and then a creeping in his tummy. He knew that things always happened for a reason; he heard voices telling him: *You caused your baba to die. You cause illness and sickness and death. You cause fires.*

Elijah looked at Mum's tummy. He tried to use lasers to see what was inside of her. She stroked his hair. 'Come on; please don't cry,' she said. 'It's not a bad fire. Just an accident. Come on; let's wait outside while Dad clears the smoke. The fire's out now. Don't cry, Elijah.' But he wasn't crying. Not any more. He was looking at her face in the lamp-light, the smell of smoke stuck to his insides. Her face was completely clear of freckles. She didn't have a single one. Not a single freckle! The angels that had been protecting her with their kisses had gone away. He looked at Mum with wet, frightened eyes. His heart thumped. They weren't protecting her any more. He heard the voice inside him, louder than a smoke alarm:

You frightened all the angels away. Nothing can stop me now. I will kill the baby in her belly. I will kill her too. Just like I killed your baba.

CHAPTER 27

Elijah,

I'd never known love like I had for you, Elijah, and I could tell that someone wanted to hurt you. Every time I went to the window I noticed the red car, sitting there outside and watching us. Something terrible had changed inside me. All I could hear was people whispering. Shouting. Sometimes the cruelty of life is in its continuation, Elijah. The world carried on. Only I was changed. I became terrified and heard voices, not only from God but the devil himself.

I kept you far away from that window; I would have done anything to protect you. Anything. I watched you curled over and soft, new and innocent. You were unaware of the danger, full of dreams and wide eyes. I was so worried of the damage they might do to you, my perfect little baby, full of goodness and hope. Elijah, my insides were rotting.

I paced the flat with you in my arms, looking at me with wide, wide eyes. You were so hungry, Elijah, and I fed you as much as any woman fed any baby. But it was so hard, Elijah. Making bottles.

A thing as simple as that. And, still, you cried and cried. I knew that I needed help. Fear plucked at my insides and sent me spinning. I wanted so desperately my baba and mummy, and my siblings, most of all Rebekah, but there was no way of going home with no husband and a baby I didn't care for properly, a baby I loved so much but couldn't keep safe and warm and full of milk. I wrapped you up in a jumper – one of your baba's – and we ran outside, past the door with the terrible men and terrible smells, and down the stairwell full of urine and writing and dark corners. We ran all the way to the high street – and running felt different, frantic, like we were running for our very lives from the devil himself. My insides were twisting with every step, my heart pounding like my feet on the pavement. I prayed the entire journey for forgiveness from something I didn't fully understand. We ran to the only place where I knew we'd be helped. The only place where rotten-on-the-inside women could be helped.

Deliverance Church was empty when I pushed the doors open, but the candles at the front were lit and flickering softly. I carried you wrapped in Baba's jumper, the last of him, the very bones of your baba. Bishop was at the front, reading *Time* magazine, flicking the pages quickly. 'Welcome,' he said, as if he'd been expecting me – us. 'How are you, Deborah? I've been praying for you. I haven't seen you since the funeral, but I've been praying.'

I nodded and pulled you closer to me. I tried to act as normal as possible, with my unkempt hair, wild eyes and wrapped-up-in-a-jumper baby.

He pushed his hand towards me and I touched it, drawing my hand away quickly, without waiting to see if he could tell how dirty my fingers were, how dirty I was. I felt as if he could see into my bad heart; that he knew at once what kind of woman I was. I felt badness all the way through me, Elijah, right to my core.

This Bishop was close to God and God had probably whispered secrets straight into his ear. He could see how terrified I was, how badly I held you, how you weren't strapped up high on my back like you should have been.

Close up, even in my raw state, I noticed how the Bishop looked even smoother. His beard was clipped neat and tidy around his mouth and he had pink, pink lips like your baba after too many hours playing the saxophone. A woman with a sour face stood behind Bishop. It was only when she coughed that I noticed her, too. She was holding a glass of water on a tray. She had a high forehead and her features looked squashed on the bottom of her face. She didn't smile at all, and I wondered if she, as a woman, could see how broken I was.

'Oh, that.' Bishop waved at her and she brought the tray. He took the glass and a sip, then replaced the glass on the tray. The woman went back to the shadows behind him. 'I mean her. She is my assistant. Not one of my twenty-seven wives – I'm no Fela! I'm only married to my work. To Jesus himself. Now,' Bishop walked closer to me, so close I could see the tiny crumb of biscuit on his bottom lip. 'What can I do for you, my sister?'

The words poured from my mouth. 'I'm sorry for disturbing you, sir. It's my baby. I am not finding motherhood easy, and I fear for him. I'm not coping well alone in England, and without my family in Nigeria. There's something wrong with me – with my health. I so want to be good, but I need help –' I said and took a big breath – 'with my baby. I am not a good mother.' My eyes fell down. 'After my husband, after my husband was killed . . .' I wanted to tell him everything, Elijah, about the red car that followed me everywhere, and other things, Elijah, that I can never write down, things between me and God and you, because only we were there; but I didn't dare speak of it. I was certain that a man of God would not help such a woman.

Bishop almost smiled, kindly, and snapped his fingers and the woman behind him came forward again. At first I thought maybe he hadn't heard me. But then he looked at you wrapped up and nodded. 'Let this poor woman sit down in my comfortable office. Can you not see she is concerned about the welfare of her child? What a stress for you to suffer, madam. Let us help you. She needs our help, here at Deliverance Church.' He looked at me. 'You have heard about our services. We can help anyone. Do

265

not worry, sister; you have come to the very best place. I am a doctor of souls, a medical man for the spirit. A pharmacist for human weakness.' His voice was soft and sure. I pulled you, wrapped up in the jumper, towards me and felt your breath on my face. Relief is a powerful force, and it blew right through me to my rotten core. Everything would be fine. I would protect you from any harm. I would be a good mother, the Bishop would help me with my grief and rottenness and he would help me be whole again.

CHAPTER 28

A small noise woke Nikki from a dreamless sleep. A tinkling sound; a tiny bell. But there was only Obi snoring in the darkness and the feeling of life moving inside her: the kicking, which was increasing every day since she'd first felt it. She touched Obi's back, his skin sleep-warm, wanting to wake him up and for him to put his hand over her stomach, whisper that he knew it would be OK.

'Why didn't we try sooner, then?' Nikki had whispered.

And Obi smiled. 'We were so tired,' he said. 'Simply exhausted.'

She lifted his hand to her face, placed his fingertips on her cheek. 'I don't feel tired any more,' she said. She thought of Elijah, of the baby inside her, imagined them both together.

Elijah had been fine, quieter than usual, but no further outbursts as Ricardo had predicted, as Nikki had worried. She'd underestimated him. Maybe, when the baby came, he would handle it well. She could see him already: a loving, protective older brother. They'd spent the afternoon in the kitchen, eating and talking; while Elijah quietly drew pictures, Nikki and Obi had talked about the baby, how it would be, how everyone would love the baby. 'You'll be such a great big brother,' said Obi, and Elijah had looked at Nikki closely and drawn a picture of a family: Nikki and Obi and him, all holding hands. A giant star above them and dark blue sky. He'd drawn dozens of freckles all over Nikki's face. 'Where's the baby?' Nikki had asked. Elijah looked up at her. 'The baby's not here yet,' he said.

The darkness became darker and Nikki's steady heart beat quicker. A noise was on the edge of things: something metal, something shining. Elijah's smile filled the darkness, but something about it felt different. She touched Obi's skin and his back was no longer warm, but cold and clammy, sticky, like there was a layer of worry coming out from his insides.

Something felt very wrong. Nikki had the sense that there was someone nearby, and she sat bolt upright. Obi groaned and turned. A shape hovered in the darkness.

'Elijah? Is that you?'

He moved closer and Nikki recognised his outline. Her heart slowed to almost normal. Almost. 'Elijah, you scared the life out of me. My goodness, I thought you were a burglar!'

Obi sat up. 'What's going on? Are you OK?'

The bed moved underneath them as Obi shifted his weight. Elijah came closer. As Nikki's eyes were beginning to adjust to the darkness, she could see something in his hand. 'Elijah, are you OK?' He looked hurt, and what was he holding? The something was shining and metal, like the taste inside her. Nikki heard a baby cry, from far away. A wail. From somewhere else. It filled every part of her.

She reached for Obi's arm but Obi's eyes had not adjusted to what was in front of him, of them.

'I am not Elijah,' he said, and he walked towards them, the knife in his hand stretched out for Nikki's stomach. And she saw it then, in those seconds, how wrong they all were about everything, how little any of them really understood.

Elijah was not himself. His eyes were different, and there was something behind them: a terrible shadow.

'I am not Elijah,' he said again.

Nikki was screaming before she realised and her own voice sounded far away, in a dream, trying to escape. Obi was shouting too, and then a light was switched on. It happened suddenly, but everything slowed down. Nikki's heart beat quietly, drawing everything towards it. Obi reached across her, and Elijah moved forward. Elijah's eyes were shining like the metal of the knife, and there was something behind them that scared her more than she'd ever felt fear. She folded in half, doubled

over, put her hands in front of her tummy and
Obi fell over them, but it was too late, the knife
pushed through and she felt it cutting to her very
centre.

CHAPTER 29

Elijah,
As I sat in the office, a feeling of hopefulness spread across me like jam. I had the feeling, Elijah, that he could help us both. I would be such a good mother to you. How I loved you, Elijah. I should have come here straight away, I thought, when the spinning started, when your baba had left. I should have come to Bishop after it happened. The church always helped its own. Cleansed us. Washed our sins away, the sins of others. I was one of God's own children, and the church was my family. Bishop was my brother.

'Now, tell me precisely, what is it I can help you with?' The Bishop looked at my clothes and bag very closely, like he was asking them a question.

I felt your mouth next to my breast, the hot air coming out, soft and warm. 'I have had bad luck, so bad, and now I feel as if I'm no good to him, to my baby.' I looked at the Bishop and his expression was soft and warm as your little breath. 'A car full of men has been following me. I get confused, since Akpan died. He was in the street, in the road.' I gulped. 'It was that red car that hit him. What was inside it . . .'

My eyes began filling with tears so large that, when they splashed down on to your face, you were startled and began to cry. 'Please, child,' said the Bishop, with his kindly voice and good heart.

I started crying so hard, the Bishop's face blurred in front of me and became another face – almost exactly Uncle Pastor. 'I try but I can't feed him properly, and he's not safe.'

The Bishop put his hand up in the air. 'It's OK; please don't cry, sister. I can see what a great job you're doing as a new mother. Motherhood is not easy and it sounds as if you've had a terrible time. Terrible luck. But that is what I'm here for. Now, let me see this lovely child.'

I opened Baba's jumper. You were curled around in a tight ball. I felt so relieved, the weight of fear on my shoulders was gone, and right there in the church I felt, for the first time since you had been born, that I'd be worthy to be your mother, that you would be mine for always.

Bishop leant forwards and saw you. He frowned.

'Your husband dying: that is a terrible thing to happen to anyone. Sister, you don't need to be upset. I will help you. Your luck will change, no doubt.' Bishop put his hand over mine. 'Now, tell me, have you taken this child to see anyone else? A medical doctor, maybe? Or perhaps a social worker?'

I shook my head. 'There's nothing wrong with

272

the baby – it's me who is not coping,' I whispered, but the Bishop was too busy looking at you.

'And your family? Do they know that you have come to see me? Friends? I'm sure your friends have recommended you come to see me?'

'My family are in Nigeria. I want to get home to them – as soon as I feel better, as soon as I'm coping a bit more. When things get better. I'm sorry to admit that I haven't yet told them of my husband's death . . .'

Bishop almost smiled. His face was so kind. 'You are in the right place. I can certainly help you with any spiritual problem. In the absence of your father, I'll become like your father. In the absence of your husband, I'll take care of you as if you are my own wife. You do not need to worry. I will treat this child like my own flesh and blood. I will help him, and I will help you.'

The relief I felt, little Elijah!

You opened your eyes and blinked.

Bishop's expression didn't change. He kept looking at you, but not in the way of a person admiring a new baby. He looked up and down and over your little body, moving arms one by one, then stretching legs out one by one, letting them snap back into place. He opened your eyes widely with his thumb and finger. Wide eyes looked out. Bishop looked for a few seconds, then seemed to remember something important. He suddenly gasped. Then he looked at the woman in the shadows behind him with lowered eyebrows, and the woman in the shadows behind him gasped too.

'What do you think is the problem with him? I myself can see straight away, but then, I'm an expert. I saw this many times in Akwa Ibom State when I first realised I had been blessed with the gift of healing. I have dealt with this issue for over twenty years and I know what the problem is, and have a one-hundred-per-cent success rate in healing this. But I need to see what you think. What would you say is the problem? Is there anything specific that is concerning you?'

'The problem is with me, Bishop. I'm not coping. I feel so alone. Since my bad luck started . . .'

Bishop smiled and put his hand on my shoulder. 'You need to understand something.' He took his hand away and my shoulder felt warm. 'The problem is not with you. These bad things that have been happening: it is very clear to me – in fact, very clear to anyone – why they've been happening. The problem is not with you, sister. The problem is clear to me. I'm an expert in such matters. The baby is not well. Not himself.'

I looked down at you. You were breathing so quickly and your face was still wet from my tears, but it might have been sweat. I felt your skin and it's true it was clammy. Were you sick? Was I such a bad mother that I hadn't noticed?

'Have you taken him to see any other specialists? Are you sure you haven't seen any of these white doctors? Because, let me tell you, some of them are charlatans. They will take your prescription charges and give you placebos; do you know placebos? Tablets with nothing but air! And they do not realise that healing comes not only from the cells, the body, the organs and immune system, but it comes from God in his grace and wisdom. Treating the body without the soul is like cooking rice without adding salt: no point. And you are lucky, hearing the voice inside you, telling you to bring him here to me, the doctor of souls. Now, this is very important: did you tell anyone at all?'

I shook my head. 'I didn't think it was him – I thought it was me that was unwell.' Relief washed through me as I looked at you. If you were sick then you could surely be easily fixed and I might be a good mother after all. A sick baby is surely easier to heal than a no-good mother? He could help us, this man of God. I could trust him. He would take away the pain I'd been feeling for so long. A voice whispered inside my ear. Heal me; heal us, I prayed. Elijah, I imagined being better and going home to my family and Rebekah's laughter and my parents, who would take care of us both.

'That is good. I see you are a wise woman bringing him first to me. I cannot say it will be easy, but I do think I can help this baby. Of course, you know that he is full with wizard?'

I pulled Baba's jumper over you and pulled you towards me. 'You are mistaken, sir; it is me that is ill. I have voices, and things are not clear . . .'

Bishop sat back in his chair. His eyes were filled with pity. 'Madam, let us look at the facts: this child is inside you when bad things begin to happen. Your husband dies in the street. A young man and run over? These things don't happen for no reason, and you, as a Nigerian woman, understand that, of course. And this red car follows you and you become quite unwell. And other bad – or worse – things, as well?'

I closed my eyes, Elijah, but the men were behind them, waiting. I snapped them open quickly.

'Madam, you should know that luck like this arises from some force greater than we know, than we can understand. Have you forgotten yourself – where you come from and what you believe?'

I held you so tightly, Elijah. I had seen cases in Nigeria where the child was denounced as a witch. I had seen *End of the Wicked*. Who hadn't? I had seen true witches in Nigeria and the way they took possession of a child's body until they were exorcised. I knew that the pastors who dealt with witchcraft had the biggest following and the most full church. I had seen. I hadn't forgotten, but I didn't want to believe it.

'This baby needs our help and protection. This child needs saving from the evil that is residing inside him! As his mother, you have that duty, and, as his Bishop, so do I. In fact, as a Bishop with a long history of service, I can honestly say I don't think I've seen the level of wickedness that is contained within your poor son . . .'

I began to sob loudly. The Bishop had to be right! Everything fell into place – otherwise, what sense did the world make? You were in danger, Elijah! You were full of the bad man. God, in his anger, had turned his gaze from us and let the devil in, and he'd filled you with wizard, I was sure of it. That must have happened, for only the devil would make me hurt like that. My little love, who I loved more than life itself. Your life was in danger.

Elijah, these things must seem strange to you – how us Nigerians believe so strongly that bad things happen as a result of spiritual attack. Growing up as you are in England, these things are so foreign and will not make much sense. But you should know how frightened I was. How terrified that you would be harmed. How much I loved and wanted to protect you.

'Don't worry for that, sister. I am an expert in delivering children from evil. In Akwa Ibom State, I acted as Bishop and cured over a hundred witches and wizards, drove them from their bodies. Now, don't cry; this situation is easier in England. We have access to the very best equipment, medicine. The evil wizard is sitting inside your baby's brain and I can get to him with the strength of God. Now, I cannot promise it will be easy, but the path to enlightenment is never easy. And Jesus will save us from all evil. I will save this child and drive the wizard out. He will be safe with me. The most important thing is that you tell nobody.

These English do not understand God as we do. They do not believe in the devil. And, worse, I hear that they take children – African children – and experiment on them, or give them to barren white couples, or Madonna. No, I will help you. I will save your child.'

How I cried. It felt as if someone had taken a knife and pushed it inside my stomach and was turning it slowly around. But, after the pain, the Bishop was still there with kindness in his eyes. And suddenly I felt as if there might be hope after all. If you were sick, then maybe he could help. I trusted him with my life, Elijah, and I even trusted him with yours. I thought of the badness that was happening to us, the voices in my head. I would have done anything that made me a good mother to you. Anything.

'Can you help us?'

'Of course. I won't even charge the usual rate for a sister like yourself. I will only charge the minimum price for exorcism. It would not be fitting to take money from a sister. In this instance, there is no way I am taking more than a hundred. Not even if I have to go short this month. The church roof, God willing, will not fall down and the choir will not mind missing a few meals. Those children I support in the churches back home will not mind missing a few days' worth of food. No. You, sister – you get the back-home price.'

I stood, suddenly. 'I do not have a hundred pounds. It is impossible.'

'Aha!' Bishop jumped up and out of his chair. 'It is impossible to keep a church running in Deptford. It is impossible for me to attract as many followers in England to listen to God's words as I had in Nigeria. Is it impossible for me, a young village boy from Delta State, to command the following of thousands in my church? From all around the world? It is impossible for a mere human being to have God's power in his very hands, but I do. Right here! All these things are impossible. Oh, I'm sure a woman like you manages finances well. If you cannot manage a simple thing like money, how can I – how can God – trust you to manage a baby? God needs to have trust in your abilities as a mother, otherwise he will not interfere and will simply let the devil take you. That is the simple reason a wizard has taken over your child. I'm sure you are the kind of woman that would lay down her life for her baby. If you knew the evil in him, the devil that's residing in his tiny body, I know you would not make such a comment. And, as you know, the good name of the church is the primary reason for my helping you. A Bishop who is able to help in such matters has the largest following. Of course, it is the Bishop's reputation that attracts followers, and so is the most important factor, but still he must command a nominal fee, otherwise he would be a laughing stock and lose his flock as quickly as if the shepherd left the gate open and the sheepdog fell asleep! This fee is a nominal fee for you as my sister, but I must insist on it. Think of the bigger picture! By saving Elijah, by protecting your only child from evil, I will attract a larger following and, in preaching the truth of God, I will therefore save their souls too. I know I can help this child . . .'

'I'm sorry, sir; I didn't mean—'

'Now, I am not offering this price for exorcism around the market or street; the church would be falling down in no time. If you want the medicine to help your son, it will be one hundred. Now, get out. I am a very busy man with plenty of other wizards to fight. You – you can take your chances with this evil wizard. I hope you can sleep at night, sister.'

I prayed, Elijah; how I prayed! I can't describe the effect of the Bishop, but it must have had something to do with how much I missed Uncle Pastor. We are all a product of our past, Elijah; you know that more than anyone else. The more I prayed, the louder the voices became, and how you cried! It couldn't be true. You couldn't be full of wizard. I stroked your curls and looked at your body, and saw in your eyes how painful it was for you. My own heart was breaking with each cry. I told myself to carry on and treat you as normal, and maybe the wizard would leave us and find another baby whose mother had failed, not praying enough. I knew how to look after babies. Babies needed to be carried around all the time. They didn't like to be unwrapped or cold – it scared them. They liked to sleep with their mum, and smell their mum, and have milk from the breast of their mum whenever they wanted it. How I wanted to feed you, Elijah! And yet some fear stopped me: fear bigger than anything, the smashing of my heart inside me until I was screaming, you were screaming.

'Stop!' I shouted. 'Stop! Stop!' I imagined Bukky, who would have had her baby by then, fat and happy on her back, her baby's open mouth getting milk from her breast. How I missed my Uncle Pastor. My baba. My family. How scared I was of what was living inside you. How terrified I was for you. How terrified I was that another loved one would die, that the bad men would return. Fear is bigger than anything else, Elijah; it grows faster than fire and kills all other feelings until it is pure and so dangerous. I'd always imagined love as the most powerful of all the emotions. But fear surpasses love, in the end, and that is what makes us so human.

Elijah, my love, my world.

I remember holding you underneath the window and showing you the stars. I sang songs and nursery rhymes and you looked at me with big eyes and I saw, deep inside your body, that you were there. I could help you. I smiled and gave you sips of medicine and you smiled, all gum, and it made me laugh out loud. I let you finish drinking and then we lay down together on my bed and I watched you trying to catch the moonlight in your tiny fist. You kicked your legs and blew bubbles and I tickled your tummy until you laughed yourself to sleep.

CHAPTER 30

Nikki was aware of people rushing around and lights turning on, shouting, and so much blood, but everything slowed down inside her, and she was back in the past and Rosy-Ify was slipping away from life. Obi pressed something on to her with one hand and in the other was the phone and he was shouting and Elijah was standing there with a knife and he looked so far away and then he was rocking in the corner of the room, back and forth, back and forth. 'What have you done?' she said to Elijah and herself and Obi, and the sharp air around them, the world. 'What have you done?' She sensed Elijah in front of her still, a small, frightened figure, shaking, with wide, terrified eyes that had seen too much already, things that could never be unseen: a small boy, alone. Then she closed her eyes for the shortest of times and remembered a beautiful dream. Her baby was there in her arms, gold-specked eyes and soft, clean skin, alive, breathing, smiling. Alive.

When she awoke, they were at the hospital already, with a woman drawing patterns over her stomach.

She looked at the ceiling. The paint. The light. She looked to the side of her and around the room: full of beds but empty of people, and curtains half closed around each bed, a sink next to the wall, a yellow bin. Obi's eyes were glued to the screen. Nikki couldn't look. She wished he would hold her hand, but didn't have the energy to reach out. Instead, she focused on the impossibly white bandage over her side, its edges taped down. She tried to let herself feel pain, but all she felt was numbness. Nothing.

'It all looks fine.' The woman drew and pressed. 'There's a strong heartbeat and everything is fine. You were very lucky.'

Obi exhaled and looked at her with dry eyes.

But she didn't exhale. Nothing was fine. Nothing would ever be fine ever again. 'Where's Elijah?' she said, sitting up.

Obi didn't answer for a moment, and simply blinked. 'With Ricardo.' He shook his head. 'I just can't believe it.' His words sounded like they belonged to someone else, as sure of himself as he usually was.

The technician wiped her belly with hard tissue and pulled her T-shirt over the bandage.

'What happened?' Nikki asked.

'You blacked out, but it was probably stress-related. Elijah had some kind of dissociation. He . . . He . . .' Obi's voice dropped down. 'He tried to hurt you, Nikki. He tried to hurt you and the baby. Something must have triggered him. He wasn't himself. I don't know what happened. I tried to stop him.' Obi held his breath. 'It happened so quickly.'

She touched her side, the soreness. 'It doesn't feel that bad.'

He crossed then recrossed his legs, tapping his foot. 'We accepted this risk when we said yes to Elijah. He's had multiple carers, numerous moves, and we knew he'd been affected by physical as well as emotional abuse and neglect. And, of all the categories, neglect was the riskiest in terms of brain development, but with time new neural pathways can develop.' Obi stopped talking and stood up. He paced back and forth, his eyes focused on the floor. Eventually, he looked up at Nikki and sat beside her. 'I've dealt with scenarios at work—'

Obi stopped talking again. His eyes were red and his lips were dry. He looked very alone, even though he was sitting right next to Nikki. She wanted to touch him, but her hand didn't move. He tapped and twitched and rubbed his head, but he'd run out of words.

Nikki cried softly next to him.

Obi saw her looking down at her stomach and turned away. Each of his breaths was a sigh. He looked like a man who had no answers at all. The world was a completely different place.

CHAPTER 31

Elijah,

By the time you were eighteen months old, I'd gone from not wanting to believe you contained a wizard, to wanting, with my whole being, to drive it out of you and save my little Elijah. Your cot was like a boat in a storm. I was so unwell, Elijah, hearing voices constantly, not sleeping, unable to eat, and I knew everything was down to that wizard destroying us. The insects were crawling around inside me.

'The wizard is so strong in this one. Back in Akwa Ibom State, I found a wizard as strong as he. Wow! That wizard resisted so hard. I had to try a range of medicines and, you know, in Akwa Ibom these were hard to come by. But the good thing was we could use muti, and that muti is strong magic to help these wizards out. The sorcerers are so frightened of muti. When I think of Akwa Ibom, my heart becomes as round as the moon. I'm sure you know the feeling for home, sister. Let us cure this child so that his family will be proud to have him visit Nigeria. Have you noticed any bad dreams? I am sure you will be suffering bad luck and bad health with this one around.'

I nodded. My dreams were becoming terrible waking nightmares that I was living right inside. My eyes were red and blurred and my cheek was twitching again and again, my hands shaking continuously.

'He is full with wickedness. Now, the medicine has run out? I can't believe the fighting of this one, staying inside the baby. It is at home in your son. It will take some very strong power to remove this wizard. Don't worry for that, sister; I'll help with the removal of this bad thing. Hold my hand and let us pray.'

The church was empty at night, except for a woman always in the shadows who dealt with the bookkeeping. The Bishop told me to always come at night, and on Sundays he'd preach how he was helping our most vulnerable member and exorcising the evil and powerful devil from that person. My Elijah. So it was, we were in shadows, running from the flat to the church and back to the flat. He gave me medicine at first, and told me it would cure you. And I gave you that medicine every day, despite the way it made you sick and your bowels irritated. I prayed so hard, Elijah, all the time. But the voices were stronger than ever. I felt like scratching my own face off, screaming. I could see how sick you were, how sick the evil spirit was making you. You were sick all the time, my little son. So sick that you no longer even cried.

'In the name of our saviour, Jesus, this baby will be healed! We need a miracle, dear God, tonight. I call on you, as your faithful servant, a man who has devoted his life to your teachings, who has devoted his life to spread your words: please, Father, save this small boy from darkness. Return Elijah, our son, from the hands of the devil. Remove this demon that has chosen to reside in his body. Put your power in my hands!'

He let his hand lift up off your head and things shifted slowly back inside me. Everything seemed clearer with Bishop around. I could picture Uncle Pastor and home and Mummy and Baba, and I knew, if I could just make you well, just save you – then we could return to Nigeria and everything would be fine.

'I need to give him stronger medicine. But, of course, that will attract a larger fee.'

'I cannot pay; I have nothing else. Please help me, Baba Bishop. Please, I'm begging you. Help my son.'

'I cannot guarantee your safety around this child. Wizards tend to build up to bigger crimes. At first, yes, you have bad health, poor finances and terrible dreams, but who knows what is next? The wizard in your son may cause another death. He has killed your husband; what next?' He paused for a few seconds. 'He may even fly to Nigeria, wherever your family is living, and cause death in your family.'

I held the side of the table and looked at you,

but all my eyes saw were Mummy and Baba, my sisters and brothers, Uncle Pastor and home.

'It will cost five hundred pounds. Now, that is the discount rate for my expert services. It won't be easy, sister. Not an easy thing and you'll have to stay strong. The wizard will try and trick you, make you think that it's left and you're somehow hurting your baby, instead of helping him. But, if you really want to help this child – and, of course, your family in Nigeria – you need to be a strong woman. Trust me, the doctor, the only one who can help you. The forces of Lucifer cannot win. The devil will never beat an opponent such as me.'

'I have no money,' I said repeatedly. 'I have no money.' I begged, Elijah. I begged on my knees for Bishop to allow me to pay him later, but he simply waved me away.

'If God cannot trust you with your finances, then how can he allow you the gift of a healthy child? Come back to me when you have five hundred pounds, and then I will see how committed a Christian you are.' He looked at me in that special way that he did, as if he could see inside my body. 'Of course, once he is cured, your luck will turn right around and then I expect you'll want to take him back to Nigeria.'

And so it went, Elijah. I tried not to eat or use electricity, and saved every penny that came my way to give to Bishop. We did our best to beat and starve out the wizard. You would cry and cry, and Bishop would hit harder, for it was the wicked spirit and not you who wanted us to stop. 'A sorcerer is an abomination to the Lord!' Bishop cried. 'The hand of the witnesses shall be first against him to put him to death, and afterward the hand of all the people. So you shall purge the evil from your midst!' I tried with all my being, little son. But no matter how much poison we had you drink, or how we smacked your body to remove him – no matter at all – the wizard remained. How my heart broke in two when I looked in your eyes, little son. I could see you were far away from me. I wanted you back so desperately I would have done anything.

'This will work,' the Bishop had said. He handed me a small bottle of liquid. 'It is for the bath, not for his milk.'

'The bath?'

'It is strong medicine that will draw the wizard out. In Akwa Ibom we use it pure and bathe the witches in it directly, but it is difficult to come by, so just add it to his bath. And make sure you rinse the bath carefully afterwards.' He handed me a pair of rubber gloves. 'Do not touch the medicine. It is very strong.'

When you woke later that evening, I had made your little bath, tipped in the medicine that Bishop had given me. I looked at the Bishop's card, Blu-tacked above our bed, and touched it to feel Akpan's leftover fingerprints. Akpan believed in the Bishop. I knew he'd know how to help us. I lifted you up and took off your Babygro. The drink was beginning to work and your lower half was covered with foul-smelling diarrhoea: a sign, the Bishop had said, that things would be working. The medicine made my eyes water and made everything smell very clean. I picked you up and walked you to the small bath. Your skin was cold, even through the rubber gloves I was wearing, and you were very thin. I could feel your bones on my fingertips like the keys of Baba's saxophone. I lifted you over the bath and dipped your legs in slowly.

Your scream filled my heart and cracked it. You lifted your legs out but there was sudden sizzling and screaming, screaming, the skin on your feet changing colour, turning pink in front of my eyes. Burning.

I pulled you out and looked at your face. Your face was a giant scream, as though the world had never known pain. I wrapped you in a towel and another towel, but the smell came through it, and I knew you were burnt.

The bath was full of medicine.

The medicine was acid.

CHAPTER 32

The first night was always the worst.

Elijah felt in a dream because he couldn't remember what happened. He knew the wizard had come back, though, because he had blood on his hands and Ricardo was crying and washing his hands at the same time. They were in a new place with two grown-ups, who were not like parents but more like doctors. Ricardo said they were specialists in extreme behaviours. Elijah was in their bathroom, sitting on the side of the bath. The bath was the colour of an avocado, which was a squishy fruit that Mum put in salad. Once, she said she'd give him a pound if he ate a slice, and he said he'd do it for twenty, and she'd laughed all afternoon.

'Will Mum and Dad come and get me later?' he whispered. 'Where's Mum and Dad?'

Ricardo kept washing his hands, even though they looked very clean by then. 'I'm not sure, Elijah. I know you'll definitely be staying here for tonight.'

'I want to go home.' His voice came out strange. Nothing felt real. Elijah sat down.

'I know you do. But something very bad happened and, to make everyone safe, we have to keep you safe here tonight. And tomorrow morning we'll all sit down and talk together, so we can decide what to do.'

'But I want to go home now.' Elijah started to cry. He didn't want to cry because Ricardo looked so upset, like he might start to cry again, and Elijah hated making people cry. It was the worst thing ever. 'The wizard came back,' he whispered. 'Didn't he?'

Ricardo knelt in front of him. 'What wizard, Elijah? What wizard? What are you talking about?'

Elijah sniffed and tried to look away. He couldn't talk about the wizard. He would never see Mama again. But how could he stop the wizard, all alone? Elijah looked into Ricardo's eyes and took the biggest breath of his life, made his stomach hard as rock.

'I am full of a wizard. A sorcerer,' he whispered. He closed his eyes and breathed out slowly. 'An evil wizard. Wizards are millions of years old. They roamed around at the start of the world. Wizards were here before humans. Before dinosaurs, even.' Elijah became suddenly quieter. 'Wizards bring sickness and bad luck and death.' He opened his eyes again. 'And, at night, it creeps out of my skin and flies into the air before choosing a victim.'

'Do you mean that you think a wizard is living inside you?' Ricardo's eyes were darting all about, searching Elijah's face. 'Or do you mean that I am

293

actually talking to a wizard. Because you seem exactly like a little boy called Elijah to me. Wizards aren't real, Elijah. They're just not real.' Ricardo didn't move, then shook his head slowly. 'Who told you that, Elijah? Was it Mama? Was it Bishop?'

Ricardo didn't believe him. Elijah started to cry again. 'I am a wizard. There is a wizard inside me. Sometimes it does bad things.'

'Oh, Elijah, you know you can tell me anything? It will help, Elijah. It will help you and help me and help the rest of the team, and even help Deborah, your mama.'

Elijah looked up, but he could see in Ricardo's eyes that he did not believe him. Ricardo did not believe in the wizard, so how could Ricardo help anyone at all? Elijah was alone with the wizard. He would always be alone with the wizard.

Ricardo squeezed him close. 'You aren't a wizard, Elijah. You aren't,' he said, his voice breaking again. 'But I don't want you to think about that right now. All you need to know is that everyone is fine and you're safe. Mum is fine.'

'Mum?' Elijah stood up in front of Ricardo. Because Ricardo was kneeling down, their eyes were exactly the same level and he made his eyes look straight at Ricardo's. 'Mum is hurt?'

Ricardo moved his eyes away from Elijah's and he knew then that something very terrible had happened. He knew that the wizard must have hurt her. He started crying properly, really crying. Ricardo tried to hold him but he didn't want to be touched. Everyone he touched got hurt. The wizard might still be inside him and it might hurt Ricardo. It hurt everyone. *You deserve to rot in hell. Go back to the arms of Satan, where you belong.*

'Elijah, you're safe now. Things will seem better tomorrow, I promise. All you need to do is stay here tonight and get a good night's sleep, then we will sort everything out tomorrow.'

'I don't want to stay here. I want to go home.'

'I know, Elijah. I know. Come on.' Ricardo opened the bathroom door and waited for Elijah to follow him into a bedroom. The two grown-ups were outside and said goodnight as they walked past. He didn't say anything to them. He didn't even look at them. The wizard would try and eat them if he recognised their faces.

'I want to go home,' he whispered again. But Ricardo put him into a small bed with a teddy bear, and tucked the cover up right by Elijah's ears.

'Try and sleep, little Elijah. Things will be better tomorrow.'

He left the door open a bit and Elijah let his eyes begin to see. The room was not a child's room. There were no toys and on the wall was a wooden board with a million holes from old pins. It might be an office. He tried to shut his eyes but he was too scared. What happened to Mum? What did the wizard do to her? Was the baby OK?

He searched the air for magic dust but the air was empty. There was no moonlight, no flashes of

295

tiny fish at the bottom of the ocean, just a universe of emptiness and nothingness.

Elijah's teeth were shaking together and he cried and cried, but then he heard banging. Then shouting. 'Let him come down; this is ridiculous! This will cause more problems than we had before! Call the police – what can they do? Arrest me? – but I'm taking him home.'

Granddad! Elijah sat up and opened his eyes and listened. His heart sped up. He was coming up the stairs, swearing and shouting. The two grown-ups were talking to him. 'It's probably best to wait till tomorrow and go through the proper channels . . .'

Granddad burst into the room and removed half of the darkness. His white hair was a halo around his head and Elijah knew at once he was an angel sent by God to protect him, just like Mama had told him. 'Elijah. Little grandson.' He rushed over to the bed and lifted Elijah into the air and kissed him all over his wet face. He smelt of coconuts.

'I am filled with badness.'

'Don't talk about it now. You need to come home. Get your jumper.'

Granddad turned to talk to the two grown-ups while Elijah put his jumper and jeans over the top of his pyjamas. 'I don't care what Ricardo says. This is our son and I'm taking him home. Don't worry; I'll take full responsibility.'

'But it's completely against the rules – we might have to phone the police.'

Elijah looked up at Granddad in the half-darkness, his soft white hair making him look like the most important angel of all. Granddad didn't care about rules. He pulled Elijah's arm and they went down the stairs and outside into the night. They walked quickly down the road, through the cool air. Granddad held tightly on to Elijah's hand. They waited for the night bus, number thirty-six, and Granddad used his bus pass. When they got to the top deck, Elijah watched the night out of the window, the world full of shadows. He imagined the sound of Mum's fairy stories, the laugh from Dad's tummy, and blood everywhere. So much blood.

'The wizard is back,' he said to Granddad. Granddad had to believe him. Granddad was Nigerian and went to church and sometimes smelt exactly the same as Mama. But Granddad looked at Elijah closely, straight into his eyes.

'Open your mouth,' he said. 'Wider.'

Elijah stretched his mouth as wide as he could until the corners of his lips began to hurt.

'As I thought,' said Granddad, tipping his head this way and that. 'There is no wizard inside you. No wizard at all.'

CHAPTER 33

Nikki was up before sunrise. Her stomach was not as sore, but she kept studying the square patch of white gauze that the nurses had put on to the wound. She had called Daddy six times already. Elijah was asleep. Elijah was very shaken, but he was a strong boy. Daddy wanted to talk, face to face, as soon as possible. Ricardo had called at eight thirty, before he'd even got to his office. Nikki paced around the kitchen, stopping to rotate her swollen ankles. 'They're coming today for a meeting. All of them. Do you think they want to take Elijah back into care?' She wanted Obi to come towards her and hold her and stroke her hair, but he didn't move. He looked like a broken man, folded in half, smaller somehow. He looked at the floor and stared, dry-eyed. 'I want Elijah home,' she whispered. 'I'm scared, but I want him home. They might take him away; they could, couldn't they?' Her voice broke. 'And what if he does it again?' She imagined Elijah's eyes looking for her. His tiny voice. 'Say something,' she said.

Obi didn't answer. Nikki looked down at her crumpled clothes, snatched up from the bedroom floor in a rush. Obi had showered and dressed as usual. His face was smooth: no stubble. She had even heard him take a phone call.

Nikki stepped backwards. 'Please,' she said, but she didn't know what she was pleading for.

Obi looked up at her, briefly, with glazed eyes.

'But, if he does come home, it might not be safe,' said Nikki. 'What if he does it again?' She held her stomach. The baby kicked her, hard, as if it was angry with her. As if she wasn't a good mother to her child, even when it was inside her body. She tried to ignore the stinging of her cut.

'It's Elijah we need to worry about. Not us. How safe will he be if he doesn't come home? Elijah will spend the rest of his life in care.' Obi stood up. 'How did this happen? We have let Elijah down.' His voice was distant and his body turned away from her.

Nikki began to cry again. 'Please, Obi. Please don't be angry with me any more. If you need to blame anyone, then blame his birth mother.' She felt the heat rising through her. 'What happened to him to make him like this?'

She walked over and stood in front of him. She could see his eyes water the tiniest bit as he looked away. Or maybe she imagined it. 'All I know for certain,' he said, 'is that it wasn't Elijah's fault. We needed to keep everything textbook.'

Nikki blinked. 'All I know,' she said, 'is what I feel. Life isn't textbook. It's messy.'

She reached her arm towards Obi. 'But you're right, we have to try to stick to the advice. We have to find out everything we can about Elijah, about children like Elijah.' She shook her head. 'We don't know anything. Not really. They never told us anything specific.'

Obi looked at her for a long time, as if he was deciding something. He had the tiniest frown. 'Elijah must come home. We have to get this right,' he said.

Nikki frowned. 'How can we get this right, if we don't even know what happened to our son?'

Obi shook his head and lifted his arm as though he was reaching for Nikki's, but then dropped it back down again as though he simply didn't have the energy.

When all the social workers arrived, Obi was talking once more, but too loudly; how they wanted Elijah back! Elijah, their son, who she loved more than she thought it was possible to love. But there was a voice inside her that she couldn't talk to the team about. What if he attacked her again? Or Obi? Or Jasmin? Or the baby? What if next time she wasn't so lucky? Ricardo was sitting next to her on one side and Obi on the other. Across the table was a new social worker they'd never met, a specialist foster-carer, Mike, who Elijah had been sent to stay with until Daddy had insisted on picking him up, the new manager, a sour-faced woman with broken veins across her cheekbones, and Chioma. Chioma was the only person at the table smiling.

'You've had a terrible shock,' Chioma said. 'We're all here to find out exactly what triggered this and how we move forwards. We're here to help.'

'We don't want to talk about disruption,' said Nikki. She circled her arms over her bump.

Obi nodded. 'We just need a plan to make sure he is safe and that we can safely look after him. He will need psychiatric evaluation and we want a post-adoption support plan.'

Nikki nodded and went on, 'But we are also worried about what else Elijah might do. We'd like to know exactly what isn't in the reports. In fact, we want all the reports. We need to know what happened to our son. You told us some of it, but we never expected this.'

The sour-faced manager leant forwards and put her cold hand over Nikki's. 'This is a terrible thing that happened,' she said. 'We haven't kept anything from you, I can assure you.'

Ricardo nodded. 'We talked about the fire, and the suspicion that Elijah caused the fire. In terms of the reports, you can have access to what we have – all of Elijah's reports. But I'm afraid that you can't see all of Deborah's reports, unless they relate to Elijah, as that is Deborah's private information. And you need to remember that we only know what we ourselves have been told.'

Obi didn't say anything; he looked far away.

Nikki looked around the room at all the faces, and she suddenly didn't trust any of them. 'I want everything.'

The manager let go of her hand.

The new social worker was writing frantically and had a frown stretching from the bridge of her nose to the top of her forehead.

Ricardo turned towards Nikki. 'We've shown you everything that we thought was relevant. Elijah's full C.P.R. You met the medical officer and we also discussed with you his extreme trauma, how it might affect him.' He stopped talking and cleared his throat. 'But last night Elijah said something very worrying to me. And it seems that more has come to light since the birth mother's last assessment.'

Nikki watched the scribbling pen. Obi's breath beside her was shallow. She thought of Elijah, alone in a strange room in Granddad's house, only two roads away, and her stomach twisted. She thought of her baby.

The manager sat forwards. 'But before Ricardo goes on, I just want to say that this doesn't really change anything. As far as we're concerned, nothing would have been handled differently. We would have given you all the same advice. As an organisation, we're proud to work in a completely transparent way—'

'What has come to light? What does that mean? What did Elijah say?' Nikki thought of Elijah's face and smacked her hand hard on the table. The social workers stopped writing. Everyone looked up at her face.

After what seemed like minutes, Ricardo spoke. 'Elijah believes he is a wizard, or is possessed by one.' He bit his lip. 'That's what he's been trying to tell us.' His face creased. 'He believes he brings bad luck to everyone around him.'

Nikki stared. Obi didn't move. 'He was shouting something when it happened,' Nikki said. 'From the Bible. He's done that before.'

Ricardo went on, 'This fits in with what we've learnt about Deborah. I'm afraid it's what we suspected, back when Elijah first mentioned the wizard. We couldn't jump to conclusions. It seems that Deborah was more involved with the church than we previously thought and there was certainly some ritualistic abuse happening. The leader of Deborah's church was arrested but fled to Nigeria, though they are currently looking for him.'

'Ritualistic abuse? What do you mean? What happened to Elijah?'

'Well, we have given you all the information as we had it, but it would seem that the birth mother and the church leaders were trying to exorcise a demon from Elijah's body. They believed him to be possessed by evil. And it was the methods they used to exorcise that were abusive. We believe that, in addition to neglect and to the physical abuse that you already know about, he was poisoned and bathed in acid. We knew the scars on his body came from physical abuse, but we had no idea about the nature of it.' Ricardo's voice was breaking. His face looked very young all of a sudden. 'He was tortured.'

The world became very slow and the air sticky to breathe. 'And you knew this?' Obi's hand was on her arm. 'Acid? Poison? You knew this and didn't disclose it?'

'No, we didn't know the extent of the abuse,' said Ricardo. 'Maybe we never will. We only know what the birth mother has told us, because a lot of it may have happened when Elijah was preverbal.'

Nikki's head was spinning. She would like to kill her son's birth mum, and whoever else was involved. She imagined what Elijah looked like as a baby, how frightened he must have been. She thought of Elijah's face. She felt sick rise in her throat. Everything blurred. She was terrified of what Elijah had been through, of how that would show itself. And she was even more terrified of losing him.

'Our son,' Obi said. She looked at his face. Obi, who was so sure of himself, who was sure of everything and the centre of safety, Obi was terrified. Nikki could see it then. 'He's our son,' said Obi.

'He's with my dad until he can come home later today. He's not going back into care.'

The new social worker sat up. She kept fiddling with a piece of her curly hair, winding it around her finger and then letting it spring back. 'Nobody is sending Elijah back into care. And that would have to be a decision led by you.'

Ricardo nodded. 'It sounds as if you're both committed to having Elijah home as soon as possible, no matter how difficult the challenges you've faced.' He smiled at Nikki.

But she was concentrating on Obi. His face was blank. He opened his mouth to speak but then closed it. Nikki felt her heart beat in her neck.

Chioma spoke. 'Right. This is good. You're angry and sad and a little frightened: that's completely normal. And I for one agree that you need to see more information if this is ever to work.' While Chioma was speaking, the social workers' pens slowed down, as if even pens were affected by her hypnotic voice.

'I've got to know Elijah very well during our sessions and I've also been in touch with Doctor Peters, from C.A.M.H.S. – who sends his apologies for not making this meeting.'

'C.A.M.H.S.?' Nikki sat up.

'Child and Adolescent Mental Health Service.' Mike spoke for the first time. He was a thin man with acne scars and tired, grey eyes. 'We had Elijah assessed by the team shortly after he arrived at our house. He's had a psychiatric evaluation before, of course, but, in view of what happened, we had him reassessed in case he needed admitting.'

'Admitting?'

'Doctor Peters reviewed him,' said Chioma, her soft voice calming down Nikki's heart. 'And he felt that we are doing everything right.' She reached across the table and touched Nikki's hand. 'You are doing everything right. But Elijah needs more intensive support, and Doctor Peters wants to see him in clinic to discuss treatment options, which may include medication, though Elijah is still very young.'

'What do you think?' Nikki pulled her hand out from underneath Chioma's. People kept touching her hand as if it would help.

'Well, as a team, we've discussed things and we think – I think – it's so difficult to unpick. Elijah may have mental-health issues, but it may all be down to attachment. And the best treatment is play – funnelling care as you have been: make sure that you are the only ones that cuddle Elijah; if he's hurt, then you make it better; play with him constantly. He needs to feel safe and know he'll be living with you forever, no matter what.'

Obi looked up then. 'What about his delusions? I mean, he thinks he's a wizard, for God's sake. Surely that is a mental-health problem?'

'Well, he's very young and he's been told that

he is a wizard, we think, by people he trusts. But he's also acting out traumatic experiences. He's hurting very, very badly and he's doing exactly what he did with the fire. He's starting to feel safe, and attached, and wants to test to see if you'll send him away.' Chioma looked at Nikki and then back at Obi. 'Everyone in his life has sent him away.'

Obi sat up straighter, pulled his shoulders back. 'We'll never send him away.'

'Then you have to make him believe that.' The other social worker stopped writing. 'If this placement is to work, we'll need regular reviews and involvement from C.A.M.H.S. as well as you, Chioma. We can offer you a structured programme of support, both practical and financial help, if required.'

Chioma looked at Obi. 'And it's important to understand that, even with the best will in the world, sometimes placements break down. And it's nobody's fault. Some children are simply too damaged to be able to cope in a family setting.'

Ricardo spoke quickly. 'But we don't want that to happen here. And we're a long way off from that discussion, in my opinion. Of course, Elijah reacted badly to the pregnancy news – worse than we thought – but we can help you through this. I'd suggest that it's high time we show Elijah his life-story work, and start going over his history with him: show him photographs, tell him all about his birth family. He's been so resistant to it in the past, but I think we have to really push him now. It might help or it might not, but we have to try this. I can provide some support.' He rubbed his face. 'I'm still working two jobs, covering my other manager who's on sick leave —' he smiled '— but, whenever I can, I will come here to do the life-story work with you.' He nodded. 'There really was nothing we kept from you. I'll try and get you access to the birth mother's health reports, at least, and I agree with Chioma: be open and honest with Elijah, about everything. He needs to understand Deborah loves him, but is mentally ill. That she put an idea in his head, but it was a bad idea, wrong, and all he has to do to make the wizard go away is to stop believing in it.'

Nikki looked at them all around the table and hugged her middle. Her breathing slowed down. She thought of the baby inside her, of how she'd ever tell the baby and explain what nearly happened. She felt a kick. The baby was strong. A strong baby: Nikki knew that, was certain of it. But Elijah was not strong at all. She wanted him with her, on her lap, in her arms. She wanted to whisper in his ear that she loved him and that it would be OK. She wanted to take away the pain he'd suffered, the abuse.

'We just want him to come home.' She thought of the dogs beyond saving, the ones who had been so abused that there was no chance they would survive. The ones who were taken from the rehoming kennels and put down.

Obi kissed her hand. His hand was steady and strong, his kiss firm on her skin. She held her head up. A look passed between them that she would remember always. It was Obi's eyes looking to hers to see what to do. She realised, for the first time, that she would have to be the stronger one. That her strength made Obi stronger.

CHAPTER 34

Granddad didn't wait for Mum and Dad to come over with Ricardo to pick Elijah up and take him home. 'There's nothing wrong with your legs, is there?' he asked.

Elijah shook his head.

'Come on, then.' He tucked Elijah's coat around his shoulders and they walked out into the day. Granddad watched Elijah pinch his nose.

'What's all this nose pinching, Elijah?' Granddad smiled and took Elijah's nose between his thumb and forefinger. 'The wizard's gone. I checked – remember?'

Mum opened the door and rushed out, pulling Elijah towards her, lifting him off the ground. 'Elijah!' She kissed his cheek and pressed his back towards her. He felt the hardness of her swollen belly. 'Ricardo's here,' she said to Granddad, reaching through the gap between Elijah's arm and body. 'You should have waited for us to collect him.'

'Well, we're here now,' said Granddad. 'Anyway, I'm going home. Call me later.'

He gave Elijah's shoulder a squeeze and turned

to walk away, but Mum ran after him, hugged him and kissed his cheek before he left. Then she walked back into the hallway and picked up Elijah's hand. With his other hand, he pinched his nose and he kept his mouth shut. He would not let the wizard escape.

At the kitchen table sat Dad and Ricardo. The kitchen curtains were half closed and it made the room look different. The air was yellow and Elijah could see specks of dust dancing around in front of him. Dad jumped up and hugged Elijah and pulled him on to his lap. Elijah tried not to cry and no noise came out but huge tears rolled down his cheeks and on to Obi's shirt.

'Do you want a juice, Elijah? A biscuit?' Mum kept touching, asking if he wanted things. He shook his head.

'I think we need to get talking straight away,' said Ricardo. 'What do you think happened, Elijah?'

Elijah shut his mouth so tightly that he bit his tongue. He focused on the pile of papers that Obi had left on the table beside his laptop computer, which was shining silver.

'I think that you thought the wizard stabbed Mum. I think that's what is going on in your head. But I want to tell you now very clearly that there is no wizard. Wizards are simply not real.'

Elijah crumpled in half. He pinched his nose shut completely. Mum rushed over and pulled his hand from his face. 'It's OK, Elijah. It's OK. We can all get through this. Me and Dad love you so, so much and nothing will ever change that. Nothing. You're home now. You're safe now. You can make the wizard disappear completely by just not believing in it. It doesn't exist if you don't believe in it.'

Wizards are real, Elijah wanted to shout.

On Tuesday, Ricardo came round again. Elijah wasn't at school because the doctor said he should have two weeks off. Ricardo wore jeans with a rip on the knee. 'I'm sorry your appointment with Doctor Peters was cancelled last week. I understand you're going on Monday? Anyway, I'm sorry you haven't had the appointment yet because I'm afraid today is going to be a difficult day,' he said. 'We're going to look at a very special book and I need to start telling you a story. It's a very special story because it's your story, Elijah – your life story. And I know that you've done some life-story work in the past, but this time we'd like to do more. I know you had a special life book at Nargis's house and that you didn't want to read it then, which is fine. But now we think it's very important that you start to read the book with Mum and Dad. Very important.'

Dad's hand was Elijah's back and they were sitting on the comfortable sofa. Mum was sitting next to him, the other side, with her arm around him too, on top of Dad's. Her arm was freezing cold. Even though she was right there next to him, he felt alone.

'I don't want to.'

Mum lifted her hand up and stroked his hair. 'It's OK,' she whispered.

'I know you don't, Elijah. Nargis told me how you found life-story work very, very difficult. Most children find that it really helps, you know. We're going to read a little bit. Just a bit. It might help you to stop being scared.'

'Is it about Mama?'

'Some of it. But most of it is about you. And most of the time Mum and Dad can read it through with you, but I thought it might be nice if I'm here while we read the first bit. Today we'll just read through a tiny section of the book and then I'll tell you any hard words and then we'll stop. OK?'

Elijah didn't nod his head but he didn't shake it either. Ricardo took the book out from his big bag. It was blue plastic on the outside and had stars on the cover. Elijah's photo was on the front page and he was smiling, but Elijah remembered that day. Darren had held him down on the ground and pushed his face into the mud and, with his other hand, burnt him behind his ear with a cigarette. Nargis had taken dozens of photos. She had said that some were for his life-story work.

Elijah looked at his life-story book. He turned the front page. At the beginning was a photo of Mama. She had a round tummy and he was inside it. His eyes burnt. He wanted to climb inside that photo and right back inside Mama's tummy. In

313

the photo, Mama was not smiling and her arm muscles were hard and tight, her legs bent slightly. She looked as if she wanted to run away.

> Elijah. You were born at Lewisham Hospital, weighing eight pounds and two ounces. You were a healthy and happy baby boy. This is your birth mother, Deborah. You grew inside Deborah's tummy.

Ricardo turned another page. There was a photo of a man wearing clothes like the clothes that Granddad wore, only the man in the photo was blurred and Granddad was always bright.

> This is a photo of your birth father, Akpan, who died when you were very small. Akpan was tall and had soft skin, just like you. Deborah says that he liked jazz music and he used to play the saxophone.

Elijah looked up at Dad. He didn't want to cry, but there was something very sad about the picture of the saxophone that Ricardo must have found and stuck on to the page below Akpan's photo. His birth father did not look like Dad at all.

'Your reading is getting very good, but some of the words are super-hard so I will read this next bit out,' said Ricardo. He looked at Elijah and smiled, but Elijah couldn't smile back. His heart was stabbing him.

When you were a baby, the doctors and nurses had some worries about your birth mother, Deborah. She found it difficult to cope with looking after you because she was very confused. You were a lovely baby and she loved you very much but, even though she loved you, she found that it was too hard for her to keep you clean and safe and warm, like you deserved, and like all babies deserve. Your Mama, Deborah, has an illness in her brain and that means everything got jumbled up and it was difficult to know what was real and what was not real. It was hard for her and hard for you too. You didn't have the things that babies need because Deborah couldn't give you those things. She didn't give you enough milk, or keep you clean, and she didn't cuddle you to show you how much she loved you. And the illness in Deborah's brain got worse and worse until she had voices inside her head that weren't really there and they told her to hurt you. You were a good baby, just like you ARE a good boy. You liked to smile and play and cuddle, but you didn't get the things you deserved and so you became confused and sad. It is not your fault that Deborah couldn't look after you. You deserve LOVE and to be SAFE and to live forever in a FAMILY.

Elijah rocked back and forth. He wanted to close his ears because he knew Mama could keep him safe and he knew Mama loved him. Mama knew that babies needed milk and cuddles and clean nappies. They had it all wrong. Mama would never ever hurt a baby.

Dad stood up and walked to the window, looked out.

'Shhh,' said Mum. She stroked his head and he closed his eyes and he rocked and rocked until he heard Ricardo shut the book.

They went to Chioma twice a week, so it felt like Elijah was seeing her all the time. They played with the sand and, when they went to clean it up at the end, Chioma stopped them. 'Can you leave it, Elijah?'

He looked at her.

'I can read sand,' she said. 'Just like how some people can read tea leaves, I can read sand – it tells me how you are, deep inside your body.'

He looked at the sand. There was nothing different about it. They'd built a few castles and other shapes. But something made him put his hand out and mess it up and the castles were quickly flattened.

'Elijah!' Dad shouted. 'That was silly.'

Chioma didn't shout. Instead, she said, 'Also, I'm really good at reading why children do things.' She smiled. 'Wow, Elijah, you really don't want me to see inside your body, do you? You must feel like something very bad is inside you. Ricardo told me how you think there's a wizard.'

Chioma looked at Elijah. But he didn't want to talk to her about the wizard.

She didn't wait too long for him to answer, but opened the door and said, 'Excellent work today. I'll see you all next week.' Mum looked at Dad and they both raised their eyebrows.

That evening, they were all together and Elijah was trying not to think about Mama, but she kept popping into his mind like a giant star. He thought of the book that Ricardo had – a book full of reasons he couldn't live with Mama. It was very hard, but he would do anything to make Mum smile. 'I will look at it, if you want me too,' he said.

If only he could make the wizard go away for good. If Mum and Dad sent him away, Mama would never find him. And if he had to live in a children's home then she'd never be able to live with him. Only children could live in children's homes. He wanted Mum and Dad to love him again. He wanted to be a good big brother. And, most of all, he needed Mama. Only Mama could save them all from the wizard. He remembered Ricardo telling him that he'd tried to hurt Mum, but he knew it was the wizard that had tried to hurt Mum and his own baby brother or sister. He hated the wizard more than ever. Elijah put his ear to Mum's round belly and he felt her smile.

She squeezed his back. 'Knew it would help,' she said.

Dad nodded. 'Every week we'll read a little bit more and it will help you to understand.'

Elijah looked up.

'What is it?'

Elijah made his tummy hard. 'Can I go to church with Granddad? I think he will let me.' He knew that Granddad's church would be safe. He would pray and pray and try to fight the wizard himself. Maybe he would find a Bishop who would help him cut the wizard out.

Mum and Dad flicked their eyes at each other.

'You tried going to church with Granddad once before and it just made you even more scared . . .' Then Mum's eyes found Elijah's. 'OK, if it will help.'

They listened to the show on the radio about tigers, who were the biggest and strongest cats in the world. A mum tiger sensed danger and carried the baby tiger in her mouth until it was safe. 'Tigers must love their babies a lot,' he said. And Mum pulled him closer and, when she did, the wizard was quiet. It couldn't even laugh.

CHAPTER 35

Chanel and Jasmin and Daddy came over for lunch. They had stayed away for a while and, apart from speaking to her on the phone, Nikki hadn't seen Chanel in days. They hugged as if it had been a year.

'Are you OK?' Chanel whispered into Nikki's ear. She nodded. She was OK. They were coming through it. Elijah hadn't acted out since that awful night. He was still very subdued, but seemed less nervous, and her love for him didn't feel any different at all. In fact, it felt stronger, as though knowing what he'd been through made her feel even more protective.

Chanel rested her hand on Nikki's bump and smiled. She turned to Elijah. 'How are you, little man?' Chanel handed Elijah a bag. She turned to Nikki. 'A tracksuit we saw in JD Sports.'

Nikki raised her eyebrows.

'Thank you, Aunty Chanel,' said Elijah. His voice was still quiet, but he didn't look like his face was in pain any more. Slowly but surely he was looking more confident again. His skin was beginning to shine.

'Can we go and play?' Jasmin led Elijah by the hand, straight up the stairs, before Nikki had time to open her mouth.

Daddy laughed. 'Kids, eh?' He smiled.

'Game of chess?' asked Obi. Daddy nodded. He looked at Nikki. 'Sounds good.' They sat at the coffee table opposite each other and Obi set out his wooden chess set. Nikki and Chanel disappeared into the kitchen and Nikki put the kettle on for yet more herbal tea. She'd stopped drinking strong coffee as all the books had recommended, but what she wouldn't do for an espresso!

'How are you?' asked Chanel.

'I'm really OK,' said Nikki. 'Really.' But then she burst into tears and Chanel jumped across to her and held her close. 'It's OK.' Nikki removed herself from Chanel's hold. 'I'm just being silly. It was probably just some freak thing that happened and will never happen again; I mean, it was our fault and we're not going to let it happen again, but it was so scary, Chanel. And what they told us, all that he's been through . . .'

Nikki found herself telling Chanel everything: how much she wanted the baby; how Obi had seemed to think all the blame was on her; how, at first, he hadn't wanted to hold her hand in the hospital and how she needed him now more than ever. And how much she worried about Elijah. She told her what the social workers had said, about what he'd suffered.

'Acid?' asked Chanel. Her mouth was open wide. 'Well, it's no wonder he's messed up. In fact, I'm surprised he's coping this well. Little love!'

Nikki nodded. 'I know. I hate her,' she said. 'His birth mother. Then I start to feel sorry for her. It's so mixed up. I wish I could only see the good in people. Obi keeps trying to rationalise why she did it—'

'Why do you think she did it?'

'Obviously she has quite serious mental-health problems, but it's more than that. It's not so important now why she did what she did, but we need to figure out what to do about it, how to handle things from now. I read Obi's boring books and we're following the advice of the social workers and Chioma, but they all contradict what Obi's dad thinks.'

'He has weird views about life. You shouldn't take the advice of a crazy old man over the professionals.'

'I know, but he is talking sense to me. He says there's no point telling Elijah that wizards don't exist, because they do—'

Chanel rolled her eyes. 'Oh, for God's sake.'

'I know it sounds crazy, but he does actually believe in that kind of thing. He says, to dismiss the idea of a belief system, just because it's alien to us, is to deny identity, and Elijah will never belong unless his identity is accepted.'

'Well, what does Chioma think?'

'Chioma says it's nonsense – we mustn't indulge

his belief in any way or it'll reinforce his sense of loss and cause further trauma.'

'That sounds like it makes more sense . . .'

Nikki sighed. 'She also thinks that some children are too traumatised to ever be able to live in families. Which is too horrible to even consider.'

Chanel smiled. 'But you can take advice from both of them, you know? Make your own mind up. Take the professional advice from Chioma about how to deal with things, and take the optimism from Obi's dad. I'm sure, along with his crazy beliefs, Obi's dad also thinks that any child can be helped at any point – which I agree with. He's so idealistic. That's where Obi gets it from.'

Nikki laughed. 'Obi *is* the same. They're so kind, both of them. And Chioma, even though I wish she'd stop saying that families aren't the right setting for all children.'

'You do see the good in people,' said Chanel. 'You always have.'

Loud laughter came from the other room. They followed the noise to the living room where Daddy was dancing and shouting, 'Checkmate! Checkmate! You may be younger, but I am far more intelligent. My brain cells are still pretty quick.'

Elijah and Jasmin ran down the stairs. Jasmin giggled really loudly and danced around with Daddy shouting, 'Checkmate!' then 'Loser! Loser!' to Obi.

'Jasmin!' shouted Chanel. 'Stop being rude.'

Elijah was quiet. He sat down next to Obi, but

322

Nikki thought she could see the corner of a smile appearing on his face.

Things were somehow getting a tiny bit easier for Nikki. She stopped feeling so scared. She'd hidden anything that could be harmful. Her cooking knives were in the highest cupboard, and locked away. Even though she barely slept because the skin across her stomach felt like it was going to split and her back was probably broken, these things were just part of having a healthy baby and, when she woke in the morning, her first thought was Elijah. Elijah crept into their bed that morning and snuggled up towards her and her ever-increasing bump, and Nikki couldn't stop smiling. Obi turned over and threw his arm around her and Elijah, and the baby had kicked her so hard that Obi's hand had slipped and he'd laughed and pulled them all closer together.

'We're seeing Ricardo today again,' said Nikki. 'I really think it's helping. What do you think?'

Elijah nodded. He moved closer to her. His skin was so soft and warm.

Nikki kissed his head. She felt so tired. She wanted to travel back in time and have Elijah grow inside her, too, and give birth to him and make sure no one ever, ever hurt her son. 'I'm glad,' she said. 'I'm so glad. Do you think you might be ready to talk about the wizard now?'

Elijah looked up at her. 'I never ever would hurt

you, Mum,' he said. 'Will you still love me when the baby comes?'

'We'll love you forever,' she said. She looked at his face, his skinny arms, the way his chest dipped a tiny bit in the middle. He looked like a child who'd swallowed the goodness of the world, not one who was filled with horror.

As she showered, the baby kicked her and she could make out a tiny foot just below her ribs.

CHAPTER 36

Little heart,

There were years in the middle that I hardly remember and that I find hard to write about, even to you, Elijah. I always said that there should be no secrets between us, but now I know that life is full of secrets we don't even tell ourselves. The words on this page make no sense to me now.

The years passed, Elijah, with me scraping money for the Bishop. At first, it was all the money I'd been saving for the trip home to Nigeria. Akpan and I had saved as much as we could, but Bishop had it all. Then I was borrowing from neighbours, claiming benefits, even begging so that he could continue doing his best to get that stubborn wizard out of your body. There was no longer any chance of returning to Nigeria. After the acid bath, I thought the wizard had gone. You clung to me for the entire time it took for the skin on your little feet to grow back. But, as soon as your body healed, my dreams returned. The spinning. The insects. Bishop said the wizard was killing you, and I spent every night praying that you would be spared, that the wizard would leave your body and you'd return to me once more a small boy, my little son, my love.

Bishop preached every Sunday, his congregation increasing every week and his reputation growing as a saviour of souls. People visited the flat – official-looking people. First midwives, then health visitors, then social workers, mental-health workers. But none of them could help with a wizard living in a boy. This was a Nigerian problem, and only a Nigerian solution would do. Everyone knows that if a spider bites you in a forest then the only place you will find an antidote is that same forest. But, even with the Bishop's help, things became worse and worse, and there was still no sign that the wizard would leave us. You were five years old when things became worse than ever. You had started talking at three, copying the words I said to you, but then you became a quiet boy, unusually quiet. Sometimes you sang, but it wasn't nursery rhymes that I recognised, but a strange low humming sound that made the whole world feel sad. I knew you were in there, Elijah; my sad boy, wanting to get out. I knew that deep down you were still there.

'Mama,' you said one day. 'Mama, can I go to school?'

You had seen the children outside the window walking along the path with their hair neat and their schoolbags swinging. I wanted you to go to school so desperately, Elijah, but you were too sick to send outside. Too full of wizard. And the red car was there following us, or parked outside our flat. The health visitor and social workers were calling more and more often. I pretended to be out. But then, once, they found me in. It was a lady who had a face the same shape as a horse, and I couldn't hear her very well but she said she was going to hold a child-protection meeting as she had a few concerns, and that they had spoken to my neighbours, who also had concerns. It was not true! She smiled at you across the room and asked if you were OK, and what activities you liked to do. You looked at me with sad eyes, Elijah, and looked back at the woman. 'I like to be with Mama,' you said.

When she left, I ran all the way to church and fell on to my knees in front of the Bishop. But, instead of helping me up, of helping us, he looked around and then stepped backwards. 'I think you need to see someone else,' he said. 'Join another church. I cannot help you.'

I stood and looked at the Bishop with my face full of tears. God spoke through him. God couldn't help us. The devil was winning. When we returned home, Elijah, I held your arms close to your body and looked straight inside your face. 'You are a wizard, aren't you? You are full with wizard.'

You looked at me for the longest time, and then you spoke, your voice soft and clear. 'I'll be a wizard if you want me to, Mama.'

I could see in your eyes the tricks you were using,

that the wizard was using to kill you, and to kill us. I knew the wizard was winning then.

The moment when I woke in the mornings, when everything was quiet, even my heart, was my favourite time of day. I let my head travel backwards to my warm Nigeria, with my smiling sisters and the courtyard with my mummy cooking or wiping her shining pots. But something always snapped me back – back to the cold flat, with no money for the electric machine. I could see you were pale, and losing even more weight. You looked at me with knowing eyes. I could see badness in them. The devil himself. The red car parked underneath the balcony every night and I knew they would take you forever. The way your mouth curled slightly at the edges, like a secret half-told . . . You grew like a weed . . . You spoke hardly any words . . . Some days, you simply sat in your bed and rocked back and forth until it was time to lie down once more. I tried not to watch you. I focused on praying and praying and, when you were well enough, you joined me, both of us praying and praying. But nothing changed. The terrible dreams continued.

I had to do something. Elijah, the depression had taken hold of me for so long I could barely stand up; but, with the strength you gave me, I found the courage from somewhere. I imagined another life for us, and the image of that – of us in Nigeria, where we were meant to be – well, that image broke through real life and stood me up. I didn't need the Bishop any more. I didn't even need to be in the church. God spoke directly to me, anyway, telling me I was his special angel and he could help me save you from the evil inside. I had seen the treatment of witches and wizards and sorcerers. I knew that pastors at home would beat the wizard out, or burn it out, or poison it out. I had tried the special medicine with you, but it hadn't worked. The wizard was killing you. Soon, there would be none of my son left at all. I had to act. I suddenly knew what I had to do. You told me. The voices told me. God's voice. I could hear God's voice above all others:

The wizard is killing him. Only you can save his life.

I looked at your small body. My son, my little heart. I would have taken my own life if I thought it would help save yours. I knew with such clarity what the Bishop would have me do, what I could do. I was your mother. I knew you better than I knew life itself. I was a committed Christian and I could pray and act. Akpan had left his screwdriver in the drawer. He was forever fixing things – small things, only. I remembered Akpan, your baba, so fondly, even though by then he'd been gone and dead for years too long. I looked at you, picked you up in my arms. You looked back at me, slowly blinking. 'Are you in there, Elijah? Mama is coming to save you.'

I had to release the wizard.

The screwdriver was tiny, really. Meant for delicate things. Small things.

Your head bent backwards and your eyes did not open. 'Elijah!' I shouted. 'Elijah!' You began to shake. Shakes on shakes, like a woman who had just given birth. Then you stopped suddenly and were too still. 'Elijah! Elijah!'

There was no sign of wickedness, no sign of wizard or evil. The room was so quiet I could have heard a pin. Your skin was grey, like the outside sky. Like a pigeon.

At first I thought you were dead, the wizard had killed you, and I was getting ready to kill myself. A pot of tablets flashed in front of my mind; I heard them shouting for me. I would eat them all. But then you moaned, a sound like a dog that had been kicked, and I knew that God was with me. God had not forsaken me. You might live.

I grabbed the sheet from the bed and wrapped you tightly, held you close enough that I could feel if you were breathing. You needed a doctor, I knew. But the spinning and the voices, the men and the dogs . . . How would I take you all the way to the hospital? It was far – the nearest in Lewisham, and a bus ride away. I had no money for the bus. I felt you sucking air from me to you. 'Shut up!' I screamed to the voice in my ear. *The wizard has killed him. The wizard has killed your son. You have killed your son. You.*

'Shut up!'

God, lead me to the hospital and a doctor who can help my son, I prayed. He is nearly dead from the wizard and he needs Your help. Please, Jesus, let me take him to safety. I prayed for what seemed like hours. My hands were numb when I took them apart.

I prayed all the way down the stairwell, which was moving sideways. I prayed all the way past those men who saw you and stopped whistling, then laughed hard. I prayed all the way to the main street, where I stopped a white man in a red car and screamed, showed him my grey Elijah. The red car.

He drove me all the way to Lewisham accident department and I prayed all the way, while he swore. 'Fucking hell! Fucking traffic, get out of the way! There's a sick kid in here! Fucking hell, lady, you should have phoned an ambulance! God, if that kid dies in my car . . . Fuck!'

The staff ran out as soon as the man got out of the car and shouted, 'Help! We need some help! Emergency!' Nurses with blue pyjamas, doctors wearing shirts and stethoscopes around their necks, all running to pull you from me, run you inside.

I ran and shouted to God. 'Please, Jesus, let my child live! Let him, oh dear Jesus! God, let this boy live!'

They ran into a room full of machines and took the sheet off your body until you were naked. 'He will be too cold! He is too cold! Jesus! Heavens! Give him a blanket! Please, give him a blanket! Nobody would give him a blanket, you see, and that's why he nearly died. He was so cold. So cold.'

I prayed and prayed, Elijah. Later, I heard them in the small office next to me. They were meeting, a lot of women who looked the same: white, horse-shaped faces, coloured-beaded necklaces, ugly shoes. I watched them walk into the room, one after the other, carrying steaming drinks in front of them. I recognised one of them. 'There is some concern about the old burn on his head,' one said. 'Other old injuries. We need to do a full skeletal survey.' The wall was very thin and a gap in the door meant every word floated right out, even though someone had written *Confidential meeting in progress* on a piece of white paper and stuck it on the door. The ward was empty of parents, except for me. It was quiet time, as if the children had any other time. They were all so sick that every minute was quiet. Too quiet. I could only hear the beep of the machines and the women's confidential voices.

'Do you think it's one of those spiritual-healing things? I keep hearing more and more about it. So awful. Not that that's definitely what's going on here.'

'Yes, I agree. It's tricky, though, as it's one of those practices that's culturally normal. We need to be particularly sensitive to that. We can't know that's what this is. It may have been some sort of cupping.'

'Isn't cupping Chinese?'

'I've had some experience of this kind of thing before. I mean, look at Climbié. And there was the headless torso, thrown into the Thames. That was some kind of black magic – ritual abuse, wasn't it?'

'That was the foster family. And this is the birth mother. Also, it's very different, taking into account the birth mother's mental state. This is not really about the church and cultural beliefs, much more about the mental-health issues.'

'Which make the birth mother vulnerable . . .'

'Well, we need to be so careful how we present it, and make sure we're fully aware of cultural norms.'

'Child abuse is child abuse.'

'Agreed; but we can't separate the family from their culture. We need to be sensitive. Anyway, did you see Margaret last week? You know she's moved to Tunbridge Wells. Right by my house – well, a short drive away. Her daughter's passed the eleven-plus to get into Tonbridge Grammar School. She's so delighted. All those school fees and tuition finally paying off!'

They carried on talking as I picked up your tiny hand and kissed it hard, so it would remember. 'Keep safe,' I whispered. 'The wizard will not find you now.'

They led me to a room which had a *Do Not Disturb – Meeting In Progress* sign stuck to the window. Inside, on chairs arranged in a semicircle, were four women I had never seen before and a police officer, who had taken off a flat black hat and put it on to her lap, tapping it like a drum with her fingers. The doctor was there, standing by the window that only opened a few inches to stop people from jumping out – but what if there was a fire? How would they escape?

'Deborah,' said one. 'We need to talk to you about some very serious things.'

'I am Mama Elijah,' I said. 'That is how we take a name in my country. We take the name of our first-born child.'

The room was quiet enough to hear an aeroplane fly in the distance, above, through the tiny window gap. The spinning had stopped, but I felt as if my body would suddenly stop, too. I had never felt more tired.

Another woman sat forwards. She had buck teeth and eyebrows that grew all the way across. 'Deborah, we need to talk to you about what's going to happen.'

I looked at the air in the window gap. It wasn't enough. I felt the start of the spinning at the back of my head. The voices in my ear were quiet at first. I felt the screwdriver go through the evil in Elijah. I felt it go inside him and inside me. And everything was still and quiet and the world was full of nothing except me and my son once more. But then – oh, there was so much blood. So much blood from such a small thing.

I turned my ears down low and prayed over and over: Dear Lord Jesus; please, sweet Lord; dear God, hear me now. Please, dear Lord . . .

But it was no good. The spinning got faster.

'Deborah,' said the police officer. 'We will need

334

to take you to the police station and get a statement from you, but first we need you to understand that Elijah, when he leaves this hospital, will not be returned to your care. While his injuries are being investigated, he will be taken into foster care.'

I let the room start to move – slowly, at first, the ground coming up to reach the ceiling. Then the ceiling back to the ground. I knew this would happen. They would take you from me. They would take you, and the wizard would climb right back inside your body.

I looked around the room and tried to focus on things: the small table with three old cups of coffee, the insides stained; the noticeboard with a picture of a pair of hands washing; the strip of light and the smoke alarm on the ceiling.

'Deborah, we need to know that you understand. Deborah?'

The room stopped spinning suddenly but everything was back in the wrong order. 'My name is Mama Elijah.'

The policewoman put her hat on and leant forwards. 'We need you to come with us now. Is there someone we can call to stay with Elijah? Also, we will need to speak to your husband. Can you call him now, please?'

'I cannot call Akpan. He is dead.'

The women looked from one to the other then back at me. 'OK; well, we need you to come, please.' One stood and waited for me to stand after her, but I sat.

'I cannot leave Elijah. He is in danger. I cannot leave him.'

The policewoman sat again and removed her hat. 'Can you call psych?' she said to the other woman, who left the room. 'Now, Deborah, this is really important. What do you mean, Elijah's in danger?'

I looked at the woman. Even though she was police, and everyone knows that police are thieves who like nothing more than treating human beings like animals, she had a small cross around her neck and I knew she was a Christian. She might help me. 'Elijah is sick.'

The policewoman nodded. 'We know he's sick, Deborah. The doctors and nurses are doing everything they can to help him.'

The room was spinning so much I could hardly keep my eyes open. I whispered, 'He needs saving.' I looked at the woman and her cross. I thought of your face, your skin, like the earth from home, the moon swelling like a heart in love.

CHAPTER 37

Doctor Peters leant forward in his chair and lifted one of his legs on top of the other, showing a striped sock.

'Your social worker tells me that you've been hearing voices telling you what to do.'

Elijah looked at Mum. She nodded. 'Only one voice tells me what to do,' he said.

Doctor Peters shuffled some papers on his desk. 'Well, I think we'll hold off on the medication front for now.' He looked at Dad. 'I've seen this kind of thing in my practice in Devon – sort of delusional thought in young people – but I'm reluctant to treat someone so young.' He looked at Elijah. 'After all, it's the age of make-believe and also imaginary friends. Hearing and even seeing someone else at your age is not indicative of illness.'

Elijah had no idea what he was talking about. He focused on Doctor Peters' stripy sock, and the pale white skin above it.

'Have you been to Devon?' Doctor Peters asked.

Elijah shook his head.

'You ought to get Mum and Dad to take you.'

He smiled. 'There's very little that can't be cured by fresh air and ice cream, I find.'

Mum was rubbing her tummy in the chair beside him and Elijah thought he heard a sound at the back of her throat. Dad coughed.

'Well, that should do for now,' Doctor Peters said.

'That's it?' Mum stopped rubbing her tummy.

'Yes – I'll see you all again in two weeks. My advice is you carry on with the play therapy and get in touch if there are any major issues. But also plenty of ice cream.' He winked at Elijah.

'Elijah, would you wait outside, please?' asked Mum. 'We just need a quick chat with the doctor.'

Elijah shrugged, said goodbye and left the room. He put his ear to the door but could only hear Mum and Dad shouting questions, until he eventually heard Doctor Peters' voice: 'Now, let's all calm down. You're making far too much of the wizard business. He's clearly just a troubled boy.'

Elijah knew the codes so well that, when Jasmin had flashed her torch three times then one slow time the night before, he'd known to expect her knocking for him that morning to walk to school together. What he hadn't expected was what happened after they got through the school gates and said goodbye to Mum: Jasmin had led him by the arm towards the small fence at the back of the playground and they'd climbed right over. 'Where are we going?'

'It's a secret.'

Elijah followed Jasmin into the woods. The air smelt of honey.

He followed her footsteps, trying to step inside her footprints. They walked and walked and didn't talk, but Elijah watched Jasmin's every step. He thought about Mum and what the school would say when they found out that Jasmin and Elijah weren't there. But Jasmin didn't look worried at all. She never looked worried about anything.

'Stop here,' said Jasmin. Her face twitched around and up, looking at the light through the branches. 'Perfect,' she said, sitting down on an old log.

'Why don't you want to go to school?'

'Sometimes I'm just not in the mood,' said Jasmin. 'Anyway, I only want to miss a little bit.' Jasmin turned her face to Elijah. 'All the time, you're quiet now. Are you thinking about her?' she asked. 'Your real mum?'

'Nikki is real,' Elijah said. But his eyes filled with tears.

'I'm talking about your other mum. The one whose tummy you grew in. Is that why you don't want to play after school? Is that why your face is always sad?'

He looked at Jasmin and the forest around them. She was his best friend. He'd never had a friend like Jasmin, not even Ricardo. He felt around inside him for the wizard, but there was nothing. Emptiness. 'I have a secret to tell you,' he said.

He couldn't believe he would tell Jasmin. What if she didn't want to be his friend any more? Who wanted to be friends with a wizard? But maybe she already knew. He looked at her face, her shining eyes, the trees around them. He made his tummy as hard as rock. 'I am a wizard. I have superpowers and I can fly and make bad things happen. I can freeze people's brains and start fires with laser eyes. And I can fly. It's true; I can actually fly.'

He held his breath and waited. Jasmin looked at him and blew air towards his face. She didn't say anything for a few seconds; then she looked back towards the school. 'We'd better go back,' she said.

'You don't believe me,' he said, 'do you?'

'Of course I believe you.'

Elijah's mouth dropped open. 'Really?' He was right, he had to be right, and Mama had been right about everything all along. And Jasmin believed him.

'That's why you've got a scar like Harry Potter. He's a wizard and he's got a scar on his head just like yours.' She reached out towards him and touched his forehead. He closed his eyes and let his whole body fill with the smell of honey air and the softness of Jasmin's fingertips and the feeling of being believed.

'Anyway,' whispered Jasmin as he opened his eyes, 'I'm actually a mermaid. And I can breathe underwater.'

★　　★　　★

340

Mum borrowed a small grey dog called Bertie from Battersea for the afternoon so they could all take it for a walk. Bertie yapped and ran around, chasing its own tail until Elijah couldn't help laughing. Dad held his hand one side and Mum held the other, and Granddad walked a little in front of them because he always walked really quickly.

The park was full of children running and kicking balls and riding their bikes. It was a sunny day with no wind, but one little boy was trying to lift his kite in the air and his Dad was running alongside him, throwing it up into the sky. Elijah couldn't feel the wizard creeping around anywhere. They walked through the park and stopped at the park café for Dad to buy four lemonades, then they sat on a bench next to a big tree.

'I love this tree,' said Mum. She put her arm around Elijah and rested her glass of lemonade on top of her belly. It made Elijah smile.

'Me too,' said Dad. He looked at Mum over Elijah's head. 'What's your favourite kind of tree, Elijah?'

'I like all trees,' said Elijah. He sipped his drink.

Mum, Dad and Granddad looked at where Elijah was pointing with his eyes. Bertie had his leg cocked up to one side and was using the tree as a toilet. Granddad chuckled. They watched Bertie run around and around trying to chase a squirrel, then the sky changed colour to almost the same shade as Bertie's fur.

'We better walk back before it starts pouring,' said Mum.

'And especially how slow you walk these days,' said Granddad.

Mum reached towards Dad, waiting for some help up from the bench, but his phone began ringing and he pulled it out of his pocket.

'Hey!' Mum shouted, but Dad was busy walking ahead, talking on the phone. Mum let her arm drop and sat still.

Granddad took the dog's lead from Mum's hand. 'We'll let him chase that squirrel a bit longer.'

Mum got up slowly by herself and walked after Dad, but he was already far away. She was beginning to walk differently: side to side, instead of forward. The baby was growing bigger.

'So, how was the doctor?' Granddad put the lead on top of his lap. 'Mum and Dad told me you went to see the new doctor.'

'He doesn't believe in wizards,' said Elijah. 'Where is Devon?'

'Is that where he's from?'

Elijah nodded.

'Well, no wonder. People in Devon don't believe in anything except cream cakes. Anyway, it doesn't matter. I told you already that there is no wizard inside you.'

'Only you and Jasmin believe in wizards. Everyone else says they don't exist, that if I stop believing, the wizard will go away, like Tinkerbell. But I don't know how to stop believing something that is true.'

Granddad twiddled the lead on his lap and looked at Bertie running back and forth. 'The world is a strange place. It's OK to believe in different things. Lots of people around the world have different beliefs, and that's fine. Do you feel like there's a wizard inside you all the time?'

Elijah shook his head. 'It comes sometimes, but it's always waiting.'

'I can't see one inside you.'

Elijah shrugged. 'It always comes back.'

'I don't think so, Elijah. I think the wizard is gone.'

Elijah looked at Bertie. It was beginning to rain; giant drops landed on top of them. 'No.' He shook his head. 'And I have to show Mum and Dad or they won't be safe, and they won't be able to help me. I have to prove it.'

Granddad pulled him closer, kissed the top of his head. 'You don't need to prove anything. It's OK for people to believe different things.'

'I will prove it,' said Elijah, quietly.

'I love you,' said Granddad. 'My little grandson. And God loves you too.'

They went every week to Chioma. Sometimes they played and sometimes they talked. They saw Ricardo at home. Mum and Dad showed Elijah things from his life-story report and told him things about Mama that Elijah didn't want to hear. Sometimes he felt very angry. He couldn't believe that there was no wizard living in him. He knew there must be because Mama couldn't have been wrong. He couldn't have hurt Mum without the wizard. But everyone told him how Mama was sick and how it was Mama who hurt him, even though she didn't mean to. But Elijah didn't believe it was true. The wizard was not just an idea Mama had put in his head. And it didn't make sense that Mama put the wizard in his head, because all Mama wanted, even more than Elijah, was to get the wizard out.

One week, Mum and Dad said they thought it would be better to go into Ricardo's office, because they had to read him something really hard, and they wanted to do it in the safest place possible. Ricardo opened a file on the table. 'This is the report written by doctors who specialise in grown-ups who have something wrong in their brain. Your mama is very sick, Elijah. And she believes things because she is not well.'

Elijah looked at the report. 'If Mama is sick then everyone from Nigeria must be sick. In Nigeria, everyone knows that wizards exist.'

Ricardo smiled. 'Well, you're right in one way, Elijah. Lots of people believe in wizards in Nigeria. But the vast majority of people in Nigeria, as in the rest of the world, would never dream of hurting a child. Nobody in the world, not your mama and not your church, should hurt a child. You're just a child, Elijah, a wonderful boy. There is no wizard in you. And Dad, Granddad, Chioma, they're all from Nigeria, the exact place your mama is from.

They would never hurt you trying to take a wizard out. Mama is ill and she hears bad voices telling her to do bad things, but those voices aren't real – it's just her mind playing tricks.'

Elijah closed his eyes. The wizard's voice was real. He heard it all the time.

'Mum and Dad need to read something very difficult with you today. It might not make sense at first, but we will talk it through afterwards.' Ricardo nodded at Mum and Dad, who came over to the sofa where Elijah was sitting and sat next to him on either side. Mum lowered herself carefully, keeping her back straight and bending at her knees. They put their hands on top of his as Ricardo read.

Deborah states, 'There is a wizard living in my son and I need to drive it out.' She is also suffering from auditory and visual hallucinations and paranoia that a 'red car is constantly following me and they want to steal my son and use his body parts for magic.'

Elijah was removed from her care after an alleged accident that resulted in Elijah being admitted to Lewisham Emergency department with a head injury and subsequently transferred to King's College Hospital for emergency neurosurgery. The mechanism of injury was never fully explained but on skeletal survey Elijah was discovered to have old fractures and be severely malnourished. He was placed on the child-protection register under the categories of neglect, physical and emotional abuse, and Deborah was transferred to the Bethlem Psychiatric Hospital for assessment and treatment.

The room started spinning around. Elijah started to remember something. They were in the flat and it was cold. The moonlight burnt a patch on to the threadbare carpet. Mama was getting something from the drawer. He saw it coming and he heard her voice. Her face was above him but it looked different: hard.

'Get out of my son!' she screamed. 'Get out of my son!' Her voice was so different from the voice he heard inside him.

She was pressing on to his head with something so very sharp and hard that he almost couldn't speak.

But he somehow managed: 'It's me, Mama. It's Elijah. I'm not a wizard,' he said. 'I'm not a wizard.'

Suddenly, time changed and Mama walked up and down beside him like a leopard in a zoo. She wore stiff fabric that made a creaking sound when she moved. Her hair was not combed, and she was carrying an empty bottle of Coca-Cola, which she kept putting to her mouth as if she'd forgotten it was empty. The hospital was like a space ship: all buzzing, beeping white machines and men in masks. A television screen showed waves in different colours, a pattern, numbers. He was above the bed, looking down at his six-year-old body. Needles the size of earthworms were being pushed into his middle, his neck.

'Put the albumin through the intraosseous line. Syringe it in quickly.'

'Get the cooling mat – pack ice around his head.'

'His pupils have blown – push through some mannitol and furosemide.'

'Get neurosurgery down here quick.'

'Somebody speak to his mother.'

He could see everything. In the next bed, a baby was asleep with a tube in his nose, like Elijah's. He had squiggles on his machine that were the same size every time. His numbers stayed exactly the same. His mama was there, holding his hand, watching the squiggles and waves. The baby was not floating in the air above his bed at all.

Mama knocked over the tray of drugs by her side and, when the tiny glass bottles crashed on to the floor, she just walked over them, crunching them like they were fresh snow. A nurse lowered her mask, took Mama's arm and moved her towards the door; she led her out and told her in the corridor that the doctors were doing their best, and they were a good team, but it was important for her to stay calm – out of the way, and calm. The nurse didn't ask her about what happened, about how they got there. It was only later, after the X-rays had been done, and Elijah had been examined all over, that they began to look at Mama with a stare. He could see everything from above, on the ceiling and through the wide-open curtains in his head.

He watched the doctors working and the nurses drawing up drugs and attaching plastic tubes and sticking down lines. He hurt all over and the hurt was bigger than the world.

'What appears to be the problem with this chap?'

The doctors were more interested in what he looked like on the inside than the outside, and spent a long time looking at scan pictures of what they called blood flow and nerve bundles before waving Mama back into the room. He remembered a rash that spread across his body like the sun setting and brought all the doctors running, putting in more drips and wires and tubes, getting medicine that made him float on the waves on the small screens.

'We want you to look in the mirror, so that you can see the hurt, Elijah. But if you don't feel ready, that's fine.' That nurse was called Florence. She had a smiley face drawn on her badge and her breath smelt like coffee. He nodded. She gave him a small plastic mirror and he held it up. Slowly, slowly, Florence unwound the bandage from his head. Underneath, there was a red line that looked like the zip of his Sunday trousers. Around the edges of the zip, bits of Elijah were bright pink. He moved the mirror around and around until he could see outside the room to the corridor where doctors were walking past, and a cleaner.

He looked for ages. But, by then, Mama wasn't there. She was completely gone.

Elijah opened his eyes. He could hear far away shouting. 'Elijah! Elijah, son, are you OK?'

'It's just a faint and nothing to worry about, but we'd better call a doctor, just in case. There's a first-aider in the office, Nikki; will you go?'

Elijah heard Mum's voice loudly. 'No. No, I'm not leaving. Call an ambulance. Elijah, can you hear me? Elijah! God, what's wrong with him? What's wrong with my son?'

And then suddenly the loudest scream in all the world cut through the voices and Mum's questions and Ricardo's rushing around and Dad's calm. It was his voice.

Elijah screamed and screamed and screamed. He kicked and punched until his knees and knuckles were bleeding and he had no more energy, so that all he could do was fall flat and simply breathe, fast breathing, like a trapped mouse.

Mum and Dad held him so tightly for what seemed like hours and hours, Mum's bump pressed hard against him, but it wasn't long before Elijah's voice stopped screaming and he opened his eyes. He looked at Mum and Dad. 'Mama hurt me, didn't she? Does Mama love me?'

Dad came to his room that evening to tuck him in. He smiled, but Elijah didn't smile back. He couldn't. 'Come on, now,' said Dad, rubbing his hand on top of Elijah's head. 'We can get through this.'

Elijah opened his eyes as widely as they would allow. 'You don't believe in wizards,' he whispered.

'No, Elijah, I don't. Wizards don't exist. Wizards are not real and I won't have any more talk about it.' Dad's face changed. Became harder.

Elijah hugged his knees to his chest.

'I am telling you,' said Dad, leaning down until his face was directly opposite Elijah's face, 'that you're perfectly safe. There is no such thing as wizards. I am telling you a fact. Your birth mother was mentally ill. One of her persistent delusions was that you were possessed, and she tried to physically force the wizard out of you in the most unforgivable way. But wizards are myth.'

He pressed his face against Elijah's cheek, then kissed him, but Elijah tried to pull his head away.

'Wizards are real,' he said. 'I can prove it.'

Dad sat up and pulled the blanket up around Elijah. 'Wizards are not real and you are not proving anything. Now, it's been a long day, Elijah. You're safe and sound now and I want you to have sweet dreams tonight. Goodnight. Tomorrow we'll play football.'

Dad smiled again before leaving the room. Elijah lay looking at the darkness. He dreamt about

Mama and heard her voice in his heart. *We invented the meaning of love, you and I, little son.*

It was real. It was true.

That night, Elijah dreamt. Mama was above, looking at him, and her face was flat. He could smell her: burning plantain. Her eyelids had dropped and her cheek skin was hanging from her bones. 'Give me back my little baby,' she whispered.

He reached up and said, 'It's me! It's me!' but she didn't hear.

'Little Nigeria,' she whispered, 'when you come back to me, I'll take you home. We'll save the money and leave this place. An aeroplane ride: in no time at all we will be back with our family, who will help us and save us. Uncle Pastor will protect you there from any other wizards entering you. We will build up your strength with Mummy's cooking and, before you know, you will be a round and running boy with straight legs and a straight back, and my balance will be returned. I will be restored and the spinning will stop. There will be no more insects crawling around inside my head. Times will be different – better. How I love you, little son of mine.'

She stopped whispering and leant down. Her words sounded so clear. When she touched Elijah's back, her hand was soft. He looked at her next to him; she was sitting down. Her other arm was behind her back. She rubbed him and he felt every movement on his spine through the T-shirt he was wearing. He wished she'd lie down next to him and they could both close their eyes and go to sleep together and never wake up. Leave the wizard to do whatever it wanted. It was pushed all the way down inside Elijah now that Mama was near. Mama's love was so strong, it might be enough. Elijah let her rub his back and he looked at her face. She looked straight back at him. He felt the corners of his mouth turn upwards.

'Mama,' he whispered. 'It's me. Elijah.'

Suddenly she leant forward and there was hardness in her face. She thought it was the wizard talking.

'Get out of my son!' she said and she pulled her other hand in front of her. A screwdriver was there, the one she sometimes ran up and down the back of her leg, pressing herself so the hurt on her outside was more than the hurt on her inside. He wondered if she was going to press herself. She looked at his eyes and leant close. Closer than before.

'Mama,' he whispered. 'It's me. Elijah.' His voice sounded strange coming out – a quiet breath. His throat was still dry from burns a few weeks before. Maybe his throat would always be dry.

'Get out of my son.' Her hand was pushing his body down into the carpet. 'Get out of my son!' she screamed, and he couldn't see her face at all. All he could see was the screwdriver above his eyes. It came slowly and pressed. The screwdriver hurt was stronger, biting. The pain filled every corner of him. He wanted it. Elijah wanted it to carry on, him and Mama and the pain pushing the hurt out, there on the carpet. Just them. She positioned her body above the screwdriver and began leaning onto it. She was praying. He thought of crying, but with Mama there next to him, there was no reason to. Whatever happened, she was there next to him.

CHAPTER 38

Little one,
There are places in this world that are stranger than dreams. When I first arrived, I remembered the Centre for Mentally Ill Destitutes in Lagos, where you could hear the patients screaming from the end of the road. I felt such a sense of panic that it was as though my face belonged to another person. The Greenfields Women's Psychiatric Hospital was a long set of rooms, each filled with wild-eyed women who had stories to tell but would never tell them. I shared a room with three such women. The first, Nicola, a depressive, had a smile on her lips that appeared to be glued there. Even asleep (I crept out of bed one night and peered over her face), her smile remained, as if she was not real and only the smile was. The second shared a name with my sister, Miriam, and was Yoruba but she'd never been to her own country. Imagine that. She liked to ask me questions all day and got me to teach her the odd words of our language.

'E'karbo,' she said, as I entered the room. It was getting annoying hearing back the words I'd taught her, in her thick English accent. She sat on my bed. I was having a day when I didn't feel like talking. They had reduced the tablets they were giving me twice a day: a small plastic cup full of pills that made me think less about you being full with wizard, and imagine you healthy and running after a football. I gobbled them up like sweets. They said I was becoming addicted. But the tablets were the only thing that numbed my stomach until the twisting knife stopped turning and the picture of your face covered in blood became softer.

'When I get out of here,' Miriam sang in her voice like a thick English coat, 'I'm going to get totally fucked up. My boyfriend will sort me out. You should come with me; I mean, we can get some good shit where I live. Best medicine in the world!' She put her face next to my ear. 'Anything you want. Crack, crystal meth: that is some good shit.'

I closed my eyes. Miriam told me about the place she went to for drugs, but I already knew where it was: the door, a few doors down from ours, with comings and goings and sweet burning smells. I tried not to think of you growing up in a country where Nigerian children could end up like Miriam, on drugs and cursing with every breath. Not my son. Nigeria does not produce such caricatures. Not even for rich oyinbos. Thank God that she'd never made it to Nigeria – she would have been beaten black and blue for such language. The market women would have dragged her weave straight out of her hair. But then, if she'd been in Nigeria, she would never have ended that way, Elijah. Of that I'm certain.

The third woman was not a woman at all, but a young girl who was quiet and had eyes that moved too suddenly. Her body was so thin I could see her insides and she had a layer of soft hair on her face like down on a newborn chick. Every night, the nurses came in and held her down and put a tube into her nose while her body twisted and turned, trying to get away from it. 'Come on, now, dear,' they said. 'Jody, dear, we need to get this into you and the sooner you lie still, the sooner it will be over. Really, if you didn't keep pulling out your N.G. tubes, we wouldn't be in this situation.'

After she'd writhed around for at least half an hour, her body usually gave up and she lay flat – too flat, like she was made of cardboard. And they'd put the tube down and then hang a bottle of sour-smelling milk above her all night. Instead of sleeping, I watched it drip, imagined you.

Doctor Phillips was not scared of anything. I could see in his eyes that stared straight at mine that he wasn't scared of me, not like the nurse who kept one arm behind her back the whole time and the other nurse who looked at the door whenever he came into a room that I was in. It's a terrible thing for people to be frightened of you, Elijah. It makes everything seem frightening.

'How's it going, Deborah?' He had his long legs

crossed in front of him and I could tell by his mismatched socks and scuffed-up shoes that he was not married. Either that or his wife was a lazy woman. I thought of Akpan, how his socks always matched. Funny the things you remember.

I smiled in as normal a way as possible. How could I tell him that I wanted to die? That they had taken you from me?

'Fine,' I said. 'I'm much better, thank you. Can I see my son, Elijah, now, please?'

I held my breath, but the doctor's face told me everything. He uncrossed his legs and sat up in his chair. There was a pile of notes on a small table beside him: my notes. I recognised my name, even though my eyes were blurred from the tablets, my head full of fog. The notes looked too big, bursting out of the folder.

'Deborah, mental illness should be no different from physical illness. Think of it as a bad break in your arm. It will take doctors and medicine and perhaps a long time to treat, but ultimately your arm will function as it did before. You will, in time, hopefully, be able to do all the things you did. But I have to tell you, Deborah . . .' He sat forward and put his arm over mine. Was that the broken one? It didn't feel broken. It felt fine. I moved it suddenly and opened and closed my hand. My hand felt bigger, giant almost, like another person's hand. It made me smile suddenly, then wonder why I was smiling.

In Nigeria, it didn't matter if you were mad with

357

sadness or with evil spirits or with marijuana drug. Mad was mad. I would be in the Centre for Mentally Ill Destitutes, if I was lucky. Or, if not, walking on the intersection of the road with urine covering my legs, one shoe on, one shoe off.

'Do you understand what I'm saying to you, Deborah? You have a serious condition. But not an untreatable one.'

'Am I sick?' I lifted my arm up and down. My arm was floating away from me.

'Yes, Deborah. You're very unwell. We think you have a serious condition which causes you to hear the voices. It makes you believe things that are not real.'

It panicked me, Elijah, that this stranger could think my thoughts. Did he know about the red car? About what was inside it?

'The voices are real,' I said. 'I can hear them very clearly. I am not a lunatic. I am spiritually gifted. My husband told me that a long time ago.' The fog lifted enough that I saw your face, Elijah, covered with blood, a bedroom full of drawn-on men, and Akpan's black shoe. I sobbed.

'We never use that word: lunatic. One in three people suffers mental ill-health at some point or other. And I know that in Nigeria things are very different. But here in the U.K. you will have access to proper treatment in this hospital and, when you're stable, you'll be able to be cared for in the community. You've been suffering a long time, Deborah, and now we know what's wrong we'll be able to help you recover. The medicines we use are so effective, we hope it won't take long at all to stabilise you.'

I looked around the room. If I was home in Nigeria, they wouldn't have given me an official diagnosis of anything. I'd have been taken to the Centre for Mentally Ill Destitutes, where my sisters would have come in every day to wash me and refresh my hair. There, in that place, the only people who talked to me was the girl who would not eat and Miriam, who had taken so many drugs her eyes did not look in the same direction. The doctor had his eyebrows raised, waiting for me to speak.

'Thank you, doctor,' I said. But I did not believe him one little bit. It was not mental ill-health that caused the voices. I had a spiritual gift. It was the voice of evil, and sometimes of God. Akpan had told me himself. I had a gift that they were trying to destroy. I was under spiritual attack.

I thought of Uncle Pastor and everything we believed. This doctor was insane. But I could play a part, Elijah. I was a clever woman, even with my imbalance. And I knew, in order to get you back next to me, I'd do anything.

But I suddenly thought of something. If they gave me medicines to stop the voices, how would I protect you? How could I possibly protect my own son when I couldn't hear the evil wizard talking to me? The wizard would surely kill you – take away my son forever. Had it worked? Had

I driven out the wizard with the screwdriver? I would never know unless I heard those voices. The quiet voices, whispering. God's voice. I suddenly knew what I needed to do.

I would have to be very careful. I would do everything they said in that prison. Eat the tablets. Talk. Tell Miriam about her own country. Ignore the bird girl being held down flat. I would do anything to save you. Anything at all.

At night, I could hear the flat bird girl wait until the staff had held her down, and then rip and cough and drip her sour milk on the floor underneath her bed. After that, she pushed her fingers into her mouth and vomited into her pillowcase. She was not a skilled vomiter. The church women would have been able to vomit by merely thinking of it – no fingers required. They could teach her a thing or two. Rebekah would have fallen over with laughter.

'Are you awake?' Miriam was next to my bed. I could smell her unwashed armpits. I closed my eyes tightly and pretended. I was getting good at pretending. I thought of you every second. 'Psst! Psst! Sister, are you awake?'

Suddenly she climbed into bed with me and pressed herself against my body. I sat up and moved away. 'Get out!' I whispered. 'What are you doing?'

But then I saw that her face was full of tears.

'I'm sorry,' she whispered. 'I just can't sleep. I can't. I really need to take my medicine. On the street, I mean; the medicine helps me. This shit here doesn't help. They're killing me.'

I looked at the door. I thought of calling a nurse, but something in Miriam's face stopped me. I noticed for the first time how young she was. How broken.

'What's wrong? What do you want me to do about it? Go back to bed, silly girl. Go back.'

She shook her head so fast. 'I can't. They're killing me. Let me sleep with you. Please. I know I'll die if I stay alone. I need my medicine.' She had scratched off lines of her skin and bled tiny droplets on to the white sheets.

'I have enough problems,' I said. 'Go back to bed.' I didn't tell her about you. I didn't speak about it to any of the other women. I didn't want your name in their mouths.

But something stopped me from pushing Miriam out of the bed, Elijah. Maybe it was the way she looked so frightened. Or maybe it was the way I was so frightened. Either way, she slept in my bed that night and every night after that. When the nurses had done their twelve o'clock checks, she'd sneak across the room and climb in, and I'd move over, allowing in the smell of unwashed armpits and terrible breath. And a few nights after that, the bird girl climbed in bed with us both, lying next to me, so tiny and fragile I didn't dare move in case I crushed her. We twisted and turned, us three. We were not a soup full of sisters, but still, for a short time, we were not quite so alone.

CHAPTER 39

Even though things were getting better, it was hard not to watch Elijah, to study him and his behaviour, over-analyse everything. Nikki had to force her eyes to look away, to make them focus on the clock, or the window.

And Elijah would look up with sad, kind eyes. When Daddy and Jasmin and Chanel were there it was better and felt almost back to normal, but when it was just the three of them it was still too quiet. Obi was making a real effort, but a couple of nights she had woken to find the bed next to her empty, Obi poring over his papers in the kitchen. Once, he had even pretended not to hear her when she told him to come back to bed. And Elijah had changed too much. Nikki began to panic. She'd kept her emotions in check so far, but now they were spiralling away from her.

'I'm going over to Chanel's, but I won't be long. Shall we play a game later?' she said to them both, father and son sitting side by side, yet not close. 'How about Guess Who?'

'Yes, please,' whispered Elijah. His voice was so small. He looked at Nikki's tummy and back up at her eyes. She wanted to scoop him up and whisper into his ear that she loved him, but he seemed far away. His quietness scared her.

Nikki walked out; Chanel was waiting for her. 'Where's Jasmin?'

'She has a play date. Come on.'

Chanel was wearing a pair of pyjamas that had a picture of a cherry on the front and lettering underneath, which said, *Bite Me*. Nikki smiled, despite herself. She followed Chanel up to her flat, where they sat next to each other on the couch.

'How's it going?'

Nikki opened her mouth to talk, but all that came out was a giant sob. Chanel moved quickly towards her, put her arms around Nikki and held her. She let her cry and cry. Chanel smelt of cigarettes. 'What now, love? What now?'

'I feel like a cigarette,' said Nikki, unravelling herself from Chanel.

'What! Miss Goody Two-Shoes? You've never smoked in your life!' She laughed. 'And I don't think now is the right time to start . . .' Chanel pointed to Nikki's tummy.

'It won't matter, anyway,' sobbed Nikki. 'I'll probably still lose the baby, like I lost all the others.'

Chanel held her so tightly she could barely breathe. 'There, come on, now. You let it all out.'

Nikki leant back. 'I mean, nothing is the same. Nothing. Obi is worried all the time and he was always so sure of everything. If Obi's not sure, then I just don't feel safe. He's not even reading his books any more. And Elijah is so sad-looking, so worried and quiet.'

Chanel nodded.

'What he's been through, Chanel, he might never recover fully. We might never make him happy. I feel such a failure – to Obi, to the baby, to Elijah. How can I call myself a mum?'

Chanel snorted, and put her hand up to her mouth.

Nikki stopped crying. 'Are you . . . Are you laughing at me? Really? Are you laughing? Because, if you think this is funny . . .'

Chanel stopped laughing. 'Always, "Poor Nikki". Poor Nikki this; poor Nikki that. I'm sick of it.'

Nikki sat up. She started to stand, 'I'll go then, shall I?'

Chanel pushed her back down on the couch. 'Sit yourself down. Listen for once.'

Nikki sat down and looked at Chanel.

'You are the best mum I know,' she said. 'Jasmin would give anything to have a mum like you. The best. Any child would be lucky to have you, but Elijah wasn't just lucky. He needed you. Now, I don't believe in God and all that bollocks, but I'm telling you that the only mum I know who could love him as much as you do, is you. And I know how much you love him every time I mention his name. The way you look at him . . . I wish, I wish for a second that I could look at Jas that way. And she wishes it too. And this baby will be born and this baby will be fine. I just know it. So get a grip.

Stop feeling sorry for yourself. You've got everything you ever wanted, and so what if there was a blip? You're a lucky cow.'

Nikki's mouth dropped open. She had no words to answer Chanel. None at all. She sat still for a few minutes.

Chanel moved closer to Nikki and put her arms around her. She stroked her hair. 'And, as for Obi, Obi loves going into battle, but this is new territory for him, and for all of us. But you all love each other and you all want this baby. It will be fine in the end, you wait and see.'

Nikki closed her eyes, let Chanel hold her.

Chanel whispered in her ear. 'You won't lose this one. You're seven months gone already. You won't lose this one. I promise.' She moved her head away and took a big breath. 'The doctors know what they're doing now.'

'Do you really think so?' asked Nikki.

'I know so; yes, there's a lot at stake, but I don't believe you can't cope. Look at how you've got through what happened. Thousands would have given up, but not you and Obi. And not Elijah. He's strong too, you know? Do you remember when we were little, and you fell off the top of that climbing frame?'

Nikki nodded. She was still taking in Chanel's words. 'It frightened the dinner ladies to death,' she murmured.

'God, it was so high. And you literally landed on your head. I remember it like it was yesterday.

And you just stood up, without a single tear in your eye, turned around, lifted your nose in the air and climbed right back up again.'

Nikki remembered. It had been a cold day, and the bars of the climbing frame had made her fingers numb.

'I was standing right next to the dinner lady who watched you fall and then get up. She looked at you and spoke to the other ladies. "She's made of really strong stuff. Won't let anything beat her, that girl."' Chanel kissed Nikki's cheek. 'Go home,' she whispered. 'Be a mum. Be happy.'

The next few days, Nikki heard Chanel's words wherever she went. She even dreamed them. Chanel was right, of course. Her sister was often wrong, but she was right about the important things, especially how much Nikki loved Elijah. She let herself begin to feel lucky again, to be his mum, to be a family. She felt more confident.

'Elijah, stop pinching your nose,' Nikki whispered. 'It will get very sore.' He had started doing that again. He was very quiet and he kept closing his eyes like he was far away.

'OK, Mum.'

She kissed his head. 'You really miss your mama, don't you?' she said.

Elijah looked straight at her eyes. He didn't move a muscle but his eyes filled up with tears. He looked surprised.

'It's OK to talk about her, you know. You used to

talk about her sometimes. You can talk about anything with me or Dad, because we're your parents forever. And our job is to keep you safe, always.'

Elijah smiled. He dropped his hand into hers. They were in the living room with Obi and it was late afternoon. Ricardo had phoned and arranged a meeting for the next day. Elijah had been nose pinching, but it seemed to be getting slightly better, though he sat unusually still most of the time.

Nikki made her voice light. 'Shall we have a new book tonight? We've finished *Treasure Island*.'

'That would be really nice. Thank you.'

'*Treasure Island* is one of the only novels I've ever read all the way to the end,' Obi said. 'But I prefer non-fiction. When you're a bit older, I'll start reading you some of my research papers.' Obi laughed. 'You don't need pirates when you have the *New Law Journal*.'

Nikki noticed that Elijah wasn't laughing with Obi.

As she tucked Elijah in that night, she kissed his cheeks and pressed her hands together underneath his back. 'Now we're locked together,' she said.

He smiled. 'You can have a cuddle in my bed if you want.'

Nikki climbed in beside him. 'Of course!' His body was so warm. She held him close and hummed a few nursery rhymes. His eyes did not close at all. 'Aren't you tired?' she asked.

'Not tonight,' he said. He turned his body to face

hers and put his hands on top of her stomach. 'I'm sorry for what I did,' he whispered. 'I'm really sorry.'

'We're going to be all right,' said Nikki, kissing his hands and then his head, patting her own stomach. 'All of us.'

Elijah pulled up her T-shirt. Nikki's skin was ghostly white in the lamplight, the skin on her stomach stretching and changing shape. Elijah rubbed his hands together and blew inside them. Then he gently put them on Nikki's stomach and laid his cheek on top. He closed his eyes and Nikki watched the rise and fall of her stomach as she breathed, her son's face. She couldn't work out what he was thinking. His eyes looked different from before. Sad, but not frightened any more. Whatever strange thought had entered his head, whatever memory had caused him to attack her, was gone from his eyes. He must have worked it through. It was a sudden explosion of all that had happened to him, and now there was calm to build upon.

'I'm sorry,' he whispered to Nikki's skin. 'The baby is safe now, isn't she?'

Nikki's eyes shone. 'She is,' she whispered.

Then he looked at Nikki very closely.

'What are you doing?'

'Looking at your freckles. You've got lots and that's really lucky.'

Nikki laughed. She closed her eyes and tried to hold the moment deep inside her heart.

CHAPTER 40

Elijah,

Time was passing and I was winning. I smiled and smiled. I planned to get out as quickly as possible and track you down, find you and rescue you. I'd make sure that the wizard had left your body and would never return. I wanted to get a message to Bishop, but there was no way of sending letters without the nurses checking every detail and, in order to play their game, I pretended to be compliant. When they put me in a special nightshirt and had me sign a form, I didn't really hear the words they spoke: 'Affecting short-term memory . . .' I simply nodded and smiled. They took me to the small room and put stickers on the side of my head. I didn't really understand what was going on.

The first sticker went over the side of my head and the second went over the very front. The stickers were small and smelt a bit like Flash wipes. They were attached to a small machine that a nurse had covered with a towel. Two doctors were in the room talking over me, as if they couldn't see me lying there.

A needle pushed into my arm and the doctors stopped talking. They put a mask near my mouth with foul-smelling cold air blowing out of it. A nurse squeezed my hand.

'First, they'll put you off to sleep and then give you a medicine to stop your body moving at all. Then they'll give the treatment and we'll wake you up in about ten minutes. OK?'

I closed my eyes, ready. I didn't care what they did to me, Elijah. I closed my eyes and imagined a deep sleep and no dreams. I imagined your beautiful face with brown eyes and felt the coldness travel up my arm and then there was nothing.

When I woke, my body was too still. I moved my fingers slowly and opened my eyes. The room looked the same, but something was not right. The doctors were still talking and the nurse was still holding my hand, but I could feel something bad in my heart, turning the blood hard. I closed my eyes again to look for your face, but suddenly I realised you were gone. Elijah! I searched inside myself, my mind running over memories like hot stones, and there was nothing. The place in my head which held pictures of you was empty! You were gone! I searched my mind and my thoughts and my head, but you weren't there. 'Elijah,' I whispered. 'Elijah!' But you were gone from inside me. For the first time since you had been born, I felt emptiness in my core that was greater than the sky. It was greater than everything. It swallowed me up. I shouted. I cried and cried. They had taken you from me again. Elijah, my son, my little Nigeria. Nothing would be the same any more. I was broken into sections and you were gone. My love, my heart, my centre. Elijah, England took you from me, my little Elijah. My little Nigeria.

CHAPTER 41

Elijah opened his eyes and did not blink. In his bedroom he saw the antlers that Granddad had screwed to his wall, making shapes in the darkness like a hundred tiny knives cutting his room to pieces, the world to pieces. It was late. He could hear Dad's soft snoring and Mum groaned in her sleep every so often, which is something she'd only done since it happened.

Since the wizard tried to hurt her baby.

His baby sister.

They said that the wizard was something Mama had dreamed and, because she was sick in her head, she couldn't tell the difference. But how could Mama's dream get inside Elijah's head? And now they told him that Mama hurt him badly. Every time he closed his eyes, he remembered and he wanted to scratch out the memory, but he couldn't. It waited there for him like a wolf under a tree. He had to make sense of it. 'There is a wizard,' he said aloud. 'There has to be.' But he couldn't feel anything at all. There had to be a wizard. If there was no wizard, then he had hurt Mum. He had hurt his sister. And he would never have hurt Mum, or his sister. It could only have been the wizard. Mama: the wizard was real because Mama loved him. And if there was no wizard then Mama hurt him for no reason.

If there was no wizard then Mama didn't love him at all.

There were only two things of which he was certain:

Wizards were real.

And Mama loved him.

He felt a pain so sharply in his shoulder that he called out, but nobody came; the snoring noises continued. He watched the magic dust gathering in the air. He knew what he had to do.

Elijah stretched out one foot, then the other. He pulled back the quilt and stepped into the darkness. He walked to the window and opened it, letting the cool air come up to his face. It was a perfect night. The stars were bright enough that he found very quickly the best one where Mama would surely be looking. Their eyes in the same place. He thought of Mama. And Mum and Dad asleep, a baby between them.

A flash opposite caught Elijah's eye and he realised that Jasmin was up and looking out of her window too. She waved and flashed her torch. He didn't wave back, but he was glad she would see it. A witness to prove that Mama was right. To prove that she'd loved him all along. He didn't think much about afterwards, about what might happen. But a fluttering at the back of his heart wondered if it might be possible, if it might just be possible that he could live with Mama again, once they knew the truth. He and Mama could live nearby, or even share a room at Mum and Dad's house, so that Mum and Dad could help with things like dinners and going to school, and Mama could help with wizards and praying. They would make a very good team.

Jasmin flashed her torch again and again. She was using the special code and she flashed the torch three times quickly then one slow flash. He knew that meant she wanted to knock in the morning and walk to school together. But there wasn't a code for what he wanted to reply: that wizards were real and he would prove it. A code to tell her not to worry, and that he knew what to do; that, in the end, it would all be all right. Elijah looked up at the patch of sky. He could see Mama's face in it, beautiful and soft. He lifted himself up to sit on the window ledge and pushed his feet out, dangling his legs over the edge. He closed his eyes and breathed in the fresh air. It was cold but, inside his body, he was hot. He knew that the wizard would be inside him, even though he couldn't feel it at all. He felt empty, hollow, like the inside of an old tree. There were knives in his head, and insects crawling. But he didn't worry. He was certain of two things:

The wizard was real.

Mama loved him.

He opened his eyes and looked over to Jasmin, who was flashing and flashing but it wasn't a code at all, just flashes. He could see her mouth open wide and she was banging on her window. Her hand was spread out like a starfish and she had her face pressed to the glass. She was saying something. Shouting. He saw Aunty Chanel's bedroom light turn on and then Jasmin's bedroom door open and Aunty Chanel rush in. Aunty Chanel ran towards the window. Her hand went up to her mouth and she ran out of the room. Jasmin stayed up against the glass, flashing her torch and shouting. Elijah smiled. Her face was beautiful, even pressed against the glass. His best friend, surrounded by a map of the whole world that she would see. He put his thumb up, to show that he was OK. He caught some moonlight in his hand. He breathed the magic air.

He took a long look at Jasmin. He could see she was crying all the way across the street. She had stopped shouting and was looking. She didn't put her thumb up at all, but lifted her torch next to her face and flashed it five slow times: I love you.

Elijah felt his whole body fill up with warmth. He took a cold breath and closed his eyes, pressed himself down on the window ledge. He heard his own bedroom door open, and Dad shout. He turned his head quickly to see Dad's strong Nigerian face. Elijah looked straight at him. 'Dad,' he whispered, and smiled the biggest smile he could. Then he pushed himself off and up in one movement until he was away from the window and the house and in the sky itself. And then he was flying.

CHAPTER 42

The Children's Intensive Care Unit buzzed and beeped and alarmed with screeching noises and nurses running to and from bed-spaces. There was a row of children, sicker than Nikki could have ever imagined, children who looked unreal, plastic, with tubes poking from their mouths and noses and arms and necks, surrounded by machinery, bags of blood and fluid, which Obi kept looking at. But Nikki couldn't stop looking at their eyes, half shut, eyelashes filled with some sort of thick, clear substance, which could have been Vaseline, or it could have been tears so cold they had frozen.

'Too busy,' said Daddy, who sat next to Nikki, her hand in his. 'When will the doctors come to us? This ward round is taking too long.'

Nikki looked at Elijah. His eyes, too, were frozen half shut, suspended somewhere – like the rest of him, like them all – between night and day, or life and death. She wanted so much for him to open his eyes and look at her, and cry warm tears. A tube came out from his nose and connected him to a breathing machine that made sucking noises and then beeped. It was quite therapeutic, the noise of the machine. Especially during last night. She'd spent the night with her head resting on the side of his bed, curled over her bump, despite the nurses' insistence that she rest.

'I don't want to rest,' she'd said. Nikki didn't want to do anything else but be next to Elijah. The baby was pressing on her bladder; she had to force herself to go to the toilet, and she ran back, squirting alcohol gel on her hands on the way. She didn't want to waste time washing her hands in the toilets. What if . . . The thought was too much to bear. The baby inside her kicked, as if it sensed Nikki's mood. Impossible, Obi had said. But nothing was impossible, she thought, looking at Elijah. Her beautiful son, with his eyes stuck half shut and three tubes sticking out of his neck carrying his blood in and out, the shape of them making him look like he was a strange exotic flower. My son.

'Is it that same doctor?' Daddy squeezed her hand and looked over Nikki's shoulder at Obi, who alternated between waiting by the bedside and pacing the corridors outside, his face puffed up from crying. 'He was nice.'

'They're all being nice,' whispered Obi. 'That's their job. But I liked the one who was really honest.' He turned his head away. Nikki had noticed that he couldn't look at his dad, or her. It was as if he'd gone into a bubble. She reached behind her and took his arm, pulling him round her.

'I'm sorry,' Obi whispered. 'I'm sorry for all of it.'

Nikki looked at him. 'You can hold his hand if you want,' she said. 'He might be able to hear us.'

Instead of Obi pulling away, as Nikki had thought he would, he leant towards her. 'Do you think he can hear us?'

She turned. Seeing Obi cry was almost the worst part of it. His face had given up already; it was a different face, one that couldn't fix everything, that got things wrong sometimes. Very wrong.

'I got the letters from Ricardo, written to Elijah. He told me to read the latest one, if we had the chance.'

Nikki let go of Daddy's hand. 'What do you mean? What letters?'

'The letters from her – from Deborah. She's been writing to him all this time. Ricardo kept them. The letters,' said Obi. 'Oh, Nik, the letters . . .'

Nikki looked at Elijah and listened for the sucking ventilator noises and she looked at the screen above him with the waves. She looked back at his face, his soft skin, the shape of his ear.

'I don't want to see them,' Nikki whispered.

The door near the bed-space buzzed and Chanel and Jasmin were there. Chanel was wearing, for the first time since they had been adults, a white shirt and pair of jeans – no rips – and trainers. Her face was drawn and grey, the patches underneath her eyes almost hollow. Nikki realised she wasn't wearing any make-up. Not a scrap.

Jasmin stood beside her, her ponytail perfectly still as she looked at Elijah. 'Why have they made him into a robot?' she said. And then she began to cry. Chanel held her.

'I saw him jump down,' Jasmin said, 'and I tried to flash my torch and I told him that he couldn't really fly, not really, just like I'm not really going to America, not really, but he wouldn't listen; he just jumped right out the window and I saw him smash.' She sobbed. 'Mummy, I saw him. I'm not really going to America, Mummy, am I? I don't want to go to America, Mummy; I want to stay with you . . .'

'Shhh . . .' Chanel hushed Jasmin's head and pulled her close, kissed her. 'You're not going anywhere, baby. Not ever. Come on, Jasmin. Let's say hi to Elijah and then get a cup of tea. OK?'

Jasmin went to the other side of the bed, ignoring the nurse who was injecting something into a bag of fluid. She bent down to Elijah and kissed his cheek. 'I meant what I said with my torch,' she said between sobs. 'You're my best friend.'

Chanel took her back to the door, where she turned and looked at Nikki and put her hand over her heart, before opening the door and ushering Jasmin out.

Daddy looked up at the nurse. Another nurse had come and alarms were beeping on Elijah's monitor and people were rushing. 'I think I'll leave you both to have some time,' he said to Nikki. 'But I need to speak to you first.' He looked at her. 'He needs to hear those letters,' Daddy said. 'He doesn't think his mother loved him. That's why he jumped. He was trying to prove there was a wizard inside him. He told me he wanted to prove it.' His voice was breaking. 'I should have said something, stopped it . . .'

'You couldn't have known what he was thinking,' said Nikki. 'None of us did.'

Daddy sat on the end of the bed, ignoring all the rushing going on around him. He picked up Elijah's hand, careful not to dislodge the tubes coming from it.

'You are the best grandson a man could ever ask for,' he said. He began to cry. 'Don't worry, little Elijah. The wizard is gone now.' He bent over and kissed Elijah on the forehead, at the point where the bandage met his skin. 'The wizard is gone now.'

Daddy kissed Nikki on the way out and put his hand on Obi's shoulder, then left the ward without looking back.

Obi picked up Nikki's hand and squeezed. He smiled, kissed her tears. Nikki looked at the letters he took out of his coat pocket and nodded.

He started to read, his voice clear and unbroken, louder than the alarms, louder than the machines:

'Elijah, this will be my last letter. I need to go home. I want to be near my family and feel the sun on my face, smell the fiery air and walk barefoot on warm red earth. I want to

feel my heart swell with the music of your baba
and sing with the words of Uncle Pastor.
I want you to do some things for me, Elijah.'

Obi paused and sniffed. Nikki leant closer to him to see the letter. She rested her head on his strong shoulder. She wanted to see her writing. Nikki gasped.

The words that Obi spoke were there in front of them, but they were surrounded by scribblings and drawings of demonic faces, piercing eyes. Nikki's breathing slowed down to almost nothing. The entire border of the page was a mess of lines and squares, horrible pictures drawn in biro – scratched so hard the paper had ripped in places. It shocked Nikki to see Deborah's pictures. It made her think how difficult it must have been to get the beautiful sentences out, to force the important words to stand out. Nikki focused her eyes on the sentence at the centre of the page:

I need to go home.

Obi looked at Nikki. He kissed her nose, then her cheek, and pulled her closer to him. And, with his other hand, he lowered the letter and began to read again, his words strong and true and sure, and so kind – the kindest words he'd ever said – and filled with emotion and love, and Nikki loved Obi then more than she'd ever loved him before.
She bent down and put her cheek next to Elijah's.

She breathed him in, whispered, 'I will love you forever,' closed her eyes and tuned out all the alarms and bleeps. She listened only to the sound of Elijah inside her heart, telling her that he loved dogs and laughing like a child should, and the voice of Obi reading to their son:

'I want you to visit Nigeria one day, and find your family.

I want you to be a good son for your new mum and dad, as you were to me and Baba. And grow up safe and tall and happy. Because that will make me prouder of you than any woman who ever lived. Come find me one day, Elijah. Find me in a place where women are kings, and where we will look at the stars together and you will tell me everything. I will tell you all about how much you are loved.

I will be waiting for you there.
Deborah.'

There were running footsteps and machines starting up, and someone shouting, and moving in front of Elijah. 'What's happening?' Nikki opened her eyes, sat up.

The numbers on the computer were all changing. Everything bleeped a high-pitched sound. A doctor and two nurses were by the bed. One of them closed the curtain around the bed-space. A red trolley was wheeled in, with tiny drawers. A cardboard tray sat on top, which a nurse put syringes on, with bright labels attached to them. A bag of fluid appeared, a box that had the words *CRASH BLOOD*. A drawer was taken out of the red trolley; inside was a metal blade with a green handle and long thin plastic tubes. A green bag attached to oxygen was put on Elijah's pillow and a nurse took him off the ventilator and hooked him up to the green bag. Elijah's chest bubbled. Everything alarmed. One nurse pulled back the covers and stuck stickers on top of Elijah's skin, then attached him to another machine, switched it on. Nikki saw the pattern of Elijah's heartbeat on the machine: the pattern was changing, the squiggly lines becoming bigger.

'What's happening?' said Nikki. They were inside the curtain. 'Do you want to stay?' a nurse asked them. Nikki nodded. She looked at Obi and searched for something in his face that told her everything would somehow be OK. She thought she heard a baby cry. 'What's happening?'

The nurses looked to one another. They were flicking through his notes, looking at the alarms, pulling on aprons and gloves. The nurse with the green bag stuck a long thin tube down Elijah's breathing tube and suctioned out fluid. She put the breathing machine back on. Nikki could see the outline of more nurses and another doctor appearing behind the curtain. She could see one of them pick up the telephone and another pull a red emergency bell. Time slowed down.

One of the nurses stood over Elijah on the

opposite side of the bed. 'Elijah's heart isn't pumping properly,' she said. 'It's slowing down and we're giving him some medicine to try and speed it up. OK?'

Obi pulled Nikki towards him. He held her so close she could barely breathe. Then he let her go and moved their chairs a few inches forwards, right next to Elijah's bed, and they both touched him. Elijah, waxy and grey, his chest rising artificially high with each breath. The shape of his eyebrows, his curled eyelashes, perfect lips. Nikki looked at their son. The nurse was giving an injection of something into one of the lines in Elijah's neck. Then the line on the monitor flattened. She pressed her fingers against the side of Elijah's neck. Nikki wanted to pull her off and shout:

LEAVE MY SON ALONE!

'He's arrested!' The nurse climbed on to the bed and, with one of her hands, she started pushing down hard on to Elijah's chest.

Nikki screamed. A nurse stood next to them and helped Nikki up from the chair, then moved the chairs back out of the way. 'You can stay if you want,' she said. 'Elijah's heart has stopped and we're trying to get it started. There will be lots of people rushing around, but you can be with him. If you want?'

Nikki looked at Obi. His face was wet with tears. A doctor came in and began pushing some more medicine into Elijah's neck. Another nurse stood over Elijah's body and squeezed a bag of blood into him.

Nikki didn't want to see it. She wanted to close her eyes and not ever see her son being pressed down into the bed so hard, listen to the sound of his bones cracking under the weight of the nurse's hand. She didn't want to see blood squeezed into his little body. She didn't want to see Obi's face wet with tears. But she walked forwards, anyway, pulled Obi with her, reached out and held Elijah's hand.

It was cold. So cold.

She watched Elijah's skin glow bright then dull: a candle blown out in darkness.

'I don't regret it,' she said. 'Not even now. I don't regret a minute of it.' She looked up at Obi's face. 'I'm not sorry at all,' she whispered.

Nikki held Elijah's cold hand and lifted it, kissed him. She told him in her heart that she loved him, and always would, and she understood. She understood. She looked at Elijah's little hand in hers, studied the lines on his palm, the shape of each of his fingers, his short half-bitten nails.

The nurses and doctors around the bed were starting to look at each other. 'We've had no change,' they said. The nurse next to Nikki put her arm on her shoulder. 'We are doing our very best, but Elijah's heart is not responding to the treatment,' she said.

His heart is broken, thought Nikki. She looked at him, blocking out all the medical staff. She had never seen a more beautiful face. For some reason, his scar had almost disappeared and his skin looked perfectly smooth, untouched, fresh and new. Obi exhaled next to her. She thought of Elijah's wide-open, loving eyes, his kindness, his hand in hers. 'He was ours for a while, wasn't he?' she whispered.

'Is everyone agreed?' The doctor holding the green oxygen bag looked at everyone's face, disconnected it; the nurse pressing on Elijah's chest stopped moving her hand, rested it on top of his heart, looked at Nikki and Obi.

Obi made a sound that came from somewhere deep inside him. Nikki made no sound at all. They left, one by one, until only one nurse remained. She pulled the sheet up to Elijah's face. 'I'm going to let you have some time,' she said. 'But I'll be right outside the curtain.'

She left and drew the curtain back around them. Nikki didn't move. Obi sobbed. Then she climbed on to the bed, right next to Elijah, and got underneath the sheet. She looked at him, focusing on a tiny ringlet curl at the nape of his neck. She pressed her body against his and held him, his arms, his back. She kissed and kissed his face and held him tight, put her head next to his chest, listening carefully for the sound of his heartbeat.

CHAPTER 43

I can hear the sea come in and out, the whoosh of water on sand. The colours of Nigeria are behind Mama, but I'm not looking at her photograph.

The air smells of burning rubber, sugar cane, sweat and heat. It is throat-burning hot. The heat weaves patterns, and light washes the colour from every-thing. Mosquitoes buzz around my head, sometimes landing on my chest; I flick them quickly, slapping hard. But they bite me anyway. I feel the bite, strong, on my chest, making my whole body jolt upwards every so often, then sink back down.

Nigeria is brighter and louder than England. I can tell that already. The light changes and the washed-out brightness gives way to colour: the green of the trees, the blue of the sky, the yellow of the sun, the red of the ground. I have never felt hotter. The heat fills a hole that was there. I hear Yoruba. I recognise Mama's language, but not the words. But Dad lifts his head, and smiles. The mosquitoes are biting and biting my chest. I tell Mum. But she holds my hand. 'Stop biting him,' she whispers to them. 'Don't hurt my son.'

And suddenly Mama is there right in front of me and her arms reach forwards. I run like I've never run before, my legs faster and faster until dust is rising up behind me in a cloud. The sun burns my neck and back and makes everything smell warm. I can hear waves whooshing in and out. Mama's arms wrap around me and I breathe in her skin, the smell of burning sweet plantain, and she's so soft. Softer than anything I've ever felt. I run my hands over her skin and lock my arms inside hers. Our eyes look and I see my reflection inside her eyes, small and not frightened at all, and the whole world is safe. She sings and laughs and behind her I see two men waving, and one is Granddad and I don't know if the other man is Baba or if it's Dad; maybe they are the same now, but he's strong and big and happy. Chioma is playing in the sand with lots of children and Mum is here too, with my sister high up on her back like a Nigerian baby, and they're smiling and laughing and Mum's face is not sad at all; the hurt is all gone. I feel all at once in a rush what it is to have a sister. Jasmin and Chanel are not here, but I somehow know they are in America and eating hotdogs and Aunty Chanel is married to a cowboy and Jasmin has her own horse. She's waving at me. And Ricardo is in Brazil on the beach wearing new flip-flops, and he has a son there all of his own, a small boy from Brazil who looks a little bit like me but who didn't have any family at all. That's not like me. I have so much family. They are all around me now and I am full with the sound of them, the sun burning all of our heads, making us laugh together. The mosquitoes stop biting my chest now. I am glad. I look at Mum and Dad. 'Thank you!' I shout. 'It doesn't hurt any more.'

And then Mama pulls me even closer until I'm part of her own skin again, and our blood is the same and she whispers to my heart, in my own language:

'Little Nigeria, I love you like the world has never known love.'